PENGUIN BOOKS

MAN OVERBOARD

Monica Dickens, great-granddaughter of Charles Dickens, has written over thirty novels, autobiographical books and children's books, and her works are beginning to be adapted for television and film. Her first book, *One Pair of Hands*, which arose out of her experiences as a cook-general – the only work for which her upper-class education had fitted her – made her a best seller at twenty-two, and is still in great demand.

Although her books arise out of the varied experiences of her life, she has not taken jobs in order to write about them: working in an aircraft factory and a hospital was her war work, not research. When she joined the Samaritans, it was the work of befriending distressed fellow human beings which she found compelling, although her novel *The Listeners* came from that experience.

She set up the first American branch of the Samaritans in Boston, Massachusetts, and lives nearby on Cape Cod with her husband Commander Roy Stratton, who has retired from the U.S. Navy, and her horses, cats and dogs. She has two daughters.

MAN OVERBOARD

Monica Dickens

PENGUIN BOOKS
IN ASSOCIATION WITH
MICHAEL JOSEPH

Penguin Books Ltd, Harmondsworth, Middlesex, England
Penguin Books, 625 Madison Avenue, New York, New York 10022, U.S.A.
Penguin Books Australia Ltd, Ringwood, Victoria, Australia
Penguin Books Canada Ltd, 2801 John Street, Markham, Ontario,
Canada L3R 1B4
Penguin Books (N.Z.) Ltd, 182–190 Wairau Road, Auckland 10, New Zealand

—

First published by Michael Joseph 1958
Published in Penguin Books 1962
Reprinted 1965, 1968, 1978

—

—

Made and printed in Great Britain
by Hazell Watson & Viney Ltd,
Aylesbury, Bucks
Set in Linotype Times

To Roy

Chapter One

'I AM like Mark Twain,' Ben said. 'I give up smoking every morning.' He took a cigarette from the case she held out to him.

Rose smiled in a photographic way, because a man at the other end of the bar was looking at her. 'It seems so silly to make good resolutions you don't mean to keep,' she said, in a voice that did not match the smile.

'Oh, I don't know.' Ben gave her back his own smile, which Rose had once told him was ingenuous, but which now, glimpsed in the mirror behind the bottles at the back of the bar, looked merely fatuous. 'It's good practice for next month when I won't be able to get cigarettes duty free any more. You know what I'm going to do when I get out of the Navy? I'm not going to buy a packet of cigarettes until I get a job.'

'That won't stop you smoking mine, though.' Rose turned on him with a sort of unwilling fondness the eyes which a waspish critic had described as painted ping-pong balls. 'I'll keep you in cigarettes if I must, Ben – but not in anything else.'

'You've already told me that.' He slid down from the bar stool. 'Twice. Come on, let's get out of here. There's an imbecile girl in the corner trying to work up enough nerve to come and ask for your autograph.'

Rose stepped gracefully from her stool and spent enough time smoothing her dress and collecting her bag and gloves for the girl to muster a last-minute spurt of courage which brought her trembling to Rose's side holding out a card which said: '8.30 to 10.30 in the Golden Bar. Peter "Fingers" Yarrow at the piano with favourites Old and New.'

Close to, the girl did not look so foolish. It was only an adoring humility that had slackened her jaw and glassed over her eyes. 'Miss Kelly – would you mind?'

Rose turned over the card and signed her name with the flourishes she had acquired since people started wanting her to write it for them on programmes and menus and scraps of paper torn from the cash account pages at the back of their engagement books, smiled at the humble girl without seeing her, and walked out of the bar without looking to see if Ben was following her.

He followed her, keeping far enough behind so that people should not see that he was shorter than Rose when she had heels on. He need not have troubled. No one was looking at him. They were looking at Rose and telling each other: 'Isn't that Rose What's-her-name? You know, that girl we're always seeing on television?'

When Ben first saw Rose Kelly, he did not immediately realize why she looked familiar. He had only seen her once, on his mother-in-law's television set, when Rose had been sweeping emotionally from side to side of the screen in a draining little drama about the wife of a pilot who couldn't get his wheels down.

Some time later, when he had another week-end leave in London, he saw Rose come into a restaurant. She made a good entrance, pausing for a second at the door with an air of standing on tiptoe and holding her breath at the joyous wonder of life. Then she moved into the room with just a tiny inclination of her clean and graceful neck in acknowledgement of the gauntlet of glances through which she passed between the tables. Two men came in behind her. There was usually a man or two tagging along behind Rose, even at purely feminine functions like fashion shows. If you saw a man with his bowler hat held on his knees like an offering, self-consciously crossing and recrossing his legs by the reception desk of a Dover Street coiffeur, you might guess that Rose was upstairs having the camera-catching golden streaks put into the front of her billowing brown hair.

Ben kept glancing at the corner table, where Rose sat vivid and alive, with a huge white collar accentuating the bright apricot glow of her skin, which was at the same time artificial and convincing, like a rose in a nurseryman's catalogue. His daughter Amy, better informed than her father about many things that went on outside the Navy, told him who Rose was.

'You saw her in that play last time you were at Grandma's,' she said, 'A knock-out, you said. What a knock-out.'

'I don't sound like that.'

8

'Only sometimes.' Amy was charitable. 'Don't stare at her so, Father. It's a bit rude, in a restaurant.'

Amy, who was never the same child for more than a few weeks at a time, was having one of her old-fashioned periods, when she called Ben Father, and was rather stiff and formal with him. Since it made her more docile too, in a beaten down Victorian sort of way, it was one of her easiest disguises to cope with; but it made her rather dull, and the lunch, which was a celebration of her tenth birthday, was not being very gay.

The corner table, where Rose sat with a slight, pale man in a bow-tie and an older man in an unsuitable country jacket, looked much livelier. In restaurants, other people's tables always looked more interesting to Ben than his own. And yet if he were to join another table, the charm would disappear, like the illusory sheet of water which shimmers on a dip in the road on a hot day and dries up as your car approaches it.

Ben was thirty-five, and he had found out long ago that the fascination of a group of strangers fades as soon as you become part of the group. The discovery, however, did not impair his enjoyment of other people's lives at a distance. Without envy or discontent, he was an appreciative Peeping Tom, yearning after houses glimpsed from a train, basement kitchens, shadows moving behind a blind, lighted front rooms seen from a street at dusk before a silhouetted figure drew the curtains on the intriguing interior.

Misery might be in that house beside the railway, and shabby poverty in the kitchen. The shadows behind the bedroom blind might be having an ugly married quarrel, snapping at each other in grubby underwear. The people in that softly lit front room might be so bored with each other that they longed to get out. As long as you kept your distance, however, the illusion held.

Ben knew that after two cocktails and a bottle and a half of burgundy, Rose and the two men would feel as if the world were running down by the middle of the afternoon, and be unable to work, and regret the lunch; but that was not part of the picture which enchanted him now. His own lunch with Amy was dull, and their afternoon at the Victoria and Albert

Museum, which was Amy's current fad, would be even duller; but he wondered if Rose, looking across the restaurant, was thinking what a charming picture they made, the broad-shouldered man with the square, sailor's hands, and the long-haired child with the pointed chin, and wishing she were at that domestic table instead of the sophisticated one in the corner.

By the end of lunch, Ben was ready to risk breaking the spell of distance and find some excuse to speak to Rose. She was the most beautiful woman he had ever seen, much more beautiful than Marion had ever been, even before her indulgences began to spoil her looks. He might never see Rose again, except on a television screen, and anyone could do that.

'How's your autograph collection coming along?' he asked Amy.

'I gave it up long ago. You know that, Father. I simply didn't have the time.' Amy folded her napkin precisely and arranged her spoon and fork in the dead centre of her empty plate.

'Pity. We could have got Rose Kelly's today. She looks approachable.'

Amy sat with her thin, freckled hands on the table, ready to get up when he did.

'I tell you what,' Ben pursued, 'why don't you get her autograph anyway? You could sell it at school, if she's as famous as you say she is.'

Amy's eyes brightened. She thought very highly of money.

Ben pocketed some of his change, folded the bill over the rest, in case the tip was too much or too little, and they stood up.

'Too shy to go and speak to her?' he asked unnecessarily, for he knew that Amy was not. Pushing the child in front of him, since he was more shy than she, he approached the corner table, trying, for the benefit of the other people in the restaurant, to look as if they were going to greet an old friend. Rose looked up and smiled. Her teeth were as white as the astonishingly clear whites of her huge eyes.

'Forgive us for butting in,' Ben said, 'but my daughter refuses to leave the restaurant without your autograph.'

Amy did not let him down. She dutifully handed over a piece of paper and the stub of pencil she had found among the geological collection in her coat pocket.

Rose looked at Ben, and he was suddenly acutely conscious of his blue suit. He remembered the fitter at Simpson's remarking casually through a mouthful of pins that no one was wearing blue any more, and he remembered hearing somebody say that a naval officer out of uniform always looked slightly wrong.

Rose wrote her name on the paper and gave it with her devastating smile to Amy. 'What's your name, dear?' she asked. Rose had no use for children, as her nephews and nieces could tell you, but no one outside the family knew that.

'Amy Francis. This is my father, Commander Benjamin Francis, Royal Navy.'

Rose's globular eyes turned to Ben with increased interest. She had not had a naval officer yet. 'Sit down and have some coffee with us,' she said impulsively. The two men with her exchanged a glance, and the youngest one signalled to a waiter to bring up chairs. Disliking him not only for his narrow pink bow-tie and his babyish mouth, but because he was having lunch with Rose, Ben had to give him credit for the fact that the waiter intercepted his signal at once, even though his back was half turned.

Lukewarm coffee was brought and Amy accepted a Coca-Cola, which she began to drink at once, with her eyes modestly cast down over the straw. It was clear that she was not going to help Ben out with the conversation. He had got her into this, and she saw no reason to abandon her suppressed Victorian child act.

Rose introduced the two men. The younger one, whose youth was slipping away rapidly with his hair, was Bob Whiting, 'who produces most of my shows'. The older one, who had a rustic face and tangled grey eyebrows, was Arnold Petter. 'He's going to write a new series of plays for me. I have my own show every week, you know.'

'I know,' said Ben, who didn't.

'It's quite a problem finding writers with new ideas,' Rose said.

'I'm sure of that,' said Ben, who had never given the matter a thought.

'The new ideas,' said Arnold Petter, in a mewing, querulous voice, which did not match his general air of having just come from the bull pen, 'seem to be confined, from what I've seen of you on the screen, to the sacrificial orgies of brave little women whose men are not good enough for them.'

'Don't be a stinker,' Rose said. 'Let's have some brandy.'

They had the brandy. The producer and the author talked to each other while Rose entertained Ben, and made a few abortive attempts to entertain Amy. When the child did not react, Rose made a small grimace and said: 'How well-mannered she is. Utterly delightful.' She had a deep, plummy voice, with a trick of pouncing emphatically on certain words, which was like a nudge or a tap on the arm.

'I've been watching you two,' she said, 'and thinking what a charming picture you made.'

You too? Ben thought. Do you watch other people too, and kid yourself you'd like to be them? It was inconceivable that he should have found a kindred spirit in this glorious creature whose world was so far removed from his. It was a magazine-story adventure, unconnected with reality. And yet here he was, sitting opposite this glowing flesh and sparkling hair, and she was smiling and talking to him, and he was barely conscious of what she said, because he was imagining, with a thrill that was almost apprehension, what it would be like to touch her.

'Most fathers,' Rose said, 'when they take children out to lunch, have that *hunted* look.'

The verbal nudge jerked Ben's eyes away from the scented swell of her breasts, and he laughed. Rose laughed back at him, holding his eyes. He let himself go with the tide. It was absurdly schoolboyish to be falling in love with an unattainable star, but Rose seemed to want it that way, and as if to indicate that she was not so unattainable, she invited him to bring Amy to the television studio when he was next in London.

Then Amy said: 'Father, we'd better go if we're going to have any time at the museum before it closes', and Rose said: 'What a *thrilling* way to spend your birthday', and kept her

12

hand in Ben's for a warm and intimate moment as they said good-bye.

The producer and the author bade him a faintly cynical farewell, and Ben reeled out of the restaurant, wondering what the sub-lieutenants in his course at the submarine school at Gosport, who considered him a back number already on his way to the scrap heap, would say if they could see him now.

All the next day, which he spent in the familiar surroundings of H.M.S. *Dolphin* at Fort Blockhouse, Gosport, Ben had a curious feeling that his world had suddenly changed. He had always been an easy-going optimist, believing that things usually worked out for the best if you let them alone, but this was more than optimism. It was drawing back a curtain, opening a door. It was like walking from a deep patch of shade on the north side of a house, round the corner into warm and blinding sun.

It was a complete break in the monotonous stretch of days and weeks and months which he had ambled through at the submarine school while the Admiralty was making up its mind what to do with him. He had thought of himself as the forgotten man of Blockhouse, glad to be forgotten when so many were being remembered and found redundant, but so bored at times with the prospect of being a shore-based sailor who might never go to sea again, that he would almost have welcomed the novelty of being thrown on the beach to fend for himself.

But something exciting had happened now. Life was suddenly the youthful, exhilarating thing it had been in the year after the war when he came home from Australia and met Marion, and the fatigue and austerity and the strange, bleak sense of anti-climax were blotted out behind the dazzling light of a hopeful future.

There had been few girls since Marion, and none of them stimulating. Well-worn Portsmouth hacks, self-centred London girls with jobs, unmarried girls of his own age, who were getting desperate, and showed it. Never anyone like Rose. Half an hour with Rose had made even the most commonplace actions, like catching a train or crossing a road, suddenly full of significance. She had turned on the lights, and although Ben told himself a dozen times that there was nothing in it, that he would take Amy to the studio and Rose would not be there and he would never see her again, he could not convince himself. His world had changed, and by the end of the evening, he found that he could not go to bed without telling somebody about it.

As the recipient of this staggering news, he made an unsuitable choice in Frank Daniels, a joyless bachelor who was spinning out an indefinite time at Blockhouse preparing for the Admiralty a new technical study of torpedo control, which was boring its author as much as it would bore those who had to read it.

Frank had been at Trincomalee with Ben during the war. They had been together in a T-class submarine, and had once nearly drowned together, an experience which had given them a basis for an ill-matched friendship, which they had renewed in a tranquil way when they found themselves together at Gosport.

Finding Frank in the ante-room, Ben fetched whiskies from the bar. When he brought them over, and Frank had put aside the *Illustrated London News* and resigned himself to the fact that Ben wanted to talk, Ben said: 'Frank, an astonishing thing happened to me today.'

Frank, who had a noble but immobile face with expressionless eyes, like a bust of Julius Caesar with hair on, kept his head in a listening position to imply, without the bother of words, that Ben might continue.

'I met a girl,' Ben said, looking down at his blunt fingers and feeling that he was being absurdly boyish. 'Oh, not just an ordinary girl. A knock-out. She's a television star.'

'Hardly your line, I should have thought,' Frank said, raising his glass to unlimber Roman lips.

'I know. That's what makes it so crazy. I met her in a restaurant. I picked her up, in a way. She didn't seem to mind.'

'She wouldn't,' Frank said, when Ben had told him who the girl was. 'I read the tabloids. The woman is –' He waved his hand dismissively. Frank did not use words like hot or sexy.

'Oh, shut up. You don't believe that filth, surely.'

'I have a healthy respect for the printed word,' Frank said

14

flatly. His hand went hopefully towards the *Illustrated London News*, but Ben had not finished.

'Anyone with a name gets mud slung at them,' he said. 'This girl is famous. She's a great actress.'

'Have you ever seen her act?'

'Only for the last few minutes of a play. Have you?'

Frank nodded without comment.

'Well, anyway –' Ben was not going to have his glory tarnished. 'I met her. She's wonderful, and I'm going to see her again. And I have this curious feeling – I don't suppose you'll understand – that everything's suddenly changed. I had one gin before dinner. I feel as if I'd had six. I've felt like that all day, as if I were on the threshold of something.' He caught a slight throaty tremor in his voice. The curious feeling was with him very strongly. It was like the exalted alcoholic illusion of being on the verge of a great discovery.

'The only threshold you're on,' said Frank, picking up the magazine and holding it before him as a barrier against any more disagreeably emotional remarks, 'is the door to civvy street. What scheme did you go for?'

An Admiralty Fleet Order had given officers the chance to apply for premature retirement sooner than stay to grow old in their present rank if they were passed over for promotion. A request for retirement did not mean that you would get it, any more than a request to stay ensured that you would be kept. The Fleet Order appeared to be a device which would enable Their Lordships, faced with the necessity for getting rid of nearly two thousand officers, to say righteously: 'We didn't axe anyone without giving them the chance to ask for it.'

There seemed to be a catch in it somewhere, but no one at Gosport had been able to figure out what it was. The problem of whether you were worse off applying for Scheme A or Scheme B had been tormenting officers and their wives all through October. It seemed that you could not win either way, so Ben had solved the problem by not applying for either scheme, following the safe old Navy doctrine: 'Never volunteer for anything.'

'Poor old Kenneth didn't apply either,' Frank said tonelessly,

15

without lowering the magazine. 'He had a tactful little communication from Their Lordships today. You're next, I imagine.'

'Why not you?'

'Oh, God, they'll never sling me out. They can't get enough people to write their beastly text books. I'll moulder along until I'm as much a fixture at the Admiralty as the plumbing. And about as antiquated. You'll see. Only you won't be around the Admiralty then.'

Since the reduction programme started, Frank had been prophesying the axe for everyone except himself, as if he were going to be left to run the Navy single-handed. Wetting his fingers, he turned over the pages of the magazine and began to read an article on Micronesian cooking pots. 'It's going to be pretty tough for you boys out there,' he said, without raising his marble eyes. 'I hear they're having a bad time finding jobs, and it'll get worse as more of you come out. What would you try for?' He asked the question less from interest than from habit, for it was one which officers everywhere were discussing that winter.

'Oh, I don't know. Not a chicken farm. Or a stone quarry. Or a non-existent uranium mine. I hope I'd have the sense not to be swindled out of my gratuity. There'll be a lot of sharks about waiting for the innocent N.O. with his touching faith in human nature. I'd sell something, I suppose. Cars, radios, stocks and shares.'

'Brushes, more likely,' grunted Frank, but Ben was seeing himself in a narrow-trousered charcoal suit, entertaining Rose on an expense account.

'It might be rather fun,' he said.

Frank grumbled at him. 'You're always so damned cheerful. A bloody Merry Andrew. I remember you in the sea that time, hanging on to the rope of a Carley float with your one good hand and laughing your silly head off.'

'What did you want me to do?' Ben stood up. 'Sob on your shoulder? You were too damn wet already.'

Frank did not bother to answer. Ben said good night and left him there, static and running to fat in the chair where he sat night after night until the steward collecting ash-trays and dirty glasses began to trip over his legs.

On the staircase, Ben put his hand into his pocket to feel once more the folded picture of Rose which he had torn from the cover of a magazine he had found on the station bookstall. How awful to be Frank. How wonderful at this moment to be Ben.

When Ben was next in London, Amy did not want to go to the television studio, so Ben went alone. He had written to Rose, and she had told him, in a letter which now lived in his note-case alongside the folded photograph, that he and Amy were welcome to attend a rehearsal of her show. 'I shall be delighted', was what she had written, and by the time he reached the studios, which were a group of converted warehouses in a part of London all but inaccessible by any kind of public transport, Ben had read and reread into that conventional phrase every possible variation of meaning.

When he arrived at last, after a ten-minute walk through streets where children played in the shadow of blank walls topped with jagged glass, and mysterious small parts were being made in flimsy, humming sheds, Rose's rehearsal was over. She was drinking gin in a small, bare room to which Ben was conducted through a mass of passages by a man with no collar or tie, and a brown waistcoat which some needlewoman in the family had rebacked in a vivid satin.

In spite of the letter from Rose, and Ben's continuing belief that his life had taken a turn for the better, there was still, as the waistcoat charged upstairs two steps at a time and scuttled round corners as if bent on shaking him off, the possibility that she would not be there. Things like that happened, as Ben knew all to well. The more you looked forward to something, the less likelihood there was of its ever coming to pass, or if it did, of its coming up to scratch. Twisting himself sideways in the narrow corridors to pass harried men with bright-brown moustaches and girls with hair trussed up in rubber bands, Ben was not thinking bitterly about life's disappointments. To an optimist, they were never so bad as an outsider might think, unless a misplaced sympathy made them so.

That was one of the things that Marion had never been able to understand. When some eager scheme of Ben's misfired, or when it rained when he had been looking forward to tennis, she had worn herself out saying What a shame, when he was already half way to a new scheme, or cheerfully telephoning people for bridge. Ben never knew whether she was aware of how irritated he was by her unwanted solicitude, or whether she genuinely ... But this was no time to be thinking about Marion, when the half-and-half waistcoat was skidding to a stop, crying triumphantly: 'Here you are, Captain!' and opening a door to show him Rose, coming towards him with her wide smile and both hands held out.

There were other people in the room with her. Rose introduced him to them emphatically as *Commander* Francis, and he had the idea that she would have been gratified if he had turned up with three gold rings on his sleeve. The others seemed to be actors and actresses, or people connected in some way with her show, but Ben was scarcely aware of them, for Rose blotted out all other life for miles around.

She was wearing a white sweater and a tight black skirt. She was more beautiful even than Ben had remembered. In that dingy room with the damp, green walls and dusty carpet, among the little group of unremarkable people with limp handshakes and indoor complexions, Rose glowed like an incandescent gas mantle.

Ben stood bemused and happy while she fetched him a warm drink in a small glass, the wrong shape for gin and tonic. She was quite possessive with him, and so the other people accepted him with no more than the lift of an eyebrow, the downward tweak to the corner of a mouth. If Rose wanted to give the impression that she knew him quite well, that was fine. Ben played up, and found himself talking to her with some ease, or rather listening, since Rose did most of the talking in any company. She did not mention Amy, so Ben did not bring out the story he had prepared to cover up the child's lack of interest.

Rose seemed glad to see him. It was fantastic, better than anything he had dreamed when he had imagined himself watching her in the studio from a distance, waiting for the bounty of a word of recognition. The first drink had been strong, because the tonic water was running short. Ben accepted a second, and his brain began to shout noiselessly: 'This is terrific. She likes me!' His brain was standing straddle-legged on a wall, telling the open-mouthed crowds below that Rose Kelly was still standing by him, still talking to him, when she could have been talking to any of these other people in the room, who worked with her and were her kind.

The door opened. Heads turned, Ben's among them, as the producer, Bob Whiting, came in. He wore offensive pale suede ankle-boots, and a pistachio bow-tie, even narrower than the one he had worn in the restaurant.

'Aha!' cried Bob Whiting, so that all the room might hear. 'The gallant Commander. How are all those gorgeous sailors?' He affected a perverted lisp, and there was some laughter, which sounded sycophantic. He was evidently quite a big wheel at the studio. Someone brought him a drink, and Ben noticed that the others glanced at him out of the side of their corner conversations, as if checking his mood.

'Well, Rosie,' Bob Whiting stood in front of Rose and Ben, with his childish mouth smugly pursed. 'So it wasn't just ships that pass in the night, I see.'

'Don't be a stinker,' Rose said lightly. 'Did you get that straightened out, about the close-up? You were right about the man on that camera. See if you can't get him changed next week. Please, Bob?' Her saucer eyes appealed to him confidently. She liked him, that was the terrible thing. Ben was afraid that they were going to slip into the kind of easy, esoteric exchange he had watched them enjoying in the restaurant, and he was about to climb down off his mental wall and say: 'Sorry, everybody. I didn't make it after all', when Rose took some keys on a silver chain out of the pocket of her skirt and said: 'How about getting the car, Ben? It's at this end of the car park. I'll meet you at the door.'

Had she merely forgotten to tell him, or did she not want Bob Whiting to know that Ben did not know what kind of car she had? No matter. Ben took the keys as nonchalantly as if he had handled them many times before, found his way down the staircases and along the baffling corridors, and nodded good night to the front view of the waistcoat, crumpled over the evening paper. In the car park, he tried the ignition key in the dashboard of all the cars that looked as if they were owned by a woman until it fitted and turned in a pale-blue coupé with an endless bonnet and a rear seat designed for midgets.

Backing it out, he scraped a bumper with a noise that threatened to bring not only Rose but the whole studio running out to see where the crash was. Nobody came. Ben moved the car forward to free it, and when he had backed it clear, got out to see the damage. This was his lucky day. Rose's car was unharmed. The car he had struck, an ancient, hump-shouldered model with vulnerable bits of rusted metal sticking out at both ends, had the front bumper twisted out and up like a wild eyebrow. Glancing round, Ben kicked the bumper roughly back into shape, and climbed quickly back into Rose's car as a figure in a muffler and duffle coat turned into the car park, obviously destined for the heap of old iron.

Rose was already at the door, in a fur coat that looked like mink, when Ben drove cautiously up. Before he could get out of the low seat to open the door for her, she had stepped into the car beside him, eclipsing the smell of new leather with the heady, mysterious scent which emanated from her hair and her skin and her furs.

'Where are we going?' Ben asked.

'I thought you were taking me to supper.'

'Of course,' Mentally he reviewed the contents of his notecase. Would they take a cheque at the kind of place where Rose would want to go? The average naval officer was not often enough in town or in funds to become known at any of the smart places, and Ben was an average naval officer. There was his club, of course. . . . My God, no. He laughed inwardly at the idea of taking Rose to that temple of muted propriety, where people would not even turn to stare at the dazzle of her, but would keep their heads bent over the sole or the steak and kidney, and talk in rapid undertones, to prove she was not there.

No, they would not be eating now. They would be sitting with glasses of port and *crème de menthe*, while the barman in the ladies' lounge yawned behind his hand and wondered whether he should try for a job somewhere that was not so slow, and where Admirals' wives would not address him as Steward.

20

'I'm afraid it's too late to get anything to eat at my club,' Ben said, swinging the racy car through the unfamiliar streets under Rose's guidance. But she had already planned that they should go to a 'funny little place I belong to'. In a mews in Knightsbridge, they went into a narrow room like a railway carriage, which had tables along the side walls, with a three-piece coloured band knocking themselves out in an alcove.

The whole place was so small and the band was so loud that conversation was not easy. Ben did not mind. He was content just to sit beside Rose and get the scent of her and the occasional touch of her bare arm on his sleeve. She was busy at first looking round and waving to people she knew; but after the drinks came and they had eaten their melon and were having a second drink while they waited for more food, Rose suddenly took a deep breath, stared ahead of her and said: 'Tell me about your wife.'

Ben was startled. He had not realized that Rose was interested enough to want to know where she stood. With the noise of the band, he could not even be sure that she had said that.

'Sorry?' He bent towards her.

Rose frowned at having to repeat a question which had cost her some slight effort to ask. As she repeated it more loudly, the band abruptly stopped playing and a woman two tables away turned with interest to see who had said that to whom.

'I'm not married,' Ben said quietly, and the listening woman turned away in disappointment because she could not hear.

Rose's face cleared. She relaxed against the back of the seat, studying Ben with her wide-open eyes. Then she frowned. Her frown was no more than a slight drawing together of her eyebrows, which barely wrinkled her creamy forehead. 'But the child –'

'My wife is dead. She died three years ago in a car crash.'

'How dreadful for you.' Rose did not look away, as most people do when surprised with tragedy, but continued to stare at him. If she had read the newspaper stories about Marion three years ago, she had forgotten them, and Ben was not going to remind her. He had never discussed the truth with anyone except Marion's mother. If he ever mentioned Marion, even to

21

his own parents, who knew the truth and preserved it like a chronic sore, he always paid her the belated and unmerited tribute of talking as if her death had been the sad loss which Rose assumed it to be.

'Amy lives with her grandmother,' he said. 'She has a big, ugly old flat in Bayswater. That's where I stay when I'm in London.' He began to tell Rose about Marion's mother and what a wonderful woman she was, but Rose did not want to hear about Geneva Hogg and how much she had done for Amy.

'Let's dance,' she said, as the band began to jerk and thump again.

Although he guessed that the waiter bearing two steaming savoury dishes through the swing door was headed for their table, Ben stood up at once and followed Rose to the dance floor. Cold food was a small price to pay for the chance of holding Rose in his arms.

When they danced, she was too tall for him. Ben danced well enough, but Rose soon said that she was hungry, and led him back to the table. Later, after several more drinks, they danced again, and Rose took off her shoes, placing them neatly on the little platform beside the grinning drummer, and some of the other women laughed and took off their shoes and danced in their stockings.

Like this, Ben and Rose could dance cheek to cheek. Her cheek was like a rose, he told her, and she nestled her firm breasts closer against him and did not seem to think him as banal as he sounded to himself.

When the dance was over, Rose went back to the table with her shoes in her hand. It was all right for her to take her shoes off here. People did that kind of thing. But they could not always come here. What would happen if Ben took her to the Savoy or the Berkeley, or any of the places he knew to take girls? She could not take her shoes off at the Savoy.

When they were in her flat, and it was so late that Sloane Street lay as silent under the windows as a deserted canal, Rose took off her shoes again so that she was the right height to kiss.

Later, Ben staggered through the pillared doorway that faced the wrong end of the Broad Walk, and shying away from the dark cavern of the lift, climbed the stairs to the second floor where Geneva Hogg lived in dilapidated disorder. Amy was sitting in the kitchen in a woollen dressing-gown with her hair in plaits, waiting for him. She did things like that sometimes. It was unnerving. While she heated the milk for the cocoa he did not want, Ben went to the sink and surreptitiously wiped the lipstick off his face with a smelly dishcloth.

When Ben went to the television studio the next evening, the man in the satin-backed waistcoat had been replaced by a much less obliging person in a beige pullover the same colour as his hair.

'Miss Kelly said for you to go along to her dressing-room,' he said in a sceptical way, as if no good could come of it. 'Show you the way?' The idea was ridiculous. 'I've got my job to do here. There may be a boy.' He put his sandy head round the corner of the stone corridor. 'Boy!' he shouted without conviction.

No boy came, so Ben set off alone, following vague directions. In spite of, or because of what had happened last night, he was more nervous than he had been yesterday. Then he had only been afraid that Rose would not be there. Now he knew she would be there, because she had her show tonight, but having had time to regret the whole thing, would she still want to see him?

Last night had been – well, odd, in a queer, unsatisfactory way. Ben had seldom yet had cause to doubt his adequacy in the preliminary skirmishes of love. Marion had not complained. The Portsmouth hacks and the desperate thirties had been all too easily excited, and unwilling to stop outside the limits of compromise. But Rose had been satisfied with so little. Ben had only just been warming up when she pushed him happily away and breathed: 'Darling – now I shall sleep tonight!' and moved towards the alabaster box on the mantelpiece where she kept a comb and lipstick secreted, as she did in every room of the lavish flat, including the kitchen.

It had been marvellous, of course, just to have held her in his arms and to have had the few disciplined kisses which were more than he had dreamed of; and yet, as he hummed downwards in the polished lift, which would trap you with its automatic doors if you were not nippy, he had found himself asking, like the virgin bride: 'Is that all?'

Soberly the next day, it came to him that the disappointment was not his, but Rose's. Although she had been polite enough to simulate content, she had been disappointed in him. She had only asked him to make the arduous trek out to the studio today so that she could tell him to go away and leave her alone.

Perhaps it was just as well Ben could not find her. Wandering lost in the inner recesses of the labyrinth, he was rescued by, of all people, Bob Whiting. Bob had a sheaf of papers in his hand and was going somewhere very fast, but he stopped and pivoted in the suede boots, and gave Ben a slap on the back that nearly drove his spine into his breast-bone.

'How's the Commander?' he asked in an offensively hearty tone, which managed to convey a subtle derision of the entire Royal Navy. 'You're going the wrong way, cock,' he said, without asking where Ben was going. 'She's on the next floor. I'll show you.'

Ben would have loved to say that he was looking for the manager's office, or the men's room, or anywhere except Rose's dressing-room; but he could not waste any more time stumbling about on his own, so he followed Bob to a peeling green door which had Rose's name on a card.

Bob knocked and opened the door in the same movement. Rose was sitting in a yellow silk dressing-gown at the shelf under the long, smeared mirror, doing something to her eyelashes. She pulled the neck of the dressing-gown together, then said: 'Oh, it's you', and relaxed.

'Me and the gallant Commander.' Bob stepped aside to let Ben into the room. Rose smiled at him, and Ben stood there just inside the door, smiling back in a foolish kind of trance. Suppose this was a bedroom, his head was saying. And she was sitting at her dressing-table and turned round to you like that with her lips parted. And it was your bedroom too.

Bob looked from one to the other of them, shrugged his hock-bottle shoulders, and went out, banging the door.

Ben still stood for a moment transfixed. What would she expect him to do? Then she got up, and he saw that she had her shoes off. She stood before him proudly, with her hands at her sides and her chin tilted, and he was reminded for a split, disconcerted second, of how he had seen her on the television screen, standing before her make-believe husband.

'Well, Ben,' she said. 'Are you afraid to kiss me?'

Yes, he was afraid. Afraid of finding that, like hothouse strawberries, her lips looked better than they tasted.

Chapter Two

IN the weeks that followed, Ben was with Rose whenever he could get to London, and both the satin-backed waistcoat and the beige pullover began to accord him the confidential nod reserved for habitués of the studio. Frank Daniels, who was not so uncommunicative that he did not enjoy dropping an odd nugget of gossip here and there, had told a few people at Gosport about Ben's liaison with the glamorous Rose Kelly, and the word had spread as rapidly as might be expected.

Ben's stock went up like a skyrocket. The sub-lieutenants in his course, who had previously shown no more interest in him than in any of the other instructors, now treated him with a new mixture of respect and ribaldry. At a Monday class, and especially on Tuesday afternoons, when Ben was back from his long 'Friday While', the innocently polite inquiries of: 'How was London, sir?' were underlaid by a current of subdued but meaningful noises made by the tongue inside the cheek, or the breath between pursed lips.

When he told Frank Daniels about this, Frank had spread his nostrils in disapproval and said: 'I'd run the swine in.'

'Maybe,' Ben said, 'but at least they've stopped thinking of me as their palsied grandfather.'

The ratings at the submarine school also took a new view of Ben. They were more respectful about Rose, but also more forthright. Able seamen would approach him with autograph books. 'It seems that you know Rose Kelly, sir. Might I trouble you, next time you see her –'

'Could you get us a picture of Rose Kelly, sir?'

'Could you fetch us back a signed photograph? – for my little daughter, of course, sir.'

One of the mess stewards, a grizzled pensioner, took to breathing into Ben's ear as he set down the soup: 'My compliments to Miss Kelly, and will you tell her from me there's one down here as thinks she's an angel?'

All in all, Fort Blockhouse approved, and was proud of Ben. So was Amy's grandmother, Geneva Hogg, in whose uncomfortable spare bedroom, cluttered with the overflow of clothes and furniture from every other room in the flat, Ben stayed when he went to town. Geneva, an indomitable old widow who was not aware that she looked her age, liked a name as well as anybody. If Ben had to get mixed up with a woman – and God knew the poor man needed a bit of fun – it might just as well be someone famous.

Amy was glad about Rose, because it brought her father to London more often, but for no other reason. On the two occasions when Ben and Rose had taken Amy out together, Rose had remembered or invented some appointment, and disappeared before the afternoon was half over, and Amy had only then started to enjoy herself. Rose was doing her best, but she had a theatrical way of sinking to one knee and enveloping Amy in scented furs which would make the most oncoming child draw back, and Amy, though poised for her age, was too self-contained to be oncoming.

Once, when she was seeing Ben off on the train at Waterloo, she said: 'If you marry again, do I get any say about who you marry?'

There was no time to discuss this, because the train began to move, and Amy, who was playing the part of a bride of the first world war, was left waving gallantly on the platform, with her knock knees, and her red beret slipping backwards off the long and beautiful hair which was the best thing Marion could have bequeathed to her.

Amy was always in Ben's mind when he and Rose talked of marriage, as they did occasionally in a friendly, unexcited way, as one might plan a possible holiday. Ben had not yet explained to Rose how precarious was his position in the Navy. Rose would not want to hear that. She liked the Navy. That is, she liked her idea of it, a sort of old-fashioned, hearts-of-oak conception, trailing power and glory.

Ben could not see Rose as a Navy wife, living in a flimsy furnished house at Gosport, or a stone cottage at Rothesay; but Rose could see herself quite easily, and she appeared to enjoy the vision.

She would not give up her work, of course. Having got so far, it would be madness to throw away her success. It would hardly be fair on her public. After all, some of them wrote to say that they had bought television sets for the specific purpose of being able to welcome Rose into their home every Sunday night. Think of that. Ben thought of it, and remembered how he too had toyed with the idea of sending Rose a fan letter the first time he saw her on the screen. He would have sent it if he had known she took the letters so seriously.

If they were married, she said, it would have to be a week-end kind of marriage. They could have a housekeeper to take care of Amy. And think how proud Ben would be to have a wife who was not just one of the service mares with a limited conversation and a seated skirt to her tweeds.

Rose's conversation was also limited – to the subjects which interested her – but her skirts were never seated. Of course Ben would be proud of her, and familiarity had not made her any less dazzlingly beautiful, although she had turned out to be not nearly as sexy as she looked. That might be quite a relief, though, in the long run of marriage. Ben's experience with Marion had taught him what an oversexed woman could be like as a wife. It had not cured him of the habit of marriage, however. He would like to marry again. He was lonely. He hated his bachelor cabin at Gosport with its all-male smell of shoes and cigarettes. And Amy could not go on living with Geneva for ever.

But did he want to marry Rose? The world into which she had taken him was so refreshingly different from the stagnant limbo of his present Navy life, and he was still, when he looked at it objectively, so staggered with the idea of himself as the cavalier of a goddess over whom millions of women sighed and millions of men drooled every week, that he was unable to understand clearly whether he was in love with her.

Sometimes, and especially when he was watching her among other people, he thought that he was. Sometimes, and especially when they were alone together, he thought that he was not.

Was she in love with him? Impossible to say. Sometimes she said that she was, but it sounded more as if she were speaking words from a play than from her heart. Studying himself in his cabin mirror, which had been hung in the place least likely to get either day or artificial light, Ben wondered what Rose saw in him that she could not have found in any of the men who were queueing up behind him for the chance to take her out and to spend more money on her in one day than Ben made in a week.

Romantic-looking men, too, like that actor with the swept-back hair, who would lean from his willowy height to murmur things that made Rose purr, and who could not tell you the time of day without making it sound poetic. Ben's hair was so thick and unruly that it had to be cut very short all over his head to make him look like any sort of a naval officer. It was so many years since he had seen it long – that time when it had grown out in hospital while his shoulder wound was mending – that he had almost forgotten its rich brown colour. It was nondescript now, like a small, furry animal that camouflages itself among the dead leaves of the hedgerows.

His skin had never completely lost its tan. That was better than being sickly pale, like Bob Whiting; but his face was too square, not narrowing enough towards the chin to give him that lean-cheeked look a girl like Rose might go for. His eyes were a conventional blue, with stubby lashes and no mysterious depths. His nose – Ben rubbed his chin, wondering whether there was time to shave before he caught the London train – his nose had been his beauty, short and straight and classic, until that chief bosun's mate in the United States Navy had knocked it sideways for ever in the semi-finals of the middle-weight championships at Subic Bay.

Why does she want to marry you? Ben asked the face in the shadowed mirror. The face could not say.

That Sunday evening, he was waiting for Rose among the cables and cameras and lights and grey flats of scenery in the big studio where an army of young men in sports shirts and crêpe-soled shoes were making the final preparations for her show. Bob Whiting came down from the little eyrie where he sat before a row of screens, controlling the three cameras and organizing their different shots into the polished production the public saw.

From up there in the control booth, he talked to the technicians on the floor by means of the headphones they wore, but before they went on the air, his instructions to Rose and the rest of the cast came through the talk-back loudspeaker which everyone in the studio could hear. Bob was not charitable, and he often broadcast in this public way remarks that made the supporting actors feel homicidal. Rose, however, was a valuable property, and had developed enough temperament to match her star position, so when Bob felt like speaking his mind to her, he came down to the floor to do it.

When he had finished telling Rose that she had hammed her scene with the seducer at the final run through, and she had finished telling him that since his mother had been on the halls, he ought to know what a ham was, Bob patted Ben on his short, stiff hair as if he were a dog, and asked: 'How's old faithful?'

Although he had grown accustomed to the sight of Ben around the studio, Bob still treated him as if he were a barely permissible joke. He lost no opportunity for veiled innuendo against the Navy or its gallant Commander, whom he now referred to familiarly as the Gall. Comm. The only reason that Ben had not punched him on the nose was that he knew that Bob was vital to the success of Rose's show. She could not have managed with a less cunning producer. Bob could get out of her what he knew the public wanted her to give, and he knew her limitations as well as he knew the limitations of his own digestive system.

Bob had weak eyes, and when the fierce white lights were on, he wore a silly-looking eyeshade with an elastic high up the back of his head, like a snood. He looked sideways at Ben from under the shade and said: 'These must be nervous days for you, skipper. When are they going to sling you out?'

'What do you mean?' Rose turned her headlamp eyes from

29

one man to the other, the false lashes which were part of her television make-up standing up on her lids like a doll's. 'Who's going to sling Ben out of where?'

'Their Lordships of the Admiralty. Out of the Navy,' Bob said. 'They're running down their numbers – didn't you know? In two years, they'll have cut down the hump of captains by one in three, so your Gall. Comm. is less likely to make captain than to make a bowler hat. Ask him.'

Damn the man. How did he know so much? Ben could cheerfully have dragged the eyeshade down over Bob's face and smashed his fist into the lot. Rose's thickly-pencilled eyebrows were drawing together into the nearest she would let herself get to a frown. Her glistening, painted mouth was turned down. 'Why didn't you tell me this, Ben?'

'Well, there's nothing in it, really, I –'

'You never tell me anything. Don't just stand there and grin at me. You're so damned inarticulate about anything that really matters.'

Bob hoped, and Ben feared, that she was going to give him a full-scale trimming on the floor of the studio where in half an hour's time she would be convincing her enraptured audience that she was a sweet little farm-girl from Cumberland, all but ruined by the city's lure; but Bob was disappointed, and Ben relieved, by the arrival of the make-up girl to remove Rose for touching-up.

Bob laughed. 'She didn't like that, did she?'

'Why couldn't you mind your own business?'

'Oh, I don't know,' Bob said airily. 'It's about time someone warned her, if you hadn't. Rose doesn't read the papers, or talk about things that go on in the great world. It wasn't very sporting of you, sir, to hook her under false pretences.' He peered at Ben from under the eyeshade. 'Or is it possible that even you don't know what she's up to?'

'Oh, look here,' Ben said uncomfortably. 'I wish you'd shut up and leave Rose and me alone.'

Turning to get away from Bob, he tripped over a large metal junction-box, where several thick cables met in a writhing tangle. Bob caught at his arm to steady him, and turned him round again.

'Don't you know about Rose, then?' he asked, not spitefully, but with a sort of baffled surprise that Ben found more un-nerving than spite. 'Rose thinks that a naval officer is a pillar of respectability. That's why she thinks she'll marry you. Poor darling, she's never really known many respectable people. Her family is – well, my God! – and Rose was Well, my God, too, until some boy friend pushed her out of Canvey Island and into a modelling job. She came here as part of a shampoo commercial. You know, the girl who's disgusted with one side of her hair and delighted with the other half.' Bob pulled two faces to illustrate. 'Somebody spotted her and tried her in a small part, and she was just so damned beautiful that she never looked back until she found herself where she is now.'

If Bob had intended to spoil Rose for Ben, he had failed. Bob was experiencing a feeling of tenderness towards her that had never been engendered by the fancy little life history she had thought up for him. Suddenly he wanted more than any-thing to marry her and make her feel secure.

'Our Rose may not have much above the ears,' Bob went on, 'but she's cute enough to know that her kind of success doesn't last long in this game. Television audiences get sated. They get sick of their dream girls and lover boys because they see too much of them. And Rose has no talent. It's my job to make sure that the dim-wits out there are too dazzled by the looks of her to spot that. But I can't go on doing it for ever. That's why she wants what she thinks you could give her. Mrs Commander, Mrs Captain, Mrs Admiral. It wouldn't be much use to her to be the Mrs of an ex-N.O. who's out there grubbing for jobs with the rest.'

As Ben opened his mouth to speak, Bob held up his hand. It was a white, fleshy hand with a huge amber signet ring on one of the fingers. 'Don't curse me,' he said. 'You'll live to thank me. What do you want with Rose for a wife? You won't be able to look at her all the time, you know. The lights will be out. Haven't you found out yet that she's as cold as a witch's –'

'Shut up,' Ben said roughly. He felt himself growing hot and shivery at the same time.

'Well, it's true,' Bob said calmly. 'I've tried. But Rose –' He made a face. 'She just wants to play around a little to satisfy her ego that she's desirable. Nothing more.'

'By God,' said Ben, his anger mounting in him like a fever, 'if you were in the Navy, I – I'd axe you.' It was the worst thing he could think of at the moment.

'I'd be delighted. I was, for four years in the war. They couldn't let me out fast enough. I got as far as leading seaman,' Bob said. 'Not bad, considering that all my officers loathed me.'

'Bob!' A disembodied voice materialized through the talk-back. 'Are you coming up?'

Bob snapped his hand to his eyeshade in an impeccable salute. 'I might add that the loathing was mutual.' He walked away, weaving a path through the cables and cameras and perspiring men with the neatness of habit.

Ben sat down on a chair. His legs felt weak, but he was not angry any more. The man's a swine, he told himself, but his inner voice lacked conviction. For no reason that Ben could understand, there was something about Bob that was beginning to be faintly likeable. Rose liked him too. Perhaps they would all end up in a furnished flat south of the river, with Bob as the friend of the family keeping Rose company while Ben was out pounding the pavements in search of a job.

The tempo of the studio suddenly quickened. Ben had seen enough television shows produced to recognize that swift transition from 'Loads of time before we're on the air' to 'This is it, chaps'. People who had been lounging stood up straight. The cameraman with the broken shoe-lace abandoned his attempts to knot it and climbed up to his perch on the big dolly camera. The last battery of lights was switched on to flood the first set with colourless brilliance. The diverse attentions of some forty men and girls were concentrated in unison towards the island of lights which enclosed the corner of the farmhouse kitchen with the black iron range and the wooden clock and the carefully-battered chairs.

A middle-aged actor, with whom Ben had once had a beer at the studio canteen, sat at the table in a corduroy waistcoat and a collarless shirt, with his boots stuck out over a palpitating sheepdog.

'Can't you stop him panting?' the actor said, squinting into the shadows beyond the lights. 'The brute wouldn't be panting at seven o'clock in the morning.'

'It's the lights,' somebody said, and a man standing near Ben in plimsolls said sentimentally to no one in particular: 'Poor creature. It isn't right, you know.'

A square-hipped woman with a moustache, who was the dog's trainer, came forward into the light, stroked the dog and gave it something from her closed hand, like a sailor palming a fag-end, and was sent shambling off sideways by Bob's voice booming at her: 'Get off the set!'

Suddenly Rose was there. She never came on to the set until the last minute. Ben got up and moved forward to where he could see all of her. She was looking towards him, and he smiled and moved his hand a little, but she did not smile back, and he did not know whether she could see him beyond the lights.

She was wearing a check gingham apron tied tightly round her tiny waist over a dress with a neck cut somewhat lower than is customary in the Border Country for milking cows before breakfast. Her hair was caught demurely back with a ribbon. Ben, who had watched the dress rehearsal, knew that later when she was all but seduced in a married man's apartment, it would be brushed into a more sophisticated arangement, to signify her transformation from clod-hoppery, as when the mouse-like secretary in a film suddenly takes off her glasses and is revealed as a raving beauty.

Rose looked round the set in a dissatisfied way, and then went outside the flimsy door through which she would make her first entrance. Ben moved sideways so that he should see her come in, and knocked into a music stand which fell with a clatter. Several people shouted: 'Quiet, please!' and an unseen voice grumbled: 'Who's that infernal man?'

'He belongs to Rose,' someone said.

As Ben tiptoed out of the way behind a piano, he heard the first voice say: 'I wish she'd keep 'em in the bedroom.'

The floor manager, who was very young, with a headset over unruly yellow hair, began to say in a rapid, self-conscious monotone, as if he was proud yet embarrassed to be the only one talking: 'All right, everybody. Quiet, please. Settle down, everyone.'

They settled. Ben watched the set. Listening to Bob's voice through the headphones, the floor manager raised the board of papers in his hand, and swept it down dramatically. The door opened and Rose stood there, just a simple farmer's daughter, as poised and glowing as she had been when Ben first saw her, making her entrance into the restaurant.

Rose's weekly show was a toothsome mixture of soap opera and a Lonely-hearts column. The short plays were supposed to be based on actual letters sent in to Rose in her capacity as everybody's girl friend. Before the play, an announcer, chosen for the sincerity of his soft moustache and compassionate eyes, would read, in a voice suitably charged with controlled emotion, the letter whose story of courageous suffering or despair or triumphant love was to be illustrated on the screen.

It was always a woman's problem. Even when it was a story about a man losing his sight, or going to prison to protect a guilty friend, the drama was always presented from the point of view of the woman in the case, because the woman was Rose.

Taut production by Bob, and accomplished acting by the rest of the cast gave the show enough gloss to get by. Men watched it because it had Rose. Women watched it because the contents were skilfully geared to make them think: This could happen to me, or: This might have happened to me, according to their age.

Many women wrote to Rose, longing to see their own troubles mirrored on the screen. They did not know that she never saw the letters. Many of them could not have been made into plays without violating the moral code, and the others were too dull or esoteric to make good entertainment. Occasionally a sure-fire situation came in, but most of the letters read on the air were composed, to match a play already written, by a morbid man called Bates, who had a flair that amounted almost to genius for sounding like an overwrought but courageous woman.

The play tonight, however, was based on an actual letter sent in by a homely girl from Wales, who longed to get off the farm and on to the boulevards. Sweating blood, a writer had made a play out of what might have happened if she did, the chief inconsistency being that the girl was now as beautiful as Rose Kelly, which would seem to remove all her problems. The scene had been shifted to Cumberland, so that no one in Wales could point a finger at a neighbour and say: 'She wrote that letter.' Television logic reasoned that it did not matter if some lonely girl in Cumberland was stigmatized, since the accusation must be false.

Ben did not follow the play very closely. When Rose questioned him afterwards about her performances, he could never give a coherent opinion of what had been going on, because he was too busy watching her and hugging to himself the thought: She's mine!

Well, almost his. And more his than any other man's at the moment, as far as he knew. As she moved about the make-believe kitchen, waiting on her father, giving back soft answers to his grumbling, dropping on one knee to bury her sad face in the dog's coat when the man went out, Ben was not thinking about what Bob had told him.

He was thinking: This is how she would look moving about my kitchen. Even first thing in the morning, she would look like this. I could buy her a gingham apron. This is how I would see her every day before I went to work. I could get her a dog.

Watching her, treasuring his plans, he forgot that Rose never got up until ten o'clock in the morning, and that she did not like dogs.

Chapter Three

IT came in a long, buff envelope, with 'N.C.W. Branch, Admiralty' stamped in the left-hand corner. Ben did not have to open it to know what it was.

He kept it in his pocket all afternoon, and when his classes were over he went to his cabin, sat down on the sprucely-made bed and slit the envelope with a pen-knife. This was not something that could be dragged open with the side of a thumb-nail. This was something that would have to be preserved, along with his birth certificate and his marriage licence and Marion's death certificate, until Amy and her children threw it out with the rest of his papers after he died.

I am commanded by My Lords Commissioners of the Admiralty to inform you that with regret they find it necessary to terminate your employment on the Active List as a result of the planned reduction in the size of the Royal Navy.

Well, there it was, and My Lords Commissioners had apparently decided to cut down on commas as well as commanders.

It was not a surprise, for he had already had the semi-official letter beginning: 'My dear Ben,' from the captain he knew slightly in the Naval Conditions and Welfare Branch. No one could say that the Admiralty did not soften the blow, but for Ben it was still a blow, every bit as painful as if it had come out of the blue. Even after the captain's friendly letter, there had still been the faint, unreasonable hope that perhaps there was some mistake. The captain had taken his name off the wrong list, a list of special people, whom the Navy could not spare.

Ben had never been anybody special. He had always been in the middle, in any group. At school and in the Navy, he had neither failed examinations nor passed them with honours. In games, he had always been a reserve for the team, never in the team itself. The middleweight semi-finals at Subic Bay were the nearest he had ever got to personal glory.

It was the same in the war. Other people did spectacular things, like sinking the *Karlsruhe*, and crippling the *Lutzow*, and finishing off two out of three Italian liners in convoy with only four torpedoes.

Ben had done his job in submarines adequately and with a reasonable degree of fortitude, but he had never had the luck to be in at the death of any of the big prizes. The ships he had sunk were cargo vessels and coasters; the risks he had run were the everyday hazards of the war at sea. Even his ditching had been an inconspicuous affair of a British mine in an unexpected place. No tales to tell afterwards of German machine-gun bullets popping the water round his head and a grinning Prussian face leaning over the rail to jeer at him.

Other people came out of the war with Mentions and worthwhile gongs that tacked letters after their names. Ben only had the regular campaign medals, and a set of confidential reports that were satisfactory; neither outstanding nor peculiarly bad. If anyone at the Admiralty wanted a little light reading to while away the half-hour before the tea-tray came, they would never pull out Ben's file.

He folded the letter and replaced it in its envelope. What comfort to tell himself that he was only one of hundreds of commanders who would read these same words in the next two years? Only the outstanding and the very lucky would reach the rank of captain. There was something so ordinary about being axed. That was what hurt.

After all I've done for them, he told the mourning crowd. Did I want to join the Navy in the first place? You know I didn't. But I've worked like a dog for them. Given them the best years of my life, and what do they do? Sling me out with a lump of money which I'll probably squander on some hopeless venture, and tell me: 'Thanks very much, it was nice knowing you, but don't come round any more.'

He sat on his bed for a while, trying to work himself up into a high-class state of gloom, for this was, after all, a momentous point in his life. Then he got up with a sigh, changed into dog robbers and went into the town to get drunk.

Telling Rose was not easy. It had not been so bad telling Frank and the rest of the crowd at Blockhouse. They knew already, because someone had seen the buff envelope and passed the word round. Naval Conditions and Welfare did not write to a commander to tell him how the ducks were standing the winter in St James's Park.

Everyone was very nice to Ben, and wanted to buy him more drinks than he could stand after last night's solitary debauch in the Gosport public houses. Their friendly regrets were genuine, but a certain brooding look in the eye showed that a part of their thoughts were on their own predicament, which Ben's had brought that much closer, as they asked themselves: Who will be next?

Rose's thoughts were almost entirely with herself, with only a passing consideration as to how Ben felt. By the time he saw her, he was not feeling so bad. His natural optimism had taken charge and twisted his head round so that he was not looking back to the lost years of his naval career, but forward to whatever this new civilian life had to offer. A dozen possible jobs played pleasantly round his head. He was not qualified for any of them, but everyone had to start somewhere. If he was an employer, he would much rather train an industrious chap of thirty-five than a goon of seventeen who lived only for clocking-off time.

Although he was not yet out of the Navy, he was already beginning to feel less a part of it. With no future in it for him, it was impossible to sustain any interest in the business of H.M.S. *Dolphin*, so he had decided to take the chance the Admiralty had given him to bow himself out at the end of the month.

When Rose had finished expostulating: 'They can't do that! They can't just throw you out in that high-handed way. I'll write to my M.P. Who is my M.P.?' Ben told her of his decision.

'Oh, no, darling.' She turned to him with one of those swooping movements she did so well. They were in the little kitchen of her flat, cooking supper with the maximum of disorder, but Rose could swoop in the most confined and cluttered space without knocking anything over.

'Why not? When you've got to go, you've got to go, and I'd rather do it now. If I hang on until everyone else is out too, it will be that much more difficult to get a job. I'll be that much older too.'

'But they *want* you to stay till the end of next year. They said so.' Rose could interpret even an official letter her way. She put her wrists on his shoulders, hanging her hands over his back because they were greasy, and trying to hynotize him with the brilliance of her eyes. 'Stay till then. Perhaps they'll change their minds by that time.'

Ben shook his head.

'Well, but anything might happen by then. There might be a war, or something. Stay a little while, Ben. I like you in the Navy.'

'I know you do,' Ben said. 'What you mean is that in another year you probably won't know me any more, but I may as well be called Commander Francis while you do.'

'Now you're being silly.' Rose drawled the last word and turned away from him to fiddle with a pan on the stove.

'How about marrying me?'

She jerked her shoulders at him impatiently. 'Don't ask me that now,' she said. 'We're not discussing that.'

'Would you marry me if I hung on in the Navy until they threw me out at closing time?'

'Oh – I don't know.' Rose fussed with the potatoes, shaking them and turning them over and over so that none of them had a chance to get brown. 'I can't think about that now. I'm all upset by what you've told me. And you're not helping me by being so pigheaded.'

'I've merely made up my mind.' Ben poured himself a drink. 'I don't think that's especially pigheaded. It's my life, and I don't see why I shouldn't do what I like with it.'

As if summoned by a cue line in a play, Rose dropped the spatula and turned round. Ben set down his drink hastily as she came at him with open arms.

'It's our life, darling!' she declared, as if that were also a line from a play. It probably was. 'Don't try to slip away from me.' Rose could not bear to let any man leave her under his own steam. If an affair was to break up, it had to be her idea.

She put her arms round Ben, and he kissed her. She responded with unusual warmth and murmured some rather suggestive things. It was hard to tell whether she meant it, or whether she was merely acting out a love scene, for sometimes when she seemed to be passionate, she would jerk abruptly out of his embrace with a remark as irrelevant and composed as if they had been simply shaking hands.

She was pleasantly passionate now, and Ben was stretching out a hand to turn off the gas flames under their supper, when Rose said in a small, preoccupied voice: 'If we got married when you were out of the Navy, could you still be married in uniform?'

'Oh, I don't think so.' Ben left the gas taps alone. 'A bit off, that would be.'

39

'The swords,' Rose said dreamily, 'and the gold braid. It would make some marvellous pictures.'

The next morning, Ben went down to Southampton to break the news to his mother and father. He had not written, because they were not very good with letters. They were apt to read into them all sorts of things that were not intended.

It was better to tell them himself, and to try to cheer them up. They would be heartbroken, or at least they would say that they were. They used words like heartbroken and sick at heart in a rather loose way. Their lives would not be completely shattered, but they would be very upset to think that the Navy did not want their son. Ben's mother would shut herself into her room with the telephone and his father would go down to the Nautical Club, to broadcast their distress to the retired maritime community on the east bank of Southampton Water. That was why Ben had not already warned them that he might be selected for what the Admiralty politely called Premature Retirement. His father, who read the papers from end to end as part of the illusion he fostered of a busy day, was aware of the Service cuts, but Ben had allowed him to go on believing that this was something that happened to other people's sons, not his. No sense in their going about telling everyone that they were sick at heart before it actually happened.

He supposed that he should have gone straight from Gosport before he went to London to tell Rose, but he was cowardly enough to want to take his candy before his medicine. Even when she was annoyed with him, Rose was lovely. Ben had no idea whether he wanted to spend the rest of his life with her, but he still took enormous pleasure in having the right to her company whenever he wanted it, which was whenever he could get to London.

He had sought to refresh himself with an evening with Rose before he tackled the effort of Saturday and Sunday with his parents. If only he had a sister, or Matthew were still alive. Ben was everything they had, that was the trouble. It was not strictly true, for they had each other, and a few depressing relations, and their clubs and their newspaper competitions and their narrow, busy social life; but they told themselves that it was true, and that was what made the trouble, both for them and for Ben. They were inevitably disappointed in him, and he, recognizing their self-deception, could not help being disappointed in himself for not being able to live up to it.

Since their eldest son had lost his life off Heligoland in one of the first submarine actions of the war, they had declared that they lived for Ben. This was an exaggeration, for they saw so little of him that if he were the breath of life to them, they would have suffocated long ago.

'He is my life,' Ben's mother was wont to say, and his father had been known to embarrass people by intoning: 'Everything I ever wanted for myself is centred in that lad,' and unhooking the wire earpiece of his spectacles to wipe away the moisture.

They were going to be hurt by Ben's news. It was not his fault, but without accusing him, they would make him feel that it was. As he sat in the train and watched Surrey go by, he wished that it would not pass with such speed. That child perched on the embankment fence would not wave him on so gaily if she knew how reluctant he was to arrive at the prim stucco house in the Southampton suburb which never felt like home, and which he could barely enter without wishing to leave.

He was sitting on the right side of the train, as he always did when he made this journey, for there was a house on that side he had to see.

His parents had lived in or near Southampton for as long as he could remember, and he had travelled on this line hundreds of times, and knew all its landmarks. Over the years, he had learned quite a lot about the people who lived along the line. He had seen farms and cottages swallowed up by expanding towns. He had watched, with as much interest as if he had money in the venture, a man build a small factory on waste land at the end of a cinder track, and gradually enlarge it with shed after shed until now it was quite a proud concern, with cars as well as bicycles waiting outside, and a paved road, and all the windows lit at night for twenty-four-hour production.

He had seen houses change their character with different owners, and whole streets deteriorate from semi-detached respectability where housewives fought the railway for the whiteness of their curtains, to bomb-scarred, untenable slums with boards nailed across the broken windows.

He had watched the progress of the lean man and his muscular wife as they painstakingly landscaped a garden neglected for years, and then created a model turkey farm at the end of it. He had sorrowed over another garden, once beautiful, but gradually reverting to weeds and jungle, because the gardener left during the war and the old man in a flat cap who used to potter with a trowel had disappeared, presumably to the grave, and the old lady who used to sit and watch him from a wicker chair retired behind her curtains and was never seen out again. Did she live alone? She was still alive, because her bulky shadow could occasionally be seen on the blind of a dimly-lit downstairs room. As the train racketed by the unheeding house, Ben looked anxiously to see if there was a collection of unopened milk bottles on the back doorstep.

There was one house on the London side of Basingstoke which never changed. The same family had lived in it for as long as Ben could remember, and the house itself remained the same, neither prosperous nor down at heel, unaffected by wars or weather or the growing up of the family whose biography Ben had constructed from glimpses snatched as the train crossed the bridge over the road which ran by their front gate.

The house had first begun to fascinate Ben when he was a boy, making the journey to London and beyond to the second-class public school preferred by his father to the local day school, which could have provided a comparable education, but not the cachet of 'sending my boy away to school'. Matthew was away at Dartmouth. Ben must go away too and learn to stand on his own like a man. Once when Ben had had pleurisy and was not man enough to go back to school without his mother accompanying him to warn the matron about his chest, he had tried to share his interest in this house with her.

The little wood went by, the huge elm in the middle of the field, the sides of the bridge rose up – 'Look, Mum, there it is!'

'Where, dear?' She peered out much too late as the train took the curve and the house was gone. Stimulated by a glimpse of the two girls in the garden – the boy would be at school, for Ben was late going back this term – he told his mother some of the things he knew or had made up about the family. Sitting back in her corner, with her gloves on and her ankles crossed, she had wagged her head at him, marvelling at his imagination without making any effort to share it.

'You always were a fanciful child, Benjy,' she told him, and when he paused in his enthusiastic story, she began to talk about where they would have lunch when they changed trains in London.

Ben did not point out the house to her any more when they went to London together. She did not remember about it, but Ben went on watching and noticing and imagining, until he built up a sort of distant intimacy with it and the family who lived there.

It was an early Victorian house of darkening red brick, with many gables, ill-matched chimneys, and weathered white paint round the windows. The side nearest the train was bulky with ivy. Once they had stripped it all off, but it grew back again in two years, up to the crooked iron S which held the top part of the house together.

There was a garden all round the house, lawns and shrubs and evergreens, with a small, neglected orchard where the washing lines hung, and a group of tall trees near the road where the children had made a ramshackle house among the branches. There was a moss-blurred driveway, some out-buildings at the back, and two untidily-hedged fields with the gateways trampled to mud or caked earth according to the season.

The house had obviously been built before the railway, perhaps by the great-grandfather of the present owner. What bad luck for the first generation to have their peaceful corner of countryside invaded by the mechanical dragons of the London and South-Western Railway. The family did not seem to notice the trains now, for they seldom looked up; but it must have taken their ancestors a long time to get used to them. Ben could imagine that first owner, with mutton-chops and tweed knicker-bockers, waging a furious war when the railway was first mooted: writing letters to *The Times*, signed 'Indignant Land-owner', bullying his M.P. about opposing the Railway Bill, stumping among the workmen who were laying the lines, prod-

ding at things with an ash stick and threatening to shoot anyone who put a foot on his land.

When the first trains began to go by, and the children in their
big hats and cumbersome clothes ran out into the garden to
shout and scream at the novelty of this marvellous chugging
monster which snorted clouds of steam and sent the rooks
cawing round the sky, the father would watch dourly from an
upstairs window, shaking his fist and saying it would not last.
He kept a gun in the bedroom in case of thieves, and his faded
wife, worn out with child-bearing, lived in terror that he might
take a pot-shot at the late train when it woke him in the
night.

The railway was there to stay, and gradually the family grew
used to it. For a few months perhaps the children stood by the
fence like the little smock-and-knickerbocker group in *The
Railway Children*, and waved to the trains, but as the novelty
wore off they went back to their old games, and the father
stopped writing letters and did not wake any more in the night.

Perhaps they talked occasionally of moving, but they loved
the house and so they stayed. They assimilated the trains as a
part of life, and each succeeding generation assimilated them
too, and only hated the railway when another maid left because
of soot on the laundry, or yet another foolish dog lost its life
on the rails.

The mother of this present generation kept horses in a stable
behind the house, and there was a horse trailer under an open
shed. That implied a certain amount of money, although
nothing else about the family spoke of wealth. Perhaps her
husband was always complaining that she spent too much on
the horses, but she had a little money of her own and did not
see why she should not spend it how she liked. Ben sometimes
saw her in the yard, doing things with buckets and pitchforks.

When the children were young – the two girls younger than
Ben, the boy about his own age – there had been ponies. Now
that they were grown-up, Ben did not see them on a horse.
Perhaps the mother's enthusiasm had discouraged them. He
had once seen the elder girl ambling down the road, slopping
long-backed in the saddle, as if she had learned nothing from
her mother.

The girl got her long back from her father. He was a lean and stringy type, seen sometimes in overalls, hammering and sawing around the house. It was probably he who had pulled down the ivy, but inefficiently, so that it started to grow again immediately. He had dug a pond once in the front lawn. It had never held water.

The other sister was small and lively, but the son was as tall as his father. Ben had watched him grow from a gangling youth into a presentable man, who for years now had been seen only occasionally at week-ends, once getting out of a car with two small children and a plump girl who must be his wife.

Quite an ordinary family, but fascinating to Ben because he only knew them in his mind. Perhaps they disliked each other and were each discontented in their separate ways, but he preferred to believe in them as he saw them. They represented something which he had never had, even when Marion was pregnant with Amy and had come as near as she ever could to domestic serenity.

As the train passed the familiar landmarks, Ben leaned forward so that he should not miss anything that was going on about the house. There was a new horse in the field. It threw up its head and ran as the train approached. The next time Ben came by, it would have seen so many trains that it would not twitch an ear.

Greedily, with a swift, practised eye, Ben took in all the details. A bucket tipped over outside the stable. A cat mewing to get in at the kitchen door. A hanging, broken branch which the father should get at with his saw. Too cold for there to be anyone in the garden. Yes, there was. A girl in an old sheepskin coat. Not the pretty one with whom Ben was in love, but the older one, throwing a stick for a dog which bounded in a flurry of dead leaves. She looked up for a moment as the train rushed by above her, then the side of the bridge rose up and she was gone.

Ben sat back in his seat. Why did she look up at the trains, the untidy one with the long, schoolgirlish legs? The others never did, and she never used to when she was younger. For a fraction of a second as he passed over her garden, it had seemed that she caught his eye. Did she see him through the space he had wiped on the steamy glass and wish that she were Ben, going somewhere, envying him because he was on the move; just as he envied her because she was playing in the leaves with a dog and he was travelling sedately to Wavecrest, Firbanks Avenue, where there was no garden worth the name, and no dog, and a difficult two days ahead of him?

Lunch was cooking as Ben arrived at his parents' house – he never thought of it as home. As he stood on the doorstep between the pair of curly Chinese dragons which fitted so ill with the square concrete and stucco house and the geometrical flower-beds, edged with looped wire, he could smell beef roasting. Well, that was something. He was to be given the prodigal's welcome, with Yorkshire pudding and all the trimmings, although his mother would overcook the beef and it would be tasteless as slate when they had it cold for lunch tomorrow. Perhaps he could get away early.

The front door was locked. Ben had a feeling that the doors of the house by the railway were never locked. Firbanks Avenue was a quiet street, on the way to nowhere except a disused gravel-pit, and there were no mental institutions nearby, and nothing in the house to steal except Ben's father's oriental souvenirs from the days when he was in the P. & O., but there were double bolts on all the doors, and little chains and pegs fitted to the windows to stop them being opened from the outside far enough to get an arm through. This also meant that they could not be opened from the inside far enough to get an arm through, or to get any appreciable amount of air; but Ben's mother did not shake dusters or mops out of windows. She shook them on to a piece of newspaper. His father had once had malaria, which had never recurred, but had given him an excuse to keep out the good sea air and enjoy a comfortable stuffiness.

Ben would not use the electric chime – his mother's pride – so he thumped on the frosted glass at the top of the door, and heard her quick feet coming tap tap along the linoleum.

'Don't bang on the glass, dear,' she said automatically. She wiped her hands on her apron and stood on tiptoe to kiss him, for she was very small.

All the way from London, Ben had rehearsed how he should break the news. Better perhaps to tell them as soon as he stepped into the house rather than let them think that this was just a friendly visit prompted by nothing more sinister than filial affection. If he let them preserve that illusion any longer than necessary, there would be a double-edged accusation hanging in the air. Not only had he let himself get kicked out of the Navy, but he had let them welcome him as if everything was all right. He would tell his mother immediately, and then she could go running in to his father crying: 'Tommy, Tommy, the most disastrous thing has happened!' and his father would puff out his cheeks and look as if he had been struck by lightning, and they could get the worst of it over right away perhaps, and then get on with lunch.

'Mum,' he began as she helped him off with his coat, but she was not listening to him.

'I quite thought we would see you yesterday,' she was saying. 'I was surprised when you phoned to say you wouldn't be here till Saturday, with the week-end half gone.' No matter how glad she was to see him, she invariably managed to make him feel guilty for not having come sooner.

'I'm sorry,' he said. 'I had to go to London.' He would let her finish fussing with his coat, brushing the collar with the edge of her hand and squaring up the shoulders on the hanger, and then tell her.

'Tommy! Benjy is here!' she called, although Ben's father was already opening the sitting-room door and could see for himself.

'Well, well, well,' he said, rubbing his hands and nodding his head. 'So you're here at last, Benjamin. Quite a sight for sore eyes.'

'He didn't come last night, because he had to go to London,' Mrs Francis told him, as if answering a question they had been discussing at some length.

'I've come to tell you, Dad,' Ben began. 'I –'

'Come in, come in,' his father said. 'Don't stand there like a stranger.'

Another moment was lost, and Ben followed his father into the sitting-room. His mother came too, taking off her apron.

She never wore it in the sitting-room in case someone came unexpectedly to call, although, as her husband never heard the door chimes, and nobody without gelignite could get into the house unless she shot back the bolts for them, there was not much chance of her being caught off her guard.

They all sat down on various pieces of the embossed suite of furniture which had managed to remain as unreceptively convex as when it was bought five years ago. Ben's mother sat on the edge of the chair with her ankles crossed and her hands clasped, and looked at him with her bright, beady eyes. She was a spry little woman with a magpie look about her greying black hair and a taste in clothes which ran to the sulphur-yellows and heliotropes and that sickly colour which was once foisted on to a loyal public as Marina green when the Duchess of Kent was married. Only her skin was grey and colourless, and appeared more so because of her bright clothes and hats. She could have refurbished it to match her apparel, but in her code you did not do things to the face God gave you.

Ben's father sat in his chair with his thick thighs apart and his torso laid between them like an egg. He too looked at Ben through his round spectacles, and Ben took a deep breath and started to say: 'Well, the axe caught up with me at last.'

As he spoke, his father spoke too, in his louder boom. 'Sun's over the yardarm.' He pushed himself upright and went over to the cupboard under the gramophone, from which he produced a new half-bottle of gin, and broke the seal. It was always a new bottle, bought expressly for Ben's visits. A generous gesture in a frugal household, but one which succeeded in making him feel that they thought of him as an alcoholic who would not come at all if he was only going to be given beer.

He poured pink gins for himself and Ben and a small gin and orange for his wife, which she held up to the light with her head on one side as if it were a ruby wine before sipping at it with puckered lips.

'Welcome aboard,' Ben's father said, and Ben said: 'Glad to be aboard, sir,' and looked into his glass to find the words to tell him that except as a visitor he would never be aboard one of H.M. ships again.

'So you went to London,' Mr Francis said, stretching out his

48

short legs and leaning back in a man-to-man way. 'Went to see Rose Kelly, eh?'

Ben had not originally told them about Rose, but they had found out about her from Geneva Hogg's sister, Marion's Aunt Florence, with whom Ben's mother had maintained a regular correspondence, although since Marion's death she had lost touch with Geneva, whom she had never liked.

She met Aunt Florence for lunch at Stewart's once a year when she went to London to do her Christmas shopping. Between Christmases, they exchanged animated letters, mostly about the illnesses and bereavements of people unknown to each other, but none the less interesting for that. Then there had been the juicy piece of news about Ben, and when he had come to Wavecrest one week-end to mention casually that he might marry a television star, they had already known about Rose and been able to get in first with: 'Why didn't you tell us?'

They were familiar with Rose's appearance on the television set which perched insecurely on narrow, pointed legs in the corner of the sitting-room, and Mrs Francis's first reaction had been: 'Why did you have to pick another one who was so – you know?' Sexy was the word she might use to Ben when she was roaming chattily round his room at night when he was in bed trying to read, but she would not use it in front of her husband.

Rose would not go to Southampton and Ben's parents seldom went to London, so that they had never met. Rose was not curious about the parents of Ben, or anyone else. She was not interested in the contents of people's lives which did not directly affect her. Ben's parents were curious about her, but not enough to make them drive their little car all the way to London or to do what they called 'facing the trains', so that they talked about her with a certain amount of suspicion, as if she were something that was being kept from them. Ben wished that they could meet, for Rose, who wanted everyone to like her, would be very charming and gracious, and would captivate his mother out of telling his father and people on the telephone: 'I fear the worst.'

'We saw your lady friend on that thing last week,' Mr Francis said, jerking his head to the set whose existence he would not dignify with a name. He watched it by the hour, but would never admit that television was here to stay.

'She was good, didn't you think?'

'So-so. Pretty girl.' He drained his glass and set it down with a little gasp. 'When are you going to make an honest woman of her, Benjamin?' He did not think that his son was living with this woman, but it was just as well to be jocular about it, in case he was.

'I honestly don't know,' Ben said truthfully.

'An actress,' his mother said. 'I don't know. It worries me sick to think what kind of wife she would make for a naval officer. If only she was on the B.B.C., it wouldn't seem to matter so much.'

Now was the time to tell them that he would soon no longer be a naval officer, but his mother was off to the kitchen to dish up the lunch, and if Ben told his father while she was absent she would say that they were trying to keep things from her.

He could not mention it during lunch either, because the commotion with knife sharpeners and vegetable dishes and tipping the platter to extract the gravy from under the meat, and a long and inconclusive discussion as to whether this new butcher was any better than the Co-op, made any serious announcement impossible.

When they had drunk their coffee, from the little lacquer cups which were so narrow that you hit your nose trying to get to the bottom of them, and before his father could knock out his gold-banded pipe and say: 'How about taking a turn down the road to look at the sad sea waves?' Ben stood up in front of the tiled stove in the fireplace and said: 'I'm being axed from the Navy.'

His father looked stunned and his mother clapped a flowered handkerchief to her mouth, and they both said: 'Why didn't you tell us before?'

Ben's mother was sick at heart all the next morning, and would not go to church because she said she could not face the neighbours.

'Oh, look here, Mum.' Ben rather wanted to go to church with her. It was one of the few things they did together which gave him the illusion of being a closely knit family. Also it would get him out of the house in case his father wanted to renew last night's discussion of whether he should stay in the Navy as long as he could, or get out next month. Unconsciously echoing Rose, his parents wanted him to stay. Not being realists, they believed in putting off until the last minute anything that was unpalatable. If the newspaper carried nasty headlines about Russia, they read the front page last.

'Even if you have telephoned half the neighbours,' Ben said, 'and they've telephoned the other half, there's nothing disgraceful about my being axed. It's happening to everyone.'

'You are not everyone. You are my son. You don't seem to realize what a crushing blow this has been to me,' his mother said, eating barley sugar as a substitute for the breakfast she had declared herself unable to face. 'I would never have the strength to go out in this wind.'

'After all I'd hoped for. All I'd planned,' Mr Francis intoned. He was prowling about this morning like a ghost in the wrong house, unable to settle to anything. The Sunday papers were still unopened, a thing unheard of.

'Why harp on it?' said Ben, looking at the clock and wondering when he would have the courage to tell them he was not staying for lunch. 'It doesn't help. I felt badly about it first, I must admit, but I'm not sure that I give a damn about it now. It's a new chance, after all. I might make my fortune. One day we may all be glad the Navy threw me out.'

'How can you talk like that?' His father stopped in his prowling, stricken on the green-and-beige hearth-rug. 'The Navy was your life. They've taken your life away from you.'

Ben was silent. Only his listening thoughts heard him answer the old man: It wasn't. I never was a career man. The Navy happened to me because of you – on top of other things. You wanted it to be my life, but there were always so many other things I wanted to do. Now it's too late for most of them.

Too late to be a doctor, a lawyer, a chemist, an architect – all the careers which his changing enthusiasms had considered for his moderate talents when he was still at school, and looking for a life without regimentation, or discipline from anyone except himself. When he left school, the war had come, and imposed regimentation and discipline on everybody. Ben applied for a commission in the Air Force. At least you could be on your own sometimes in a plane.

In January 1940 his elder brother was lost in a submarine in the North Sea. Ben withdrew his application and joined the Naval Reserve. There was nothing else to do, it seemed, if he were ever to meet his father's eyes again.

The Navy was something Mr Francis had always wanted for himself, but his eyesight kept him out. He had spent most of his life at sea, however, as a purser on passenger lines. A mediocre man, with less ambition for himself than for his sons, he had eventually risen from tourist-class purser, but he had never climbed higher than the cabin class, where for countless voyages back and forth across the Atlantic, his humourless anecdotes had bored the five or six passengers who had the misfortune to sit at his table. Widows had tried to draw him out, pretty women in irresponsible sea-going mood had tried to tease him. All in vain. It was always a relief on the last night of a crossing when Mr Francis was too busy to come to the saloon for dinner.

All his hopes and dreams were centred in the clever, genial Matthew, the very cut of a naval officer, as his father called him, our future First Sea Lord. When Matthew was taken from him, the hopes and dreams were transferred to Ben. As Matthew had been in submarines, when Ben was a sub-lieutenant, he chose submarines too. What difference did it make? There was a war on, and it was at least something he could do to please his father, ploughing his way through the hazardous seas in the troop-transport liner in which he had once held his sober little cocktail parties, where his *hors d'œuvres* were more exciting than the conversation.

At the end of the war, when everyone was trying to get out and there was a scramble for jobs, Ben had transferred to the regular Navy. His father desperately wanted it, and he had to have a decent job if he was going to marry Marion. She was not the type who would live in a caravan until you found work, or to get up at half past five to send you off fed to a factory.

School and the Navy were all he had ever known of life beyond the threshold of home. Now he had a chance to find out what else was going on in the world. How could his father talk about his life being taken away from him? When he got away from this house and could think straight without his confusion of irritation and pity, Ben believed that he was going to find that what the Navy had done was to give his life back to him.

When he told his parents that he must get the bus for Gosport before lunch, his mother put on a little act of bravery. She braced her small body in the cerise wool dress, jerked her chin up, and said: 'We don't want to interfere with your plans. I had made an apple pie for you, but I dare say your father and I will manage to eat a little of it.' Stepping rather high, like a pony, she went upstairs to telephone her sister in Reading and tell her about Ben, and spoil her day too.

Mr Francis went to look out of the bay window which faced across the sandy road to the Carsons' house, where there was a flag-pole in the paved garden, and red and green running lights on either side of the gate.

'You know what did it, of course.' He turned round, and his voice was matter-of-fact, discounting argument. 'It was the scandal. The Admiralty has all those newspaper clippings about your wife.' He hardly ever said Marion's name. 'They would be attached to your confidential reports, and they've counted against you.'

'That was more than three years ago. None of it was my fault anyway. They couldn't hold that against me.'

'Then what else have they got against you?' Mr Francis looked defeated. His head sagged forward on his short neck, and you could see what he would look like at eighty. 'You've had a fine career. Never put a foot wrong, as far as I know. A good war record, and command of two subs since then.' He looked at the wall by the fireplace, where photographs of all Ben's ships hung in chronological order, with the date of his service in them printed underneath.

With a disappointed little snort, he turned from the pictures and sat down heavily in his armchair. 'I don't know why this should happen to me,' he said in a wondering, child-like way. 'I really don't.'

'Please understand, Dad,' Ben made one more effort. 'You shouldn't take it this way. It's happening to everybody.'

'So you tell me,' his father said mulishly. 'So you tell me.' He picked up the newspaper and rustled it over to the page where he was pursuing, with every expectation of winning a speedboat or a six-cylinder car, a weekly competition to choose the six smartest cocktail dresses from some thirty small and ill-defined fashion photographs.

'Edna sends us all her deepest sympathy,' his mother announced, returning from the telephone. Ben hoped that he was not going to start getting letters of condolence from all the people to whom his mother had announced the tragedy. If Aunt Edna had the nerve to write patronizingly, after what the magistrates had said about her son, he would answer her on black-edged paper.

'Well, Benjy.' His mother stretched her pale lips into a gay little smile. 'You'll want to be getting along, I suppose. Daddy, shall we have the cold beef, or would you rather finish the curry? There's still a spoonful of chutney left, I believe.'

If she had begged him to stay on bended knees, with tears streaming down her face, it would not have had as much effect as this bleak little speech. The thought of them at their Sunday lunch in the chilly little dining-room, passing things to each other across his chair pushed in against the table edge was more than Ben could bear. When he told his mother that he would take the afternoon bus, and she realized that her apple pie had not been cooked in vain, her face lit up and she turned swiftly for the kitchen, uttering little exclamations of joy.

Chapter Four

'It makes me feel such a swine,' he told Geneva Hogg. 'I do nothing for them. I don't go there often enough. I want to get away from the place as soon as I arrive, and when I say I'll stay two hours longer, they're in heaven.'

'Don't let it get you down,' Geneva said. 'That's parents for you. Only yours are more helpless than most.' She set down the two coffee cups, slopping into their saucers, stirred them, licked the spoon and sat down opposite him by the gigantic fireplace where Ben, ignorant of the price of coal, had built a huge and incandescent fire.

The fireplace was gigantic because everything had been planned on a large scale when this was built as a three-storey house for one family. It was a typical Bayswater house of that period: solid, big-windowed, with cowled chimney-pots set together in rows, a heavy cornice round the unseen roof, and just enough embellishment in the way of a pillared porch and black and white marble steps to give it an air of unpretentious prosperity.

The house was plastered on three sides and decorated in the cream colour beloved by London painters because it quickly becomes dingy and needs renewing. The back was plain sooty brick, because no one was supposed to see it except the servants when they came up from the basement to hang out the washing.

When there were no longer any servants to tackle a house of this size and therefore no families able to live in it, the land-lord had converted it into four flats by the rudimentary method of dividing the big rooms by flimsy partitions. The moulding on the ceilings and the carved plaster friezes were cut off short by the new walls, so that the rooms always seemed to be what they were, just pieces of larger rooms.

In Geneva's flat on the second floor, the partitions had been knocked up in a very arbitrary way, and the rooms had queer shapes and were in unexpected places. The bathroom, which was like a condemned cell, was on the other side of the kitchen, which had one corner less than a right-angle from which the dirt had to be hooked with a finger, since it could not be got at with a broom. Amy's bedroom and the spare room where Ben slept were higher than they were long, like upended shoe-boxes. Geneva's bedroom had three doors and windows and practic-ally no wall space, so that she had to keep most of her clothes outside in a top-heavy wardrobe which loomed at the end of the corridor, blocking the light. The pitch-dark corridor wandered like a canyon between the rooms, pushed out of the way in the middle by the side of the lift-shaft. Groaning like the souls in purgatory, the lift crept up and down in a wire cage festooned with dust. At night it crouched in the basement making restless ticking noises.

The drawing-room, dwarfed by its wide, draughty windows that looked to the Park over the tops of the Bayswater Road buses and by the mammoth fireplace whose mantelpiece was out of Amy's reach, was the shape of half an octagon. All the small, amorphous rooms were filled with pictures and furniture with which Geneva could not bear to part when her husband died and she moved here from the country, but the drawing-room was the most crowded of all.

'I like to have my things where I can see them in the room where I live,' Geneva said, and had crammed them all in until there was scarcely any room for living. Getting to the other end of the room was hazardous. There was only one electric outlet from which a multiple plug sent fraying wires in all directions to trip you up and send the lamps flying.

It was mostly Ben who knocked the lamps off their rickety tables and stands, and Geneva's clumsier friends, like the ham-handed Major. Amy was too nimble and too familiar with the flat to knock things over, and Geneva, though neither neat nor nimble, moved among her beloved shabby possessions with the instinctive avoidance of the blind. She loved her flat, with all its quirks and inconveniences. She had not cared for her square flint house at Maidenhead any more than she had cared for the husband who had tried for twenty years to make her conform to his brutally rigid code of behaviour, and who had died without achieving it. His name had been against him from the start. Having allowed him to impose that on her, she was not going to let him get away with anything else. He would have crushed the spirit of most women. Not Geneva. Her spirit, unlike her skin, had preserved its elasticity. At seventy-two, she was stripped down to her driving mechanism of restless energy, with a cracked laugh and an opinion about anything that came up, especially when she knew nothing about it.

Slightly raffish in appearance, with her sparse ginger hair twisted into airedale curls, and a liking for big, shiny handbags and jewellery which clanked at her bony neck and wrists like a spectre's chains, she was no one's idea of a cosy grandmother. Amy and she loved each other with an independent, uncritical love which gave more than it demanded. Ben loved her too. She was one of the things he and Marion had fought about.

Ben had wanted to invite Geneva out to Malta, or to stay with them at Portland. Marion did not want her because she said that her mother always had one gin too many at cocktail parties.

Geneva lifted her skirt a little to let the warmth of the fire get at her spindly legs, and leaned back to pour her coffee back from the saucer to the cup. The coffee table was a round brass tray on legs, which gave forth a thin, resonant sound when you picked anything off it. It could never be used as a tray, because without it the legs collapsed and could not be put together again.

Ben drank his coffee quickly. It was gritty and slightly oily, in spite of the new percolator he had given Geneva. He could make better coffee himself with an old tin mug and a can of condensed milk, but Geneva liked to do things for him. Ben's mother would seldom sit down before lunch because of the Upstairs, but Geneva loved to drop whatever she was doing at any time of day and sit with him like this, talking, wasting the morning away, with the laundry unsorted and the sink full of breakfast dishes.

'Another thing,' Ben said, 'that makes me feel guilty. I'm fonder of you than of my mother.'

Geneva neither protested at this nor fished for flattery. 'It's because I'm not your responsibility,' she said. 'Poor Sybil is.' She had referred to his mother as Poor Sybil ever since she first met her at Ben and Marion's wedding in that unfortunate royal blue three-quarter-length dress.

'With parents, you see,' she went on, 'it's like this. First you are their child. Then all at once you find the balance has tipped up and they are suddenly your children. It's hard to say exactly when it happens. With my parents, it was after my honeymoon, when I found out my mother had told me the facts of life all wrong. In your case, it was probably when they lost Matthew. That must have taken away a lot of the old dears' stamina.' Geneva was older than either of Ben's parents, but she referred to them as if they were a bygone generation.

'God, yes.' Ben leaned forward and looked into the quivering heat of the fire. 'They were pathetic. I remember going home that time. They hadn't written to me, oddly enough. It was the one time Mum didn't rush to send bad news through the mail.

Dad had got leave, but he was in uniform. One of his old ones, a bit shiny. He'd been quite robust at the beginning of the war. He can't have been much more than fifty, but when I saw him then, he had sagged, and suddenly seemed much older in a feeble, rather childish way. My mother wasn't talking much. She just blurted out: "Matthew is dead," and then they both sat there and stared at me helplessly, waiting to see what I could do about it.'

'Yes, I can see it. So you had to go into the Navy. I can see why. A toy for a crying child. Now the Navy's putting you out and taking their toy away from them. Naturally the poor old souls are upset.'

'Won't they set just as much store by me when I'm a company director?' Ben stretched back in the worn armchair, whose seat was so near the ground that it would take a block and tackle to get you out of it in a hurry. 'I have a feeling I'm going to be terrifically successful.'

'You'll have to, if you're going to keep that Kelly girl.' Geneva laughed. It amused her to think of Ben and Rose. When she laughed, it was sometimes like the cawing of rooks before a storm, sometimes like the clamour of barn-yard fowl. 'Or is she going to keep you?'

'Apparently not. She says I have to get a job.'

'What as? I wish you'd go into shipping. Jack Friedman could get you in with his lot. He'd do it for me.'

'No more ships. I want something new. God knows what, but I'll find something. I'll make a tardy but brilliant career, and set the old folks up in a fine house on the Beaulieu River, with maids.'

Amy came noisily into the room in a thick blue school overcoat with the collar turned up. She had been playing in a hockey match. She was in the fourth eleven, and she was very sporting at the moment, because she was in love with a girl called Fiona Maclaren, who was captain of the first eleven. She wore her long bronze hair in tight pigtails and affected a slightly rolling walk.

She leaned over the back of Ben's chair to kiss him, and ran her small hand through his short hair. 'Feels like stroking a dog,' she said with satisfaction. She came round the chair to stand straddle-legged in front of it, smelling of cold outdoor London.

'I've been promoted,' she announced in the terse, tight-lipped voice she used for talking about hockey. 'I played left wing today. When Miss Ascott said: "Amy Francis on the left wing", I almost died. Poor Brenda Sims is still right half. She'll never get anywhere.'

Ben, who had played hockey for various naval teams, was aware of the subtle social distinctions between positions on the field, but Geneva asked: 'Why is left wing any better than right wing, where you played last week?'

'Oh, Grandma, surely you've lived with me long enough to know that. It doesn't matter who plays right wing, because no one ever passed to you on that side. In the first eleven they do, of course. Not in the fourth.'

Ben had not seen Amy since the letter came from the Admiralty. Geneva had told her the news, and he asked her what she thought of it.

'It's hard cheese,' she said, in her new hockey language, 'but Miss Maynard says there'll be another war soon, so you'll be back in before you know it. I hope so. It will be a pity not to say: My father, Commander Francis, any more. Or could I still?'

'I don't think so. I'll call myself Mister.'

'The Major doesn't.'

'The Major. That's different,' Geneva said, and they all laughed. They usually laughed when they spoke of the Major. He was a disreputable friend of Geneva's who had been hanging around for years with his spattered veins and wobbly knees. He came in and out of the flat unheralded and at will, sometimes bringing a bottle in case Geneva was down to the last dregs of whisky or gin.

'Well, I'll buzz off,' Amy said. 'I have to oil my hockey stick.' She banged out of the door and went stamping and whistling down the passage to the kitchen.

'Don't worry,' Geneva said. 'It won't last.'

'Grandma!' Amy's voice came thin and piercing from the other end of the flat. 'Gregory's here!'

'Oh, my God.' Geneva clapped a hand to her forehead. 'I

forgot it again. Tell him to come in here!' She raised her voice in a shout which cracked on the last word and set her coughing.

A young man in a green coat embroidered with the name of a laundry appeared in the doorway. 'Basket's empty, Mrs H.,' he said. 'Looks like you've fallen down on the job again.'

'Oh, Greg.' She ravished him with one of her special smiles. 'Couldn't you make just a few other calls and then come back? I've been so busy, I haven't had a moment to do it, and if I don't send the sheets this week, Amy and I will be sleeping in blankets like refugees. And the Commander, too, if he slings his hammock here. The Navy's through with him.'

'Is that so, sir?' Gregory turned his round, black head to look at Ben compassionately. 'I'm sorry to hear that.'

'Oh, don't be.' Geneva flapped a hand at him. 'He doesn't give a damn, any more than you did when they threw you and your ulcer out of the Air Force. How is it? Been acting up again?'

'So so. I get my turns.'

'You should have gone to see that man I told you about. I said I'd pay. These National Health people will kill you. You will come back, won't you, Greg?' She put her head on one side, charming him like a pet bird that does not know what it looks like in the moulting season.

'If you'll get that basket packed right away. I've only a few calls to make round here, and I'm not coming back for the fun of it, even for you, Mrs H.'

'Of course, of course. I'm on my way already.' Geneva made no attempt to move.

The laundryman looked at her suspiciously, said: 'All the best, Commander', and went out.

'Ask Amy to give you some coffee!' Geneva called after him.

The polished black head reappeared round the door. 'You want to kill me?'

'Oh, of course.' They nodded solemnly at each other, in silent homage to the ulcer.

'Quite the nicest man,' Geneva said when the head withdrew. 'Of course, it wasn't the Air Force that gave him the ulcer. It was his wife. She's a bitch on wheels, from what he tells me. Had all her teeth pulled out when she was twenty-five because she couldn't stand the drill. I can imagine what she looks like in bed at night.'

'Even if you know all the details of his private life,' Ben said mildly, 'do you have to tell him about mine?'

'Why not? He takes a great interest. I hope you're not going to be touchy about being kicked out of the Navy. I'm beginning to think it may be the finest thing that could have happened to you. You were getting rather stuffy and parochial. I hope you'll get out as soon as you can, now you've got the chance. Poor Sybil and the old man are crazy to want you to hang on like a drowning man. Why waste your time?'

She got up, but it was not to do the laundry. It was because when she was working herself up about something, she could not talk sitting down. She had to move about, touching things, jerking the furniture about; or stand shifting from foot to foot, clasping her hands, twisting her necklace, scratching her thigh.

'You're not a coward. Get out and see what you can do,' she exhorted Ben. 'Don't listen to those timid old Jessies at Southampton or to that glamour girl you're chasing, who just wants to keep you in storage at Gosport where you won't meet any girls who don't look like the back of a bus. The Navy says they're through with you. All right, tell 'em you're through with them, and let them find some other stooge to teach the infant class. There's other things in life besides being called Sir and having all that pretty gold stuff on your hat.'

'Perhaps I'll get a job where someone will call me Sir.' Ben was half ashamed of himself for saying this, but he was always honest with Geneva. 'I don't care about the scrambled egg, but it may be a bit tough at first, not being an officer.'

'You see – that's what the Navy's done for you. Made you think you're somebody.' Geneva put on a mocking face, then she suddenly took it off and reached out a hand to stroke the top of his head in Amy's fond gesture. 'If it's going to be tough, Ben, do it quick.'

'As a matter of fact,' he twisted his head unobtrusively away as one of the big rings caught him on the ear. 'I've already told Their Lordships I want to get out next month. I didn't tell you or Rose or the old folks, because I wanted you all to agree to it first. You see, I am a coward.'

'You're not. You're just too lazy to enjoy arguments. Not like me.' Geneva smacked her lips, smudged at the corners with the mulberry lipstick that never would stay where she put it. 'I thrive on 'em.'

'Why did you tell the laundryman I'd be moving in here? You can't take on me as well as Amy.'

'Why not? You ought to be with her, and you can't pay a decent rent until you get a job, if you're going to invest all your gratuity for Amy. You'll have to pay me something, of course.' Geneva tightened her lips practically. 'I'm flat broke. I'd been thinking of taking in a lodger, only I couldn't stand a woman; she'd want to wash her stockings in the bath and hang them on a string, and people would talk so if I had a man.' Geneva felt that she would never be too old for scandal. 'A son-in-law would be different though.'

'My parents will want me to live with them,' Ben said gloomily.

'You'd die. We'll think up some excuse so as not to hurt them. They won't like your being here, any more than they like me having Amy. She tells me that when she goes to see them they make veiled little hints about how badly I bring her up. No wonder I practically have to drive the child there with a whip.'

'I would never have let them have her,' Ben said. 'I was a pretty stolid child. I could take it, but I would never let Amy be so bored. I don't know what I would have done without you, Geneva. You've been wonderful to her.'

'Stuff,' Geneva said. 'She's been the making of me. Kept me young.' She stood on a frayed tapestry stool to look in the mirror which hung over the mantelpiece, tipped forward because it was too high, so that she saw the top of her thinly-covered scalp and a foreshortened view of her deeply-lined face. 'Even if I didn't love her,' she said, addressing him from the footstool, 'I would have done anything to make up for what her mother did to you.'

'What do you tell her about Marion?'

'The same as you do. That she was killed in a car. I don't say who was with her, and she's never asked. She doesn't seem to take much interest in Marion, except as a sort of tragic death figure. When I told her last month that it was the anniversary of her mother's death, she stuck a black ribbon bow on her picture with cellophane tape and put a pot of those awful little dried flowers people sell in the street in front of it. She rather enjoyed it.'

Geneva fell off the stool, stumbled in her tarnished brocade mules, and stood on one leg like a pelican to take off the slipper and rub at her long, yellow foot.

'Will she ever find out the truth?' Ben asked her.

'Not unless someone tells her. Your poor mother might, in a fit of exhibitionist honesty.'

Listen, Ben told his mother in his head, if you ever tell Amy that Marion was killed driving with a Chief Petty Officer she'd been sleeping with for months, I'll shoot you.

'SUBMARINE COMMANDER'S WIFE KILLED, LOVER ESCAPES,' the headlines had said. The bloody man had talked at the inquest. It could have been hushed up. He had not been asked ꞁɔ tell more than the details of the accident, but before the coroner could stop him, he had dashed into an orgy of confessing – or was it boasting? The local Press had picked it up, naturally, and the London papers got it. Whether or not the Admiralty had preserved the cuttings, pinned to his confidential reports like dirty washing, Ben knew that his parents had kept them. They never wanted to forget how much they hated Marion.

'Geneva,' he said, 'did Marion ever come to this switch of relationship with you – of feeling that you were her child?'

Geneva laughed, her cawing laugh, which was her least amused one. 'She felt that way all her life. She used to scare me even when she was a baby by looking at me cynically when I was feeding or changing her, as if she thought I didn't know what I was doing. I didn't, most of the time. She patronized me. I was rather a nuisance to her, I think. When she was at school I always said the wrong thing to her friends or wore the wrong sort of hat on Speech Day. When she first brought you to meet me, she behaved as if she was ashamed of me.'

Ben remembered noticing that and putting it out of his head, as he had tried to put away discoveries about Marion that dismayed him, after he was committed to marrying her. He had not known that Geneva had noticed it. She had welcomed him that day as if he had been one of the family for years.

'It wasn't until I met you,' he said, 'that I was finally sure I did want to marry your daughter. I like you, Geneva. Let's have a drink.'

'Oh, do let's. How gay. It isn't nearly twelve o'clock.'

As Ben threaded his way through the furniture to see what Geneva had in the sideboard, he said: 'Are you sore with me for being kicked out of the Navy? Everyone else seems to be.'

'Hell, no. I think it's a damn fine thing. You'd have been impossible as an Admiral. Hearty, perhaps, and liking your port, but dreadfully *passé*, wanting to revive the era of the battleship, and things like that. I'd have been dead, anyway, so – oh, go away, Greg.' She waved her slipper at the laundry-man, who appeared once more at the door.

'You haven't done it,' he accused her. 'I can't wait, Mrs H. I'm due back at Purley before one.'

'Why do they always have laundries in such impossible places?' Geneva hopped, putting on her slipper, and made for the door. 'Please wait, Greg.' She looked up at him, blinking her stiff eyelashes in what she thought was fascination. 'It will only take a minute. Have a gin with the Commander.'

Gregory made a vomiting face.

'Of course not. Amy!' She went down the passage, yelling. 'Bring some Ovaltine at once. It's an emergency.'

'My spies at headquarters,' said Frank Daniels, raising a gin and tonic to his lips with no more enthusiasm than if it were medicine, 'tell me that a resettlement officer is coming down next week to help you chaps into a happy and profitable retirement. Too bad you won't be here.'

'He's come already,' Ben said. Encased in his bubble of phlegmatic indifference, Frank was always several days behind with the news. 'I've avoided him, though. I'd rather struggle along on my own, although they tell me he has some nice lines to offer in the way of sanitary inspection, or personnel officer in a cement works on the upper Tyne. Kenneth told me he felt like a discharged prisoner being helped to go straight. I already feel like a bereaved widow, the way that new man Parkins treats me.'

Lieutenant-Commander Parkins had been sent to relieve Ben at the submarine school. He treated Ben with nervous deference, as if he were apologizing for being still in the Navy when Ben was going out. Ben kept trying to corner him for a drink and talk about what he might run into with the course; but the new instructor did not drink, and he seemed anxious to keep out of Ben's way, as acquaintances avoid a bereaved person when they are not sure how to express their sympathy, or whether to express it at all.

It was Ben's last night at Gosport, and he was as thankful to be getting it over as Parkins would be tomorrow to have him out of the way. Ben was at the bar in the ante-room with Frank Daniels and some other officers who were buying him drinks, trying to ensure that his last memories of the place would be the splitting hangover he took to the station tomorrow.

Several people came up to Ben and slapped him on the back, and unlike the craven Parkins, who shied off the subject like a startled faun, found some joke to make about being axed, and said simple, hearty things like: 'Here's to a bowler hat.' Many of them were unsure of their own positions, and they felt superstitiously safer if they voiced their doubts, as people will swear that they have failed in an examination, even when they know they have done well.

Ben had dreaded this last evening, afraid that he would feel envy for these officers who would be drinking here tomorrow, while he would be in town ploughing through the Situations Vacant with a cup of Geneva's coffee at his elbow. Now, curiously, he found he did not care. After a few drinks, he began to feel almost sorry for the others, because he knew his fate and they did not. It seemed to him that he had not felt so bad after he received the Admiralty's letter as when he was wondering whether it would come.

He was headed for the new world. They were stuck behind in the world of routines and regulations, important enough while you were a fixed part of it, but diminishing behind you as you approached the way out. He was like a boy leaving school, suddenly mature across the widening breach between him and the pimply ones who will still wear the blazer next term. No regrets. No nostalgia. Not until the novelty of freedom wears off does the boy pull out his blazer with the frayed binding and ponder on the happiness of the prison.

Ben got a little drunker. Not foolish, but nonchalant enough to satisfy the general idea that old Ben must go out with a bang. Before the evening was over, three officers came in together. They were from a submarine which had just returned from exercises. Pale, tired, relaxed in the familiarity of each other's company, they brought with them an air of reality and achievement which seemed alien to the idle, smoke-hazed room. They were in clean uniforms, but as Ben watched them come up to the bar, he saw them in the thick white sweaters, the tattered jackets, the bashed-in headgear of a submarine crew at sea.

'Good cruise?' Ben asked one of them.

He answered non-committally. It had been a tedious, un-eventful exercise. He wanted a whisky and a lot of sleep. Ben knew how he felt. He knew the fatigue, the disoriented sensa-tion when you first came ashore, as if the earth were pushing the sole of your foot into your knee joint, the lingering indiges-tion. The three men who had been at sea together wandered up to the bar, keeping together from habit, not because they were talking. Ben stayed a little apart, leaning on the bar, stroking the side of an empty glass, not wanting and not able to join them.

He was far away from them. He was in the control-room, the centre of a submarine's world, and all around him was the casual presence of men he knew well. Like a wave of sickness, the memory of that unique brand of shut-in companionship came back to him. He was not remembering the faces of men. It was just the familiar, predictable sound and smell and move-ments of them. Fifty fathoms under the sea, there was an uncomplicated security unmatched above the surface.

In a submarine, men with whom you had little in common on shore became your closest friends. You were dependent on each other. You worked and ate and slept together, and shared the jokes, crusted with repetition, and talked and argued and sometimes unleashed surprisingly private thoughts in the ward-room when the ship was surfaced at night. Tongue-tied men became articulate. Dull men were occasionally almost witty. Pigheaded sticklers for Navy dogma relaxed into real people.

The older ratings fathered you, because they knew more about the job than you did. Each one had the sober pride of a specialist, and there was a great respect between you. The younger ones were more like sons, seeking advice, trusting you with their problems. A wife was unfaithful. A gossiping neighbour was trying to make trouble. A child was very sick, but the patchy letter forgot to say what the sickness was.

The war had nothing to do with it. What mattered was not the training or the hardships, the escapes, the triumphs, the risks. The Navy was a continuity, running before and through and beyond war. It was a dependence of men on each other. This was what had been important. This was what Ben was losing. Frank Daniels was behind him. Ben straightened his back and turned round. He put on a smile, but Frank, with a perception unapparent in his passive face, muttered: 'Don't let anyone see you care.'

'I don't.' Ben widened his smile. 'I swear it.' But as he spoke, he heard Amy's blithe voice telling him: 'There'll be another war soon, so you'll be back in before you know it.'

A world calamity staged for the sole purpose of putting Benjamin Francis back into uniform again? 'I hate my guts,' he said to Frank.

'Why worry about that?' Frank said. 'I often feel the same. I take a dose of salts for it, myself.'

Chapter Five

'I THOUGHT you said you were going to give up smoking,' Rose said.

'I am, tomorrow.' Ben put away the packet. 'I didn't say that, anyway. I said I wouldn't buy any cigarettes until I got a job. Bob gave me these.'

'Sponging now.'

'Just one of his little charities. Helping the unemployed.'

Bob Whiting had been much more friendly towards Ben now that he was out of the Navy. When Rose was difficult, which she was in increasing ratio to her success, it was almost as if they were in league, the lover and the colleague both trying to guard themselves against her egotism.

Once when Rose had fought with Ben before a rehearsal and fought with Bob during the rehearsal, the two men had gone off together afterwards and left Rose, who hated to drive herself home, to fall back for escort on her male lead of that week, who disliked her as much as she disliked him, but disliked the Underground even more. Bob and Ben had ended the night in the Ambassadors, and had met Jayne Mansfield. It was many days before Rose would forgive either of them.

Bob had dropped his sneers, and no longer referred to Ben as the Gallant Commander. He called him Ben old boy, and had even negotiated for him a job of sorts, but Rose said that she would have nothing more to do with him if he took it. She would not have Ben scuttling up from the basement when somebody yelled: 'Where the hell are the seagulls?' She was not going to be seen leaving the studio with the junior assistant to the assistant manager of Sound effects.

Although he was living in London, Ben did not go often to the television studio. The novelty had long ago worn off, just as the novelty of Rose herself was wearing off and bringing to the surface the beginnings of an old-shoe relationship, which was less glamorous, but much less tiring. Her glowing beauty never ceased to enchant him every time he saw her, but the excitement of having a girl who looked like that was giving place to a tolerant fondness that recognized the sweetness buried too deep under the humbug. He now wanted to protect her from her own absurdities.

Rose had other men round her, but they came and went like July butterflies, while Ben was more or less a permanency. He had learned not to mind too much about Rose's other men, for he could not cure her of her habit of picking up admirers as easily as a naval uniform picks up lint. When she wept to him sometimes after she had cast them off, and cried: 'Oh, darling, I've been unfaithful to you!' he was not crazed with jealousy, because he believed that technically she had not erred. Unlike Marion, it was only men's scalps that Rose wanted. She constantly had to prove her power; then she would return tranquilly to Ben, almost as if he were a husband.

They still talked of marriage in a leisurely way, and there were many times when Ben felt sure that if he could land a decent enough job to support his pride against Rose's earnings, they could get some happiness out of it. Other men had married famous women and kept their self-esteem by leading a life of their own and letting their wives get on with being famous by themselves, taking only a background part in the career that brought the fame. And there was always the sustaining thought that Rose would surely not be famous for ever.

It was no longer a thrill to Ben to be seen out with a woman whom everybody recognized. At first he had liked it when taxi drivers slid back the front window to say something appreciative, but now he wished that they would leave the window shut and keep the draughts out. In public places, he used to enjoy his position on the edge of the stares, and to relish the glances of envy from other men, but he was growing tired now of tagging along behind Rose. He was not going to walk through marriage one step behind her, holding the mink on the edge of the crowd which clamoured for her autograph, waiting out of camera range while she posed for a picture, stopping with her at tables on the way out of restaurants, while she sparkled at people whom he did not know, and to whom he could find nothing to say when he was introduced.

Although he had told her not to, Rose still persisted in introducing him as Commander Francis. At parties, people sometimes followed this up with a polite: 'Where are you stationed, Commander?'

Rose did not like him to say: 'I'm out of the Navy,' so he would give random answers like: 'Wapping Pier,' or 'Mumbles Lighthouse'.

Afterwards Rose would complain: 'Why do you tell such silly lies?'

'Why do you keep calling me Commander?'

'It sounds better,' was her crisp reply, and she would study him for a moment with the stupendous orbs narrowed to the size of ordinary eyes, as if she were speculating whether he was fit to be seen out with her.

If things went on like this, the day would come, Ben knew, when someone would address him as Mr Kelly. The thought of this spurred his ambition. He must find himself a niche in life where there would be people who would say: 'There is Benjamin Francis. He's married to someone or other. Somebody one knows.' He must be able to walk before Rose into restaurants and tackle head waiters on his own. He must hear people call Rose Mrs Francis, in a natural way, not as if it were some temporary and faintly comic joke.

With this in mind, he began to apply for jobs that offered: 'Excellent prospects for right man', and 'Unlimited opportunities for advancement'. He answered impossible advertisements for posts like Advertising Manager, or Senior Consultant in Management Accounting, or Assistant Sales Manager with Extensive Experience of Marketing a Variety of Merchandise. He was not surprised when he received no answer from many of the firms. When there was one, it was the bleakly familiar: 'The post has been filled,' or the more courteous brush-off: 'We will keep your letter on record in case a suitable post arises.'

'I'm starting at the top and working down. I'll let you know when I reach office boy,' he told Geneva, as he sat down once more at the scarred dining-table and pulled his typewriter towards him. It was a pre-war portable that had been half-way round the world with him, and had suffered greatly from the sea change. It shifted the paper sideways towards the bottom of the page, and was apt to write everything in capitals if you did not watch the shift-lock key like a hawk and catch it as it started to go down. When he was composing an application, Geneva would sometimes come behind him and rest a painful bracelet on his shoulder and protest: 'You can't say that. It's a lie.'

'It doesn't matter. They'll know it's a lie if I don't give references, but they might respect my ingenuity. It's all part of the game. The advertisement says: "Since the company's approach to its more unusual problems is adventurous, the post demands a resourceful personality." What is more resourceful than a lie?'

It started as something of a game, whiling away the too-empty hours of freedom with the advertisement pages of the newspapers in the Paddington library, pouring himself a beer and drafting and redrafting masterpieces of persuasion to try to trap an employer into granting him at least an interview.

It was not long, however, before the game sobered into reality, as Ben became increasingly aware of two serious facts. One was that he must find a job as soon as possible if he were not to dribble away his meagre retired pay in supporting himself and Amy and catering to Rose's ideas of where to go and what to do in London. The other, still more depressing, was that jobs for an ex-naval officer of thirty-six were not easy to find.

It was small comfort to know that there were many men in the same boat. In one of the few interviews Ben achieved, the nonchalant man swivelling back and forth on the other side of the desk had said: 'I had three of you chaps in yesterday. One poor devil was a group-captain with three kids, two of them at public school. The hell of it is, we owe our lives to blokes like you; but this firm's a profit-making concern, not a charitable organization.'

Ben read a newspaper article in which he and the other ex-officers were referred to as The Lost Men of Britain. Everyone was sorry for him, it seemed, but what use was that? He did not want to be treated like a paraplegic charity case. He wanted a decent job.

He was too old, too inexperienced, too bare of academic qualifications. His technical knowledge of such things as engineering and radio and radar was no more than basic. In a submarine, there had always been an engineer officer and highly-qualified technical ratings to depend on. The Navy had cast Ben out fit for nothing more useful than to command a submarine, and if there were any commercial firms engaged in undersea projects, they were not advertising the fact.

Ben went to several employment offices and had friendly or irritating chats with sympathetic or superior clerks; but neither the sympathy nor the hauteur yielded any success. With his experience of handling men, which was one of the few saleable attributes he could lay claim to, Personnel was the thing to go for, they told him. But for each vacancy for welfare officer or personnel manager, there were dozens of applicants, mostly ex-officers, falling over each other to get in first.

One day, when the sun came out over icy pavements which bit like iron through the trodden-over boots of the old ladies creeping towards Whiteleys, Ben crunched across the park through the thin, dirty snow and wandered into an employment bureau in Kensington.

It was a small and unprosperous concern, two flights up over a chemist's shop, with the linoleum showing its threads on the stairs. The office was just one room with two kindly women and a thin young girl who had a typewriter in an adjoining cubicle the same shape and size as a train toilet. It had the same kind of basin, too, deeper than it was wide, with a cracked glaze and awkward taps from which the girl filled the kettle to make tea. Ben knew about the basin, because once when he was the only client in the office and the girl was tired, sitting in a chair without her shoes and twisting her chilblained toes, he made the tea for all of them.

It was obvious at his first visit that Ben had come to the wrong place from which to be launched on his meteoric career; but after his second visit, when he and Miss Arkwright and Mrs French and Jessie had enjoyed an all-round unburdening of some of their hopes and dreams, Ben and the bureau became very attached to each other. He often walked across the park, more for the exercise and to see his three friends than for the hope of finding himself a job.

If there was anyone in the office, which was not often, Ben would wait on one of the hard chairs on the landing outside. Then he would go in, with a bunch of flowers or a bag of jam tarts, and draw up a chair, and Miss Arkwright would give him one of the filter-tipped cigarettes, 'named after my darling Sir Larry', which were one of the few things on which she spent money for herself.

Mrs French, a motherly lady with soft white hair and a fancy for brown dresses with glimpses of lace at the neck, was at the desk which dealt with the affairs of employees; but in Ben's case, Miss Arkwright, who handled employers, and even Jessie, who did not handle anything except the typewriter and the tea-pot, chipped in with ideas and advice. Nothing ever came of it. The bureau dealt mostly in domestic posts, and as there were few people who wanted to be maids and almost as few who could afford to employ them even if they could find them, business was steadily dropping off. Sometimes they talked with mouse-like courage of widening their scope. Miss Arkwright had once found a hosiery buyer for a desperate department store, and they had never forgotten it. They had wanted to have the contract framed to hang on the wall.

Miss Arkwright was gentle and dovelike, and should have found a husband long ago. She intimated once that she had lost a lover in the war, but no one, including herself, seemed quite to believe it. It occurred to Ben that if he could introduce her to Frank Daniels, she would make a wonderful wife for him. Frank loved to wear knitted cardigans and woollen gloves, and Miss Arkwright was always knitting. If a client came in, she would stub out her cigarette and thrust needles and wool into a drawer of her desk, looking up with her bright, businesslike smile, as if she had been putting away important papers connected with the bureau's crushing load of work.

It was her sister's children for whom she knitted. Her sister had produced babies in a regular but improvident fashion, and Miss Arkwright's life outside the office was devoted to auntly services. Before that, it had been her brother's children, who were now grown-up and needed mufflers rather than matinée coats. Like Georgina Hogarth, Miss Arkwright had always been so busy with other people's children that she had never had the chance to find a man to give her some of her own.

The three women in the little office with the grimy window between them and the perpetual noise of traffic in Kensington High Street grew very fond of Ben. They were always glad to see him, and they tried their hardest to help him, although the nearest they came to finding him a job was to arrange an interview with a lady who wanted a personal bodyguard for her daughter, which fell through when the lady telephoned to say that the daughter had run away and married the man against whom she had desired to guard her.

Ben grew fond of the three women, and found himself almost as concerned about finding a husband for Miss Arkwright as about finding a job for himself. He even went so far as to write to Frank Daniels, suggesting that he should come up for a week-end in town, during the course of which Ben planned to stage a meeting with Miss Arkwright. After an interval, Frank replied that the Admiralty was sending him to Scotland.

'No time to get to town, even if I wanted to,' Frank wrote, not knowing what he was missing. Surly devil. Perhaps Miss Arkwright was better off with her nieces and nephews, one of whom had been expelled from two nursery schools and was claimed to be a proper tartar.

One evening when Ben breezed into the office near closing-time and found the women pulling on rubber boots and dabbing at their noses with little velour puffs, they greeted him with twittering excitement. Something wonderful had happened. Miss Arkwright had answered an advertisement for an Appeals Organizer for a charitable organization. A gentleman called Sweeting – such a pretty name – had telephoned at two o'clock – 'No, it must have been two fifteen, because I was naughty enough to get back late from lunch' – and an interview had been arranged for Ben the next day.

'We didn't want to tell you until we'd heard from him,' Mrs French said, beaming at Ben as if he were her favourite child. 'We wanted to surprise you, and we were afraid of disappointing you in case he never answered Phoebe's letter. We've been trying to reach you all the afternoon. Your mother-in-law said she didn't know where you were. "For all I know," she said, "he's run away to sea." She's very humorous,' Mrs French added doubtfully. She did not like jokes about Ben and the Navy.

'I went to the cinema,' Ben said.

'To the cinema, on a day like this!' Jessie exclaimed. 'Oh, but of course, you didn't know. How could you? You couldn't of course.' Jessie often asked questions of herself and answered them in the same breath, a habit acquired from living with a large family who never listened to each other. 'Isn't it exciting, Ben? Yes, tremendously so.' She stretched her mouth in a wide smile beneath her gaunt cheeks. She was in love with Ben, but it did not matter. She had a young man with whom she was properly in love, with holding hands and kissing and looking at three-piece suites in shop windows. Her feeling for Ben was deliberately unreal, like an enjoyable dream of Tony Curtis. It was sufficient just to be daring enough to call him Ben, and to take more trouble with her hair and the seams of her stockings in case he dropped in.

Miss Arkwright was sitting in the chair by the gas fire, zipping up stout boots. Her expression was smug. While Jessie and Mrs French babbled, she told Ben the details tautly, as if she negotiated thousand-pound-a-year jobs every day of the week. She was the one who had done it. She had seen the advertisement. She had written the letter. She had talked on the telephone with the great Sweeting and had been shrewd enough not to say anything that would put him off.

'A real gentleman,' she said, stretching her feet out to the fire for a last warm-up before she joined the frozen queue for the bus. 'I think you'll enjoy working for him.' The boots began to smell a little.

'Steady on,' Ben said. 'I haven't got the job yet. An interview's only the start. What do I know about raising funds?'

'You've always claimed you could bluff your way into anything.' Miss Arkwright turned her large doe eyes on him reproachfully. 'You wouldn't go and let me down, surely?'

'You will go to see him?' Mrs French asked nervously. If he failed them now, it would be the end, after all their efforts for him, and Jessie making a novena at Saint Patrick's. Bulky in their outdoor clothes, they all looked at him, their white-haired boy, the pride of the Phillimore Employment Bureau.

He hastened to reassure them. 'And I did once pass round the hat for old Corky's silver wedding,' he added. 'I made a good job of that, even though his wife never liked the tray.'

'There you are, you see!' Miss Arkwright turned off the gas fire and stood up, pulling a felt hat down over her fluffy hair. 'You can do it. Go to it.' She grasped her umbrella before her as though she were presenting arms. 'Go in and win.'

'The very best of luck to you, my dear boy,' Mrs French said moistly. For two pins she would have kissed him.

'Ditto from yours truly.' Jessie tied a long woollen scarf over her hair and flung the ends back behind her narrow shoulders. 'I'm sure I'll never get any work done tomorrow for thinking about you.'

Ben found himself shaking hands solemnly all round. Then he left them, galloping down the treacherous stairs two at a time, their sailor knight off to the jousts.

Geneva and Amy were almost as excited as the three women

in the Phillimore Bureau. The Major was at the flat when Ben reached home, and they drank to his success in large martinis.

'When you get dug in there,' the Major said, 'you might look about you and see if there's a trifling little job for me.' He had not worked for years and did not intend to, since his wife had left him enough money to sustain life, but he frequently talked about what he would do if someone would only give him half a chance. 'I might be useful to you. Give you some tips. I know all about these shows. Colossal expense accounts. You'll be doing all your business over lunch at the Savoy Grill, I dare say.'

His smile was canny. The Major was a man who prided himself on knowing a thing or two. He had a loose, discoloured face, bruised purple in the cold weather, and black hair streaked painstakingly but inadequately across his skull. His figure was still carefully martial, the shoulders braced, the growing paunch manfully sucked in. When he expounded his inside information about life, he would bend and stretch his knees like a stage policeman. He bent them outwards now, but since he was on his third martini, he could not stretch them again, so he continued downwards into an armchair, knocking his glass off a little table.

'I don't think so, sir,' Ben said, while Amy, who was being domesticated today, went silently to fetch a cloth. 'This outfit sounds pretty genuine.'

'Of course it's genuine,' Geneva told the Major sharply. 'Don't try to crab everything everybody else does, you idle old rascal. This is the first real nibble of a job Ben has had. You should rejoice with us.'

'I do, my dear, I do,' the Major said. 'And if you will kindly bring over that cocktail shaker, I shall rejoice with even better heart.'

Amy had a holiday from school next day, the relic of some bygone anniversary which had never been relinquished along with the piece of empire it commemorated. She insisted on accompanying Ben to his interview. Nothing that he could say would dissuade her. She would no more let him go alone than if he were a four-year-old child wanting to travel across London by himself, although she did make the concession that she would not follow him right into Mr Sweeting's office.

Everybody in the flat helped Ben to dress for the occasion. The Major had passed out the evening before and spent the night on the sofa. His recuperative powers were remarkable, and after monopolizing the bathroom for half an hour and using Ben's electric razor and a quantity of Geneva's talcum powder, he appeared at breakfast in the kitchen ready to tackle a large whisky and water. After breakfast, he polished Ben's shoes for him with the spit-and-rub technique he had learned from a long-ago batman. Amy laid all her father's ties out on his bed and picked out the one which seemed to be the most persuasive. Geneva went over the collar and lapel of his best suit with cleaning fluid, and drawing her mouth into a hundred tiny puckers, removed Rose's powder and two of her strong hairs from the shoulders.

Rose had telephoned last night, but although Ben had wanted to share his excitement with her, the general hysteria surrounding the forthcoming interview had still left him enough sanity to wait until he got the job. If he failed, she would be more discouraged with him than she was already. If he got the job, he would swoop down on her and carry her off in astonishment to a champagne dinner.

Ben established Amy in a café near Victoria Station with a chocolate milk shake and a plate of hot buttered toast. He hovered for a moment by the table where she crouched with sucked-in cheeks over the straw.

'Are you scared, Daddy?'

'In a way.'

Amy looked up at him and raised her hand in a grown-up gesture, startlingly reminiscent of her mother, to pin up a short wisp of the long chestnut hair which she wore today in a pony-tail, to make her look older. 'Remember you are a naval officer,' she said.

Walking towards Grosvenor Place, Ben passed a public house which was just opening. He would have welcomed a drink for the strange dryness in his mouth and the hollowness inside his waist, but Mr Sweeting would not care for whisky on his breath, and peppermints afterwards would be just as incriminating.

Waiting to cross the road, he looked at himself in a shop window, and saw that he appeared the same as usual. A man no longer boyishly young, but far from being irrevocably mature, of medium height, with broad shoulders and rather short arms, wearing a soft felt hat, a tweed coat over a grey flannel suit, and shoes that shone like an advertisement. From the looks of him no one would guess that here was a Navy throw-out, on his way to the first important testing of himself as a civilian, with a stomach that seemed to have done nothing at all about the bacon and eggs he had put into it three hours ago.

He adjusted the hat to a better angle. What would such a man be doing here at this hour of the morning if he were not going to see Mr Sweeting? It was much too late to be coming in on the train to work unless he were the very highest class of executive, and the soft brown hat and the tweed coat denied that.

What business had a man at Victoria Station late in the morning? The women, that was easy. They had come up to shop from the country or the suburbs. For a moment, Ben saw himself in a red-brick house in Reigate with a wife who looked like that girl over there in the coat with the high fur collar cuddling her neck, who would not be so busy buying things for the children and the house that she could not find time to slip in a little something for him.

The men were more difficult. There were crowds of them about, going in and out of the station, or hurrying in every direction along the pavements, as insanely purposeful as ants. They must be going in or out of offices in the neighbourhood, or travelling to or from factories south of the river. But what would they do when they got there, and where would they go when they left? Ben's imagination struck, protesting to him that it knew nothing about the world of affairs, at Victoria or any-where else. And yet in a few months, if his luck held – he could never think of himself as anything but lucky – he might be one of these men striding with a brief-case in and out of the station, looking as if he knew what he was about. What would he be doing at Victoria Station in the cause of charity? Going to Brighton, of course, comfortably on the noonday pullman, to see a rich old widow about her donation.

Mr Sweeting's office was in a converted Belgravia house. Waiting in the reception-office where the sleek, straight up and down girl had shown him a chair and returned to her ivory-coloured, noiseless typewriter, Ben began to think that the Major might have a point when he talked about large expenses. There was an air of muted luxury about this outfit which did not come from paring down your budget.

Ben was early for his appointment – Miss Arkwright had suggested, as if it were a highly novel plan: 'If I were you, I wouldn't be late' – and he sat with his hat on his knee and looked at a picture on the pastel wall. It was a dark water-colour of the back of a row of little houses, all exactly alike, separated from each other by a narrow space that would barely let a bicycle through. Under the identical gables were tightly-shut bedroom windows, and in the foreground house, under the window, a sloping roof covered what looked like a lean-to kitchen with three wooden steps slightly askew outside the back door. Snow lay on the roof and along the window-sills and was piled in a little drift between the steps and the house. Against the dark wall of the kitchen two windows and the top half of the back door shone with a warm yellow light.

There was someone in the kitchen, indistinguishable as either a man or a woman, with one arm hanging forward and down as if the sleeve were being rolled up. A man washing at the sink after work. A woman preparing supper. It was a poor house, a house probably ill equipped to keep out the weather which had brought the snow. The bright kitchen was perhaps only a small stuffy room with grease behind the stove and people who had nothing new to say to each other, but as long as you remained outside, it had the secret charm of any lighted place at night.

The artist had caught this covetous feeling of being outside and wanting to go in, because he knew he was not going in. Perhaps the man or woman had looked out of the window as they rolled up their sleeves, and seen him standing in the snow in a cap and muffler making a sketch for his picture, and envied him the adventure of his creation, because they were not going out to share it.

A discreet buzzer. 'Mr Sweeting will see you now,' the flat

girl said, and Ben pulled himself out of the picture, wrenched at his persuasive tie, and followed her along the soft carpet to the door at the end of the corridor.

Mr Sweeting was a large, middle-aged man with a pouched eye and an easy but somewhat elusive manner, as if his attention was only half engaged. His suit and shirt were good and the appointments of his office elegant, down to the last polished leaf of the trailing plant in the window. The Major intruded into Ben's head again with his observation about the Savoy Grill. It was easy to imagine Mr Sweeting lunching there.

Ben sat in a comfortable chair and waited for him to start the ball rolling. After the preliminary pleasantries, Mr Sweeting fell silent, looking unhurriedly through some papers on his desk as if he were alone in the room.

Perhaps he did not know why Ben was there, and was waiting for him to elucidate. Could one plunge in and say: 'About the job –,' or must one sit humbly and let Sweeting play cat and mouse with one's nerves? Remember you are a naval officer, Amy said from the café two hundred yards away, and Ben straightened his back and looked at the cigarette-box which was open on the desk. He had not had a cigarette all morning. Geneva had run out, and the Major smoked cheroots.

Mr Sweeting did not offer him a cigarette. 'Can't find the letter,' he said at last, looking up about two inches to the left of Ben's head. 'Let's see, I think the agency said you were in one of the Services.'

'The Navy. I was retired as a commander,' Ben said, trying to make it sound impressive.

'Well, that's against you for a start.' Mr Sweeting had a thick, catarrhal voice. After he spoke, his mouth remained slightly open. 'The Navy is a strenuously efficient organization, though not, I regret, a profitable one.'

He drew out a large, crumpled handkerchief and blew his nose with a noise like an enraged elephant. When he had finished gasping and sniffing and stowing away the handkerchief, he continued: 'Our organization is efficient too, of course. At the top. At the lower levels, we are served by all kinds of well-meaning amateurs whose charitable instincts sometimes fail them if they think they're being treated too militantly. We had a lieutenant-colonel once.' He shuddered, looking beyond the opposite wall into memory. 'Ghastly failure. An entire ladies' committee walked out on him and went over to tuberculosis. What do you know about women?' He shot the question at Ben suddenly, without bringing down his eyes or changing his tone.

'Women, sir?' Damn, he had said it. He had vowed not to, but with Mr Sweeting holding the reins of this situation, it was almost impossible not to treat him like a senior officer. 'Well –' He spread his hands. 'The usual amount, I suppose. Do any of us know what really makes them tick?'

'Don't ask me.' Mr Sweeting declined to be won over by this sprightly platitude. 'I'm asking you. You ever worked with women?'

'Wrens. Yes, of course.'

'Did they have more money than sense and swallow half a bottle of aspirin because their deadly rival was appointed chairman of the Come-as-you-are Ball?'

'I doubt it. One of them had hysterics once. In a harbour launch. We held her over the side to cool off.'

'Very good.' Mr Sweeting's face was blank, like the sadistic oral examiner who gives no indication of whether an answer is right or wrong. He took a cigarette and lit it, coughing harshly. Catching Ben's eye, he said : 'Excuse me,' and offered the box. Before he could stop himself, Ben heard his voice say : 'Thanks, I don't smoke.'

Idiot. A smoke might have pulled you through this, and the man will think you're not convivial. He'll expect you to say next that you're a teetotaller, and that won't get you very far at the Savoy Grill.

'Tell me,' said Mr Sweeting amiably enough, leaning back and squinting at Ben through the smoke of the cigarette which hung on his open lip, 'what are you qualifications for this job?'

Ben assumed the debonair face he had practised before the mirror. 'My experience in this field may not be very extensive, but I'm confident I could do a good job for you.' He had rehearsed that. It was designed to disguise the fact that he had only a vague idea of what the job entailed.

'What do you know about research and statistics? The donation ratio between season and area and class of subscriber, and so on.'

Ben felt his debonair face slipping. Seeing Mr Sweeting's open mouth, he realized that his own was hanging open too, and shut it quickly. 'Of course.' He stalled for time. 'Research. Yes, I see, all the usual paper work. I've had plenty of that in the Service, naturally. The Navy is laid on a keel of S forms, they say.'

Mr Sweeting did not smile. He trained his pouched eyes on Ben, looking at him directly for the first time. 'What the devil is an S form?' he asked irritably.

'It's a printed form, sir. You use it to report anything from the loss of a tin opener to the grounding of a ship. There's an S form for almost everything – drawing stores, writing up the character of a rating. S.264, that is.'

'You amaze me,' Mr Sweeting said coldly. 'And now suppose you stop playing the fool with me and tell me what you know about advertising, drafting brochures, financial statements and the preparation of budgets. Take one at a time if you like.'

Ben did not like any of them. All he could say was: 'I'm not trying to play the fool, sir.'

'Look here.' Mr Sweeting leaned forward to stub out the cigarette, which was making him cough. 'You are Francis, aren't you?'

Ben nodded.

'I can't find the agency's letter. That girl tidies this desk every time I go out of the room. Do you know what they said about you? Perhaps you wrote the letter yourself? No? Well, that's something. They implied that you'd been working with charitable groups for some time. I got the impression – perhaps I'm the fool – that you'd been running some sort of sailor's benevolent association, and that most of your time in the Navy had been spent raising funds.'

Miss Arkwright, what have you done?

Ben sighed. 'Most of my time in the Navy was spent in a submarine or a depot ship. The only thing I ever raised was a beer mug.'

'I can only suppose,' Mr Sweeting said heavily, 'that the agency hoped that you would keep the fiction going, in the feeble hope that I wouldn't ask for references.'

'How could I? They didn't tell me what they'd said.'

'Then,' said Mr Sweeting, who was shrewder than he looked, 'they just wanted to bluff me into interviewing you, on the chance that I'd like you so much I'd employ you anyway.'

Ben and Mr Sweeting looked at each other solemnly for a moment, and then they suddenly burst out laughing.

Mr Sweeting's laugh was like a bronchial donkey. His sunken eyes oozed a few drops into the folds of flesh. His large body shook. He pulled out the handkerchief and mopped his face, passing the handkerchief right over his bald head and round the back of his neck.

When he had finished, Ben asked: 'I say, could I have a cigarette?'

'I thought you said you didn't smoke.'

'I said it by mistake. I was scared.'

This made Mr Sweeting laugh again. He went through the whole process of braying and shaking and wiping his eyes and his head and neck. 'Oddly enough,' he said, when he had achieved the second recovery, 'I do like you. Can't think why. You haven't said a sensible thing since you came into this office. Except about the Wren. Dunked her in the sea, eh? I wish I'd been there.'

Ben told him some more about Sylvia. With the tension broken, he felt more like himself. It was quite a shock when Mr Sweeting reminded him that he had failed to get the job.

'I wish I could help you, though,' he said. 'It's going to be hard for you to find something worth while, I'm afraid. What can you do, anyway?'

'A few things. I'm an expert at handling drunken sailors. Ask anyone. And at one time I was said to have the best periscope eye in the Mediterranean fleet.'

'At the moment, I fail to see how we could use that. Perhaps later on –'

'Meanwhile you'll keep my name in your files in case a suitable vacancy arises,' Ben quoted cheerfully. Mr Sweeting had seemed at first like a man you could not like. Now that they had shared a laugh together, he was suddenly a friend, and Ben did not mind what he said to him.

'You took the words out of my mouth.' Mr Sweeting's eyes no longer wandered disinterestedly round the room. They rested on Ben with an amused favour. 'I might find you some junior post. I'd make one if I could, but I can't play around with other people's cash. We have to save money wherever we can.'

'You might start right here,' Ben said, looking round the office.

'Don't be beastly, my dear chap. You have to spend money to get money. Don't you know that?' He stood up, smiling, and held out his hand. 'I hate to throw you out, but I've got serious work to do. I have to draft another advertisement that won't land me with another dead loss like you.'

They shook hands, and he went with Ben to the door. As Ben went down the corridor, Mr Sweeting called after him: 'Let's lunch some time.'

The girl in the reception-office had stopped typing at the sound of Mr Sweeting's convivial voice. She was surprised into asking Ben: 'Did you get the job then?'

'No. Didn't you think I would?'

She shook her well-brushed hair. 'I can always tell. I have a feeling about people. I'm sorry,' she offered, smiling for the first time.

'It's all right. I shouldn't have come after it.'

As he picked up his hat, he glanced once more at the picture. The figure in the lighted kitchen was a man. No wonder it looked inviting to see him rolling up his sleeves at home. He had a job, one that made him honestly dirty. He was not supposed to know about anything he could not do with his hands.

Amy was no longer in the café when Ben returned to her. She was standing outside with her hands tucked into the sleeves of her coat, looking anxiously along the pavement for him. She was quite tall for her age, but she looked tiny standing against the wall to be out of the way of the heedless, hurrying people, with her toes turned in and the beautiful pony-tail flattened against the steamy window of the café.

Ben came up to her grinning, but it was not his usual grin, and she said at once: 'You didn't get the job.'

'Not this time. I'll get the next. Excuse me.' A woman with a shopping cart bumped into him and glared, looking back at him as she trundled away, as if she suspected him of accosting a child.

Ben was going into the café to pay Amy's bill, but she said: 'I paid it. No, don't pay me back. You need it more than me.'

What kind of a father am I? She shouldn't have come. Seeing her sympathetic face. Ben despised himself for involving the child in his problems, and yet, knowing Amy, he knew that she would not want it any other way. Her consolation for not having a mother or a proper family life had always been the feeling that she was necessary to Ben, because she was all he had.

'Come on. It's cold.' He took her hand and put it with his into his overcoat pocket.

'Do you feel like I did when they turned me down for the junior choir?' She looked up at him anxiously as they walked away.

'I suppose so. No. No, I don't really. You cried in front of the music mistress. I didn't. I laughed. So did Mr Sweeting, because it was so absurdly hopeless. Can you see that? I don't want you or Grandma or anyone else to feel sorry for me.'

Amy thought for a moment, watching her walking feet. 'Yes, I see. Grandma will, too, if you tell her the right way. But I don't suppose Miss Kelly will.' She had stubbornly refused to call her Aunt Rose.

'I'm not going to tell her. I'm supposed to meet her for lunch. Do you want to come?' Rose would not be pleased, but he could not put Amy on a bus for home when she had been through this with him.

'No thanks, Daddy.'

'All right, let's find a telephone. If she's still at the flat, I'll tell her I've got flu, and take you to lunch instead. And a museum, if you like.'

'I've gone off museums,' Amy said. 'It's French films now.'

'Well, that's better.' Ben stopped and released her hand to pull some silver out of his trouser pocket. 'We might even manage the Curzon if you don't have cider at lunch.'

Chapter Six

'HOW could you do it? How could you do this to me?'

Miss Arkwright lowered her head, for her eyes were reddening. 'I know,' she said. 'Don't tell me. I've already had Mr Sweeting on the phone. He told me.'

'Did he tell you it was a criminal offence to make false claims for your clients?'

Miss Arkwright nodded, and fumbled in the sleeve of her apple-green angora jersey for a handkerchief. She could not speak, so Mrs French took over.

'He laughed at Phoebe, that was the worst of it. If he had been angry, she could have given him back as good as he gave. You don't know Phoebe when her dander's up. But he laughed at her.' She raised her voice to where Jessie was typing listlessly in the little closet. 'Tea's wanted here!' she called, like a ward sister calling a nurse for emergency coramine.

Ben tried to explain to them that Mr Sweeting had been sympathetically amused, but they would not be comforted. They had believed so firmly that Ben would come whistling back to them with the job in his pocket that their second-floor world was temporarily at a standstill. Jessie had broken out in a cold sore, and Mrs French had taken two sleeping-tablets last night and slept right through the alarm clock, and her husband had been late for work in the catering department at Barkers for the first time in twenty years.

Rallying a little after the tea, Miss Arkwright racked her brains and files for other possibilities. Slightly drunk with contrition, she offered all kinds of random ideas from male modelling through crowd work in films to night porter in a private hotel, all of which were rejected out of hand by Jessie and Mrs French, as being insulting to Miss Kelly. They knew about Rose, and had transferred some of their proprietary interest in Ben to her, especially since he had obtained for them a signed photograph, which was tacked to the wall, curling in the fumes from the gas fire.

Not only Miss Arkwright, but Miss Arkwright's sister and

her sister's friends were working for Ben. One of the friends, who had been teaching shorthand in a boy's residential settlement for two weeks before she was bowed out for lack of discipline, came up with the news that the warden was being bowed out too, for a different reason.

With the Phillimore Bureau's blessings – blessings that were less confident than when he had charged out to do battle at Victoria – Ben journeyed to a northern suburb to try his luck.

Was luck the right word? He did not really want the job. He had only come to please Miss Arkwright. Six hundred pounds a year and the struggling headache of responsibility for fifty boys who were mostly on probation or from broken homes – this was not the life he had planned. This was a refuge for the desperately unemployed. It bore no resemblance to the brilliant, adventurous career which had beckoned to him when he left the Navy.

As the trolleybus glided to a stop by the church with the broken spire, Ben got off reluctantly, hoping he would not get the job. It might be all right to tide him over for a few months until something better turned up; but if he got stuck in some forgotten, gloomy institution with a bunch of social workers and delinquent boys, the something better would never come his way.

He was pleasantly surprised by the appearance of the settlement. A collection of white stucco villas surrounded a large central building with a red roof and a lot of fresh green paint. There were gardens, a football field, even a hard tennis court, which was being used as a roller-skating rink by a few boys in turtle-neck sweaters when Ben walked up the well-kept drive. He spoke to them, and one of them came out of the wire cage to take him to the secretary. On the way, he showed Ben the warden's house, a modern bungalow with flower-beds tidied for the winter, and red curtains and a red front door. Instantly, Ben saw himself and Amy there. She could go to some school nearby. They could have a dog. He and she would take it on the common, accompanied by a boy or two whose problems Ben would discuss in a man-to-man way while they walked. He would have to make strict rules for Amy about mixing with the boys. Those he saw looked all right, and the one who had taken off his roller skates to go with him to the secretary's office was a spirited lad with a quick, gnomish smile; but Ben had handled enough national service ratings to know that this did not mean a thing.

Mr Prentiss, the secretary, was an eager, myopic man with enormous glasses like the ends of bottles, who seemed as anxious to help Ben as he was to help the boys at the settlement. 'I was R.N.V.R. myself in the war,' he said. 'Oh, in an office job, of course.' He touched the spectacles. 'I'd have given anything to go to sea, but – "They also serve –" I told myself.' He had a rapid, running voice, which he used in small excited bursts, like a woman telling a story.

'So you see, I can't help being prejudiced in your favour.' His wide-stretched smile revealed a lot of intricate bridge-work. 'This is no way to start an interview, is it? But I was only a lieutenant. I can't get over the feeling that I should be calling you Sir, although I believe I'm twenty years older than you.'

'Oh, no, sir,' Ben said, although he believed it too.

'I should start by finding out all the things against you, I suppose, but I'm so accustomed to looking for all the things in favour of the boys who come here that I haven't the knack. That's what sunk me with our last warden, between you and me.' There was a boy working in the outer office, and Mr Prentiss lowered his voice without slowing it down. 'I only found out the things that were against him when it was too late. However . . . water under the bridge and all that.' He had a set of keys in his pocket, which he jingled merrily as he talked. 'Let's have some coffee. David!'

The bony, red-haired boy from the outer office ambled in. 'David is doing some secretarial work for me,' Mr Prentiss said. 'The boys who don't go out to work from here all have some sort of jobs around the place. It's part of their training. Will you make us some coffee, please, David?'

The red-haired boy, who was perfectly polite although he did not say a word, favoured Ben with a careful stare before he went out. He returned shortly with two mugs of vile-tasting coffee, heated up many times, but not sufficiently this time.

'Ah, that's good.' Mr Prentiss sucked at it and smacked his thick lips. 'Nothing like a good hot cup of coffee.' When the boy had gone out, he threw the rest of it into a basin in the corner and invited Ben to do the same. 'David will learn,' he said indulgently. 'He'll come to it.'

They talked pleasantly for a while and Ben began, with mixed feelings, to think that he was going to get the job. He offered all his disadvantages, but they could not staunch Mr Prentiss's enthusiasm. He tossed aside Ben's lack of experience like spilled salt. 'I'd be here to show you the ropes,' he said. 'I've been here ever since the war. I could run the place in my sleep. Tell me just one thing. Why do you want to work with us?'

'I don't exactly know,' Ben said slowly, wondering whether he ought to produce some high-sounding philanthropic reason. 'It isn't anything like what I was looking for. Frankly, I didn't want the job at all before I came here and saw the set-up. Now I think I do. Not only because you're the first man who hasn't slapped me politely and regretfully in the face since I left the Navy, but because I think Amy and I could be happy here. I could bring my daughter, I suppose?'

'Naturally.' Mr Prentiss gave his orthodontic smile. 'I would hardly expect you and your wife to move in without her.'

'I'm a widower,' Ben said, expecting that this would be in his favour in this male community, but Miss Arkwright, of course, had overlooked the vital snag. Mr Prentiss let his artless face fall like a disappointed child.

'That's too bad, too bad.' He beat his unworkmanlike hands softly together. 'The governors stipulate that the warden should be married. The wife is in charge of the housekeeping, and looks after any of the boys who aren't sick enough for professional care. Our late warden's wife was excellent in that respect. Nothing that happened was her fault. I felt very sorry for the poor little woman, but of course, the boys come first. Look here.' He transferred his sociology from the boys to Ben. 'You ought to marry again, a young man like you, and for the little girl's sake too. Have you a picture of the kiddy? Ah, yes –' He shook his head sentimentally over Amy's photograph, and handed it back delicately, as if it were too sacred to be touched with the balls of his fingers.

'Well, I'm terribly sorry. I wanted to help you. I thought I could kill two birds with one stone – get a good man for the settlement and put you in a worthwhile job. I've felt so badly about the Services slinging out officers right and left, even though I am a taxpayer. Excuse me. That was in bad taste.' He drummed despondently on the top of the desk. 'If only you were married . . . not only because of the job here, but when I think of what my good wife has done for me – oh, hang it, you should be married, you know.'

'I am sort of vaguely engaged,' Ben said, more to please Mr Prentiss than because he believed it.

'Why didn't you say so?' the bridgework was on view again. 'When is the happy day? I can probably wangle you the job after all, if you send your fiancée along here to see me – purely as a formality, of course. I'm sure she's a pearl.'

Ben laughed. 'I'm sorry,' he said. 'It's so incongruous.'

'She wouldn't want the work? It's not hard, and she'd get her four hundred or so. That's good pin money.'

'If she did come for an interview, you'd see what I mean.'

'You mean she's not the type? She wouldn't like it here? Well, if you think that's funny –' Mr Prentiss stood up, his natural eagerness withdrawn. 'However, that's your affair. I'll say no more.' He tried not to, but his beneficent instincts would not be denied. As Ben stood up, Mr Prentiss looked searchingly at him. 'It's none of my business, I know, but are you quite sure she's the right sort of girl for you?'

Ben said nothing. Rose, Rose. What if you should marry me, and by some miracle agree to give up your sham success and come and live in the bungalow with me and Amy?

Oh, you fool, darling. You're joking.

His mind shook itself like a wet dog. He held out his hand. 'Thanks for seeing me,' he said. 'I hope you find the right man soon.'

'We'll have dozens of applications, I expect. Many of them from men like yourself. You got in first because of Miss Thomas knowing about the vacancy. How is that poor woman by the way? I hated to have to let her go.'

'I've never met her.'

'Well, if you do, try and help her, if you can. She's had a tough struggle. Invalid parents, and so on. I tried to find her

90

another job, but she's not really equipped to earn her own living. She –' Mr Prentiss looked at Ben speculatively through the bottle ends, pondering a match between him and Miss Thomas, since the fiancée sounded so questionable. He went with Ben to the door and through the passages to the main door of the building, wishing him luck and talking encouragingly and a little wistfully, as if he were loath to let Ben get out of his hands to rush off and marry the wrong woman.

The boy with the gnome-like smile was back on his roller skates. He came over to the wire netting as Ben went by.

'How did it go, sir?' he asked.

'How did what go?'

'Well, weren't you, like, after the warden's job? David come out and give us the thumbs-up. He said you was all right.'

'Thanks, but I can't come here. I'm not married.'

'Too bad. Well, I don't blame you.' The boy rubbed his hands, spat on the ground and skated expertly away.

That night Ben went out and got drunk with the Major. Geneva had sciatica, and was out of whisky. She had also quarrelled with Ben, because she had declared herself relieved that he could not have the warden's post.

Back in the fastnesses of the Bayswater Road, with the settlement so far away in distance and spirit that it seemed almost a mirage of the north London hills, Ben might have agreed with her, if she had not said it first.

'It's the deadest end I ever heard of,' Geneva told him from her bed. 'I can't see why you even went there. I thought you were going to have such a brilliant career.'

'Find me one,' Ben said. 'You can't start a career if no one will employ you.'

'And you can't start to climb the ladder of success if you begin by going down to the cellar.'

'Spare us the clichés,' Ben said. 'And the snobbery too.' The day's pain showed in her face, so he added: 'Anything I can get you?'

'Thank you.' Geneva attempted to look lofty in spite of a hair-net and the beribboned bed-jacket that she had received, with caustic ingratitude, from her sister Florence last Christmas.

'Since I am not a juvenile delinquent, I cannot hope to engage either your time or your sympathy.'

So Ben and the Major went round the bars together, cheerily enough at first, but later growing mournful. In an undefined club off Tottenham Court Road, where they paid a pound each to become members in order to get a drink, they talked of love and marriage and the sorrows of being a widower.

'I've sometimes thought of marrying again,' the Major confided, keeling forward and buffering himself with his arms on the table. One of his elbows slipped off the edge and he almost fell on the floor.

Ben heaved him upright with one hand. 'Who'd marry you?' he asked.

'You'd be surprised.' The Major's small discoloured mouth curved into a silly smile under the brave little moustache which was dyed to match his hair. 'Women have chased me all my life – when I wasn't chasing them. They've slowed down now, so have I, but the hunt's still on. A man needs a woman, my boy.' He turned to look at Ben with mournful, bloodshot eyes. 'That's the hell of it.'

'That's what I found out this morning. Have I told you what happened to me this morning?'

'Twice.' The Major moved his lips carefully round the word.

'I'll tell you again.' Ben told the story once more, making it very sad. It was sad. It was a bloody tragedy. They both felt that. They would have cried, if they had been that sort. They called for drink towards the shadows where they thought the bar was, and while they waited for it, they laid their forearms side by side on the table, sunk their necks between their shoulders and moped.

'It was the only chance I've had,' Ben said. 'My only chance of happiness. All gone.'

'What a shame,' said the woman who brought the drinks. 'That will be twelve shillings, dear.'

The Major plunged his hand into his pocket and spilled an assortment of coins on to the table. 'Leave him alone,' he said belligerently. 'Officer and gentleman. Allow me the honour at least of buying his whisky.'

The woman took what she wanted from the money and the

Major scooped the rest back into his pocket, and scrabbled on the floor with his legs spread wide and shaky to find the fallen coins. When he pulled himself upright, making the table rock and the drinks slop over, his face was deep purple. His eyes were starting from his head, and Ben wondered dispassionately whether he was going to have a stroke.

But he was only having an idea. 'Take my advice.' He got a grip on Ben's lapel and pulled himself very close. 'Carry the girl by storm. Force her to marry you. Fair heart never won faint lady, and all that sort of rot.'

Ben removed the Major's breast-pocket handkerchief and began to dab at the spilled whisky, tracing swirling patterns with it on the plastic table-top. 'Geneva doesn't want me to have the job, anyway,' he grumbled. 'She never wants me to have any fun.'

'Geneva can boil her head. It's your life, isn't it?'

'But Rose wouldn't want to come there with me. No one wants me to have any fun.'

'I do, old boy.' The Major's face glowed with compassion.

'I can't marry you. And Rose wouldn't like it at the –' The word eluded him. 'Where I was this morning.'

'Women never like where you take them. When I took my old trout to Aldershot she bitched the whole time. Doesn't mean a thing.'

'Suppose they didn't like her?'

'My friend.' The Major slapped him hard on the thigh. 'The boys will adore her.'

'That's not the idea.'

'What's the matter with you?' The Major sat up straight, swaying a little, and regarded Ben severely. 'Where are your guts, man? You love this wench, don't you?'

'Yes. Oh, yes.' When he was drunk, Ben was always violently and sentimentally in love with Rose. Hazily he saw a vision of the bungalow with the red door. The door opened and Rose came out, looking as she had in her last television show, when she had been a suburban housewife with a Mayfair suit and the kind of shopping basket women never carry in the street. 'She's really just a lovely, simple girl,' he said.

'Well, then.' The Major staggered to his feet. 'Let's get a taxi.

You can put me off at home. I have no idea where I live at the moment, but the driver will know. They always do. A fine body of men.' He stood like a doll while Ben hung his coat on him, and then he took the wrong hat from the shelf and fitted it carefully down over his ears.

'You've got someone else's hat.'

'They won't mind.' Half-blinded by the hat brim, the Major began to grope his way down the stairs to the street, getting two feet on each step before he ventured down to the next. 'Mine was a better hat.'

The night porter in Rose's block of flats glanced at Ben with an insulting lack of curiosity. Ben had thought of asking him to work the lift, but he lost his nerve. He plunged into the lift, pressed a button, got out at the wrong floor, checked himself just in time from ringing a bell marked Dr Lazarus, and stumbled down the service stairs and along a tilting corridor to Rose's door.

Rose had never given him a key. He kept his finger pressed on the bell. He had no idea what time it was, but when Rose opened the door cautiously, she was in pyjamas.

'What on earth are you doing?' she asked, stepping aside as Ben made a grab for her and lurched into the little hall. 'I was in bed.'

'Marry me,' Ben said hoarsely. 'Rose, you've got to marry me.'

'Darling, of course I will. You know that.' She patted him on the arm like a sister.

'Now. Tomorrow.'

'Oh, my sweet, I can't. Ringler told me today there's a chance of a stage part for me, in his new show. I can't think of anything else just now.'

'But, Rose –' He stared at her. She had got her lines wrong. 'This wasn't what you said in the taxi coming here.'

'You're drunk,' Rose said, not unkindly. 'Come on, you can sleep it off on the sofa.'

Before she left him, she brushed her lips across his hair. He wanted to reach out with his arms, but he fell asleep before he could kiss her.

Chapter Seven

WITH the aid of the battered typewriter and the Paddington library and the Admiralty Resettlement Office, Ben persevered with applications and interviews for all kinds of jobs he had never known existed, most of which sounded so depressing that he was almost glad to be turned down for them. He was now on the files of so many firms and organizations that if they had all fulfilled at the same time their promise to let him know if a suitable vacancy arose, Ben would have been the most sought-after man in Britain.

Meanwhile, the only people who wanted him were those who had turkey farms, fishing inns on the Welsh border, or guest-houses on the east coast to exchange for his gratuity.

'Everyone is so damned nice,' he told Jack Frazer as they lunched together in a public house after a surprise meeting in the street. 'Even the ones who aren't trying to sell you a flooded gravel-pit. They sound as if they were trying to make up for ever having said: "Good show" when Sandys decided to cut the defence budget at the expense of you and me.'

They had last been together in a depot ship at Malta. Jack, who was commanding the spare submarine crew, had been a plump and rosy, rather too hearty man with a great capacity for beer. He had been out of the Navy several months longer than Ben, and was now touring the unlovelier Midland towns selling office equipment to people who already had enough of every-thing he was trying to sell them.

His cheeks were paler now, and he was thinner and greatly subdued. He ordered the cheapest lunch, and refused a beer because of indigestion.

'I know what you mean,' he said. 'People are so decent that you almost think you've got the job until you find yourself at the door with your hat in your hand and the voice saying: "We'll keep you in mind." '

'I thought it was going to be rather a lark, being a civilian,' Ben admitted, because he thought that Jack would understand. 'An adventure, perhaps.' He laughed shortly, looking without enthusiasm at the plate of meat and vegetables that was set in front of him. It's not much fun not being wanted anywhere.'

'We're wanted, I suppose,' Jack said, 'but not at our own valuation. When I came out as a commander, I thought I was a hell of a fellow. I thought people would be falling over themselves to make me a director, and Nancy could have a decent home of her own at last. So here I am selling refills for staplers, and Nancy has had to take a job so that we can keep the boys at school.'

'There's something wrong about being an officer,' Ben scratched the brown stubble of his hair, which he was keeping short so that employers should find him a neat and clean man at least, if not a genius. 'Chaps seem to think we'd be too dumb and limited to learn anything new, and too upstage to be able to take orders from anyone less than an Admiral. They don't come right out with that, of course, but they imply it in some of the nicest ways. One man even told me I was too good for the job he had to offer. I say, Jack, I wish you'd have a beer. That glass of water looks like a disguise on you.'

'It is. I'm disguised as a sales executive with an incipient salesman's ulcer. What was the job?'

'Some kind of personnel assistant in the packing department of a huge firm that makes some ghastly thing women clean houses with. No authority and a salary that makes a commander's pay seem like a fortune.'

'You've got beyond caring about that by this time, I imagine.' Jack pushed away his unfinished plate and brought out a bottle of pills.

'I'd be a fool if I hadn't, but this chap took me for the fool. When I told him that I thought I knew how to deal with men if nothing else, he said that handling men in the Service was very different to handling men in industry, as if he thought I was going to try and shove all the packers in cells the moment I got there. 'I'm adaptable,' I told him. 'Maybe,' he said, 'but a lot of the men you'd be working with aren't. They've been in the forces, or their fathers have.'

'Resentful devils,' Jack said. 'I've had a bit of that. The high-ups are all right, but as soon as the little Caesars find out you're an ex-officer, they start thinking how to take you down a peg. However, it's a job. Why don't you have a bash at selling?'

'At the moment I don't feel as if I could sell a splint to a man with a broken leg.' Ben said. 'How did you get it?'

'Industrial employment analysts. They're a cheery crowd of people who aim to fit you into your right niche. By the time you've had to answer No to most of the questions on their endless form and had an interview with a patient psychologist, you're about ready to jump in the river; but they pulled me out and offered me this job, or a chance with an oil company in the Middle East. Why don't you try them?'

'I might.' Ben felt very depressed. It should have been comforting to talk to someone in the same predicament, and to renew a friendship with an old shipmate, but it was not. When they had last been together, they had been sure of themselves and of their future. Jack's conversation had always been full of bounce. He was deflated now and sadly changed. Ben saw himself changing too as he became, like Jack when he spotted him this morning in the street, just another tired, preoccupied man hurrying along the street with an attaché case.

He did not want to sell paper-clips. He did not want to go to the Middle East. But he did want a job. When he went back to to the flat to ask Geneva if she thought it would be all right for Amy to be brought up on the Persian Gulf, she came flying down the hall as soon as she heard his key in the door.

'Where have you been?' She pulled open the door and he came with it. 'I've found something marvellous. All your troubles are over.'

They went into the kitchen, where Geneva had a newspaper spread on the table among the debris of an apple pie she had been making. 'I had some pastry left over, and I was going to put it on the roof for the birds. I was just scooping the bits into yesterday's newspaper when I saw this fabulous thing. It leaped at me from the page, as people say when they see the name of a husband they haven't heard from for ten years. It's absolutely fate, Ben. It's simply too thrilling for words.' Her faded green eyes were moist with excitement. Her finger shook as she ran it haphazardly up and down the personal column, unable now to find the lines which had leaped at her.

'There it is – there!' She stabbed, wrinkling and tearing the paper with her finger, which had a lump of raw pastry on the nail. They leaned over the table and she read the advertisement out to Ben as he read it.

Wanted: ex-naval officer of courage and initiative. A lucrative, adventurous proposition for a bold, resourceful man.

'They want my gratuity,' Ben said at once.

'Don't be so suspicious. You're like an old maid with a sock under the mattress. Come in the other room. I'm going to dial that number for you. They're sure to have hundreds of answers. We may be too late already.'

A girl answered the telephone, a girl with an intriguing, husky voice. You could almost smell through the receiver the kind of perfume she would use.

'About your advertisement,' Ben said, with Geneva leaning on his back and breathing heavily over his shoulder.

'I'll let you speak to Mr Peale.' The girl's voice was shrouded and beckoning, as if she were promising the secret favours of the harem.

Mr Peale – the boss, presumably, but of what? The girl had merely repeated the number when she answered the telephone, without giving a name – was affable. No, the post was not yet filled. Yes, Ben could have an appointment. Tomorrow morning? 'Good show, Mr Francis. Be grand to see you. Many thanks for your call.'

He did not give any indication of what the job was, and he had rung off urbanely before Ben could ask him. When Amy came home, she found her grandmother and Ben having tea in the kitchen, and joined them in speculation.

Ben had run through a dozen ideas, and was now wavering between an arctic expedition and a secret-service mission. Geneva thought it was a sunken treasure-ship off the Outer Hebrides. Amy, drawing up a chair and plunging in at once, thought it would involve sailing the Atlantic on a raft. Could she come too? She was doing the *Mayflower* at school, and was in a pioneering state of mind. She had been complaining recently that there was nothing to discover in Bayswater except the significance of the Rima statue in the park, which last year had passed her by.

Caught up in each other's enthusiasm, elaborating and conjecturing and inventing wild and yet wilder possibilities, they did not pause to consider that Ben might not get the job. He was obviously just the man for it, whatever it was.

Whatever it was, it was adventure. For this he had been waiting. For this his luck had arranged for him to be turned down for all the lesser, mundane jobs he had sought. They read and reread the advertisement. There was money in it, and danger too, and perhaps even fame. Ben caught himself once or twice talking in the clipped tones of a hero. Amy decided to cut her hair. Geneva dreamed of their all going to live in Spain when it was over.

They talked excitedly all through supper, which was without the apple pie, because Geneva had forgotten to light the oven, and then Ben embarked on the arduous journey to the television studios, where Rose was appearing tonight as a guest star on a panel show. He had to see her. If things moved swiftly, this might be their last meeting.

'It may be dangerous,' he told Rose, throwing the remark away casually as they drove from the studios in her car. He had told her the whole story, or as much as he knew of it, in the brief, disabused manner of a half-hour detective serial. It sounded better that way, and it was the kind of language Rose could understand.

'Oh, darling.' She moved closer to him along the seat and slid an arm round his shoulders. 'I can't bear it. What should I do if anything happened to you?'

'The same as you were doing when I met you tonight, I suppose. Sign autographs for the studio audience and try to get the best-looking man on the programme to go home with you and think it was his idea.'

'Don't be a stinker,' Rose said happily. She liked Ben in this masterful mood. He rather liked himself. In spite of Geneva's and Amy's preoccupation with beards and pemmican, he was inclined more and more to the idea that he was going behind the iron curtain. The girl's voice on the telephone had smelled of top-secret refugees and smuggled arms. The fact that Mr Peale had a Harrovian instead of a Viennese accent was merely a blind.

The thought of what might lie before him, and of the kind of slouch-hat and trench-coat character he was shortly to assume, had given him more confidence than he had ever had with Rose when she was among other people. At the studio, he had shouldered his way through the crowd of infatuated autograph hunters and grunted in her ear: 'Come out of this. I want to talk to you.'

Ordinarily she would have refused curtly, without losing her public smile, but tonight Ben's voice and his grip on her arm had surprised her into going with him. He could see that she had that long-lipped ass from the panel show lined up to take her home, but with creditable aplomb, Ben had taken her coat from the man's arm, thanked him suavely for holding it, and swept triumphantly away with Rose, who was never averse to finding herself a shuttlecock between two men.

At the flat, Rose was very fond and solicitous of her hero. She shimmered about, waiting on him with sandwiches and drinks. When she had him comfortably settled, she sank to the floor in a becoming swirl of contrition and laid her arms and her head on his knee.

'I'm so sorry I've nagged you about getting a job,' she said, with a trace of tears in her elastic voice. 'Please forgive me. If I hadn't driven you to it, you wouldn't be going off tomorrow to God knows what.'

'You didn't drive me to it,' Ben said, through a salami sandwich; but she wanted it that way, so he let her go on. It was very pleasant to have her so loving. Perhaps after all she was not acting. The situation was one which was familiar to her from her plays. Since Ben had known her, she had said farewell on the screen to a test pilot, a racing driver with a damaged hand, and a blinded scientist off to try a kill-or-cure experiment on himself. But perhaps tonight her devotion was real. Ben began to let himself believe that she had really come alive to loving him.

She was wearing a low-cut dress with a plunging neckline. The producer of the panel show, which was classed as 'family', had insisted on having the dress sewn up one inch in the front before she went on the air, and she got up now and fetched a pair of scissors to remove the stitches.

'Let me do that.' Ben got up. She had taken off her shoes. She stood before him with her head on one side while he clipped at the stitches, his hand trembling a little.

When the steel of the scissors touched her bare, creamy flesh, she gave a little shiver. Ben looked up at her, but her face was completely blank and serene. She did not feel anything, and she did not realize that she was supposed to.

Mr Peale was a tall, casually elegant and youngish man, so loosely hung together that he could not help lounging whether he was on his feet or sitting down. In a chair, he tipped it backwards, curving his relaxed spine and stretching out his endless legs, with the long feet flopping in what looked like hand-sewn shoes. Upright, which he never was completely, he could not stand without resting one hip like a tired cab-horse. His hands were often cradled in his pockets. He leaned on anything that was handy.

When Ben came into the office, Mr Peale was leaning back in a tilted chair, with his feet on the desk and a telephone in his lap. It was a large, well-lit office, with two desks and a pale fitted carpet, and water-colours of aeroplanes on the walls. The pictures were effective rather than technical, but they hit Ben with a new and disconcerting idea. He had not thought of planes. Mr Peale could not expect him to fly one, but perhaps he was to be a guinea-pig for a higher and faster flight, the man who was strapped into a bucket seat with an automatic camera taking pictures of his contorted face muscles as the cramps hit him. His imagination turned and ran, but the heavy, resourceful shoes in which he had come to meet the challenge of adventure walked on across the room, making flat dents in the carpet.

The girl in the outer office had not inquired whether Ben might come in. She had merely shown him in, opening the door and announcing Ben in an off-hand way, as if she had little respect either for him or Mr Peale. She was the girl who had answered the telephone, but her appearance did not match her husky, mysterious voice. She had an untidily-cropped head with the greenish sheen of brown hair that needs washing, and a flat, unhealthy face with a few spots in the greasy areas round her nose and chin. Her figure was good, and rather consciously inviting. She was one of those girls who only comes into her own at a party when all the lights fuse.

'He's here now,' Mr Peale told the telephone, and rang off. He dropped his long legs to the ground and stood up, propping himself on the desk with one hand, while he offered the other to Ben. 'Take a pew,' he said, and collapsed gracefully back into his chair.

They talked for a few minutes about nothing at all. The victim of so many interviews, Ben recognized the technique of making friendly, meaningless conversation until the nervous applicant cannot stand it any longer, and puts himself at a disadvantage by blurting out some crude allusion to the job. Ben kept his end of the conversation going, determined to beat Mr Peale at his own game and force him to reveal, or at least hint at what was at the back of the advertisement.

But this was not courage and initiative. What would the master mind with the club tie and the spotless finger-nails think of a man who sat so humbly pretending to be interested in the Army and Navy rugger match?

'Can we get down to business?' Ben cut bravely across the small talk. He looked at his watch without seeing it. 'I haven't got too long.'

'Who has?' Mr Peale smiled agreement. 'The days whizz by. Awfully good of you to come along at all, as a matter of fact.'

His manner was disarming. Ben smiled back and admitted: 'I couldn't help coming. Your advertisement was most intriguing. What is this lucrative, adventurous proposition?' He and Geneva and Amy knew the advertisement by heart, and Amy had it pinned to the wall, over her bed.

'You liked the ad.? Mitzi wrote it.' Mr Peale inclined his head, which was small and smooth, with a clean skin and unobtrusive features, like the painted top of a ninepin, towards the outer room. 'She put in all the adjectives she knew.' He was confidential, but he had confided nothing.

'I want the job,' Ben ventured, 'if it's something I can handle.'

'Do it on your head,' Mr Peale said casually. 'Money for jam. A chance for a man to do a bit of good not only for himself but for hundreds of other poor sods. Thousands, perhaps, if the thing goes well.'

So it was to be refugees. 'Tell me more,' Ben said. 'Who's going to be helped, and how?'

Mr Peale stalled. He was more cunning than he seemed with that throw-away sixth-form voice and that round face of an inbred aristocrat on top of the long neck that rose like a flower stalk out of the perfect fold of his collar. He continued to generalize. He was waiting for something, and finally the outside door of the other room opened and a man's voice said something abrupt to the girl, and it was obvious that this was what he had been waiting for.

It was not Mr Peale who was the master mind. It was Mr Beckett. He was a much tougher customer, a disenchanted man with a square head of curly grey hair, bright with oil, and grey eyebrows and moustache trimmed like little hedges. He was not friendly. He was not even very polite. He prowled about the room, shooting questions at Ben, and clicking his teeth as if he did not like the answers.

'Sit down, Jake,' Mr Peale urged him, but Mr Beckett continued to prowl about the carpeted room, looking at Ben from every angle. Ben was in a swivel chair. He tried to keep the chair turned to face him, so that Beckett could not give Peale the thumbs down behind his back.

Suddenly Mr Beckett stopped prowling and sat down at the other desk in the window, folding his hands as if he were waiting for dinner. 'This chap's OK, Jimmy,' he said surprisingly.

'How about it then?' Mr Peale asked Ben.

'How about what? I'm prepared to do almost anything, but you haven't given me a clue.'

Mr Beckett laughed. 'You don't suppose,' he said, 'that we give away all the secrets of our business to every Tom, Dick and Harry who comes in here looking for an idea to steal?'

'In that case,' Ben got up stiffly, feeling anger creeping over him, 'I might as well go.'

'Jake didn't mean you,' Mr Peale said. 'Sit down, for God's sake, and don't be so stuffy.'

'Well, all right.' Ben sat down and looked from one man to the other. 'What do you want me to do?'

'What do you think?' Mr Beckett grinned at him. He had a long line of even teeth under the clipped moustache.

'God knows. You might want to shoot me on to the moon in a rocket for all I know.'

'Would you go?'

'No.'

'Why did you answer our advertisement?'

'Because it sounded like adventure,' Ben said. 'It sounded like the chance I dreamed of before I got out of the Navy and found out how many dull jobs there were on the beach.'

'You were in the war. Didn't you get enough adventure at sea?'

'That was different. Being under orders isn't like an adventure you can run by yourself.'

'Champion,' said Mr Beckett, bringing out into the open the trace of a northern accent which ran flatly through all his speech. 'Adventure is what we're offering you, if you're man enough to take it.'

Ben's heart leaped. I'm in. This is it. 'Tell me what I must do,' he said with simple courage.

Mr Beckett told him. After half an hour, Ben agreed to train for the job, two weeks' probation, either side backing out if they wanted to. As he left the office, dragging his feet a little and wishing he had not worn these shoes, Ben argued with his fallen spirits: It's something, after all. It's better than nothing.

Mr Beckett and Mr Peale were the directors of a company which was called the Services Investment Association. They promised to servicemen an interest of ten per cent on their savings twice yearly after the first six months, and a free life and accident policy with one of the major insurance companies. The money thus acquired was invested by Peale and Beckett in foreign industrial stocks. 'A profit for us and a profit for the serviceman,' Mr Beckett said in the smooth tones which overlaid his voice like oil when he talked about money. 'No one can lose.'

'Why foreign stocks?' Ben had asked. 'Why not invest at home?'

'A good question, sir.' Mr Peale lit a cigarette without moving his elbows and forearms from the desk. Ben's disappointment over the adventure was showing itself as suspicion, and they were trying to woo him back. 'We're investing abroad, because that's where the money is. Sweden and Germany, all those chaps beavering away in factories ... they can't miss. But there's a more subtle reason too. The clients want to know what we're doing with their money. They like the sound of foreign investments. It has that magic, millionaire ring to it, like foreign exchange. Just another come-on.'

'You mean you're trying to trick these people out of their money?' Ben rubbed his head and frowned.

'You are very insulting,' Mr Beckett said cheerfully and without offence. 'Your caution is natural, of course. I admire that in you. Jimmy shouldn't have used that word come-on. A misleading term, though it does mean what it says, if you get me. All we're doing is persuading these people to let us make some money for them; to get the habit of saving instead of spending foolishly, and to put their savings to work. Our tempting offers – the high interest rate, the free group insurance, are designed to help them to take the plunge. A bank doesn't expect to get depositors without offering them interest on their money. We operate just like a bank, you'll find, the only difference being that we offer our clients twice as much interest.'

'How do you make any money then?'

'I assure you that we do. Very tidy profits. Very tidy indeed. Money makes money. I don't need to tell you that. And the more investors we acquire, the greater our profits. That's why we need you.'

Peale and Beckett, an unlikely pair of men to come together, had started the Services Investment Association in conjunction with an ex-group-captain, and were at first operating only with the Air Force. After six months, the venture had proved so successful – 'Our clients have been so delighted,' was the way Mr Beckett put it – that they had decided to expand to take in the Navy as well. That was where Ben came in.

He was to work the naval bases, to start the ball rolling until word-of-mouth enthusiasm had the sailors piling up behind each other to join the money-spinning Association.

'Not Gosport,' Ben said flatly. 'I know too many chaps there.'

'Of course, of course. We understand. Not that you'd necessarily be working among the officers. The seamen and petty officers are the chaps with the money these days. But start anywhere you like. The field is yours.'

The secretary slouched in with some letters for Mr Beckett to sign, her falsies pushing out her sweater like cardboard cones.

'Not now, Mitzi,' he told her, but she said: 'I thought you wanted to get them in the post,' and dropped the letters on his desk.

While Mr Beckett signed them, she stood cleaning the nails of one hand with the nails of the other, and surveyed Ben with a flat-eyed and discouraging stare. Ben dropped his head and looked at his twisting hands, struggling with himself to find the snap decision that the secret-service man in the trench-coat would have made long ago and been on his way, with or without the job.

Half of him wanted to get up and tell Peale and Beckett that they could put the Service Investment Association where the bosun put the pudding. The other half did not want to leave yet one more office and go home without a job. It was not what he had hoped for. So what? Scarcely any of the posts for which he had applied unsuccessfully had been that. The Navy had not been what he had hoped for when he was a boy, and the Navy had given him a lot of good things. Could he afford to turn this down because he was squeamish about going back to his old stamping grounds as a sort of glorified insurance salesman? Beggars can't be choosers, he would be told by Rose, who was inclined to platitudes when she was lecturing him.

It was hard to turn down Peale and Beckett in any case. They seemed to like him, which was in their favour, and made it hard for him to dislike them. They talked openly with him, as if they had nothing to hide, and charmed away his objections in an understanding and cheery way that had somehow transformed the interview into a conference, as if he were already part of the firm.

When the girl had gone out, he made one more struggle to escape.

'For a man who wanted adventure,' Mr Beckett said, 'you're surprisingly scared of the chance to make some fat commissions. There's your gratuity too. You'll never find anything better to invest it in than the S.I.A.'

'Leave my gratuity alone,' Ben said. 'I want it for my daughter. It's already invested in gilt-edged. I like it where it is. Is that why you advertised for ex-naval officers?' he asked Mr Peale. It was easier to say these things to him than to Mr Beckett. 'So that you could get their gratuity?'

'Oh, my dear chap.' Jimmy Peale smiled tolerantly. He did not have the projecting teeth that usually go with a chinless face. When he smiled, his mouth made a rounded, empty shape, as if he had no teeth at all. 'What do you think we are? Of course, later on, if you want to invest some of your money with us –'

'I said no.'

'Keep your shirt on. It's pretty obvious why we want a naval officer. For a start, we want to help chaps like you who've been axed. And we want you because you know how to handle these kind of people. You've been nursing sailors along for – what? sixteen, seventeen years. It's no strain to nurse them along a bit further and show them what to do with their money. You know how to talk to them. You know the ropes, and you'll be able to get at them. You can't go trotting into dockyards, or swarming up the side of a battleship, but you can ferret around and find some ship's writer or somebody who'll give you addresses, so that you can go and see the wives.'

'Why the wives? Are they more gullible?'

'No, no, Benjamin.' Mr Beckett slipped in his name as easily as if they had been on Christian-name terms for weeks. 'There's nothing to be gullible about. But the wives are more available, and they usually wear the trousers.'

'I'd feel as if I was peddling vacuum cleaners,' Ben said. 'That was the one thing I didn't want to do.'

'That's a lucrative enough job in its way,' Mr Beckett mused, as if he had tried and enjoyed it. 'But you'll be an investment salesman. That sound toney enough for you? Selling futures, that's what it is. Selling future happiness, future security. Building an estate for these deserving women – the backbone of the country, mark you – assuring that they and the kiddies will have a nest-egg in case something happens to their dear ones.'

'Are those the sort of things I'd have to say?'

'In essence. You'll put it in your own words, of course. I envy you, Benjamin. I'd much rather be out in the field than in the office. It's the human side of the business. You'll love it.'

'I haven't said yet that I –'

Mitzi came into the office and said familiarly: 'There's another naval officer out there, Jake. He says he has an appointment.'

'Tell him the post is filled.' Mr Beckett stood up, pulling down his short, neat jacket and twitching at the three-fold peaks of his breast-pocket handkerchief. 'How about shaking hands on our future, Benjamin?'

Ben felt himself going under like a submarine. They shook hands.

Geneva took it well. 'I knew it sounded too good to be true. There's always a catch in those things,' she said, as if she had never been deceived by the challenging advertisement. 'I'm awfully glad really, Ben.' She kissed him. 'Amy and I would have had fits if you had gone into any danger.'

Geneva was a true optimist, like Ben. That was one of the reasons they understood each other so well. She was hopefully enthusiastic before the event, but when it did not come off, she buried it gladly and switched her enthusiasm without effort to the next thing that came along. She now applied herself, with the stub of a pencil and the backs of old envelopes, to reckoning up how much money she could make if she entrusted her tiny savings to the Services Investment Association, and how much commission Ben would make on her if she did.

'But you're not a naval wife.'

'Don't kid yourself, sweetie. Your Peale and Beckett would make poor old William a posthumous Admiral if that was the only way they could get my cash.'

The Major was quite excited. The S.I.A. would obviously set its sights next on the Army, and what better man than Major Hubert Grantley Flood, D.S.O. (retd) to be their agent round the camps and barracks?

'You'll put in a word for me, no doubt, when the time comes. I could do it on my head. Aldershot, Catterick, Woolwich – I know 'em all like the back of my hand. Call on me any time. I shall be honoured to work with you, Ben my boy.'

Amy, usually so ready with an act to fit any situation, looked to Ben to see how she should take this new development. She had been keyed up to play the part of the tight-lipped hero's daughter, or the fisherman's child, waiting at the cottage window with her eyes glued on the storm-tossed sea. She could not assume her new role until she saw how much her father minded.

She brought him the newspaper advertisement from above her bed. 'Shall I burn this beastly thing?' she asked, to see if he was feeling bitter. 'Or shall I keep it in my album as a memento of what might have been?'

'Keep it as a memento of what is,' Ben told her. 'I think it's the start of a new life for you and me, Amy. It's the chance for me to work for us at last. I'm going to make some money. We'll have a place of our own, a car, holidays abroad. When I take you to America, it won't be on a raft, but first-class in the *Queen Elizabeth*.'

'The raft would have been fun,' she said, and then discarded it to join him in building extravagant, impossible plans for their prosperous life together, which had to include Geneva.

'In a flat above the garage, I think,' Amy said. 'Then she could be part of us, but on her own at the same time.' For a child who had never had a proper family life, she was very alive to the subtleties of family relationship. 'I wouldn't want her to be like Jane Egerton's grandmother, who gets shoved upstairs with a tray when they have people to supper.'

Geneva laughed. 'If I'm living over the garage, you can go one better than that. When you get sick of me, you can run the engine of the car all night and let the carbon monoxide seep up through the floor.'

The ladies at the Phillimore Bureau were enchanted. Ben took them a bottle of sherry, and they drank it out of the tea-cups, although Jessie's boy friend, who was a militant tee-totaller, would half kill her if he knew.

'I'm so happy for you, Ben,' Mrs French said, doting on him with her head on one side, the sherry warming her to gentle sentiment. 'My only regret is that we shan't see you here any more.'

'I'll visit you,' Ben said, 'to bring you news of the world of finance. I may need some tips from you too, on how to talk persuasively to women.'

'Don't look at me,' Jessie giggled, as drunk as if she had had three whiskies. 'You wouldn't need to do much talking to persuade me.'

'Jessie!' Miss Arkwright wagged a scandalized finger, and Jessie clapped a hand over her mouth and giggled through it.

Miss Arkwright raised her tea-cup in a toast. 'May good fortune smile on you in your new career,' she declaimed. 'I can't help wishing you had got something through us though,' she said, giving him her sweet smile. 'You never were in our line, of course, but I was always hoping. I didn't tell you, but we always planned that if you did get something, we wouldn't ask any commission from you, even if it meant cooking the books. That was our secret.'

'I've got a job,' Ben told Rose triumphantly. She did not say: 'And about time.' Rose nagged, but when you did what she wanted, she was ungrudgingly delighted.

She kissed him and gave him her wide-eyed, searching look, lips slightly parted, sweet breath coming softly between her comely teeth. 'Oh, darling, I'm afraid for you. Is it as dangerous as you thought? You're probably not supposed to tell me what it is, but tell me, anyway. I'm like the grave.'

When he told her, she moved away, pouting, and stood running her forefinger along the piping at the top of the sofa. Her short-sighted egotism was occupied with the disappointment of not being privy to a secret. Ben had the idea that she could have borne the news that he was going to ram a ship with a human torpedo, as long as she could have been the only person to know about it.

When her mind expanded slightly to inquire for more details of Ben's new job, he did not tell her too much. She was concerned about his social status, so he tried to make the S.I.A.

110

sound as impressive as possible, stressing the shrewd, successful aspect of Mr Beckett, and the old Harrovian polish of Jimmy Peale. His own part in the business, and the financial prospects, he painted for her in phrases that Mr Beckett himself could not have bettered.

'A financial agent.' Rose tried the words to see how they would sound to describe Ben to other people. 'An investment salesman. Yes, I see. Like a stockbroker,' she said comfortably.

'Like a stockbroker,' Ben agreed, and left her happy.

Travelling down to Southampton to tell his parents that he was no longer unemployed, which would put a stop to the wistful letters from his mother telling him of situations she had seen advertised in the local paper, which would suit him nicely if he lived at home, Ben felt the old familiar excitement as the landmarks passed by, heralding the approach of the house by the railway.

When it came, with the father burning a pile of fiercely-smoking rubbish at the edge of the orchard, much too near the laundry line, and one of the bedroom windows wide open to the gusty morning with a flowered curtain streaming out, Ben felt more like reaching home than he ever did when he arrived on the draughty doorstep of Wavecrest.

Craning back to see the last of the narrow chimneys and the tops of the bare trees before the side of the bridge cut off his view, he wondered whether he would ever get the house out of his blood.

'A place you know?' asked the man to whom he had been talking, as Ben turned round and sat back again in the carriage.

'Yes, pretty well. I've never been there, actually.'

The man looked uncomprehending, and went back to his impressions of John Foster Dulles, to which Ben gave only half an ear.

Will I ever go there? I must go there some day. It will spoil it, of course. The fascination will fade like a mirage, and it will be just a house with people doing ordinary things and dogs' hairs on the furniture. But I want to know.

No chance that the father might be a retired naval officer. He had been around too consistently for as long as Ben could

111

remember. He had only seen the son once in the last two years, getting out of the car with his plump wife. The car did not look like anything you might see parked in the dockyard at Portsmouth. He might be in the Air Force, though. Ben could trespass on the group-captain's field and get off the train, at Easter perhaps, when the son would come home, to try to interest him in a little investment.

The man who hated Dulles got out at Winchester and Ben sat alone in the carriage with the morning paper still unread on the seat beside him. If he began to make the kind of money Mr Beckett promised him, would he marry Rose? Would she marry him? He would have to be away a great deal, and she would be free to go on acting for as long as the public could stand her.

It would be the kind of marriage she had been almost prepared to make when he was still in the Navy. They could have a house in the country, not too far from London. A reliable couple to look after things and keep Amy happy. There could be a pony, dogs, a house in a tree. Their friends would be the sort of people like the family who lived in the house by the railway. They might even take a house in that neighbourhood, and their friends could actually be that family. Rose would not like them, but she would still have her London crowd, the television people, and if she pulled off this stage part, people from the theatre too. She could have them down for week-ends, and they could stand about in pea-green sports jackets, drinking cocktails before lunch and making witty jokes about Ben's neighbours, and Ben would suffer them courteously and pour more drinks, knowing who his real friends were.

Chapter Eight

MR BECKETT spent most of his time in what was known as the Back Office, where the foreign investments were handled, and a book-keeper looked after the accounts of the Services Investment Association.

Cheques and cash received by Mr Peale were taken either by

him or Mitzi to the Back Office, which was only a few streets away, somewhere off the Euston Road. Ben offered once or twice to take the money round for them, to see if they trusted him with it, but apparently they did not, for Mr Peale made some excuse for wanting to go there himself, and so Ben never found out what the Back Office was like.

Jimmy Peale was astute enough, but Jake Beckett was clearly the brains of the organization, and the Back Office was where most of the serious work was done. The Front Office, with its luxurious carpet and its big windows opening on to the sooty trees of a Bloomsbury square, was not much more than a reception-room, designed to please the eye and soothe the mind with the tangible evidence of the S.I.A.' prosperity.

Jimmy was a kind of front man, a liaison officer between the field and headquarters, and he did not allow his job to tax him unduly. He was never in the office before ten, never took less than an hour and a half for lunch, and was invariably gone by four. He handled the correspondence, dealt with callers, either reassuringly, persuasively or sympathetically, according to their requirements, held long telephones with the group-captain, who was reaping a fair harvest among the airmen at Farnborough, and filled in his spare time training Ben to reap similar harvest among the personnel of the Royal Navy.

Mitzi filed her nails, read library books, ate apples and toffees, and occasionally typed letters and took a little slapdash dictation, using a code she had evolved after two weeks' stenography at a night school, which looked more like kindergarten pictures than shorthand symbols. It was soon clear to Ben, and indeed nobody made a secret of it, that Mitzi held the job more for what she did for Mr Beckett outside the office than within.

She was a costive, pouting girl with a good opinion of herself that was not justifiable to the dispassionate observer. When Jimmy Peale was talking to a client, or had slipped off to the Back Office, and Ben had nothing to do, he would sit with Mitzi and she would tell him: 'This place smells. I wouldn't be here at all if I hadn't had such bad luck.'

She had trained for six months at a dramatic school, but had to leave because of jealousy among the students. 'I was getting

113

the best parts,' she said smugly. 'I was good enough for them too. It had nothing to do with one of the instructors being in love with me, although he was, poor man. He wanted to leave too when I left.'

Mitzi was always talking about men who were or had been wildly in love with her. Ben was the captive audience for long sagas of dubious passion, which Mitzi recounted with a hypnotized look in her small, muddy eyes, and the same relish with which she sucked at caramels. She told Ben that Jake Beckett had a wife and three children whom he would eventually leave for love of her, although it was obvious from their vulgarly casual attitude towards each other that there was nothing more between Mitzi and Jake than a convenient arrangement which suited them both for the moment. Jake would drop Mitzi any time he felt like it, and Mitzi would probably drop Jake any time she could get her graceless hands on another man.

She suggested once when they were alone in the office that Ben might be that other man. She was quite crude about it, so he was able to be quite crude about turning down the offer. After that, they understood each other and became rather good friends.

Mitzi helped Jimmy with Ben's training, and the three of them had more fun over it than Ben had expected would come an embryo salesman's way. Mitzi sublimated her theatrical frustrations by acting as the guinea-pig for Ben's experimental sales talks, using her experience from the dramatic school, which perhaps had lost an actress when it slung her out. Playing every variety of naval wife, her sluggish personality came alive at last. Once, acting the part of the starry-eyed bride of a sub-lieutenant, she was almost beautiful, but only for a moment. Dropping her role to swear at Jimmy with a man's epithets for interrupting her big speech, she was just Mitzi again.

The exhausted Jimmy Peale also woke to a livelier show of spirit during these enthralling playlets. His comfortable seat assumed the aspect of a folding canvas chair with a film director's name stencilled across the back. From the unsuspected labyrinths of his ninepin head he produced an assortment of characters for Ben to practise on.

'You're an engine-room artificer's wife in a pre-fab at Weymouth,' he would tell Mitzi. 'You've got three small children and you've lost your figure and you're trying to cook a meal and keep the baby out of the coal-scuttle and you haven't any time for Ben. Got that everybody?'

Mitzi took up her stand by Jake's desk, as if she were stirring saucepans. Jimmy leaned back in his chair with his eyes narrowed and his hands folded on his stomach, and Ben went outside the door and tried to imagine himself coming up a garden cinder path.

'Action!' Jimmy called.

Ben knocked on the door, and Mitzi opened it, pushing back her hair with her wrist, as if she had flour on her hands.

'Mrs Bloggs?' Ben asked in a courteous way, neither too deferential nor too demanding.

'That's right.' Mitzi slapped backwards at an imaginary child.

'Mrs Bloggs,' Ben said, 'I have come to help you.'

'If you're from the Seventh Day Adventists, we're Chapel,' Mitzi said and prepared to shut the door.

Ben put his foot in the crack and kept on talking. It didn't matter much what you said in the face of a closing door, Jimmy had told him, as long as you kept the words coming fast enough to hold the woman's curiosity. He dried up before long and stood helplessly with his foot in the doorway, his salesman's smile replaced by his normal grin.

'Do I let him in this time?' Mitzi asked.

'I think so. He looks rather cute.' Jimmy said, so Mitzi heard milk boiling over on the stove and let go of the door, and Ben came in, patting the heads of the older children and waggling his finger at the baby.

Mrs Bloggs was back at the stove, stirring vigorously, with an unapproachable back.

'Won't she ask me to sit down?'

'Later she may,' Jimmy said. 'Not till she knows what you want. There isn't anywhere to sit, anyway. There's a cat on one chair and a pile of wet nappies on the other, and the kiddies have the others upside down to play Daddy's boat.'

Ben was stranded in the middle of the floor. He set down his brief-case on the ironing board, put his hands in his pockets, took them out again and scratched his head.

115

'You'll have to let that hair grow, Ben,' Jimmy observed. 'It looks too military for the family's best friend.'

'It looks like hell if it's any longer,' Ben said. 'Women don't mind it. They say it's like stroking beaver's fur.'

'Enchanting.' Jimmy closed his eyes. 'Go on.'

Ben cleared his throat. 'I've come to help you,' he told Mitzi's back.

Jimmy clicked his teeth. 'You're slipping. When you repeat yourself, do it in different words.'

'Can I light a cigarette?'

'Not in her kitchen.'

Ben approached the stove. 'Give me a break, Mitzi,' he said. 'I'm stuck.'

'All right, I will this time, but Mrs Bloggs won't.' She turned round and asked him: 'You're selling something, aren't you? Well, you've come to the wrong house. We've got the telly, and Dad doesn't hold with the *Encyclopaedia Britannica*.'

'You're right,' Ben said, gathering strength, 'I am selling something. But it's something that no one has ever tried to sell you before, believe me, dear lady. Dear lady . . . too much?'

'Too much,' Jimmy said, without opening his eyes.

'What I have for sale,' Ben ploughed on, 'is happiness. The happiness of your future, Mrs Bloggs. I want to make sure that the years ahead for you and your family shall be secure and free from worry.'

'Who are you kidding?' Mitzi asked, putting her hands on her prominent hips. 'With the price of everything going up, and Dad not knowing if he'll be able to sign on again at the end of his time and that child's chest – cough, cough, cough, every winter –'

'You could use some more money, couldn't you?' Ben came out with it boldly. 'You have some savings no doubt. I can tell from your home what an able and prudent manager you are.'

'The gas has just gone out,' Mitzi said uncooperatively. 'They threatened they'd cut me off if I didn't pay this month.'

'You have some savings, damn it,' Ben insisted. Then more smoothly: 'I am here to show you how you can make your savings work for you, how you can be sure that there will always be money when you need it badly. Suppose,' he coughed

116

discreetly, 'something were to happen to Mr Bloggs. Unthinkable, of course, but our lives are, after all, but a brief span snatched from the tentacles of death –'

'Not that word,' Jimmy said sharply.

'Sorry. From the tentacles of chance. Surely his last thought would be: "Thank God they're provided for." '

Mitzi snorted. 'Don't make me laugh. That time the motorbike skidded with us all on the Portsmouth road, his last words were "We'll never make it before the pubs close." Look, Mr Whatsit, if it's insurance you're selling, I've got no money to spare for that out of the housekeeping.'

'Yes, it is insurance, in a way, but there are no premiums. A free insurance policy is only one of the benefits I'm offering you. Would you like to hear the rest?'

'I don't mind.' Mitzi wiped her hands on her skirt. 'Eric! You stop that screaming and let's hear what the gentleman has to say.'

Sometimes Mitzi would allow Ben to persuade her into an investment. Sometimes she held out, and Ben would have to leave the house, being regretful, but still polite, lest the word get around the neighbours that he was no gentleman. Sometimes they all three collapsed in laughter and decided to chuck it and go out for a drink.

So sluggish as her normal self, Mitzi unearthed a surprising scope and invention when she was acting. Sometimes she was a push-over, sometimes a stubborn wife, sometimes blankly stupid, sometimes craftily one step ahead of Ben in her conviction that he was a swindler.

As the lessons went on, half in earnest and half in laughter, Ben began to find his part getting easier. Ever since he left the Navy, he had been discovering how many things he could not do. Here was something he might be able to do at last.

From time to time, Jake Beckett would come round from the Back Office to see how Ben was getting on, and they would stage a little scene for his benefit.

Their favourite was the Admiral's widow, Lady Arbuthnot, with the spaniels and the budgerigars, who made Ben stay to tea and flirted decrepitly with him over the madeira cake. She had tried to seduce him once, but that was only Mitzi reverting to type, and Jake had slapped her back to the Maltese lace tablecloth and the bird-seed, 'and while you're up, Commander Francis, would you just turn his cuttlefish round so that he can nibble at the clean side?'

It was more play than work, although Peale and Beckett insisted that it was deadly serious. Ben had a good time, but he was not looking forward to the day when the fun would be over and he would have to go out by himself and tackle the real women, who would give him all the wrong answers and get him as confused in his sales talk as an actor suddenly given a cue from the next act.

When Mr Beckett announced that he was ready to try his luck in the field, Ben did not know whether to be glad or sorry. He was proud of his progress, and the solemn removal of two of the aeroplane pictures, to be replaced by impressions of destroyers surging bows-under through tumultuous seas, was a salesman's graduating ceremony.

He would miss the lessons though. He and Jimmy Peale and Mitzi had been through so many Mrs Bloggs and Lady Arbuthnots together that they were as companionable as the cast of a play after a year's run. It had been fun, but he could not stay in the nursery for ever. Now he must venture out to prove himself against the world. It was a challenge, and something of an adventure after all to go into the houses of strangers and see how they lived and how they would treat him.

It was not going to be easy. He would have to telephone Jimmy every day to report progress, and he had a feeling that if he did not keep coming up with results, the atmosphere in the front office of the Services Investment Association was not going to be so genial.

When he told Rose that he was off to Rosyth to begin work in earnest, she gave him a rabbit's foot charm and promised to be a good girl until he returned.

'When you come back, let's talk some more about getting married,' she said cosily. It was a subject she enjoyed, since it was purely personal, and no harm could come of it, because they never reached a decision.

She kissed Ben tenderly, and waved him down the corridor towards the lift with a touching little sideways gesture of her hand, as if she were a young bride watching her man stride off to conquer the world via the eight-fifteen.

As he turned the corner at the end of the corridor, Rose dropped the lonely bride and called rather raucously after him: 'I hope you make a million!'

Ben turned back to give her the victory sign, but the door of her flat had banged shut.

He had not admitted to Rose that he was nervous, and he would not show it to Amy and Geneva, who believed in him. He had been practising on them at home, but it did not work as well as with Mitzi, because Geneva was too prejudiced in his favour, too ready to fall in with anything he suggested. After he had practised one of his sales talks on her at breakfast when Amy had left for school, it was all he could do to stop Geneva going round to the bank without doing her face and drawing out all her money.

'Why not?' she protested. 'If you don't think it's safe, you shouldn't be in it.'

'I am in it,' Ben said seriously, 'and I do think it's safe. I have to believe that if I'm ever going to sell the idea to anyone.'

'Why not to me, then?'

'I don't know. You haven't got enough, anyway, to make a worthwhile profit, and you need every penny of it. You shouldn't gamble with it.'

'I thought you said the S.I.A. was as safe as a bank. Even if it was gambling. I wouldn't mind having a little flutter on it. Ben —' She lifted her creased face, with pins sticking out from all the little ginger curls. 'I've been trying to tell you this for two days, but I was afraid you'd think me an old fool. It's possible that I shall be a little better oiled in the near future.'

'Geneva, that's wonderful! Has somebody died?'

'It's the Major.'

'Good God — the poor old chap. Why didn't you tell me? What happened — a stroke?'

Geneva shook her head, watching his face cautiously. 'He wants me to marry him. Oh, Ben —' She reached her skinny, freckled arm across the table to him. 'Please, please don't laugh. I know it's funny, and everyone will think so.'

'I don't,' Ben said. 'I think it's a damn good idea. I can't think why I didn't think of it myself.'

'Do you really?' Geneva's face lit up. 'Oh, I am relieved. I was afraid you'd be horrified at the idea of throwing in my lot with such a shocking old character. But he was sober when he suggested it, honestly.'

'I believe it. He could never have such a good idea when he was drunk.' Ben went round the table to kiss Geneva on top of the hairpins. She did not like to be kissed before she had done her face. 'The more I think of it, the better I like it.'

'You swear it?' Geneva twisted her neck to stare up at him to see if he was serious. 'I shouldn't think of it really, I suppose. Poor William must be whirling in his grave. He never could stand Hubert. He is an old rogue, I know, but I'm fond of him in an exasperated way. And I get lonely, you know, at times. I've got friends, and I've got my darling Amy, but it isn't the same as having a man, even a man like the Major. I've had you, but now that you're going to be in high finance, with everything you touch turning to gold, you'll want to go away and get a place of your own, and you'll want Amy with you. That's what brought this whole thing up, as a matter of fact. I was telling the old buffer how I'd feel without you, and he takes a deep breath and blows out his cheeks and says: "Why not let me move in?" "As a lodger?" I said. "No, madam," he replies, as gallant as you please. "As your husband." '

Ben went away to take a bath. While he was soaking in the old-fashioned boarded tub, he thought about himself and Amy and where they would live. They would rent somewhere at first, and later, if things went well, they could think of buying. Amy would have to stay with Geneva for a while until Ben got into his stride, but he could not leave her in the flat after the shocking old character moved in.

And Rose? Now he would have to decide about her, and she would have to stop being cosy and make up her mind about him. 'Let's talk about getting married when you come back,' she had said. But this time he would pin her down to talk about it in earnest.

When he came home that evening, he went into Amy's bedroom, where she was standing up doing homework, with the

120

exercise-book spread out among the china animals and photographs on her dressing-table.

'You can't work like that,' Ben said. 'What's wrong with the dining-room?'

'Geneva keeps talking to me. She's so excited. And she wants to sing.'

'You know why?'

Amy nodded, drawing a line neatly under something she had written. She was wearing blue jeans and a cotton shirt. Her legs looked very long and her waist and back looked frail, with the shoulder-blades sticking out under her plaits.

'What do you think of the news?' Ben asked, sitting down on the bed.

Amy turned round to see from his face what she ought to think of it. He smiled at her, so she said: 'I think it's smashing. She told me I could be a bridesmaid. And she told me another thing. She said that you and I were going away to live in a place of our own. Is that true, Daddy?'

'I may be able to swing it pretty soon. You and I should be together, although Grandma would love to keep you, of course.' He wanted Amy to think that she was a valued possession, wanted by everybody. He was not going to have her feeling like a dependent child for whom suitable arrangements must be made so that the grown-ups could do what they wanted.

'I'd rather come with you.' Amy sat on the bed and ran her hand over his hair. 'Perhaps we could still have the flat over the garage, and Grandma could come there when she wanted a rest from the Major. He's better in small doses. When she first told me about him – ages before she told you, by the way, but she made me promise not to let on – I was terrified that I might have to go to Southampton. I'm sorry. It's your mother and father, I know, but you do understand. Oh, Daddy!' She jumped off the bed and whirled round excitedly with her hands in her pockets, kicking out at the furniture. 'Where shall we live? Could we have a garden? Will I go to a different school? That would suit me down to the ground. I'm going to be in terrible straits with the geometry exam. Miss Harbutt says I'll never pass, but it would be a sell for her if I could leave before she had the chance of being right.'

She stopped whirling and said casually, without looking at her father: 'With everyone else getting married, I suppose you and Miss Kelly will be thinking of taking the plunge.'

'Would you mind?'

'Nope.' The blue jeans were stretched very tightly as she dug her hands deeper into the pockets.

'I don't know if she'd marry me, though.'

He was watching her to see if she would clutch hopefully at this, but she said: 'Of course she'd marry you. Anyone would. And you're going to be rich, too.'

'Maybe. With Rose's money and mine, we might have quite a decent place, and we'd find someone nice to stay with you when I was away. Rose wouldn't be there all the time, but it would be grand when she was. We'd be a proper family.'

He was waiting for Amy to give some opinion about Rose, but the child gave him no clue to what was in her mind. He must be fair to her, but fair to Rose too. If he was going to marry her, Amy must not start out with antagonism.

'Rose is an awfully sweet person when you get to know her,' he said, watching Amy's unrevealing face. 'She has to put on an act for the public. That's her job. Underneath, she's very lovable, and not a bit grand.'

'Is she?' Amy began to look more hopeful.

'Yes, and quite honestly, darling, apart from how much I like her, it would be much better for me to have a wife. A man can't give a daughter everything she should have. Nor can a housekeeper. That wouldn't be the same for you as having a — a —' He balked at the word Mother.

'I know, Daddy.' Amy came over to the bed and took his hands. 'You needn't bother to explain. You love Miss Kelly, don't you?'

'I think so. It's awfully hard to know sometimes. You'll find that out when you're older.'

'Oh, I know already. I've been in love thousands of times. It's agony. Come on, let's go and tell Grandma that you're going to be married too. That will take some of the wind out of her sails. Could you have a double wedding?'

'With the Major in a silk hat and a socking great buttonhole stealing all the limelight? Not likely.'

They laughed together, holding hands and laughing into each other's faces. Amy pulled him to his feet. He tried to ask her whether she was really happy, but she kept on laughing, and dragged him out of the room to where Geneva was spring-cleaning the dining-room with her head tied up in a scarlet scarf and a hooting song competing with the cries of the carpet sweeper.

The next day, when Jimmy Peale had slipped round to the Back Office and Mitzi had gone out for coffee, Ben was in the office alone. He took the old, creased magazine photograph of Rose out of his wallet and propped it against the telephone on Jimmy's desk. Because it was the first picture he ever had, when he was sure that he was in love with her, it held more enchantment for him than all the breath-taking photographs she had given him, scrawled over with intimate, extravagant messages. He saw himself laying it on the bar of some northern railway hotel and confiding to a stranger that he was going to marry Rose Kelly. The stranger, who had thought at first that Ben was just another commercial traveller, would look at him with new respect and call the barmaid over.

The door from the corridor opened, and a man came into the outer office. Through the open door between the two rooms, Ben caught a glimpse of him as he came in : a slack-cheeked, humourless face, an odd wisp of hair low down on the forehead from which the rest of the hair had receded, shoes like black coffins for the kind of springless feet which would tramp with equal unconcern on violets or mud.

Ben got up and went to the door. The man was standing in the middle of the room, looking about him as if he would not give you twopence for the lot.

'Can I help you, sir?' Ben put on his S.I.A. salesman's smile.

'You're not the chap I saw here before.' It was a belligerent voice, grudging, displeased, the kind of voice Ben had heard on the lower deck when a trouble-maker was aboard.

'Our Mr Peale?' Ben said smoothly. He could talk like this when there was no one in the office to hear him. 'He has just stepped out for a moment. I am Commander Francis, managing the naval side of our organization.'

'Group-Captain this, Commander that,' the man complained. 'Where's all the Generals today?'

'Out to lunch,' Ben said. 'Can I help you?'

'You can get me my insurance policy,' the man said. 'That's what you can do.'

It seemed a fair enough request, and Ben would have granted it, if he had known where the insurance policies of the S.I.A.'s investors were kept. He had no idea when Jimmy Peale or Mitzi would be back, so he rubbed the palms of his hands together and promised that the policy would be mailed as soon as possible.

'It's not good enough,' the man said, as if he had said that many times before about many things. 'I want it now, right here in my hand.' He pounded a coarse fist in his palm. 'I'm entitled, aren't I?' He jutted forward his head, fixing Ben with what would have been a sea-lawyer's eye if he had been a sailor instead of an airman. 'No messing about. You've got my money, and you've promised me insurance. That means I've got a policy, and I've a right to possession of it.'

'Of course, of course.' Ben had learned long ago not to dispute rights with men like this, for they usually knew what their rights were better than he did. 'Unfortunately all the documents are in our other office.'

'Go and get it then.' The man sat squarely down on a chair by the door and folded his arms. 'I'll wait.'

Ben scratched his head. Although Peale and Beckett had never said that they did not want him in the Back Office, they had never encouraged him to go there. The Back Office was the hub of the Association, where they spun their mysterious deals in foreign stocks, and made their staggering financial computations, which had nothing to do with an investment salesman whose place, as Jake Beckett often reminded him enviously, was in the field.

'It will mean some delay,' he hedged. 'Surely it will be more convenient for you if I –'

'If you don't go and get it right away,' the man said in a matter-of-fact voice that was more threatening than his belligerent one, 'I'll fetch a policeman to you.'

'You might at that,' Ben said, trying to keep calm. 'At least he could look after this office for me while I go round to the other one. As it is, you'll have to wait until the receptionist gets back.'

'How long? I haven't got all day.'

'That's hard to say. She's out on business.' Mitzi's quarter-hour for coffee sometimes extended for two hours if she felt the urge to do some shopping.

The man stood up. 'Lock the ruddy place up then, and I'll wait downstairs. I've not come all this way for nothing.'

Ben searched in vain for an answer. Look at me, he invited the disappointed audience of his thoughts. Here I am, the handler of men, the naval officer who's got a job because he knows how to deal with the fads and foibles of Other Ranks. You've got to laugh.

'What's so funny?' the man asked, taking a crushing step forward and peering at Ben's rueful grin.

'Nothing.' Ben reached for his coat.

The Back Office was not a patch on the Front Office as far as outside appearances went. The entrance was through a narrow door in a street of narrow doors and dirty stone steps and lower front windows half painted over to conceal what went on inside.

What went on in the Back Office of the Services Investment Association was plain to Ben as soon as he stepped through the only door on the ground floor which was not locked, and which was labelled surprisingly: 'Beckett Finance Company.' He had been to a similar office in Portsmouth on behalf of a panicky able-seaman. He knew a loan office when he saw one.

A small, yellow old man was on the other side of the counter behind the wire grille. He muttered a question at Ben through a damp yellow cigarette, but Ben waved a hand at him and went boldly through the door behind which he could hear the voices of Mr Beckett and Jimmy Peale.

Jake was at a scarred old roll-top desk, very different from his neat, expensive desk in the Front Office, which had a glide-away typewriter and a little softly-clicking locker for whisky. Jimmy was sitting on the window-sill, swinging one leg and looking out at the depressing street. He must have watched Ben come in at the front door, for they were not surprised to see him.

'What's to do, Benjamin?' Jake asked calmly. 'Did Mitzi send you?'

'She's out somewhere. I locked the place up. There's a man round there who wants his insurance policy. He threatened to call the police if I didn't come and get it.'

'Too madly dramatic.' Jimmy laughed lazily. 'What are you panting about, old boy? You look as if you'd run all the way. Sit down and take the weight off your feet.'

'No.' Ben stood with his back to the door of the small, drab room. 'I've got to get this chap's policy. He bullied me into it.'

Jake spread his hands on the desk and studied his polished nails. 'That's hardly the spirit for a senior member of the sales staff,' he said. 'You're not supposed to let the clients bully you. You're supposed to bully them – in a subtle way, of course. Perhaps you need a few more lessons to brush up your technique. Jimmy and Mitzi will be glad to –'

'Don't fob me off,' Ben said. 'What's going on here, anyway? This place looks like a loan office. I thought you were investing the clients' money. Are you making loans with it? Is that what it is?'

'Bright fellow,' Jake said. 'Of course we are. Best investment there is. We pay out ten per cent interest to the investors, and we loan their money out at forty per cent. Watertight profit. You see, we're not hiding anything from you, Benjamin. You could have come round here any time you wanted and investigated the financial side. You didn't seem all that interested.'

'Well, I'm interested now,' Ben said. 'Something smells.'

'The garbage from the hospital, probably.' Jimmy wrinkled his nose towards the window. 'Their kitchen entrance is just round the corner.'

'Don't fool with me, James.' Ben looked away from Jimmy's absurd, friendly face, which could always make him laugh and feel indulgent. 'I'm in a fighting mood. What about this man's insurance policy? Have you got it, or is the insurance a fake too, along with the foreign investments?'

'Now you're going too far, Benjamin,' Jake said sadly. 'Of course our client is insured.'

'Give him his policy then.'

'He doesn't need it.'

126

'That's his affair. Listen, Jake. Has he got a policy, or hasn't he?'

Jake looked him in the eye. 'Of course he hasn't,' he said calmly. 'I'm surprised at you, Benjamin, falling for your own line of sales talk. I thought you knew everything about the business.'

'Nobody told me.'

'OK. I'll tell you now. If you want to work with us, you'd better come out of the clouds and face a few economic facts. How do you think we could afford to insure all our clients at the premiums the big companies charge? We let them think that we do, because it keeps them happy, and if some damn fool sailor falls off the dock and his old woman puts in her five-hundred-pound claim on his life, we'll pay it, of course. No one is going to get cheated.'

'I won't do it,' Ben said. 'I won't go round telling lies to these wretched people. I'd be getting their money under false pretences.'

'Grow up,' Jake said. 'You're acting in a rum way for a man who came galloping into our office two weeks ago panting for adventure. Why don't you go home and pack your bag and go off to Rosyth like a sensible chap and get on with your side of the business, and leave the rest of it to Jimmy and me? We're not crooks, you know,' he added softly, showing his even teeth.

'You're damn close to it. I haven't signed any contract with you yet. I think I'd like to get out.'

Here went his job, his only job. How could he go home and look Geneva and Amy and Rose in the face and tell them he had chucked it? But how could he look them in the face if he went through with it, knowing what he knew? He scratched his head. His scalp was beginning to itch, as it always did when the brain beneath was in turmoil.

'Take it easy.' Jimmy Peale dropped down from the window-sill, brushed off his trousers, and leaned on the top of the desk, studying Ben with sleepy, half-closed eyes. 'We like you, Ben. You're a damn good chap, and we've had a lot of laughs together, which is more than one can say for most of the people one has to do business with in this grim world. But don't go getting any half-cocked ideas about our morals, or you'll end

127

by making a fool of yourself. Jake and I are as pure as the driven. Leave us alone, and we'll leave you alone. Come into the office tomorrow and I'll give you your expense money, and for God's sake don't let's mess about any more. There's work to be done.'

'Not by me. Find another N.O. There's hundreds of us about needing to turn an honest penny. But I want to be sure mine is honest. I'm scared, if you like. Scared of this loan office, scared of that pugnacious chap sitting in the hall round the corner waiting for his insurance policy. I'm not going back there.' Where was he going? Back to the Paddington Library, back to the polite letters of rejection, the futile, demoralizing interviews.

'You mean that?' Jake's eyes were dark and shrewd.

'I mean it. Here's the office key.' He flung it on the desk. Damn. He had pulled out the key to Geneva's flat. His effect spoiled, they watched him in silence while he fished in his pocket for the key to the Front Office.

'You're making a big mistake,' Jake said. 'You'll regret it. However,' he raised his head, his features lighting up with a sharp commercial clarity, 'to show you there's no hard feelings, should you ever think in the future of investing some of your gratuity with us, we –'

'I'd rather sew it in my corsets,' Ben said, and suddenly the atmosphere of nervous distrust cleared, and they all looked at each other unguardedly and laughed. His decision made, jobless, disenchanted, Ben felt oddly carefree. Because he was free of Peale and Beckett and their dangerous game, he felt better disposed towards them than at any time since he came into the Back Office and saw the counter and the wire grille.

He shook hands with them both. He still liked them. He could not help it. 'Say good-bye to Mitzi for me,' he said, as if he were parting with congenial hotel acquaintances after a holiday.

'Will do,' Jimmy said, and ambled to the door to open it for Ben. In the loan office, a small, hungry-looking man was talking to the yellow old man through the grille, whispering intimately, as if it were visitors' day in prison.

'One thing –' Ben turned back, and the hungry man and the yellow man stopped listening to hear what he was going to say. 'I've left a picture on your desk, Jimmy. Rose. Put it in an envelope, will you?'

'Sure thing.' Jimmy drooped one lazy eyelid. 'You going to invite us to the wedding.'

'Of course.' He probably would. That was the ridiculous thing.

He picked an unfortunate time to go and see Rose. Several things had combined to put her in a bad temper. Her West End play had been abandoned for lack of support; she had had the bitterest of her many fights with Bob Whiting, who had walked off the set and told her to find another producer; and her parents had turned up unexpectedly from Croydon and were sitting with grease-proof paper in their laps eating the sandwiches they had brought, when Ben arrived at the flat.

'Just as if it was a pub,' Rose railed at Ben in the hall, hardly bothering to lower her voice. ' "We don't want to put you to any trouble," they say. "We've brought enough food for all of us." Why can't we all go out and buy lunch, for God's sake?' She shot a disgusted glance through the half-open door of the room where her mother was sitting with her hat on and her knees apart, chewing placidly on a hard-boiled egg.

'What are you doing here, anyway?' Rose turned sulkily back to Ben. 'I thought we said good-bye.'

'We did, but – look, let me go and say hullo to your parents. They'll think it queer if we stand here muttering in the hall.'

'They think everything queer,' Rose said. 'But come on. You asked for it.' She led the way defiantly into the room, introduced Ben in a slap-dash way, and ostentatiously knelt down to gather up a very few crumbs from the rug by her mother's chair.

She had never allowed Ben to meet her parents before, although he had wanted to, and he saw now that she was ashamed of them, angry with them for being here when Ben came, and angry with him for coming when they were here.

They were delighted to meet Ben. They stood up beaming, the father brushing crumbs off his grey moustache, the mother dabbing at her mouth with a paper napkin.

'This must be the naval gentleman we've heard so much about,' Mrs Kelly said, wagging her head with arch approval.

129

'Oh, Mum, for heaven's sake –'

'No need to be embarrassed about it, Rosie.' Her father moved his yellowish dentures slightly to free a crumb. 'He's a fine-looking lad.'

'Hardly a lad, I'm afraid, sir.' Ben sat down, and the three of them smiled at each other. They were a cosy, friendly couple, unpretentious and oddly alike, with their thick grey hair, rounded cheeks and mild, uncritical eyes. Sitting opposite each other in identical chairs, their legs planted straight out and down, and their feet polite and small, they looked like Tweedle-dum and Tweedledee.

'Have a sandwich, Commander,' Mrs Kelly urged. 'I'm sure you haven't had your lunch. I brought enough for Rosie, but she's always on with this nonsense about her figure, though she's a right to be proud of it, I must say.'

'You can say that again.' Ben winked at Rose, to Mr Kelly's delight, and accepted a ham sandwich gratefully, which annoyed Rose even more than the wink.

'How about some coffee, Rose?' he asked. 'I'll make it if you like.' No harm in showing his future parents-in-law that he was perfectly at home in their daughter's flat.

'They like tea,' Rose said crushingly. 'I can make some, I suppose.' She walked away, clicking the heels of her mules on the polished floor.

Her mother was searching in a black leather carry-all which looked like a midwifery bag. 'I brought you a packet, dear, in case you were short.' She had apparently never outgrown the habit of compromising with wartime shortages. She held out the packet of tea as if it were a priceless gift, but Rose banged through the swing door into the kitchen without paying any attention to her.

Ben ate all the sandwiches that Mrs Kelly had brought for Rose, and they had a lively conversation about the old days of the war, which had been the high spot of the parents' lives. Mr Kelly had been a sergeant in the Engineers, and Mrs Kelly had been in charge of an air-raid warden's post near the Elephant and Castle. Mr Kelly talked with long-winded relish of his exploits in North Africa, and his wife told of the exciting nights when the whizz-bangers were dropping like hail all round the Elephant, and of how little Rosie used to tap-dance and sing for the people in the shelters, and of the night when someone brought a headless body into the warden's post, and it turned out to be a dummy from a shop window.

'I haven't laughed so much since the day the bed fell on father,' she told Ben, laughing again, and enjoying his laughter.

When Rose came back with the tea, which had taken her a long time to make, Ben and her parents were old friends, which should have pleased her, but did not. When the parents left for the early house at the Palladium, extracting promises from Ben to come and look them up very soon, even if Rosie would not bring him, he knew as he shut the front door behind their twin roundabout figures that Rose was going to be difficult. Remembering the many times when Marion had quarrelled with him after Geneva left them, he thought that he was fated to get on better with the parents of the women he married than with the women themselves.

When he told Rose that he had abandoned his job with the Services Investment Association, she was very difficult. 'It takes you ages to find a job, and when you do, you can't even stay in it two weeks,' she told him. 'What's the matter with you? Don't you want to work?'

'You know I do.' He tried to touch her, but she slid away, and stood frowning at him with her arms folded. She was very poised and beautiful, like an outraged heroine in a film.

Ben tried to explain. 'I had to get out, don't you see? They're not exactly swindlers, but they're liars. I can't go round telling lies to sailors' wives about insurance policies and investments that don't exist. I'm thankful I had the sense to get out before I took anyone's cash.'

'If you call it sense,' Rose said scornfully, 'to throw away a perfectly good job, the only chance you've had to make some real money.'

'I don't want to make it that way.'

'You're so smug. The perfect naval officer,' Rose grumbled, inconsistently, for she had preferred him as naval officer to a civilian. 'What are you going to do now – go to the police?'

'God, no, I wouldn't do that. Jake and Jimmy aren't really crooks. They're just – manipulators, and it may be all quite

131

legal. None of their promises are put on paper. They're just talked about by some mug like me, with his foot in the door and an ingratiating smile on his face.'

'If it's legal, why did you run out on them?'

'I told you. I don't want to tell lies. I don't want to be mixed up in their game. I thought you'd understand.'

'I don't understand anything.' Rose's enormous eyes looked at him blankly, with neither affection nor distaste.

'Don't look at me as if you'd never met me.' Ben moved towards her. 'I didn't come here to fight with you. I came to ask you to marry me.' He took her hand. She did not pull it away, but let it lie limply in his, without warmth.

'How can I marry you?' she said slowly. 'What are you, anyway?'

'At school they used to call me BF.' Hopefully he tried to turn her towards a joke.

'Don't fool. I'm serious.' Rose bit her soft red lip. A small pulse throbbed gently in the smooth hollow under her creamy neck. 'You know what I mean. As a naval officer, you had some kind of position. Now you have none, until you make it for yourself. Listen, Ben.' Her hand was still unresponsive in his. She looked at him coldly, talking in a flat voice, as if she hardly cared whether he understood or not. 'I've got somewhere. I've made myself into the kind of person I've always wanted to be. How can I marry someone who's so – so terribly just nobody?'

'Bitch,' Ben said, and dropped her hand.

Three weeks ago, Rose had slapped a man's face on the television screen, and the sound had echoed satisfyingly through a million living-rooms. She was going to do it again now. Almost impersonally, Ben watched her arm go back from the shoulder, straighten out towards him, and – crack! There it was, perfectly aimed and timed, just as Bob Whiting had taught her.

There is nothing like a blow in the face to stimulate the circulation to anger. Ben left the room without a word, grabbed his hat and coat and slammed through the front door of the flat.

Behind him, he heard Rose wrench the door open. 'Get out!' she shouted after him, as if the expensive block of flats were a tenement building. 'You stay away from me, do you hear? Don't come back until you've got a job!'

A door along the corridor opened, and a head with a turban over pin curls looked out and stared at Ben's flaming cheek. He raised his hat politely and rounded the corner to the lift.

Out in the street, he walked rapidly for some time, going nowhere in particular, bumping into irresolute shoppers, crossing against traffic lights, glowering at motorists. As he passed a large cafeteria, with steam on the lettered windows and people already going in for tea, the corner of his eye was caught by a notice stuck on the inside of the plate glass: 'MEN AND WOMEN FOR COUNTER AND KITCHEN WORK.'

As if the corner of his eye were attached to the notice by a string, he jerked to a stop, reversed his course smartly, entered the cafeteria and got himself a job.

Chapter Nine

'Is it some sort of a stunt?' Geneva asked.

'No, it isn't a stunt. It's a job. "Don't come back until you've got a job," she said. All right, I've got a job.'

'So now you can go back to her?'

'Not yet. She can stew for a while.'

'Why go back at all?' Geneva blinked her eyelids very fast, as she did when she was trying to sound casual about probing for an answer.

'I'm going to marry her,' Ben said, 'but she can wait. I'm busy at the moment.'

The cafeteria was a large and popular place of refreshment with a heterogeneous clientele of workers, shoppers, students, lonely men with strange faces, exhausted elderly ladies who could not face cooking a meal or who had forgotten what it was like to have a kitchen to cook in, and people of all ages and shapes and creeds and colours who could find no better way to pass the time until death than by putting solids and liquids into their stomachs.

The huge, low-ceilinged room with the cruel neon lighting

and the endless loaded counter was full at any time of day, and at meal-times it was jammed. The line of discreetly-watering salivary glands waiting to reach the point where the trays and cutlery were and the steel rails led to nourishment wound like a snake among the tables to the room, and sometimes right out on to the pavement, for London is the only city in the world where anyone but the destitute will wait patiently in the street to be fed.

On wet days, when even the Londoners would not wait outside, the line of fishy-smelling raincoats would, in a miracle of discipline, accommodate itself in hairpin loops within the room, so that Ben had to make detours round the walls to get from table to table with his trolley.

Ben's job, the starter's job, from which, if he was diligent, he might progress to such eclectic tasks as slicing pies or browning the tops of welsh rarebits, was to collect dirty plates, wipe the tables with a sodden cloth and wheel the trolley when it was full out through the armour-plated swing door to the back end of the kitchen, where May and her swollen arms and legs fought their day-long battle with the rapacious dish-washing machine.

On the return journey, Ben brought back wire baskets of china and cutlery and glasses, still hot and not quite dry, and dumped them down behind the counter, so that they could be dirtied again and washed again and dirtied again in the endless cycle of satisfying a civilization which believes that the machine will run down if it is not refuelled every four hours.

He also had to collect the metal trays, wipe them and return them to the end of the counter. There were wide shelves all over the cafeteria, with notices which said: 'Please Place Trays Here.' Some people obeyed, but many either ate off the trays and left them askew on the tables, or leaned the trays against pillars or the legs of chairs, whence they fell with a hollow crash under the feet of anyone carrying a load of food.

The crash of the trays was only one of the many noises which went to make up the vast conglomerate din of the cafeteria. For the first half-hour of his first day, Ben had felt as if the noise beating in his ears would meet under pressure in the middle and split his head wide open. Then suddenly the noise became a part of the background of life, like the howls and thuds and tortured creakings of a prolonged storm at sea. He could live with it. He did not mind it, any more than he minded the yellow shreds of cigarettes in slopped saucers, the discarded fat, the half a sausage chewed and spat out with all the gristle showing, the spilled ice-cream dripping from the table edge on to the floor, the cake crumbs and the sticky crumpled straws in the lemonade glasses. There was no time to mind. These things had to be dealt with, and he dealt with them, in a seamanlike and efficient way of which he could not help being proud.

One quarter of the room was his responsibility. Impossible for four people – a gangling student, an old woman, a wide-hipped young slattern, and Ben – to keep pace with the eat-and-run technique of most of the customers. You could never stand back for a moment and say: There, that's done. Everywhere you looked, there was another emptied tea-cup with its slug's trail of lipstick, another brimming ash-tray, another abandoned plate littered with the debris of some finicky eater who did not know enough to eat what he had paid for. Undaunted, Ben laboured on, determined that as long as he could stand the job, his tables should be the cleanest and most frequently cleared, his customers the most consistently spared from having to eat with one elbow in a predecessor's soup bowl.

'You'll kill yourself, dear,' said the remains of the old Polish woman who worked on the next section. 'What you are trying to do? Show us up? I don't care. Tomorrow I quit.' She moved slowly away on her skeleton legs, clattering half the dishes off a table and leaving the rest, swiping at the plastic top with a stained and dripping cloth which added its own unsavoury contribution to the smears and puddles it missed.

Ben cleared two of her tables behind her back and returned to his own. Just a little science, that's all it needs to get it squared off, he told the customers, who did not hear him, since he did not speak, and did not see him, since he was doing the kind of job which is remarked only if it is not done.

'Do you think you'll be able to manage the work?' the manageress had asked him, tapping her teeth doubtfully with a pencil. 'You don't seem quite the type.' She was a middle-aged, harassed woman in a loosely-knit black cardigan, with a girlish velvet ribbon threaded through her thin grey hair. She lived in a tiny office off the clamorous kitchen, with an open door through which disgruntled members of the staff constantly charged with complaints against the customers and each other.

'Of course,' she smiled at Ben through her built-in frown, 'we get all sorts. Students and the like. We even had a débutante once. I put her on the teas. It was not at all satisfactory. The newspapers came after her to take her picture, and got everybody upset.'

'I can do the job all right,' Ben said, 'if you'll let me have it. I'm desperate for work.'

The manageress looked down. 'Your troubles are your own affair,' she said quickly, as if she had heard too many hard-luck stories to be able to stand any more. 'I'd advise you to keep quiet about them,' she added, looking at Ben's suit, 'for there's many here that must be much worse off than you.'

After he had signed on, she took him to the cloakroom, where he took off his jacket and put on a stiff bleached apron which covered the front of his shirt and tied round the waist with tapes frayed from much laundering. It stood away from his body like sailcloth, moving a little distance apart from him, as if it had an independent life of its own.

'You don't quite look the part, I must say.' The manageress tilted her head and frowned sideways at him. 'Oh, dear, these are funny times.'

A girl came out from the women's section of the cloakroom. 'Ethel,' the manageress said, her voice regaining authority, 'this is Mr Francis. He's to work on the tables. Will you pass him on to someone out there who will show him what to do?'

The girl was heavy bosomed and dark skinned, with a starched white crescent of cap fastened with many iron pins at an impossible angle on her piled-up hair. 'Another one for the salt mines?' she said cheerfully. 'We just buried the last. What's your name?' she asked, as they passed through the inferno of the kitchen.

'Ben.'

'Hullo, Ben.' She smiled at him invitingly, assuming a slight American accent. 'Where did you come from, baby dear?'

136

I don't know much, Ben thought, but at least I know enough not to say From the Navy.

From the office of a pair of crooks off the Euston Road, he could have said, but he told her: 'From a hotel. I was a kitchen porter.'

'Oh, well.' Ethel accepted this gratifyingly. 'This will be a breeze for you. Two days here, though, and you'll wish you'd stayed in the hotel. Why didn't you?'

'I couldn't.' Ben raised his voice as they passed from the clatter of the kitchen through the kicked metal door to the tea-time roar of the cafeteria. 'There was some trouble with one of the guests.'

'A woman?' Ethel's dark gaze swept hopefully up and down his independent apron.

Ben nodded. A woman in an obliterating felt hat caught at his arm as they passed her table. 'This tea's sugared,' she complained. 'I asked for it without.'

'I'm so sorry, madam.' Ben picked up the cup. 'I'll get you some more. Show me where,' he said out of the side of his mouth to Ethel.

'I'll get it.' She took the cup. 'Madam, he says. That's a word I never heard in these parts before. No wonder you got one of the guests into trouble.' She winked at him, raising one side of her mouth to meet the wink. 'Here, I've got to get back behind the counter. Doris wants to get off. I'll give you to Sir Thomas Beecham. He's queer too. You and him will get along fine.'

Sir Thomas Beecham was a tall young music student who was labouring after college hours with trolley and dish-cloth to pay his room rent. His name was Tommy Maverick, and his growth was all towards the ceiling. There was no bulk in him anywhere, and very little sinew. His apron went one and a half times round him. His long arms and legs flopped and dangled awkwardly, like a puppet with an amateur at the strings.

His long, immature face was perpetually troubled by the complications of life. Where there were none he made them. He took Ben over anxiously and proceeded to make mountains for him out of the molehills of the cafeteria.

'You'd better come with me,' he said, 'and watch what I do,

before I let you have a trolley of your own. I wouldn't want you to get into any trouble on your first day.'

He handed Ben a cloth, the essential tool of his trade, and they worked together all down one side of the long, garish room, its pink walls and yellow table-tops flattened to the livid colours of nightmare by the panels of harsh light in the low ceiling. No cochineal or spinach water could ever have evolved such tints on the icing of the cakes. No tomatoes could have produced the blood-orange pools of ketchup which smothered the suppers which were beginning to be eaten side by side with the teas.

While he worked, Sir Thomas instructed Ben under his breath in a nervous mumble. 'It's not as easy as it looks, actually. There are all sorts of snags. Sometimes they leave a plate with heaps of food on it. They may have pushed it aside, so you think they've done with it, but sometimes they're going back to it, and it's dreadful if you take it away by mistake. I asked a woman once: "Have you finished?" and she said: "None of your business." I felt such an ass.'

Working together in their long, unwieldy aprons, they soon had the trolley stacked high on both levels with plates and cups and sliding cutlery. 'And that's another thing.' Sir Thomas leaned over the heap, fussing and prodding at it with long, knuckly hands. 'If you pack it too full, some of the stuff will fall off, and they take the breakages out of your pay. And then the cloths. That's a terrible worry. There are never enough clean ones. You have to take them out to the kitchen and rinse them out, and there isn't a proper sink, you see, like at home, because of the dish-washer, so you have to use the tap where they wash the vegetables, and there's a man there – he doesn't like it at all. He turns the hot tap on suddenly while you've got your hands under it.

'And then there's May.' He lowered his voice as they approached the dish-washing machine with their load. 'She's not a bad sort really, and the poor old soul has a crippled husband, they say, and some frightful disease that puts water in all her limbs. She'll tell you. It aggravates her, and sometimes whatever you say to her, she says something nasty. She said a horrible thing to me once. I couldn't repeat it to you. I wouldn't even tell my own brother. Some more, May,' he said nervously, wheeling the trolley alongside May's messy counter and beginning to unload the dishes.

'Of course it's some more,' May grumbled, her swollen arms flailing about among the china. 'It's more, more, more all the time. The glasses over there, *please*. You ought to know that by now. If you'd just do the job instead of gab all the time, we might all get along a lot better.'

'I'm sorry, May.' Sir Thomas plunged forward to separate the glasses.

'I'll do it.' She pushed him aside with her bulk. 'You've brought a cellar out again.' She threw the salt-cellar back on to the trolley. 'I've a good mind to report you to the manageress.'

'Oh, don't, May,' Sir Thomas said, as if he thought she meant it. 'Look, this is Ben. He's come to work here.'

'They come and they go,' May said, hurling a pile of plates into the moving racks which carried them into the maelstrom of hot, soapy water. 'What do you expect me to do about it?'

'You see?' Sir Thomas said as they pushed the trolley away. 'You see how difficult it all is? Come on, I'll get you a trolley, if you're sure you'll be all right on your own. Come to me if you get into any difficulties. I hope you'll manage. I don't suppose you'll stay though. Most of them only last a few days. Casual labour. Except me. I've been here five weeks.'

'Why don't you get moved up to a better job at the counter?'

'Oh, I don't want to. I know this job now, you see. I know where I am.' He found Ben a trolley and parted from him reluctantly, clearing plates, wiping tables with stooping, anguished care, occasionally throwing up his long, bony head to look for Ben across the room and make sure that he was all right.

When Ben had been on the job three days and was falling into the trauma of feeling that he had been here all his life and could only be released by death, a stubby, round-faced man came up to him in the staff canteen.

'I know you,' he said. He looked about him to see if anyone was listening, and dropped his voice. 'I served in the *Tigress* with you, sir. Remember me? Henry Briggs, Telegraphist, First

Class. Babyface Briggs, they used to call me. I got out at the end of the war. Regretted it ever since.'

Ben remembered him. Babyface Briggs, a wireless operator, cheerful, conscientious, knowing his job, but not much else: a boy straight from his mother's skirts, who believed everything his shipmates told him. If there was a practical joke afoot, it was always played on Babyface Briggs. There had been some trouble with a girl in Ceylon. A prostitute. Babyface had believed that he ought to marry her, and although Ben was a year younger than he was and scared stiff of prostitutes himself, it had been his job to explain to Babyface why he should not.

Over corned beef sandwiches made from two-day-old bread and cups of tepid tea, they reminisced about this and other shared experiences. Babyface was working on the big griddle underneath the open hatch between the kitchen and the serving counter. Ben did not ask what fortune had brought him here instead of using his knowledge of radio on a better job. Babyface did not like to ask Ben what had brought him to the trolley and the damp cloth.

He asked tentatively: 'You here for a lark, sir – on leave, like?'

When Ben shook his head and said: 'I've been axed. I need a job,' Babyface whistled softly through a gap in his teeth and said no more.

With a reversal of the relationship which had been theirs when they served together, he took Ben under his protective wing, proudly because he had been an officer, and with a pitying concern because his commission had unfitted him for the realities of life. Babyface was no longer the ingenuous boy, easy victim of practical jokes. He had learned a few tricks since he left the Navy, and when they were off for meals at the same time, he often managed to smuggle a freshly-grilled sausage or a thick slice of ham into the staff canteen for Ben.

'Who's your pal?' the other short order cook asked, when Ben stopped by the griddle to speak to Babyface. 'I heard you talking about the war.'

'We were in the Navy together,' Babyface said.

'Not on the lower deck. Looks more like a ruddy officer to me.' The cook slapped a fried egg on to a plate and followed it

140

with a scooping of chips from the deep fryer. 'Though if he was, he wouldn't demean himself to speak to you.'

Babyface laughed. 'An officer! That's a good one. Ordinary Seaman Francis, that was old Ben. Never went no higher before they gave him his walking papers.' He winked at Ben as the other cook turned his back to dive a dirty knife into the butter can. 'Commie,' he said under his breath. 'Don't you ever let on you was an officer, sir, or your life here won't be worth twopence.'

'Not, mind,' he explained later, when they were discussing it over the Friday plaice and chips which was the canteen's best menu, 'that he don't get a kick out of working heel and toe with you here, same as I do, him having been a sick-berth attendant with a bad record, but he isn't never going to admit that, even to his self, see?'

Ben saw. He had been out of the Navy long enough to see.

At the end of the week, Ben drew his pay packet from the manageress, who seemed surprised to find him still there, and spent most of it on taking Geneva and Amy and the Major out to dinner. Now that Geneva and the Major were officially engaged, although Geneva refused to fix a wedding date until Ben and Amy had found a home, the Major had to be included in their outings. It would have been almost impossible to leave him out, for he was constantly at the flat, turning up at all hours with a bunch of violets for Geneva, all leaf and no flower, or a small phial of cheap perfume, which she poured down the sink with her head averted as soon as he had gone, and washed it down with onion water in case he should smell it when he came back. In his new role of fiancé he was very courtly, especially when he was in liquor. He referred to Geneva as My Betrothed, or My Queen, and would seize her hand and press it to his shaky lips with a daring air, as if the next thing he planned to do was to run his moustache up and down her arm.

Geneva was torn between wanting to be kind to him, and not wanting to spoil Ben and Amy's last weeks with her. The Major had an uncanny instinct for turning up whenever there was a meal cooking. 'Irish stew,' he would say, rubbing his knotted hands as he came into the flat, and sniffing the air with his cut-away nostrils.

'I suppose you want some.' Geneva, in a frilled apron, with a wooden spoon in one hand and a cocktail glass in the other, addressed him sharply from the kitchen doorway.

'No, no, my birdie, I wouldn't dream –'

'You know you would, you cunning old devil. Did you bring your teeth?'

He lifted his top lip to gnash them at her.

'All right, I'll feed you. I've got to feed you for the rest of my life, just because I never could say No to a handsome man.' She patted his mulberry cheek with the wooden spoon and went back to the kitchen, while the Major ambled happily off towards the drink cupboard.

Sometimes Geneva would alter the times of meals so that they could eat without him, but some bush telegraph seemed to warn the Major's insatiable stomach, and he would come earlier or later, and catch them laying the table. When they were setting out to spend Ben's pay packet, he was there outside the door when they opened it, with his bowler hat at an angle and his regimental tie arching out from the knot like a stallion's neck, so they took him along.

It was the first money Ben had earned since he left the Navy. The Major got mildly drunk on the strength of it. Nothing more than a glazing eye and an inability to finish his food or the ends of stories. He was always a gentleman when Geneva and Amy were present.

Ben found himself watching the waiters with a new interest. He felt restless sitting at the table and behaving like a customer. He should have been up there on his feet with them, pushing in and out of the kitchen door with trays, and muttering close-lipped over the service tables the unfathomable dead-pan secrets that only waiters know.

The waiter at their table was slow and not efficient. He was an old man, past his job, if indeed he had ever caught up with it, and Ben felt that he could give him a few tips on the speedier handling of plates. When he was a long time coming to clear the table and take their order for dessert, Ben's fingers itched to pick up the plates and cutlery himself and carry them away.

'Why don't you?' Amy asked, when he told her this. 'That old man would be glad to get some help.'

142

'He wouldn't. He'd hate it. He may resent us for sitting here and enjoying ourselves while he's working, but he'd rather run his flat feet into the ground than have us stack a plate.'

There had been a woman at the cafeteria late one afternoon when Ben's beard was beginning to grow, who had said to him: 'You poor man. You look so tired. Let me help you.' She had got up in a confusion of handbags and shopping baskets and begun to put the dirty dishes from the table on to Ben's trolley. Her face was ennobled with the clear light of charity; but the other people at the table had stared at her as if she were insane, and although the wide-hipped girl was off sick and Ben and Sir Thomas were coping with her tables, Ben had found, perversely, that he was not grateful for the woman's help.

He remembered a time when he had taken Amy to a seaside hotel, soon after her mother's death. Amy was nearly seven, and just beginning to be conscious that other people had lives too. The hotel was understaffed. Meals in the dining-room were interminable ordeals of spinning out the sardine and beetroot *hors d'œuvres*, the suspect soup, the overdone meat, the apple pie and custard, to try to minimize the gaps between each course while the sweating waitresses pounded through the room with trays for everyone but them.

Ben was annoyed at the poor service when the hotel charges were so high, but Amy, with her new-found humanity, had suffered agonies for the overworked waitresses, one of whom had a built-up shoe. Seeing a tray, she had got up and begun to collect plates from nearby tables. The guests murmured how sweet she was, and put out tentative hands to touch her long chestnut hair, but after she had carried away the tray, she came out of the kitchen in tears, and dragged her father out of the dining-room, although they had not got further than the glued turbot. Afterwards, the manageress had tackled Ben and told him that she could not have the child upsetting her staff.

Ben had been angry at the time, and had left the hotel, but he could understand it now. For some reason that had nothing to do with unions, there was a barrier between the serving and the served, and it must never be crossed.

At the cafeteria, nobody except the missionary-faced woman

ever attempted to cross it. Mostly the customers paid as little heed to Ben and his trolley and cloth as if their tables were being cleared by automation.

The Major had said to him: 'Good God, man, what if some chap came in who knew you? You'd never be able to show your face in the club again.'

Apart from the fact that Ben had already resigned his club membership to save money, he was not afraid of recognition. People simply did not look at him, and although he sometimes wanted to talk to a pretty girl, or to throw a remark into a conversation, he very rarely spoke to the customers. He and they were in different worlds.

If he was promoted to counter work, he would have to speak to them, but they would still be in different worlds, with the space barrier of the stainless-steel counter between them. The customers would hear his voice asking: 'With sugar?' or: 'Do you want chips with it?' but they were not likely to remove their attention from the consideration of what they were going to eat to observe the face that belonged to the voice.

Amy came in sometimes for tea with a school friend. When they had filled their trays with strange mixtures of food, Ben would find them an empty table by the wall and clean it off with a flourish and tip up the other two chairs, as he had seen Sir Thomas do for his friends from the college, knowing that the British public would walk round the cafeteria all day looking for somewhere to put down its tray sooner than dispute the privacy of a tipped-up chair.

Amy, who was in a gregarious phase of being popular at school, brought a variety of friends, including the daughter of the Mayor, who was one of the trustees. It must be all over the school by now that Amy Francis's father was wiping tables in a cafeteria. The headmistress with her college gown and her study full of diplomas and netball cups must be quite shocked, but she could live with that as long as Ben paid the fees. Amy and her friends were not shocked. They seemed to like it. It gave them quite a thrill to have their tea in a place where they knew a member of the staff who would bring them more of anything they wanted from the counter, while the other customers had to fetch their second helpings for themselves.

144

Amy tried to persuade her grandmother to go to the cafeteria, but Geneva refused. 'I strike,' she said. 'I'm proud of your father for working like a dog, but I will not go to a place where I have to carry my own tray. The only time I ever went to one of those places, the crowd rushed me along the rails so fast that I fetched up at the pay desk with nothing on my tray at all and the cashier wanted to have me committed.'

One day, Ben's mother arrived. She had come to London for shopping and a matinée, and when she went to look for Ben at the flat after the theatre, Geneva sent her to the cafeteria, thinking that the shock would do her good.

Ben was near the door when she came in, looking uncertainly about her, for Geneva had not told her what Ben's job was, and she imagined that he was in an office behind the scenes.

'Hullo, Mum.' He stood before her in his long apron, limp and stained at the end of a long afternoon's work. His mother was wearing a fiery suit and an electric-blue turban which looked as if it was on back to front, from beneath which her hair fussed out in twiddled curls, some black, some grey. She stood and stared at him with round, incredulous eyes while people pushed past them, and her unpowdered face grew red, as if she were going to cry.

'Don't make a scene, Mum,' Ben said, as he had said so often as a boy when his mother had been displeased in shops and restaurants. 'Brace up. I'll find you a table and get you some tea.'

His mother put out a hand blindly and leaned on the trolley for support. 'How could you, Benjamin?' she said faintly. 'How could you?'

'I should have told you,' he said, 'but I knew you wouldn't like it. Just a temporary thing, to give me something to do while I —'

'Ben, Ben!' Sir Thomas Beecham came up wringing his hands, his long face twisted with anxiety. 'Please do something. Your tables by the wall are absolutely piling up, simply piling, and people have nowhere to put their trays. Oh, why do you have to slack off just now when it's our busiest time? You know what the next shift are like if they think we've left too much for them.'

'Calm down,' Ben said. 'I'm on the job. This is my mother. Mum, this is Tommy Maverick, the future organist at Westminster Abbey.'

'Oh, shut up.' Tommy ducked his head sideways. 'You know I'll never get *that* job. Your mother – I say, how wonderful. I'm delighted to meet you.' Mothers to Tommy were almost as sacred as organs. 'Please excuse me, Mrs – er, I can't stay. I simply must –' He panicked off, his apron flapping round his legs like a wet sail.

Mrs Francis had given him neither word nor glance. She was still staring at Ben in a kind of stupor. He led her to a table, sat her down, and brought her a cup of tea, and she rallied enough to say: 'But you didn't bring me any sugar.'

'Hang on there,' he said. 'I'll be off in twenty minutes, and we'll go somewhere and talk.' Working like a beaver to catch up on the time he had lost, for on this job and at this time of day you could not afford to take two minutes off for a chat, he looked across the crowded room and saw that she was crying, dabbing at her nose with a screwed-up handkerchief in between sips of tea. Two girls at the table were talking across it spellbound, unnoticing, but a middle-aged woman sitting opposite his mother was nodding and smiling at her, apparently trying to comfort her. Ben wondered what his mother was telling her. He could not go to her then, but when he handed over his trolley to the sub-alcoholic on the next shift, and went over to tell her that he was going to get his coat, she was not there.

'Did the lady go, who was sitting here?' he asked the middle-aged woman.

'Yes, just now. What's wrong?' The woman's face brightened. 'Didn't she pay for her tea? Poor soul, she's in trouble. Her son has let her down, she was telling me. After all she's done and hoped for him, he's broken her heart. Why be surprised? I told her. The pains we suffer in childbirth are only the beginning.'

When Ben got back to the flat, his mother was not there. Later, he telephoned her at home, but there was no answer. His father must have gone to meet her train. He imagined her telling him, crying out the bad news as soon as she hopped off the train, hanging on his arm and gabbling out her heartbreak as they went past the ticket collector and out through the crowd to the car. Damn. Now his father would start writing again to say that he could get him the job of secretary to the Nautical Club at Hamble if only he would come home.

Chapter Ten

AT the end of his second week at the cafeteria, Ben decided that Rose had suffered enough, and he went down to the television studio to see her.

It was the evening of her show, and he timed himself to arrive about half an hour before she went on the air, when she would be alone in her dressing-room, 'growing into her part', as she told people.

Ben knew that she would be more likely to be eating a sandwich. The camera fright, which Rose concealed but had never completely overcome, had the effect of making her hungry. Nobody but Ben knew about the little packet wrapped in greaseproof paper which travelled at the bottom of her cosmetic case. The sandwich was one of the most endearing things about her. The moment when she had admitted its presence to Ben, and had stood before him in a sequinned dress and full television make-up tearing at it like a hungry schoolgirl, had been more intimate than if she had taken off all her clothes.

Tonight when Ben told her that he had held a slave's job for two weeks, and showed her the unopened pay packet with which he was going to take her to supper, she might not need the sandwich. She would be so glad to hear what he had done for her sake that she would go radiantly on to the set and give the best performance of her life. That would make her still happier, and there would be no problem about the rest of the evening.

'Nice to see you back, Commander,' said the man in the satin-backed waistcoat, to whom Ben had become almost as familiar as if he were one of the staff. 'You been away?'

'I've been too busy to get down here,' Ben said. 'Working on a big project.'

'Ah,' said the man, imagining heaven knew what. 'I know how it is.'

Turning the corner into the familiar corridor which led to Rose's dressing-room, Ben ran into Bob Whiting, who was travelling fast on his small, light feet, with a board full of papers under his arm and a discontented pout to his childish mouth.

'What's the headache?' Ben asked. 'I thought you were off Rose's show.'

'I am, but the headaches are still there. I'm filling in this week for Alan Rickie as interviewer on *Who's Doing What*. God, what a mess. The people are all cranks. They have some impossible job, or they do some crazy thing like making music with spoons and a kitchen chair, or teaching parrots to recite the Ten Commandments. They're all half bats, and one of them hasn't turned up at all. Just rung up from Chichester to say he missed the train. That's what you get for relying on a man who makes model railways out of toothpicks. I've got to use that revolting girl from the typing pool who makes bird noises. She's been trying to get on the show for weeks. Catch my act,' he said, patting Ben on the arm as he turned to go. 'It'll be a riot. Nice to see you again, Ben old boy. You haven't been around lately. I suppose you've had a row with little Rosie, like everyone else.'

'Not exactly. I've been working.'

'Got that directorship at last? More power to you.'

Bob was already beginning to walk away when Ben said, to amuse him, for it was flattering to be able to make a cynic laugh: 'I'm working in a cafeteria, clearing tables and mopping up.'

Bob stopped as if he had been shot, pivoted on one suede boot and stepped back. 'Say that again,' he growled, thrusting his face close to Ben's.

Ben said it. Encouraged by the sight of Bob's streaked eyeballs, which only protruded like this when he was interested, he began to fill in some details.

'All right, all right.' Bob held up his fleshy white hand. 'Save it for the air. I want it fresh. Come with me.' He took Ben's arm in a pinching grip and hustled him protesting down the stairs and into the office of the producer of the *Who's Doing What* show.

148

'Tell that girl to stuff her bird noises,' he said, sweeping Ben up to the desk. 'Here's our number three spot.'

The producer, a dynamic type in giant horn-rimmed spectacles, slapped his thigh at what Bob told him and gave them both a drink. 'Are you sure he'll talk?' he asked Bob, as if Ben were not there. 'We don't want another lemon like that woman who put the holes in processed cheese. Have you got time to rehearse him?'

'We'll play it by ear. He'll be all right. I know old Ben. He's solid, aren't you?'

'Possibly, but look here, Bob, I don't think I want to –'

'Of course you do. It's your big chance. Get a little public sympathy for all the poor devils who've been kicked out of the Services and can't get a decent job.'

'I don't think the Admiralty –'

'Who cares? They should have thought of this before they started swinging the axe. Don't be selfish, Ben old boy. There are men out there who need you, and by ten o'clock tonight you'll be a ruddy hero.'

'I'll be out of a job if the manageress has a television set. When the débutante –'

'Don't ramble. I want your mind on this.' When Bob was on the job, his voice lost its querulous drawl. 'England expects, and all that sort of filth. We'll get you an apron from the canteen. The viewers will eat it up. Come on.' He put down his glass. 'I want to catch Rose's show.'

'I hear she's terrible,' the producer said, not without satisfaction.

'So do I,' said Bob happily. 'That's why I want to see it.'

He took Ben to a small, hot room where a television set was playing loudly to some empty chairs and a table covered in brown serge. Bob turned down the volume and they sat down and waited for the familiar sentimental music that would lead in *The Rose Kelly Show*.

'Maybe you shouldn't see it,' Bob said, 'if you're still doing the moth and candle act, but I suppose it will do you no harm to know the worst. I think the poor darling has really laid an egg this time.'

'Yes, yes.' He clapped his hands softly, as the announcer

appeared on the screen and began to read, with a controlled sympathy worthy of the B.B.C., a letter from a miner's wife whose husband had been trapped in a pit disaster. 'There she goes. This beastly thing has been in the files for ages, but I would never let her do it because it was much too grim for her to handle, and she couldn't get within a mile of the accent. As soon as she got me off the show, she persuades Pete to let her do it. You know how Rose persuades, and Pete is so astonished to find himself suddenly producing a major show that he hasn't got her number yet. Or else he's sleeping with her. I don't know.'

Ben said: 'Shut up,' not knowing what else to say.

'I know, I know. You love her, and all that vomit. But if you marry her, don't ask me round unless she's out. Rose and I are through. After doing everything she could to push me off her show, she was so mad with me for leaving it when she found out how much of the show was mine that she tried to make some trouble for me with the high-ups. It didn't get her anywhere, but you can't expect me to send flowers and good-luck telegrams to her dressing-room. Look at that! Oh, my God, look at that.'

He covered his face with his hands as the announcer was faded discreetly from the screen and Rose was revealed standing bowed before an iron gate, with black stockings on her shapely legs, and her huge eyes, with the glycerine already forming tears on the lids, staring at the camera from beneath the decoratively-arranged folds of a woollen shawl.

Bob peeped through his fingers, moaning lightly, then took down his hands and smacked them on his knees. 'She's furious,' he announced. 'I can tell it. I know that face better than my own, and I like mine better. Something's going wrong. Look, that other woman moved right in front of her as she began to speak. They've botched the whole thing. She turned on the tears too soon, and now she isn't going to have anything left when the man comes up to the other side of the gate and it isn't her man. Oh, God, she's so tied up with the accent, she's going to muff her lines.' He leaned forward and hitched his chair closer to the set. 'This is going to be good.'

Ben sat and watched the play in silence. In spite of the drab

150

costume, Rose was as beautiful as always, and considering how wrong the part was for her, he thought that she was doing nobly. Bob kept muttering gleefully: 'God, she's bad. She knows it. She's livid. I hope the critics are getting this.'

Damn Bob. It was his fault that Ben had not been able to see Rose before the show and make her happy by telling her how he was working for her. If she was worried, he could have given her confidence by saying: I love you. What woman would not act better if someone said that to her just before she went on the air? He must get to her before he himself was put to the ordeal of the cameras. How had he let himself be railroaded into this? Damn Bob again. But if Rose were to tell him: I love you, he would not care how much of a fool he made himself.

But she would not be thinking about love. She would be thinking about her show. If she was satisfied with her performance, he could tell her how marvellous she had been. If she was depressed, he would console her and tell her that it was everyone else's fault. His fault, perhaps. He should not have stayed away from her for so long. Perhaps she was pining. ...

No, no, said the voice from the third row of the empty stalls, listening to the dress rehearsal of his thoughts, now you're going too far.

'She stinks,' Bob said with satisfaction, as the commercial blasted its way in half-way through the play, leaving Rose in the chapel in widow's weeds.

'I thought,' said Ben, louder than necessary, 'that she was jolly good.'

Bob stared at him, and Ben kept his eyes on the screen, feigning absorbed interest in a working diagram of what would happen to the tubes and little doors of his digestive system if only he would put a certain pill into it.

Before the play was over, Bob switched off the set, dusted off his hands as if Rose were on them and became business-like, for *Who's Doing What* would be on the air in forty minutes.

'I want to see Rose,' Ben said.

'Later, later. No time now.' Bob hustled him off to the make-up room, where Ben enjoyed the attentions of a cool-handed girl who sent him away with unnaturally dark eyebrows and a complexion that looked as if he had spent the last six months in the Mediterranean. In the canteen, the clean aprons were too white for the television cameras, but the cook found a dirty one crumbled at the bottom of a laundry basket, yellowed with age and tea stains.

It was too long for Ben. When he took off his jacket and hitched the apron high above his waist, it still covered his shoes.

'I could never work in this,' he complained.

'That's right,' said the cook, pursing her mouth and speaking to him as a colleague. 'Nor could I.'

'Stop being so professional,' Bob said. 'It's perfect. The sloppier the better, in contrast to what you looked like as a naval officer.'

'Look here.' Ben's hands went behind him to untie the apron. 'I don't think I like this.'

Bob lit a cigarette. 'OK,' he said, breathing smoke through his curved nostrils like a delicate dragon. 'So you're going to let down two thousand unemployed naval officers. I'm glad I wasn't in your submarine, Ben. I'd have worn a Mae West all the time.'

'Don't tease him,' said the cook, not understanding, but knowing Bob well enough to know what he was at. 'It's only stage fright. Don't worry, dear.' She tightened the knot of the apron again and gave Ben a little pat behind. 'You'll be lovely. I wish I had your chance. I've been here two years, and they've never even asked me to read the weather forecast.'

In the corridor, Ben started for the staircase which led to Rose's dressing-room, but Bob switched him round a corner and through the heavy door which led to the studio. By the time the floor manager had shown him where to stand before the cameras, and had tested his voice and told him what his cue would be to come on to the set, the huge studio clock with the thin red hand sweeping away the seconds like the wing of death showed eight minutes to air time.

Ben sat on a piano stool by the wall and prayed that Rose would not be gone before his part in the programme was over. Let her take a long time removing her make-up. Let her stop for a drink with someone. If she does go, let her not go out to supper. Ben would rush straight to the flat without taking off his Mediterranean face, and if she was not there he would squat

152

in the corridor like a Maltese beggar. If she came home with the new producer, Pete – well, Pete would have to clear out. If Pete would not go, Ben would throw him out. Let Pete not be a heavy-weight.

'You're on the show, aren't you?' A small, thin woman with make-up running into lumps and crevasses on her pinched face, and hair that was either a wig or had not been combed out since she left the hairdresser, sat down on the other end of the piano stool. 'What do *you* do?' She looked down at the folds of dirty apron which swirled round Ben's legs and feet.

'I work in a cafeteria.'

'Oh? So does my niece.' The woman patted her ridged hair. 'They never asked her to go on T.V.'

'Well, you see.' It was going to sound silly, but she would know it soon enough. 'I was a naval officer, and so –'

'Oh, yes,' said the woman, losing interest. 'That's nice. I'm self-employed, myself.' She looked at him with her head on one side. She was obviously waiting for Ben to ask her what she did, so he asked her.

'I breed rats,' she told him. 'White ones. For experimental purposes, you know.'

'Vivisection?'

'It's more for psychology. I breed neurotic rats. But I know what you're thinking. There'll be people calling up the studio as soon as I get on the air. When I was on *What's My Line?* last year,' said the woman, who was apparently a professional television amateur, 'they had forty telephone calls in ten minutes. And the letters I had – I wish you could see them. Some of the nasty words, I'd never even heard of. I had to look them up in the dictionary. I expect I'll get a lot more after tonight.'

'Don't you mind?'

'It's good publicity. You can't sell anything these days without advertising, even rats. Well, thanks for the chat. I'm on first. Top of the bill.' She got up and moved towards the lighted set where Bob was talking through a headset to the producer in the control-room. The little rat breeder took her place beside him under the hanging microphone and waited smiling, showing her front teeth like one of her nurslings, supremely confident in the knowledge that in two minutes she was going to have the studio switchboard jammed with abusive calls.

Bob took off his head-set, twitched at his pale-grey tie, passed a hand over his receding hair and assumed an unfamiliar gregarious smile of welcome for the rat breeder and the public as the floor manager, crouching beside the camera in a pair of earphones that made him look like Mickey Mouse, flung a pointing arm at Bob, and the show was on the air.

Ben sat on the edge of the piano stool and watched the little woman prattling away as unhesitatingly as if she were working from a script. He was too far away to hear what she was saying. She was just a harmless, mouthing doll, and yet because of her, people all over the country who had been sitting comfortably in chairs with little tray-tables of snacks beside them were even now springing up and dashing for the telephone.

After the rat breeder came the man with the spoons and the kitchen chair. He worked himself into a frenzy, beating his insane tattoo on the chair, the floor, himself, and even the top of Bob's head. Ben stood near the set and watched him gloomily, biting at a piece of skin at the side of his thumbnail. The spoon percussion was torture, as much for the man as for the audience, but Ben wished it would go on for ever, even if it meant the end of the man, who with contorted face and rasping breath seemed already to be nearing the end of his rope.

The floor manager had signalled to Ben. This was it. He was next. He felt that he was trembling all over, but when he took his hand away from his mouth and held it in front of him, the fingers did not move at all. The trembling was inside him, cold, griping at the roots of his teeth like neuralgia. What was he going to say? His mind was not only a blank, it was not there at all. He could remember nothing about the cafeteria, and everything that had happened to him since he left the Navy was receding fast away, like the corners of a bedroom where you lie sick with a high fever.

He would be able to say nothing. Bob would be glossy and poised, as he had been with the other two – but dammit, this was his job – and Ben would stutter and gawp like a yokel and make a complete ass of himself, and tomorrow people would nudge each other in the street and whisper behind their hands.

The man with the spoons dropped them into a capacious poacher's pocket, picked up the persecuted chair and staggered off panting, as if he had run a four-minute mile. Bob said a few genial things towards the camera, turned with his hand out-stretched as Ben came on, taking small steps because of the apron, and they shook hands in a sickeningly hearty way.

Although Bob appeared so cool, his hand was sticky with sweat. Ben conquered a desire to wipe his palm on his apron, and felt his own sweat beginning to run into the pencilled eye-brows as he stood and grinned stiffly towards the camera, with the fierce, hot lights beating at his face.

'Don't be fooled by the disguise, folks,' Bob was telling the ghoulish crowd who lived out there in space beyond the camera. 'This is, or rather was, a naval officer. Commander Benjamin Francis, Royal Navy.' He looked at Ben with his curved eye-brows raised, and Ben could only nod, running his tongue over his lips, which felt as cracked and speechless as if he had been in the desert for days.

Bob was talking suavely and sympathetically about the re-duction in Service personnel, making it sound real for people who had never heard of it, or never given it a second thought. Even in his predicament, stuck in the spotlight with the small army of technicians wasting their brains and experience and valuable equipment to bring Ben's paralysed face into a million homes, Ben had enough wits left to admire the professional charm of Bob's television personality. Off the set, he behaved as if he expected people not to like him. Now, in front of the cameras, with his fancy waistcoat caved in at a relaxed angle and his soft, pink mouth jovial as Father Christmas, he was playing for popularity as if he were sure of getting it.

When Ben saw him pulling out all the stops of his unsus-pected charm, there flashed across his mind what Bob had once said about his experimental relationship with Rose. Had he wooed her deliberately like this, as if she were an unknown woman sitting before a television set? As Ben's imagination plunged away towards a series of disturbing pictures, he realized that Bob was asking him a question. Well, of course, he could not hope to stand here and listen for ten minutes. He was here to talk. Desperately he grabbed at his mind and dragged it back, and as he began to answer the question, hearing his own voice strange and stilted, he caught sight of himself on the small monitor screen at one side of the cameras.

God, what was it doing here, that sturdy figure with the cropped head and the anxious expression and the lower half of its body swathed in the ridiculous creased apron? It looked like the worst half of a comedy team. An officer and gentleman. Retired Admirals must be having cataleptic fits all over the south of England.

The figure on the tiny screen squared its shoulders and grinned, and he turned the grin away from it towards the camera. What did he care? He could not be court martialled for this. They could not even stop his pension. He had let Bob push him into this, and he might as well make the best of it. He was here to do a bit of good for all the poor blokes like Jack Frazer, peddling his way round Sheffield with a brief-case full of gummed reinforcements for the holes in ring-books.

He glanced at Bob, and Bob winked with a flicker of a lower lid, and suddenly it was a bit of a lark after all. Ben's voice began to come out more naturally, and the blank pistol eye of the camera was no longer an enemy but a receptive friend. Bob was kidding him along, asking the right questions, letting him talk freely when he saw that Ben was warming up and beginning almost to enjoy himself.

Was anybody listening, out there in the world? Ben imagined that they had all switched off, or turned the dial testily over to the B.B.C. That made it easier for him to tell them what he wanted to say. Here in the studio, there were people listening. The studio manager and the carelessly-dressed men round the cameras and in the shadows beyond were watching Ben, half-smiling, wanting to be diverted. Ben told them, with a tinge of affectionate regret, for he had a feeling that he might never see any of them again, about Sir Thomas Beecham, and the old Polish woman, and Ethel, and May, and Babyface Briggs. He tried to do them justice. He wanted them to like him for this. If they were listening, he wanted them to jerk upright with a proud smile and cry: 'That's me!'

Under Bob's skilful prodding, Ben remembered things that had amused Amy and Geneva, and told them again. When he told about the day the vegetable cook had gone after one of the counter hands with a knife and sliced all the buttons off the front of his jacket, one of the assistant cameramen threw back his head and laughed, and Ben understood, in that heady, dizzying moment of success, why Rose would never give up acting.

A boy with a loose forelock was holding up a board which said: 4 mins.

'It all sounds like a lot of fun,' Bob said, dipping his face and his voice smoothly to seriousness, 'but let's not forget what's behind it. You've served your country for seventeen years as an officer in Her Majesty's Navy. Now you're out, through no fault of your own, and you've had to take this – this, let's say unsuitable job, because although you're a man who's held responsibility and command, you couldn't get anything else. Right?'

'In a way,' Ben said. He could not tell the world that he had taken the job because he was angry with Rose. Bob was playing for sympathy now, overdoing it a bit, so when Ben answered his questions about job-hunting and interviews and rejections, he kept a grin on his face, in case anyone imagined that he felt sorry for himself. He was here to make people feel sorry for the other chaps, not for him.

As if he understood that, Bob said, with a glance at the boy, whose board now said: 2 mins.: 'It's toughest, of course, on the men who have wives and families. You have a small daughter, I know, but I understand, Commander Francis, that you're a widower.'

Why bring that up? Blast you, Bob. Now there would be letters from all the frustrated women who thought that they could get husbands by writing to strangers. He wished he had not mentioned his gratuity. If the anti-vivisection group had cleared off the telephone lines, the spinsters and widows might already be calling in. Ben glanced at the monitor set to reassure himself that the most desperate woman could hardly want to marry that aproned figure of fun.

Except perhaps Rose, who was not desperate. He had nodded in confirmation of what Bob was saying before he realized exactly what he had said.

'Wonderful, wonderful,' Bob purred. 'Our own Rose Kelly and a man who has about touched bottom in his search for a decent job. Surprise you, folks? Quite a fairy story, isn't it?'

The floor manager was going crazy. Crouched on one knee beside the camera, he was waving his arms back and forth like giant scissors, but Bob went blandly on.

'How does she like you in this outfit?' He tweaked at Ben's apron.

Something had gone wrong. Bob's face had lost its geniality. He was still smiling, but his smile was not for the folks out there. It was for himself, and catty. 'How does she like it?' he asked again.

'I don't know.' Ben had to say something, and he could think of nothing but the truth. 'I haven't told her yet about the –'

'Then she wouldn't like it? But Rose is so democratic, so human.'

The floor manager was throwing some kind of epileptic fit, almost lying on the floor, his face working, his hands clutching towards Bob, doing everything but leap on to the set and strangle him.

'I'm surprised she's not working right there at the cafeteria with you. As she has shown us in so many of her plays, a woman's place is at her man's side.'

Bob smiled sentimentally at the camera, but Ben saw that the knuckles of the hand which clutched the lapel were white, because the hand was tense. Then the boy with the flopping forelock, looking as unhappy as everyone else, was holding up a board which said: 15 secs., and Bob was shaking Ben's hand and wishing him luck. Ben walked awkwardly off the set, trying not to trip over his apron, while the floor manager, with a face of despair as if he had seen his job fly out of the window, waved forward an elderly gentleman whose face was related in every feature to the monkey he carried on his shoulder.

Without waiting to see what the man and the monkey would do and say, Ben groped past the hazards at the back of the studio and hurried towards Rose's dressing-room. The door was locked. He banged on it and called, but she was not there.

Turning away, wondering where he had left his jacket, he saw Rose come round the bend of the corridor. Although she still had her make-up on, she had changed from the black dress she had worn for her show into a scarlet dress which fitted her tightly all the way down until it came to a little fan of pleats in the front which flared and bounced before her as she tap-tapped towards him on very high heels.

She did not speak to him. Ben held out his arms, but she brushed past him as if he were air, put her key in the lock and went into the dressing-room. Ben followed her inside before she could shut the door.

'Get out of here.' Rose sat down at the long mirror, banged a huge tin of cold cream in front of her and began to spread it on her face.

'What's the matter?' Ben stayed where he was, near the door.

'What's the *matter*?' With savage tugs, Rose peeled off the strips of false eyelashes. 'What do you think? I've just come from the viewing-room. I saw you.'

'Were you proud of me?' Ben ventured a few steps forward, kicking aside the sagging apron like a clumsy Edwardian débutante. 'I didn't think I was bad, considering it was my first shot. I made one of the cameramen laugh. No one ever does that, I understand, except Danny Kaye.'

'I asked you to get out of here.' Rose began to wipe off the cold cream methodically, pulling her face about, which still did not make it look ugly.

'Don't mind me. I've seen you take off your face before.' Ben stood behind her and put his hands on her shoulders. She did not shrug them off, but she humped her shoulders and stared with chill antipathy at his reflection in the mirror above her own.

'You humiliated me. You deliberately and cruelly humiliated me. Shut up,' she said, as Ben opened his mouth to speak. 'You're going to make some stupid joke, and I can't stand it.'

Ben saw that her eyes had shifted slightly downwards to study her own face as she talked. 'I was going home,' she said, the tight scarlet dress rising and falling as her breathing quickened, 'when Bob sent me a message to stay and watch his show because there was a man on it I must see. "You might be able to use him," he said. I thought he meant on my show, of course – oh, that man is a devil – so I stayed, like a fool. I wish I

hadn't. No, I don't. I'm glad I did. It opened my eyes to just
what you are, just how low you can be.'

'You mean because he dragged your name into it? Poor
taste, I agree, but that wasn't my fault.'

'Not your fault!' She tore her eyes away from her reflection
and swung round to face him so violently that he dropped his
hands and stepped back. 'Don't make me laugh. I know you
cooked it up, you and Bob between you, to make me look a
fool. You let Bob use you to get his own back at me. I hate
you.'

She stood up. She was two inches taller than Ben in those
heels. Clean of all make-up, her skin was like a petal, like a
sun-bloomed fruit. Her lips were soft and pink, but the lower
one was pushed out sullenly. If she had been an ordinary
woman, Ben would have kissed her, forcibly if necessary, and
standing on tiptoe if necessary, and compelled the lips to melt
and part and the rubber-taut body to relax against him.

As it was, he stayed two feet away from her and said: 'Look
here, Rose, even if Bob was using me as a weapon in his private
war with you, I had nothing to do with it. I had no idea he
meant to say what he did. I was just there to try to do a good
turn for the other poor devils who nobody wants. And for a bit
of fun too, of course.'

'Fun.' Rose had an objectionable way of picking out a word
or a phrase from what you had said and repeating it as if it
smelled. She sat down again and began to put on her street
make-up, staring without expression at the face on which she
worked. 'You make me sick. I suppose you think it's fun to
have that damn-fool job, to wear that ridiculous toga. If you
only knew what you looked like in it.' She blended rouge deftly,
turning her face this way and that.

'I do. I saw myself on the monitor. I look like hell, but that
was half the point.'

'I'm surprised she's not working right there at the cafeteria
with you,' Rose mimicked, through a cloud of apricot powder.
'My public is just going to love that, aren't they?'

'Why not? It's not a bad job, apart from the pay. I do pretty
well at it. The manageress says I'm the best man she's had for
ages.'

'A dish-washer.'

'You weren't listening to the programme. May does the dishes. I clear the tables.'

'That's worse.'

'If you don't like it, it's your fault. "Don't come near me until you've got a job," you said. Well, I've got a job, so here I am.'

Rose said nothing. She was occupied with her lipstick. Then she dropped it into her bag, snapped shut her cosmetic case, stood up, dusted off the front of her dress and went over to the corner where her coat hung.

Ben was trying to untie his apron, but the strings were knotted and he could not undo them. As she came towards him, he turned his back to her. 'Help me, would you? I can't get this thing off.'

'Then you'll have to keep it on.'

'But I can't take you home like this.'

'You're not going to take me home.' Rose stood with her hand on the door-knob, her beautiful head flung back, her words coming out as clearly and effectively as if she had been rehearsing them for days with every possible inflection.

'You're not going to take me anywhere, ever again. I'm through, do you understand? I'm finished with you. This is the end.'

Ben believed that she meant it. He ought to feel sick, or faint, or violently angry. Instead, to his surprise, he experienced a curious feeling of relief, a comfortable, relaxed feeling as if he were sinking down on to a bed without a care in the world and nothing to look forward to but a good night's sleep.

'All right,' he said, 'but I wish you'd untie my apron before you go.'

Rose jerked her head with an impatient exclamation which might have been written in one of her scripts as 'faugh!' She wrenched open the door, but as she did so, the telephone on the make-up shelf began to ring, and she had to shut the door and come back into the room. Even though it spoiled her exit, Rose could not bear to let a telephone ring without finding out who it was.

'Let me.' Ben moved towards the telephone.

'Don't you dare.' Rose picked up the receiver, and made a face as she listened. 'It's for you.' She held it out at arm's length. 'What a nerve they've got, thinking you'd be in here with me.'

'Well, I am.' Ben took the telephone. 'Hello?'

'Commander Francis?' It was a man's voice, resonant, authoritative, no one he knew. 'I saw you on television. Thought I'd call up to congratulate you.'

'Well, thanks.' Ben sat down to enjoy this. 'That's awfully nice of you.' He looked at Rose. She had gone back to the door and was standing with it half-open, torn between wanting to sweep out and slam it and wanting to know who was talking to Ben.

'This is Glenville Roberts,' the confident voice said, and paused as if this should mean something impressive to Ben. Vaguely it did, but he could not at the moment think why. 'I'm offering you a job,' the voice continued, 'if you'll take it. I like your looks, and I like your guts.'

Ben maddened Rose by smiling broadly. 'What is it?' he asked.

'Come and be my private secretary.'

'I can't type very well, and I –'

'That doesn't matter. I've got a girl for that. Come and see me tomorrow and we'll discuss it.' Without waiting for Ben to agree, he gave an address in Hampstead, and Ben grabbed a make-up stick and scrawled it on the side of a box of tissues. 'You can live at this place, if you want, and I'd be glad to have your daughter too. I love little girls. Oh – not in that way, of course.' He chuckled. 'Till tomorrow then. Don't come until after eleven. I'm a bastard before that.'

'Well,' Rose said impatiently, as Ben put down the receiver, 'who was it?'

'No one you know. You wouldn't be interested.' He was not going to tell her. If he told her about Glenville Roberts, who sounded like a man with money and power, she might reconsider her dismissal of him. They might have to start all over again. Off, on. I'll marry you, I won't marry you. I love you, I don't know whether I love you or hate you. He felt too tired to face the strain of it.

162

He sighed. 'Go on, Rose,' he said. 'If you're going, please go.'

It was a shame that the telephone had spoiled her exit line. Because she could not think of another, Ben felt sorry for her and said, to help her out: 'It's been very sweet, my dear. Thanks – for everything.'

The Noël Coward line revived her. 'I'm sorry it had to end like this,' she said, on cue. 'But it's the best way, Ben.'

'Yes, the best way.' She was very lovely, so he looked away from her as she gathered her coat round her and went out.

After she had gone, he took a pair of scissors from a drawer and cut the strings of his apron. He bundled it up and put it in the drawer with the scissors, in case she wanted a memento of him. It took him half an hour to find his jacket, and then he went up to the deserted offices to look for a *Who's Who* to find out who Glenville Roberts was.

Chapter Eleven

GLENVILLE ROBERTS was an author of comparatively small output, but considerable and somewhat flashy repute. He had written only two books, but they had both been best-sellers, because they were not only brilliant in an exhilarating though patchy fashion, but minutely descriptive of some of the aspects and aberrations of sex which are not usually recorded so photographically in print.

Bishops had denounced them, and tabloid columnists, whose own minds were far dirtier than Glenville's had furthered the publicity by asking their readers, many of whom would not otherwise have dreamed of buying a book: 'Would you let your daughter read this?' and 'Why was this book ever published?'

Both novels had been made into films, which were very successful, even with the sex watered down, and on the strength of his name and his work in adapting his books, Glenville Roberts was able to pick up a thousand pounds any time he needed it by writing a film script. He had a Midas touch. Although he was lazy and without any artistic conscience, and claimed that he only worked when he was forced to pay his income tax of the year before, he made money easily, which was galling for less fruitful authors who slogged away day after day and believed in what they wrote.

He was a flamboyant man in his middle forties, with a thickening figure, a deteriorating handsomeness which he knew looked best in profile, and a large head maned with abundant coarse grey hair. His clothes were superb, with just a touch of eccentricity – a hint of braid on the lapel, a glimpse of embroidery on a dress shirt – to distinguish him from anyone else who could afford a good tailor.

Half by accident, half deliberately, he looked like a literary lion, which was gratifying for the small fry at Foyle's luncheons and publishers' cocktail parties, where most of the authors looked like schoolmasters or somebody's aunt.

Glenville Roberts had been called a genius by people who did not know what the word meant. For all his egotism, he was the first to disclaim that. He was, however, a man who had a flair for immensely stimulating prose and sudden swift sweeps of sparkling narrative which carried the reader, skipping blithely, over the patches of slipshod writing in between. His large readership was composed chiefly of skippers : those who were willing to skip the bad writing for the pleasures of the good, and those who skipped everything except the dirty bits.

Besides being the author of two best-sellers, Glenville Roberts was also a skilful journalist, possessing the invaluable ability to write an article about almost anything under the sun at the drop of a hat, whether he knew anything about it or not. The Sunday paper for which he wrote outrageous and provocative articles which sounded convincing, although they were written with a lack of conviction that would have been cynicism if he had been a cynic instead of an opportunist, had played an important share in building him up into something of a national figure.

He had appeared on radio and television, which had helped his notoriety because, like Sir Gerald Kelly, he invariably said something taboo, and like Gilbert Harding, he managed to sound entertainingly angry when he was suffering from no greater irritation than a mild indigestion.

The indigestion was one of the things that were in Ben's care as private secretary to the great man. It was an indeterminate job, encompassing many small tasks, from keeping the medicine cabinet stocked and reminding Glenville what he should not eat – it was no use reminding him what he should not drink – to discouraging bores and undesirables in the flesh, on the telephone and in the mail, and anyone at all in any medium before eleven o'clock in the morning.

The typist, Priscilla Neave, was afraid of Glenville, which made her nervous and incompetent, except when her fingers were actually flying over the typewriter, which was as integral a part of her as a fifth limb. Priscilla's skill on the typewriter and the shorthand pad was the sole justification for her conception, or the conception of any of her ancestors, Glenville Roberts said. Originally engaged to do for him everything he could not be bothered to do for himself, she was now confined to stenography, while Ben took over those less mechanical duties which used to be Priscilla's until she had driven her employer to the edge of madness which had impelled him to telephone Ben at the television studio.

In this way, Glenville could appear to put Priscilla cruelly in her place, while yet indulging the concealed pity which would not allow him to fire her. To ensure that the pity remained concealed, he was sadistically unkind to Priscilla, whose pale-lashed lids were pink by nature, and rubbed red when she had been crying over the typewriter; but to Ben he was as nice as he could be without lowering his standards of selfishness.

'Call me Glenn,' he had said, flinging out a hand when they first met. 'What do I call you – Benjamin or Ben?'

'Ben, if you like.'

'Fine. That's settled then. You want the job, I take it.' It was not a question. There could be nothing but a statement of fact on the opportunity of working for Glenville Roberts.

On an impulse, Ben had taken Amy with him. He had rushed her off as soon as she came home from school, without giving her a chance to change her uniform, which she felt put her at a disadvantage.

'I look better when I'm not in this thing,' she said, tugging at the girdle of her gym tunic when Glenville told her that she was pretty.

'Of course you do. The armour-plating is a sacrilege on a figure like yours. But never mind, we'll put you in Miss Melbourne's school, up on the hill. The girls wear what they like there. I often see them in the High Street. Quite big girls too.' He gave Ben a look that managed to be solemn and lewd at the same time.

'She's doing very well at the school where she is,' Ben said. 'I want her to stay there.'

'Oh, Daddy, no!' Amy turned on him, her bronze ripple of hair swinging with her. 'What's the point of you starting a new life if I can't too?'

'Don't worry, my dear,' Glenville Roberts said. 'We'll work on him.' They smiled at each other, and initiated a liaison that was to last with affection and understanding all the time that Amy and Ben lived in Hampstead.

It was a comfortable life. A daily maid called Mrs Bowstrom and a cleaning woman looked after the house so efficiently that Ben had little more to do with it than to pay the tradesmen's bills and telephone the wine merchant. He and Amy had two pleasant bedrooms with their own bathroom, and a small upstairs sitting-room where Amy could do her homework and entertain her friend Susanna Clarke, a sophisticated child into whose company Amy had graduated since she had moved up in the world and came home on the Hampstead tube instead of the Inner Circle.

She had not won her battle to change schools. Glenn, siding with her as he did on any dispute between her and her father, had offered to pay Miss Melbourne's excessive fees himself, a false move which had enabled Ben to insist that she must stay where he could afford to keep her.

He did not want to tell Glenn yet that it was not worth changing schools because this was only a stopping-off place for Amy and him, to take them off Geneva's hands and give them somewhere to live until Ben found a proper job. He did not tell him that he was still answering advertisements and had even risked being told that his *métier* in life was to peddle sweet bubbly drinks to tea-shops and confectioners by applying to the Industrial Employment Analysts for a test and a psychological interview.

166

If he got the chance of a decent job it would be time enough to tell Glenn, who imagined that he had given Ben the ideal job for an ex-naval officer, and thought that he had come to stay. Meanwhile, Amy was happy here, and Ben was as near contented as long patches of boredom would allow.

Susanna Clarke was an actress, like Amy. They assumed diverse roles and indulged in fancies that stopped just short of lies. As soon as they were out of school, they entered together on a complicated existence where neither was the same person for more than a few days, and their aliases were so real to them that they would not always answer when addressed by their own names.

Glenville loved them both, although he was a little wary of Susanna, who appeared to have got his number the first time she came into the house, when she produced her sister's autograph album and said: 'I suppose you'd like to write in it.'

Although he was suspect because he was famous, she accepted him because Amy did, and he was always welcome in the upstairs sitting-room, to which he made frequent trips to join enthusiastically in a lunch party between the mothers of débutantes, or the first concert of a child violin prodigy, or whatever was going on.

He had been divorced many years ago and had a nearly grown-up son whom he rarely saw and did not care for when he did. 'I'd been thinking of marrying again,' he told Ben. 'There's a woman – Clara. You haven't met her yet. She's piqued with me at the moment, but she won't stay away too long. But now that I've got Amy, I don't know that I'll bother with a wife. She's all the woman in the house I need.'

When Susanna had gone home to Belsize Park and Amy was in bed, Ben was occasionally able to use the upstairs sitting-room as a refuge from Glenn and his frequent guests. He could not often get away, except when there was a woman alone downstairs, for Glenn insisted that he should be present at all parties to mix drinks and help Mrs Bowstrom with the food and talk to anyone whom nobody else wanted to talk to.

When Glenn was not having one of his violent spasms of work, which were short but concentrated, to the exclusion of all else, like Asian flu, there was someone in the house almost every night, and often a lot of people, and it became a party that persisted into the small hours. Ben enjoyed at first mixing with people from a world that was comparatively new to him, although he had explored a small part of it with Rose. After a while, however, he found that this was the most tedious part of his job.

He might hang about the house all day with very little to do, and then when he was beginning to think about going to bed, a party would suddenly develop out of the air – Glenn's friends always seemed ready to come no matter how late he telephoned – and Ben would have to stay up for another four hours and be as tired the next morning as if he had done a worthwhile day's work.

Geneva loved to hear about his social life, and the Major never ceased to angle for an invitation to this place where it seemed that alcohol flowed out of the very bathroom taps, but Ben was soon sated with the voluble arguments and discussions in which everybody talked at once and listened to nobody, and with the half-drunken fooling that turned almost every party into a silly shambles before Glenn suddenly tired of humanity and pushed his guests hooting and laughing out of the door into the blossom-scented Hampstead night.

The pretty white house with its arched windows and fragile balconies was in one of those carefully-preserved backwaters of history whose residents are always writing letters to the newspapers protesting about new street lighting or the cutting down of trees, and agitating, in a civilized way, to get a question asked in Parliament.

Many of the neighbours were literary figures, not so well known or successful as Glenn, although, or because they had more genuine intelligence. That was one reason why Glenn had bought the house with the little paved garden in the middle of the street. There was no one famous enough on either side to outshine him, but they could supply the background that he lacked.

He had made a point of knowing everyone in the peaceful, winding street, but most of them stayed away from his parties, and those who came usually left early, because, unlike Glenn, they planned to work the next morning.

168

When his parties finally erupted into the narrow street with shouts and laughter and the banging of car doors and revving-up of sports engines, the neighbours turned over in their beds and reflected that there were other threats to their cherished preserve besides the philistine attitude of the works committee of the borough council.

To complete the picture of himself as a successful literary man, Glenville Roberts had bought a property in the country which had thirty acres of grassland and a pink-walled farmhouse. Although he had rented the outbuildings and all the grazing to a neighbouring poultry and dairy farmer, he called it My Farm.

After his first visit to the house, Ben doubted whether Glenn would ever live there for more than a few week-ends in the year; week-ends for which he would import his own companions. The farmhouse was in a lovely fold of gentle hills, with elm trees raising their cumulus shapes along the hedgerows; but it was five miles from the nearest village and ten miles from a town, and neither the village nor the town nor the scattered houses in between contained the kind of people whom Glenn would put up with for long.

But he had fallen in love with the house. That was what he told people. He had first seen it by mistake, after losing his way on the drive back to town from seeing off a Very Dear Friend on the *Queen Elizabeth*.

The phrasing was typical of Glenn. All his friends were Dear Friends, but a Very Dear Friend implied some superb and perhaps famous woman whose relationship with him had been too intimate to reveal her name. He had still not arrived quite far enough to consider it immaterial to the story whom he was seeing off, and whether they sailed in the *Queen Elizabeth* or in a cattle boat.

Before his listeners could reflect on this, they were hearing that the house had struck an answering chord in Glenn's heart as soon as he saw its dark-tiled roof rising beyond the little copse. Here he would be able to find the solitude and calm of spirit in which to finish the book which meant everything to him, his two-hundred-thousand-word novel about pre-war Berlin.

He was not particularly interested in Germany, either before or since the war, but he had chosen the locale and the period because of its sexual decadence, which would give unlimited scope for those peculiar talents for which a large section of his public valued him.

Ben had been put to work on research, which was one of the duties which had bogged down the hapless Priscilla, but Glenn had not yet got further than making notes for the first two chapters. Every time he decided to start work on the novel in earnest, a magazine editor or a film producer would come up with a tempting offer which would mean a quicker return for far less work.

Meanwhile the house was being converted from its original design as a farmer's home to a country place fit for Glenn to live and work in. He never had time to visit the house and study progress, so one of Ben's duties was to make frequent trips to the country to talk to the architect and the builder and the plumber and the electrician and the landscape gardener, and make decisions about wallpaper and kitchen flooring.

'I leave it to you,' said Glenn, who wanted to impress with the house, but did not want to bother with it until it was finished. 'You are a man of taste.'

Ben knew that he was not. His lack of eye for variations on the spectrum almost amounted to colour blindness, but the local interior decorator was making all the decisions about colour schemes and curtains. Ben merely had to give the official approval, because the decorator, who knew that Glenn was unpredictable, did not want to find himself involved later in a lawsuit for having done everything wrong.

The house was between Winchester and Andover. Glenn usually wanted the car for himself, so it was Waterloo Station again, and the London to Southampton line which Ben knew so well. His life seemed to be inextricably bound up with Waterloo and the Southern Railway.

At least once a week, at the request of the decorator, or of the architect or the builder who were infected with his caution, Ben would take a day trip to the country and snatch two glimpses of the red-brick house by the railway from whose influence it seemed that he would never free himself.

In the Easter holidays, he took Amy with him, and often Susanna as well, for their friendship did not end with the end of term. They would take sandwiches and fruit and chocolate, and picnic in the unfinished house, or in the garden if the day was warm enough.

'This is where we're going to live,' Amy told Susanna, as they sat on a broken garden bench in a sunny alcove at the side of the house. 'Glenn will be here most of the time.'

'Steady on,' Ben said. 'I have a feeling we'll still be in London most of the time.'

'Oh, no. He'll be here. He told me. And Mr Garrett is going to let me keep a pony in with his cows, and I shall go to school in Winchester. We'll invite you to stay, of course, Sue, or you could come and live here all the time and go to school with me, if your parents would let you.'

'They would.' Susanna rolled off the bench and lay on her back in the uncut grass of the lawn. 'They'd be glad to get rid of me. They never wanted me in the first place. I'm not their child, you know. I was left on their doorstep – the back one – on a wild December night.' She rolled on to her face and beat on the ground with her clenched fists. 'How many, many times they've regretted their kind impulse to take me in!'

'Susanna!' Ben said, wondering, as he did occasionally, whether this was the right friend for Amy. 'You know that isn't true.'

'Of course it isn't,' Amy said impatiently, 'but she's a found-ling just now. Don't spoil it. This evening – not now, because we're going to help Mr Garrett collect the eggs before the taxi comes – I'm going to be the rich benefactress who rescues her from her cruel foster-parents and gives her the first real happi-ness she has ever known.'

Ben had always talked to Amy about the house by the rail-way, and they had watched it cheek to cheek from the train window whenever they travelled to Southampton together. The saga of the family who lived there had captured her fancy as much as his, and on these trips to Glenn's farm-house, both the girls were avid for the glimpses of the house and the chance to observe some new detail, commonplace in itself, but fascinating when their imaginations had trimmed it.

Once they saw the son's wife playing with a toppling baby outside the back door.

'She's left her husband,' Amy declared. 'I always said it wouldn't last.' Mrs Bowstrom had been saying that about her niece.

'Nonsense,' Ben said. 'She's just there for the holidays. He had to stay in town, because of his work, but he comes down at week-ends.'

'Let's go to the farm next Saturday and see,' Susanna suggested.

'That wouldn't prove a thing,' Amy said. 'He'd be indoors. He's the indoor type.'

'But we'd see his car in the trailer shed. There isn't room for more than one in the garage,' said Ben, whom the years had made familiar with these details. 'In any case, if she'd left him, he might be there, but not her. She'd be with her own parents.'

'In Guildford. It was a local match. Yes, I hadn't thought of that. But perhaps,' said Amy, who wanted the drama of a broken marriage, 'she likes his parents best, and they've taken her side.'

The daffodils were out in the corner of the garden where the tree-house was. Once they saw the mother picking them. She was wearing a tweed skirt, perfectly square, and what was either a riding coat or a man's sports jacket. As the train went by above her, she straightened up to stare at it, the bunch of daffodils clutched awkwardly upside down in her hand like a club.

'She won't arrange them, of course,' Amy said, as they all settled back into their seats with a sigh because it was over so quickly. 'The younger daughter, the pretty one, will do that. She's clever with her hands.'

'And artistic too,' Ben said. 'She paints, and has a potter's wheel in the bathroom. There's nothing that girl can't do.'

'Daddy's in love with her,' Amy explained to Susanna, to the amused interest of a woman in the other corner of the carriage, who did not look as grand as her suitcase, which was stamped: 'E. de la A. H.' 'Perhaps when we live at the farm, Daddy, we could get to know them somehow. It can't be too far away. We could give a hunt ball, or something, and invite them, and then you can marry her, now that you –'

She coughed and looked down at her hands. Ben had told her that he was not going to marry Rose Kelly, or ever see her again, and she had received the news in careful silence, and had never mentioned Rose since.

The woman in the corner, who had been smiling to herself in a comfortable way, got up and turned her smile to Ben. 'I'm going to have lunch,' she said. 'If you're going to the dining-car, you'd better go now, because it fills up after the next stop. I know this line.'

'Oh, so do we,' Amy said. 'But we never go to the dining-car. It's too expensive. We're going to have a picnic.'

'What fun,' the woman said. 'I wish I could join you.' She went out into the corridor and slid the door shut with a nod and a smile.

'Ernestine de la Rue Harrison,' Amy said at once. 'I wonder where she lives?'

Glenville Roberts was idle about starting work, and would conjure up any excuse to postpone sitting down at his desk with the mug of sharpened pencils and the scribbling-pad from which it was poor Priscilla's lot to decipher and translate into type his vile handwriting; but once he had forced himself to start, he went at it like a demon.

He had to, because he always left until the last minute any articles that had been commissioned. As the deadline approached, Glenn would utter an oath, take a stiff whisky and plunge into a fury of high-pressure creation, yelling at intervals for Ben to bring him nourishment, for he would not let Priscilla or Mrs Bowstrom into the room when he was working.

Sometimes he would hear the call to arms late in the evening, and he would turn any guests out of the house and sit up in a silk dressing-gown which the Very Dear Friend had sent him from Sulka in New York, writing far into the night.

He expected Ben to stay up as long as he did, or to get out of bed every time he shouted for coffee and sandwiches. One day, Ben bought a thermos flask, and the next time Glenn started to attack his scribbling-pad at eleven o'clock at night, he made a great pile of sandwiches with Glenn's special low-calorie bread, wrapped them in a plastic bag, filled the thermos with hot coffee, and put the tray without a word on the corner of Glenn's wide, chaotic desk.

Glenn stabbed at the end of a sentence, made a huge black question-mark, and crossed the whole thing out in the same movement. Straightening the silk-clad hump of his shoulders, he looked at the tray and then looked up at Ben.

'What's this?' he asked. 'Are you going out, or something? Don't tell me you're on with that Kelly bit again.'

'You know I'm not. Rose and I are through. She has a South American singer now. I saw a picture of him carrying the mink.'

'Poor sod. You were well out of that. I hope you've picked something a bit higher grade this time.'

'There's no one. I'm not going out, Glenn. I'm going upstairs to bed.'

'And you don't intend to get out of it. I see.' Glenn nodded at the tray. 'Very ingenious. What's in the sandwiches?'

'Ham and chicken.'

'Delicious.' He spoke so pleasantly that Ben was taken by surprise and caught the sandwiches full on the side of his face when Glenn threw them at him. 'All right. Now pick them up.'

'I'll be damned if I do.' Ben knocked some crumbs down from behind his ear to join the mess of bread and meat on the floor.

'Then you'll have to make me some more.' Glenn picked up his pencil. 'And when I ask for them, not just whenever it suits you to bring them.'

His heavy head looked threatening, but Ben clenched his fists along the sides of his legs and held his ground and said: 'What the hell do you think I am?'

'What the hell do you think I pay you for?' Glenn's eyes flickered downwards for a moment to Ben's hands to see if the crazy fool was going to hit him.

'God knows,' Ben said. 'You could live without me, but you asked me to come.'

'And you jumped at it. I suppose now you're going to tell me that you wish you'd stayed at the cafeteria.'

'Perhaps. At least no one ever threw food at me there.'

Glenn flung down his pencil, breaking the point, dumped his elbows on the desk and ran his hands through his thick, untidy hair. 'Come off it,' he groaned. 'If you're going to be dignified, it's the last straw. I should have known better than to take on a brasshat – however tarnished. But I'm giving the orders now. You can get the hell out of here into the kitchen and make some more sandwiches, and then you can get the encyclopedia and look up some dates on the Industrial Revolution. I'm going to need them before I'm through with this thing.'

'Yessir.' Ben knocked his heels to attention.

'I'm not laughing. And you can take that away and heave it.' Glenn jerked his head at the thermos. 'Those things make coffee taste as if it came out of a sewer.'

Satisfied that he had put Ben in his place, he chose another pencil and began to write again, his cramped hand pushing the lead deep into the paper. Ben paused behind his back with the thermos, wondering whether he should hit him on the head with it. He probably would not even feel it through all that hair. Ben went out, his shoulders and neck and face hot and tingling with rage.

It was the first battle between him and Glenn, but by God, it was going to be the last. For two pins he would have woken Amy and walked out of the house; but Amy was ill with flu and could not be moved. That was the way life was. There was always something like a child's temperature or a flat tyre to spoil your big gestures.

The next morning, Ben kept out of the way, but Glenn sought him out and asked him: 'Did you throw away that thermos?'

'No.' Ben did not commit his face either to sullenness or friendship. 'I kept it for our picnics at the farm.'

'Good. I've changed my mind. I may use it at night after all. You're planning to ask for your cards this morning, I suppose.'

'I was.' If Ben had heard from the Industrial Employment Analysts that his application form had been approved, he had been going to tell Glenn what he could do with his job. But there had been nothing for him in the morning mail.

'Hang on till tomorrow,' Glenn said. 'I want you to come down to the film studio with me. We're having a story conference on this war film they want to do, and there's a chance I can get you the job of technical adviser on the naval side.'

Glenn went out to lunch and came home with a mammoth box of chocolates for Amy and a silver cigarette lighter for her father. Ben would not take it, but Glenn dropped it into his pocket and said: 'It's your birthday present. I didn't give you one.'

'I haven't had a birthday.'

'You must have had one last year. Everybody does.' He continued to be very friendly towards Ben, and Ben thawed out to the conclusion that Glenn had only thrown things at him because he had been disturbed while he was working. Priscilla told him that he had once thrown an inkwell at her when she had interrupted his work, even though it was to tell him that the boiler chimney was on fire.

The story conference was not held the next day and Ben never went to the film studio, since the war film was shelved because of objections from the War Office, but Ben and Amy stayed on in Hampstead. Amy was very happy, and Ben waited, with slightly less than his usual optimism, for something to turn up, and thought that she might as well stay happy until it did.

Chapter Twelve

GLENVILLE ROBERTS received many letters: from fans and amateur critics and cranks, from people who wanted something, and people who did not know what they wanted, but wrote just the same, querulously, as if the misdirection of their lives were vaguely Glenn's fault.

The choicer letters were answered by Glenn, dictating to Priscilla. Ben answered the others, for Priscilla was not allowed to compose. Ben dealt with the eccentrics and the beggars and the pests and the people who wanted Glenn to read their manuscripts, or wanted to sell him their life stories as material for a book.

One of the biggest pests was a girl called Esther Lovelace, who wrote about twice a week, crying: 'Oh, Mr Roberts, I must see you. It's urgent. Please let me come and see you. *You will never regret it.*'

Ben fobbed her off. He had to answer her letters, because the girl sounded so unbalanced that Glenn was afraid that she might commit suicide if he ignored her completely, and he might be involved at the inquest. There had been a case like that once, and because of the man's reputation, no one had believed that he had never laid eyes or hands on the dead woman.

One Friday, Glenn was working furiously against time to finish his Sunday article. He had known the subject all week, but he never wrote it until the last minute, and Ben had to take it to the newspaper office, since it was always too late to post it. Ben had already answered the telephone three times to the impatient Features Editor, and finally he went in to Glenn to tell him that a messenger from the newspaper had roared up the street on a motor-cycle and was waiting in the hall.

'Tell the bastard to go away. Or give him a beer, or some thing.'

'He doesn't want anything, and he's been told not to leave here without the copy. He's sitting in the hall with a crash helmet in his lap.'

Glenn groaned. 'How anyone is expected to write under these conditions . . . Get out of here, Ben. Bring me some coffee. No, make it a whisky. Tell Nellie to stop that infernal vacuum cleaner. Tell Amy to stop playing the piano. Don't they care if I go insane?'

By the time the article was finished, Amy and the cleaning woman were sulking, because they could not find anything to do that did not make Glenn shout for quiet, Mrs Bowstrom was angry because the lunch was spoiled, and the messenger had made several scratches in the polished wood of the hall floor by scraping his boots backwards and forwards. Priscilla was in tears because Glenn had flustered her into putting a carbon into the typewriter the wrong way round, and she had had to type the last page again with Glenn standing over her and swearing.

Everyone was upset, including the messenger, who had missed his lunch-hour. As Ben shut the front door behind him, Glenn came out of his room, with his hair on end and the top button of his trousers undone, and a girl in a green knitted cap came out of the little washroom under the curving stairs.

'How do you do?' She held out her hand to Glenn. 'I'm Esther Lovelace.'

Glenn did not shake hands. 'Why did you let her come here?' he asked Ben.

'Oh, he didn't.' The girl, who was small and plump, with a ladder in her stocking and strawberry lipstick smudged on her teeth, stood herself right in front of Glenn and looked up at him adoringly. 'The man on the motor-cycle let me in. I'd been watching from the garden of the empty house across the road. I often do that, to see you come out or go in.' She giggled. 'But suddenly today seemed like my lucky day – funny, on a Friday, when you think of it – so I knocked on the door and the man let me in and I hid in the w.c.'

'There's a public convenience a hundred yards away.' Glenn turned to go up the stairs, but she skipped before him and stood on the bottom step, blocking his way with one hand on the wall and the other on the banister.

'You are awful, Mr Roberts.' She giggled again. She had a simpering, freckled face with a sharp nose and swimmy brown eyes set too close together. 'I came to see you. Your letters have been so kind.'

Glenn glanced back and made a face at Ben.

'I can understand why you wouldn't give me an appointment to see you. You're afraid of your power over women. So am I.' Her hand on the banister trembled. 'But I came just the same, and so here I am, and now I've seen you in the flesh.'

'How do you like me?' Glenn became aware that the top of his trousers was unfastened, but did not bother to do anything about it. Once he had undone the button and let his stomach go, it was quite a struggle to do it up.

'I'm in love with you,' Esther Lovelace said. 'You know that.'

'Get her out of here, Ben.' Glenn pushed her aside quite roughly and went up the stairs.

Miss Lovelace stepped down into the hall like a sleep-walker, with her eyes swooning into space. 'He touched me,' she whispered. 'He touched me for the first time. I shall never forget this moment.'

She went out of the house without protest, and Ben saw her swaying away down the street, veering from side to side of the pavement. At the corner, she stepped off the kerb without looking, unaware of the car which swerved and hooted and almost killed her.

'Good thing if it had,' Glenn said, as they discussed her over lunch. 'Crazy woman. If you ever let her in here again, Ben, I'll shoot you. Amy, you remember that too. Don't ever open the door to a girl who looks like a lovesick ant-eater. If she telephones, I'm dead, or gone to Australia.'

'I don't think she'll come again,' Ben said. 'She's had her moment.'

'She will,' Amy said, without looking up from her food, 'and Glenn will see her.'

'I will not.'

'I bet you do. It's terribly flattering to have someone madly in love with you like that. You are a bit flattered, aren't you?'

'Precocious brat.' Glenn made a face at her. 'I am not.'

But he was, and he did see Esther Lovelace again. One afternoon when Ben had been out, he came in to find the green knitted cap and the limp fawn coat lying on a chair in the hall. The drawing-room was shut.

Ben shrugged his shoulders and went upstairs. Presently the front door banged, and looking out of the window, he saw Esther Lovelace tacking away down the street on her cider-bottle legs.

When Amy and Susanna came in from school, they ran upstairs to find him. 'Who's been here?' they asked. 'Glenn's asleep on the sofa in the drawing-room, and he's got pink lipstick on his face.'

Esther Lovelace did not come to the house again. She did not telephone, and there were no more letters. When Ben asked Glenville how he had managed to discard her, Glenn smiled in a foxy way and said: 'It's easy if you know how. Don't forget I've had plenty of practice in shaking off infatuated women.'

'You haven't managed to shake off Clara,' Ben said. 'She still wants to marry you.'

Clara had given him permission to say this if the occasion arose. She was a twice-divorced woman who had never been beautiful, even when she was on the right side of forty, and her pride, she said, had disappeared along with her second husband.

'Clara has her uses,' Glenn said. 'All women do.' Priscilla came into the room at that moment, and he made a tigerish face at her. She dropped her pencil and sat down with a bump and began to flutter through the leaves of her note-pad in a panic.

Ben was glad to be free of the hysterical letters from Esther Lovelace. He wondered how Glenn had managed to kiss her and get rid of her at the same time, but Priscilla told him that one evening on her way to an Indian restaurant in Soho with her father, who had to have curry once a week, she had seen Glenn coming out of a cinema with 'a poor-looking girl. Not his type at all. What do you make of that?'

'The same as you do, I suppose?'

'Oh, Commander Francis,' said Priscilla, who could not call anyone by their Christian name in less than a year's acquaintance, 'you never used to speak to me like that when you first came. I'm afraid you've lived too long with Mr Roberts.'

'You're right there.'

'You're not leaving?' Priscilla's watery eyes were alarmed. 'I'd hate to have to get used to someone new.'

'I can't stay here for ever. This isn't what I left the Navy for.'

'Mr Roberts won't let you go,' Priscilla said, pursing her small mouth. 'If there's any changes to be made, he likes to be the one who thinks of it. He was always complaining about Mrs Stokes – she was the daily woman we had before Nellie – and yet when she walked out because of the mess he made of his bathroom, you should have heard him carry on.'

'If I've gone, I shan't hear it.'

'No, but I shall.' Priscilla blinked at the thought of it. 'And where will you go, you and Amy? It's not easy to find a job when you've a child on your own. My sister Margaret –'

Priscilla had three sisters and could produce one to illustrate almost any situation. To halt the saga of the widowed Margaret, Ben said: 'We'll find something. We'll go hop-picking. Join a circus, perhaps.'

'Would you really?' Priscilla took this literally. 'I wish I had your nerve.'

Where would Ben and Amy go? It was a question to which

Ben gave a lot of inconclusive thought. Sitting in the front of the church at Geneva's wedding, his mind wandered away from the service to worry over the future of the child beside him, who sat bolt upright with her gloved hands clasped on the front of the pew, watching her grandmother with shining eyes. She and Susanna would be involved with weddings for many days after this.

Last night Ben and Amy had had dinner at Geneva's flat, without the Major, just like old times. Under the influence of the champagne Ben had brought, Geneva had beaded her mascara with a small dribble of tears and said how happy she was that they were so comfortably settled with Glenville Roberts.

'I would never go through with this otherwise,' she had said. 'I'm really fond of my old soak, apart from wanting so desperately to get rid of the name of Hogg, but you two come first with me, always.'

But Ben and Amy were fixed up satisfactorily, as far as she knew, and so she was going through with it, in a purple suit and hat, because purple was her best colour, although the Major had complained that she would look more like a funeral than a wedding.

'Mourning for my lost youth,' she told Ben, gripping his arm very tightly as they came into the church. 'But I feel a lot younger today than the day I married Arthur.' She straightened the little spotted veil over her eyes and advanced bravely up the aisle on incredible heels to where the Major, splendid in sponge-bag trousers and lavender waistcoat, awaited her with braced legs, sober as a judge.

Geneva had had him watched all morning by the best man. Although the best man had neglected to watch himself, and was swaying gently from foot to foot, the Major stood as if he were on the parade ground, and rapped out his responses with all the pride which filled his sentimental old heart because he and Geneva were going to share the last chapter of their lives together.

The following week, Ben went after a job in the personnel division of a firm near Oxford, and failed to get it because another naval officer was in ahead of him. Returning to London, he found Glenn and several friends having drinks and sandwiches before going on to a first night.

'Where have you been?' Glenn asked.

'It's my day off.' Ben was tired from the train journey on top of the disappointment. 'I don't have to tell you where I've been.'

Clara, who was always ready to fill an awkward silence, laughed a little too shrilly, and the others pretended to talk again.

'Have a drink,' Glenn said, with a touch of condescension. 'You'll feel better.'

'No, thanks. I'm going up to see Amy.'

'She's not here. She's spending the week-end with Susanna.'

'I didn't tell her she could go.'

'Oh, that's all right.' Glenn waved a sandwich at him. 'I told her.'

'Since when –' Ben saw the interested faces, amused at the sight of a row brewing between Glenn and his sailor. He shut his mouth and went out of the room.

When the party had gone, with a lot of noise in the street about who was going in whose car, Ben came downstairs again and finished what was left in the cocktail shaker. He was furious with Glenn. Whose child was it, anyway? He remembered all the times when Glenn had sided with Amy in some small dispute with her father, flattering her, joking with her when it was something that should be discussed seriously, trying to make Ben look like a kill-joy parent.

Tomorrow he would inform him who was going to run Amy's life, and in terms that Glenn would understand. He thought of the night when he had almost hit him with the thermos flask, and felt a sensation in his hands that told him it might be a very satisfying experience to take a poke at Glenville Roberts.

Mrs Bowstrom had gone home, so Ben found a cold leg of chicken and was gnawing at it thoughtfully, standing by the kitchen table, when the front door-bell shrilled on the wall above his head.

Wiping his mouth and his hands, Ben went to open the door, and found Esther Lovelace with a pictorial scarf of London over her head and her soggy eyes full of tears, which spilled over as soon as he spoke to her and ran down the channels between her long nose and her freckled cheeks.

Ben did not want to bring her in, but he could not leave her crying on the step. 'Here, now.' He guided her into the drawing-room. 'This won't do. Take off your coat and tell me what's the matter.'

She was too distraught to take off her coat or her scarf, on which a crude representation of Big Ben stuck out in a peak at the back of her head. She sat hunched-up on a footstool, looking like a refugee, and cried in a very ugly way, with words wailing out in half-coherent bursts through a wet, square mouth.

The old, familiar story. Ben had heard it once or twice from his crew's pick-ups, but he had never had it told to him by a fat, hysterical girl in a bunched-up raincoat and blunt-toed shoes, whose abandoned bawling was more childish than tragic.

Where had it happened? 'Not in here?' Ben remembered the girls' description of Glenn asleep with the strawberry lipstick on his face, and felt that if Esther nodded he would jump up from the sofa and never be able to sit on it again.

'Oh, no.' Esther glanced at the sofa with almost as much aversion as Ben had thought of it. In her room. A furnished room near Shepherd's Bush. 'Twice. The second time, the land-lady asked me to move. It hasn't been easy to find another room I can afford.'

'Do you want money?'

She shook her head. Her tears were drying up to intermittent gasps and sobs.

'Then why are you telling me this?' There could only be one reason. 'Are you –?' Ben cleared his throat. She did not help him, and he had to ask the whole question.

Sniffing, she shook her head violently again, and Big Ben twitched from side to side like a puppy's tail.

'What's the trouble then?' He got up and went to the other end of the room, not wanting to look any more at Esther's ruined and swollen face. 'You can't accuse Mr Roberts of assault. After all, you asked for it by coming here in the first place.'

'You mean he behaves like that with every woman who

admires him?' She was either criminally naïve or criminally insincere.

'No, you idiot.' The answer might be Yes, but Ben supposed that he was paid to be loyal. 'But you did, sort of, offer yourself.'

'Oh, I know I did.' She swivelled round on the stool to face him. 'I'm not complaining about *that*.' For a moment, her face was transfixed in the blank rapture with which it had left the house the day Glenn had pushed her on the stairs. Then it crumpled, and if her tear ducts had not been milked dry, she would have cried again. 'It's just that ever since – what I told you – he won't see me any more. I don't know what to do. He threatened to set the police on me if I tried to get in touch with him.'

'Why don't you leave him alone? If I was a girl – thank God I'm not – I wouldn't let him make a fool out of me.' Ben locked his jaws to smother a yawn. He wished that she would go. He was sorry for her, because she was such a fool, but it was a bit much to be playing True Confessions at the end of a depressing day. Damn Glenn. Was this one of the duties of his private secretary – to clean up the debris of his careless follies?

'I can't help it.' Esther stood up, her raincoat bulging above and below the twisted belt like bags of dirty laundry. 'I'm in love with him. You know that. I was before, and I'm even more so now.' She came over and put her hand with the bitten nails on Ben's sleeve, and pulled gently, like a child asking for attention. 'You must help me. You seem so kind. The only one in this house who is. That typist. I've never seen her, but I know she's in love with him too.'

'Priscilla? She hates him.'

'No, she doesn't. He told me.' Since Esther came into the house she had not once mentioned Glenn by name. 'She'd scratch my eyes out as soon as look at me. You're the only one who can help me. It was you I came to see tonight. Not him. I'd been waiting in the garden across the road. I saw you come in, then I saw him go out with all his fine friends,' she put her long nose in the air, 'and I knew it was my chance.'

We'll have to have the street patrolled with police dogs. 'Your chance for what?' Ben asked. 'I can't help you. I'm Mr

184

Roberts' secretary, not his conscience. Look here – have a drink, won't you?' He needed one himself. He released his arm from her clinging hand and went to the glass trolley where the bottles were.

Esther refused as if he had offered her poison, but he poured a stiff whisky for himself, and downed half of it before she came over to put her damp little hand on him again.

'I want you to be my friend,' she said, turning her eyes up at him so that the whites showed. 'I'd be a nice companion for you. He told me you haven't got a girl. I dance nicely too. Classic, of course, I don't jive, but I don't suppose you do either.'

'Why not?' Ben resented the inference that he was out of date. 'I only jive,' he lied.

'We needn't go dancing then, but we could go out together. That way I'd still be near him. I knew a girl who was jilted by a man, so she took up with his best friend and got engaged to him, and that made the first man so jealous that he wanted her back. Do you see?'

Ben saw. He drank the rest of the whisky and picked up the decanter again. 'Nothing doing,' he said.

'Why not? Don't you like me?' She tilted her fleshy chin and stuck out her bosom at him. She had no idea how unattractive she was.

'Of course,' he said nervously. 'You're a very sweet girl, but you're much too young for me – and for Mr Roberts too.'

'I'm old in experience – now,' Esther Lovelace said, dropping her voice darkly and moving closer.

Trapped in the corner between the trolley and the arm of the sofa, Ben tried to fight his way out by saying: 'I have got a girl. I'm engaged. I'm going to be married.'

'Who to?' The brown eyes sharpened, moving closer together. 'Not to Rose Kelly. I know that's over. He told me about that too.'

'I'm surprised he didn't tell you about – about Marigold then, since he's told you so much about everyone else's business.'

'I don't believe you,' Esther said. 'It's not fair to tell me lies. I thought you were a naval officer, and so honourable.'

'I was. I'm not now.' Ben put down his drink. The whisky was not helping him. He wanted only to go to bed. 'You'd

185

better go,' he told her. 'It's late, and I'm tired.' He began to manoeuvre her towards the door.

'I'm tired too,' she said listlessly. 'I haven't slept properly for days.' She dragged her feet, scuffing the juvenile shoes into the rug. Ben was beginning to feel sorry for her again, when in the hall, she grabbed his hand and squeezed it. 'Meet me tomorrow night,' she whispered, although there was no one else in the house. 'The tube station at Piccadilly. Seven o'clock.'

'No,' he said, and tried to pull his hand away, but she squeezed it tighter and said: 'If you don't come, I'll come here. He can't object if it's you I've come to see.'

Ben jerked his hand away and let her go to the door by herself. As she opened it, she turned and said with a thin, smug smile. 'Seven o'clock. I'll be waiting. I have a feeling you and I are going to be very good friends.'

When the door had closed behind her, Ben dragged himself up the stairs. His head felt as if it were hollow, and inside it, a lonely voice was shouting: 'Help!'

He did not tackle Glenn about Amy or about Esther Lovelace the next morning. He woke still tired, and he had not the strength to tell the man what he thought of him. Instead he announced that he was going to take next week's day off today, and although Glenn refused, he walked out of the house and made for Waterloo Station.

It would mean a fight when he got back, but there would be a fight anyway, because he was going to tell Glenn that he was through. First, he was going down to Southampton to ask his mother if she would take Amy for a while.

Poor Amy. He hated to do this to her when she was so happy. It would have been better if they had never gone to Hampstead. He should never have taken the job. Flattered into it, he supposed, and it had seemed a sensational climax to his farewell scene with Rose. What a fool he was. A fool and a failure. What had happened to all the high ideas and ambitions with which he had left the Navy? Six months out, and he had not had the smell of a decent job. All he had done was to walk out of the only jobs he had found. A quitter, that was what he was. A quitter. The Navy had been right to discard him.

186

The thought of explaining to his mother and father, and of their undisguised disappointment in him was unbearable. When he telephoned to say that he was coming, his mother had forced surprise into her voice as she recognized him, and said: 'Well, you're such a stranger, I hardly recognized your voice.'

When he asked if he could come down, she had said: 'You know your father and I just live for your visits, but I thought you were so busy that you couldn't get away to see us.'

'Well, I'm not busy today.' Ben had managed a polite good-bye and rung off, grinding his teeth.

To satisfy his parents, he had given them a rather grandiose picture of his job with Glenn. Now they would be disappointed in him, either for having thrown away a good chance, or for having originally been deceived into thinking it was a good chance. Either way they would be heartsick, and his mother would only pick at her lunch. They would be glad to have Amy, but in a triumphant way. They might not actually say: 'I told you so,' but they would imply it, and after he had left, they would talk about it with nodding heads, and his mother would ring people up and say: 'The child should have come here in the first place.'

Poor little Amy, playing so happily with Susanna. Playing at weddings, perhaps, in sheets and cheese-cloth veils, with no idea of what was brewing for her. She ought to hate him for this, but she would not, because she would try to understand, and that was more than he deserved. He was a failure as a father as well as a civilian. She trusted him, and he had let her down.

He felt so dispirited that he did not think he could bear to look today at the house by the railway which seemed to embody the security of generations of settled family life; a house where children who had made a mess of things could always find a refuge, and someone to take their side.

If he could have taken Amy back to a house like that. . . . He pictured the stucco bleakness of Wavecrest, Firbanks Avenue, on to whose cement doorstep he would soon be putting his reluctant foot. The contrast was too painful. He would not look out of the window. But as the landmarks approached and passed him, the yellow house at the level crossing, the gravel pit, the patch of fir trees, he found himself leaning forward automatically.

The nearest meadow was dark with lush grass. They were growing it for hay. On the broken paving outside the back door, the older girl in a white overall was washing a dog in a zinc tub. As the train went by, she looked up, tossed back her hair and did a thing she had never done before. She waved. The soapy dog jumped out of the bath-tub and then the house came between, and the side of the bridge, and it was all gone.

Why had she waved and smiled? Because it was warm in the sun and she was doing something she liked? Because she was happy today and felt friendly to everyone, even the unknown dolls being rushed south-westwards above her?

The wave was for Ben. When the train stopped at Basingstoke, he got out, convinced the ticket collector that there was sanity in not travelling as far as his ticket entitled him, found a garage and hired a self-drive car. He paid the deposit with the money he had brought to forestall anything his mother might think but not say about the extra expense of having Amy. He drove to the small station which came next on the line to the house, then using his navigator's sense, he found the narrow road which ran past the house and under the railway.

He sat outside the gate for a moment, taking in the unfamiliar view of the garden hedge and the railway bridge, and the part of the flinty road he had never seen before, running under the arch and away round a corner on the far side of the line. He almost drove straight on. He turned the ignition key, then turned it back, got out of the car and walked quickly up the uneven drive before he could lose his nerve.

It was strange to see the house from this angle, an eye-level instead of a bird's-eye view. It was higher than he had thought, and the gables and odd-shaped chimneys were not so apparent. The lawn did not look so patchy as it seemed from above, or perhaps the father had been giving it more care this spring.

A bicycle was leaning against the shallow brick porch, its back wheel partly across the doorway. The front door was open, and beyond a small lobby filled with coats and sticks and boots. Ben saw the hall for the first time, wide and rather dark, with many doors and passage leading from it, and a fireplace untidy with last winter's ashes and the charred ends of logs.

There was a good smell. Not an exquisite country house smell of flowers, or lavender or furniture polish, but a homely smell compounded of many things, like roasting meat and leather and dogs and laundry soap.

Ben stepped round the bicycle wheel and pressed the knob of the large brass bell. It did not ring. He tried the knocker, and at least three dogs began to bark from the back of the house. The tall girl came out of a doorway with her eyebrows raised, and put on a stiff, polite smile when she saw it was a stranger. She was still wearing the white overall. It was dirty in the front, and the sleeves were rolled up over arms that were awkwardly long, with prominent elbows. As she came into the lobby, she tripped over the curling corner of a rug, blushed, pushed back her straight tawny hair, and said: 'C-can I help you?'

She added as an afterthought, as if she had been told all her life not to keep people on the step, but was always forgetting it: 'Please come in.'

Ben stepped over the low stone sill. He was in at last. Now he had to say something. He grinned, feeling the grin un-natural, and said: 'I'm afraid I've lost my way. Can you tell me where the Martins live?' It was the only thing he could think of that would give him an excuse for at least a few minutes' conversation.

He wished that it had been the pretty younger sister with the curly hair who had come to the door. She would have answered him easily and smiled, liking to meet new people, and perhaps taken him into the hall and asked him to sit down while she tried to think who the Martins were. Impossible ill-luck if they should be dearest neighbours, and someone should insist on telephoning to say that their good friend Ben was on his way.

The tall girl stood shyly in front of him, her feet rooted to the stone floor, frowning and not knowing what to say. 'The Martins,' she said finally. 'I don't think I –'

A barking yellow dog with long matted hair like Nana in Peter Pan erupted into the hall, scattered rugs, and hurled itself at Ben's shoes. The girl took hold of its collar and held it panting, while she turned to appeal to the man who followed the dog. It was the father, older than he had looked from a distance, with a thin, grizzled moustache on a long upper lip, and only a fringe of hair round the bottom of his skull. Ben had never before seen him without a cap. He wore a tweed jacket with leather patches, a shrunken wool tie, and creaseless flannels held round his concave waist with a cracked leather belt.

'It's someone looking for someone called Martin,' the girl told him. Her voice held the remnants of a confused schoolgirl gabble.

'Martin ... Martin ...' The father scratched his bald skull which was the colour of scorched paper. 'Doesn't mean anything to me at the moment. What's the address? Come in, come in. We'll try to help you.'

The girl stepped back, still hanging on to the dog, who was quiet now, trying to lick the hand that held him. 'I don't know the exact address, sir,' Ben said, stealing glances round the hall to see as much as possible before he had to go. 'They only gave me directions. About three miles from the village, and up a hill and down a hill – you know the sort of vague things people tell you when they know a place well themselves.'

'The vaguest person I know around here is – got it!' The father showed his long, ugly false teeth in a surprised smile. 'Up a hill and down a hill. The Mortons, of course. Ella, you got the name wrong.'

'I didn't,' she said gruffly, as if it mattered. Why? She was about thirty. Perhaps she had lived too long at home.

'No, I did say Martin,' he explained. 'I must have read the signature wrong. Good thing you told me before I got there.'

'Why?' asked the father inquisitively. 'Are you going after the job? Forgive my curiosity. Been my weakness all my life, but when you live in a dead end like this, with the chariots of the Southern Region your only contact with civilization, you want to know everything that's going on. And of course we have an interest in the school, because of Ella.'

The girl mumbled something.

'She's the housekeeper there,' her father said, and the girl bent to stroke the dog, as if she did not like to be talked about. 'Does a good job, too, as you'll find out, if they take you on. Navy, aren't you?' Ben was wearing a blazer with naval buttons, because his father liked to see him in it.

190

'Ex-Navy, sir.'

'You're in, my boy. There's a snob appeal about having a retired officer as bursar of an outfit like that.'

So it wasn't teaching. And it wasn't a girls' school. You wouldn't have a male bursar for a girls' school. Nor a teacher either, for that matter, but Ben had not had time to think of that. This is Commander Francis, our new bursar. The headmaster would like to use his rank. Ben saw himself on Speech Day, making his number with mothers in garden-party hats. What did a bursar do that Ben could not do? He could find out, at least.

'How do I get there?' he asked. 'How do I get to the school?'

Chapter Thirteen

IT was the tinned beetroot that started it. Mrs Morton was such an unpalatable woman that if she were mixed up in some small racket, it was fitting that her hand should finally be called over something like tinned beetroot.

The trustees of Greenbriars Preparatory School for Boys lived too far away, or were too richly disinterested or too senile to question the staff appointments made by the headmaster. This was lucky for Ben, who had got in on his own bluff and the character references supplied by the Flimsies of his Confidential Reports. It had also been lucky for Mrs Morton. As headmaster's wife, she held the post of dietitian, for no better reason than that she had told her husband to appoint her, and he had made up his mind twenty years ago that his only chance of happiness was to let her have her own way.

Ben discovered the tinned beetroot when he was taking his inventory of stores, which common sense and his naval training told him was one of his first jobs as bursar. If old Hammerhead, as he had already learned to call the headmaster, who had a claw-like nose and a bony knob at the back of his skull, wanted him to save the school from financial ruin, the first thing was to check on their tangible assets.

'Stores are money,' he told Tilly Wicket, the cook, who was

as wide as she was high, but more active than any of her dispirited kitchen helpers.

'I dare say, but it's an awkward time to come into my kitchen.' Tilly was drinking tea at a scrubbed kitchen table in the lull between lunches gone and teas and suppers to start; but this was her normal greeting for anyone who did not come into her kitchen to work. 'Him that was here before you never wanted to pry into my stockroom at all hours.' Tilly never gave a name to Mr Butterick, the late bursar, who had departed under a veil, as yet unlifted by Ben. He was reminded of Esther Lovelace, and her refusal to speak the name of Glenville Roberts.

'If he had, it might have been better for everyone. No offence, Miss Wicket, but –'

'Everyone calls me Tilly,' she snapped. 'Even you.'

'No offence, Tilly, but all this stuff has been paid for by the school. I must know what our assets are.'

'You're talking very legal,' Tilly said, pouring a cup of tea for him from a pot she had made for herself which would hold enough for twelve, 'but it'll rub off. I've seen all kinds. Masters. *Mensana incorporate sano*, one of them said to me once after the corned beef went bad. Nurses. Matrons, they call themselves, although none of them could hold their own in a stand-up fight with Miss Welsh up at the hospital, where my mother is. I've had them come in here turning over my pans, hoping to find last week's scrambled egg on the bottom, and looking under my stove as if they expected to find dead mice. "You won't find them there," I told them. "In the flour bin's the place to look." I've had nurses. Don't you take sugar? Well, it takes all sorts. But things have quieted down in that department now that we've got Mrs Horrocks. She's not much of a nurse, as those poor little boys could have told you when the flu hit us like old Nasty himself, but she's a master's wife and they'd have to keep her anyway, so it saves the keep of one, and she gets a cushy job.'

'Well, we must economize,' Ben said heartily, seizing the opportunity to get back to the subject of stores. 'Thanks for the tea, and now if you'd just unlock the stockroom –'

'Don't make me laugh.' Tilly looked at him as if he had said something absurd. 'There isn't even a lock on that door, let alone a key.'

She pushed herself to her feet and led the way with her brisk, rolling walk, which listed her vast hips from side to side like shifting cargo in a rough sea. Following her, Ben took out the black notebook in which he was recording all the things he hoped to get done, and wrote: 'Lock and key for stores.' He had seen the kitchen helpers. Two of them were permanent but shifty. The other two were transient dish-washers, who were replaced at frequent intervals by the unemployment office when they fled in the night, taking heaven knew what with them.

He had not been in the stockroom ten minutes before he was back in the kitchen. 'Miss Wicket – Tilly. What on earth are all those tins of beetroot? There must be five dozen of them.'

Tilly was marshalling her vegetable helper for the potato salad. 'Very nourishing,' she said, tight-lipped. She did not talk in front of the Help.

'Who eats tinned beetroot?'

'The boys.' She shooed him with her apron back into the stone passage that led to the stockroom. 'If they're hungry enough,' she added in a lower voice. 'But I don't often have the heart to serve it.'

'Why did you buy it?'

'Don't look at me. Mrs Morton bought it. She does all the ordering. The grocer and the butcher and them send up every day to get the list. Of course she pads it, and don't think they stop her. "We've a lovely line of tinned beets", Mr Pears will say when he's got some cases he can't shift on to anyone else. He often comes up himself for My Lady's order. Oh, yes, they're *very* good friends. Don't ask me how those big boxes of chocolates and fruit get into Mrs Morton's rooms, not to mention that case of whisky last Christmas. Just don't ask me, that's all.'

Having told Ben what he needed to know without being asked, Tilly trundled back into the kitchen, calling out in a costermonger's voice to the dreamy girl who was standing by the chopping board with her mouth open and the knife poised motionless in her hand, as if she were in the castle of the Sleeping Beauty.

Ben went back to his office, which was a small room, still cluttered with the impedimenta his predecessor had not bothered to remove, on the ground floor of what was called the Old Building. This was the original square stone manor house which stood a quarter of a mile back from the road in its own small park, while goal posts and bowling screens and practice nets and a cinder running track now adorned the gentle slopes where cattle or deer had once grazed under the ancient oaks.

The house had been extended at the back with two new wings which did not match it. The stables and coach-house had been converted into classrooms. A gymnasium, an assembly hall, and masters' houses had been added at various times and in various styles to complete what was now one of the most expensive and possibly the worst-run preparatory school in the south of England.

In his office, Ben prepared a Fleet Order, which he circulated to all departments. Henceforth all requisition forms must be signed by him before anything was purchased, from a bottle of Worcester sauce to a set of new tyres for the small bus which conveyed boys to and from the station and was known locally as the Black Maria, because the boys travelling from the station in it always looked so miserable.

During those last difficult days in Hampstead, when Glenville sulked and Esther Lovelace hovered in the garden across the road like a virulent germ, Ben had slipped out through the back door and over the wall to pay a visit to Peale and Beckett at the Services Investment Association. Nicely set up now with a less squeamish lieutenant-commander canvassing the dockyards for them, they welcomed Ben and gladly offered advice.

'You're the only businessmen I know,' he told them, while Mitzi perched on the edge of Jake's desk and listened, with a wad of chewing gum in one side of her slack jaw. 'Give me a few tips. This is the best chance I've had. If I don't make a go of it, I'll re-enlist as an ordinary seaman.'

'Always glad to help an old colleague,' Jake had said, picking his teeth delicately with a slim gold instrument. 'You've been engaged to make this small boys' penitentiary show a profit, or else. Elementary. I wish I had your chance.'

Beckett and Peale had never been bursars of a school, but

they viewed the problem from the other side – what they would do if they were on the staff, with the opportunity to make a little gravy on the side. 'I can't recall ever giving this advice to anyone before,' Jake said, 'but I give it to you now, Benjamin. Be dead honest yourself. Be dead honest, but don't expect anyone else to be. Nail 'em down. Don't give 'em any rope.'

'Run it Navy style, I would,' Jimmy Peale said. 'That's all you know, anyway, old boy. Let's face it. Mitzi, get the glasses and let's crack a bottle to good old Ben's success in the seats of higher learning.'

As he typed out his Fleet Order, which he had to copy several times, because he could not find any carbon, Ben could hear Jake's flat northern voice: 'Don't give 'em any rope.' From what the book-keeper had shown Ben of last year's accounts, too much rope had been given for too long. The expenses of the school were even more staggering than the fees. Small wonder, when a dozen different people were ordering food, text-books, stationery, sports equipment, garden supplies, and the pay-roll was swollen with incubi like Mrs Morton, who was undoubtedly not the only one who was making a good thing out of it.

Not Ella, of course. There was nothing, except muddle, wrong with the housekeeping department. Ella Halliday, her name was. Ben had sometimes thought that if he ever learned the name of the family in the house by the railway, it would spoil the magic. Now he knew their name, but the magic still held. He could not wait to get back into the house.

The headmaster, nervously crossing and uncrossing his small, pointed feet, and squinting towards the finger which rubbed at the perpetually red bridge of his hooked nose, had told Ben that if the school's expenses were not cut down, he would have to appeal for donations among the capitalist parents. All the parents were rich, but some were capitalists, which was Mr Morton's word for having more money than was good for you.

'Think how shaming! There are those who could buy us out tomorrow without feeling the draught, but charity's a different matter.' He took his hand away from his nose to choose a curly pipe from the lopsided pipe-rack which one of the boys had made in Handicrafts, and his eyes straightened out again, blinking weakly, as if he needed glasses. 'I'd lose prestige. That is, the school would. There might be boys removed. Our best boys.'

'The sons of the capitalists?'

'Please, Commander.' Old Hammerhead blew down his nose like a horse. 'I don't want cynicism from you. I want your help. My last bursar failed me ... rather badly, I'm afraid.' He dropped his head and fumbled with the pipe, scattering shreds of tobacco on the desk. 'Chap called Butterick. He thought less of doing his job than of – well, no matter. Suffice it to say that he let me down. He dropped the torch. I look to you to pick it up, to raise the flag of Greenbriars on high. . . .' He wandered vaguely off into a maze of chivalrous exhortations with which he had been appealing ineffectually for years to boys who seemed to have less and less team spirit as the terms went by.

Whatever his scholastic endowments, Old Hammerhead was, as one of the boys had recorded in linesman's chalk on the back wall of the lavatories, a prize drip. He was actually also a brilliant classical scholar, and the boys who came from Greenbriars were usually a year ahead of their age when they went on to public school.

This sort of thing pleased the parents, although it would not do the average boy much good in later years when he had forgotten most of the Latin and Greek he had ever learned and remembered only that he had had to work too hard too young.

The standard in all subjects was high, and the parents of boys whose work persistently fell below a certain level were politely informed that the school would be a better place without them. This put a great strain on the dull boys, especially those whose parents' ambition was as swollen as their wallets, but it gave the school the kind of intellectual snob appeal which ensured that for every boy pushed out there were ten waiting to get in.

Throwing out the dead wood had been Mrs Morton's idea to raise the school's prestige. Her husband would not have thought of it by himself, for he rather liked boys, and even felt a mild pity when he had to give one of them back to his chagrined parents. Neither the liking nor the pity, however, was strong enough to support him in a stand against his wife. If she said a boy had to go, he went.

Feeling rather like a substandard boy himself, Ben knocked at the entrance to Mrs Morton's apartment and waited, shuffling his feet. When she summoned him, he went inside and found her standing up at the telephone in the little hall, with her black hair dragged into a netted doughnut at the back of her narrow head.

'I can't talk any more,' she told the telephone, not politely, as if she did not want to keep Ben waiting, but insultingly, as if he were an eavesdropper. He could not step back because the door was behind him, and as she turned round quickly, the rubber-tipped cane she held under her arm caught him a dragging blow across the ribs.

This cane, with which she supported a limping gait, went everywhere with her and was like another limb. With it, she pointed at boys who were running in places where they should have walked, poked holes in flower-beds and sometimes through the crown of plants while she harangued the gardener, and thumped on the ceiling of her apartment when one of the older boys, who lodged above, gave forth the sort of adolescent guffaw she hated, or put on the kind of gramophone record she despised.

The two bachelor masters, Willis and Knight, who were indifferent to most women, but actively averse to Mrs Morton, were prepared to swear that they had seen her walking as sound as a bell when she thought no one was looking. The boys claimed that she had been lamed for life when Old Hammerhead had thrown two volumes of the Latin dictionary at her and knocked her down the stairs. Mrs Horrocks, the matron, who was not only charitable, but liked to air medical knowledge, credited her with a congenital hip. Amy, after seeing the gross ginger cat which crouched all day jammed up against the glass of Mrs Morton's front window like an overblown geranium, said that the cane was a broomstick.

Whatever the truth, the cane achieved one purpose in making a nuisance of itself in any room in which it appeared. It tripped people up. It jabbed itself on to unwary toes. It hung perilously on the edges of the furniture and fell with a clatter as soon as someone reached the point of a story. Tucked under Mrs Morton's arm, if she turned round suddenly it was liable to whack you in the chest, as it had just done to Ben.

'I'm sorry,' she said, watching him straighten his coat as if she did not like the material. 'What can I do for you?'

'I don't know.' Ben was a little afraid of her cold, dark eye, which had a shallow, unfocused look, like a bird, but he was determined not to show it, although she looked as if she knew already. 'You sent one of the boys for me, and so here I am.'

Although the Mortons' private rooms were on the ground floor of the Old Building, she would never step across the hall to Ben's office. She would rather go ten times as far looking for a boy to fetch him, so that she could have the advantage of having summoned Ben and of being on her own ground.

'Busy as I am,' he ventured to add, for the boy's message had been 'Mrs Morton wants to see you immediately', as if she thought he had nothing else to do.

She ignored this. Limping with sideways thrusts of her cane which shifted two small rugs slightly to the right – would she push them back again when she went the other way? – Mrs Morton led Ben into the drawing-room, looked about for the most uncomfortable chair and offered it to him. She hooked her stick on the corner of the mantelpiece and sat down facing him.

She sat very upright, and the front of her plain linen dress was as flat as the back; flatter perhaps, because she had protruding shoulder-blades. She was not a bad-looking woman, but her hair was dragged back so tightly that it hurt to look at the skin round her temples, and she had a curious lack of expression, like a woman asleep with her eyes open. Waiting for her to speak, Ben imagined what it would be like if he suddenly fell on her and kissed her. It would be like grabbing a telephone pole. He could not imagine Old Morton, with his ducking, nervous gestures, ever getting up the nerve to embrace her. Perhaps he never had. They had no children.

'I don't suppose,' Mrs Morton said, in her flat, composed voice, 'that you are surprised that I sent for you?'

'Surprised?' Ben cleared his throat. 'Well, not exactly.' He had known that she would not like his instructions about the requisition forms. 'But I'm always glad of the chance of a chat

198

with you, of course.' No harm in trying to keep on the right side of her. Everyone in this place who wanted to keep their job knew that.

'This is not a chat,' said Mrs Morton, coming straight to the point before he could waste her time with flattery. 'It's a protest.'

'Against what?' As if he did not know.

'Against the impertinent note which you gave to my maid.' It was not her maid. It was Lucy, one of the school housemaids, who flicked through Mrs Morton's room when she had the time. 'No doubt,' said Mrs Morton, managing to look at him and through him at the same time, 'you thought you were quite a somebody in the Navy, with people saluting you every five yards, but I've been the dietitian here for ten years, and I'll not submit to changing my methods purely to satisfy your vanity.'

'It's not a question of my vanity. It's a question of economic efficiency. As I see it,' he leaned forward with his wrists between his knees and gave her a candid look, trying to make her believe that he was willing to discuss this thing sincerely, 'the only way to cut the appalling expenses is to have a central purchasing department.'

'That's you, I suppose. Forgive my curiosity, but how many schools were you employed in before you came to us?'

Ben sat back and stopped looking candid.

'Exactly,' said Mrs Morton. 'And yet you propose to decide how much we need of any given item. Well, I don't know what the others think about it,' she said, although she had undoubtedly discussed it with them and told them what they should think, 'but I for one don't like it.'

She leaned back in her chair as if the interview was over as far as she was concerned. Without mentioning chocolates or whisky, Ben tried to explain to her the advantage of centralized purchasing, but she closed her ears like a Civil Servant at the Admiralty being asked to consider the advantages of the Ministry of Supply.

Emboldened by the thought of the tinned beetroot rotting on the shelves, Ben stood up. 'I'm sorry,' he said, 'but this is the way it has to be. I was taken on to help cut down the expenses of this school, and I'm going to do it, just as I would have cut down the expenses of a ship under my command if I was ordered to.'

Mrs Morton smiled at him. Her smile was thin-lipped and almost sweet. It turned her eyes into half-moons. 'Don't talk so pompously,' she said. 'This is a school, not a ship.'

Thrown off his balance by the sudden softening of her voice, he flung at her: 'I wish it was a ship! I'd be able to do things right without an argument at every turn. I've had to fight with half the masters over this, not to mention the groundsman, and Mr Harbutt, who seems to have been playing fast and loose with the parents' money and the school funds for years.' It would do her no harm to know that he was investigating the games master's deals in cricket bats and boxing gloves. It might shake her.

She was not shaken. She looked up at him impassively, with the smile gone, but he caught the mocking shadow of it in her eyes. For an instant, he saw how she might look with the net and the pins yanked out and the black hair tumbling round that damned mask of a face. Then his vision cleared and he saw her as she was, a woman whose hair no one but a madman or a drunk would ever pull down, and he said curtly: 'If you've made out your grocery order for today, I'll take it while I'm here. I'm going into town to see the man myself and tell him that if he can't give us a better deal, I'll look for someone who can.'

'Mr Pearse? You can't do that. He's served this school for years.'

'That's the trouble. He's had it all his own way. I'm going to see all these dealers. Sharpen your pencils, boys, I'll say. There's going to be some competition.'

'Please don't rehearse it in my drawing-room,' Mrs Morton said. 'I'm getting a headache. You'll have to go.' She moistened her straight lips and turned her head from side to side with unusual nervousness, as if she thought there was someone behind her chair.

'I'll be glad to,' Ben said, and meant it, 'but I must insist that you give me your list.'

He put some force into his voice, expecting her to refuse. When she said tonelessly: 'Did I say that I wouldn't?' he was

200

left feeling as if he had swung for a tremendous tee-shot and missed the ball.

She seemed suddenly to have lost interest. Was this her way of deflating him, to pretend that an issue was unimportant if she was not winning? 'Help me up.' She put out a cold hand, laid it in his palm and got up with scarcely any pressure on it. 'My cane.' He handed it to her, and she went to the desk on the other side of the room, with a slow limp that looked so exaggerated that Ben could not even be sure if she was limping on the right side.

She handed him the long requisition form as if it was last week's newspaper to light the fire with. He was on his way out of the room when an item at the bottom of the list caught his eye, and he stopped and turned back. Got her. He had got her cold.

'Tinned beetroot,' he said triumphantly. 'Two dozen of it. No, you can't, Mrs Morton. You absolutely can't.'

'Why not?' She was standing by the desk with her back to the light, thin and unbendable, watching him go. 'It's very nutritious.'

'But the stockroom is loaded with the stuff. I've just taken an inventory.'

'An inventory?' She leaned heavily on the stick, so that one shoulder was tilted sharply above the other. 'There was no need for that. I made one myself at the beginning of term.'

'I've never seen it. I had to make my own, in any case. Basic logistics, Mrs Morton. You can't argue with the Book.'

'*Mister* Francis,' she said – everyone else called him Commander – 'I begin to see why the Navy didn't keep you.'

'I saw that long ago,' Ben said, not minding, because of the beetroot. 'Why do you think it was?'

She did not answer. Her silhouette against the window, dim on this bright day because the house had been built in that sun-shy period when all the best rooms faced north, was motionless.

Ben turned and went to the door. Before he opened it, he took out a pencil, rested the grocery list against the wall, quite high up, so that Mrs Morton could see what he was doing, and drew a thick line through the tinned beetroot.

Amy was outside the door, waiting for him. 'War to the knife,' he told her.

'Oh, good. Who's winning?'

'I am, at the moment. She probably will in the end. That sort always does.'

'Oh, Daddy, don't!' Amy flung herself at his arm, twisting both her own arms round it, so that her feet dragged sideways as they walked across the stone entrance-hall. 'Don't say things like that. You've got to be tops at this so we can stay here.'

'Why?' He stopped and looked down at her. 'Do you like it so much? You hated changing schools, I know, and it isn't especially homey for us, living with the Glynns.'

'It's all right. The Glynns do try, and I'll get used to the school. Daddy, don't you see? We've got to stay somewhere. Not keep moving about like refugees.'

Her words were like a penance for his failures. He was going to say something serious and loving, when her strained expression suddenly lifted to a friendly grin, and she waved and whistled through her teeth at a boy who was crossing the gallery at the top of the stairs.

The boy whistled back, glanced behind him and ran out of sight.

Mrs Morton was not the only one who objected to Ben trying to run Greenbriars School like a ship. Almost all the staff, except Tilly Wicket and Ella, who were on Ben's side, complained to Mr Morton. Instead of backing him up, Old Hammerhead had sent for Ben and told him: 'Go a little easy, Commander Francis. Some of my teaching staff have been here for years, and it isn't easy for them to accept new ideas. Rome wasn't built in a day, you know.' Accustomed to using more esoteric clichés in dead languages among his intellectual equals, he produced this easy one for Ben with the skittish air of a man who fancies he is speaking cockney.

'It would never have been built at all if the job had been run this way.'

'Please don't misunderstand me. You're doing a fine job. A fine job.' He rubbed his hands and smiled the forced, closed-lip smile which made him look like Punch. 'I've told everybody not to get excited. To give you a chance until we see how it goes.'

'Why didn't you tell them that I have your authority to make whatever changes I think necessary?'

'Oh, well, I did, of course –'

But he had not. He was the kind of weak well-wisher who would take all the credit for any success, but none of the blame for any unpopular methods of achieving it.

'Have you ever been unpopular?' Ben asked Ella.

They were in the linen-room, where Ella was counting the clean linen from the laundry and putting it away.

'I was once, at school.' She stood and thought for a moment, her soft brown eyes staring at nothing; then she went on bending and stretching her long back, taking the sheets from the basket and piling them on the shelves while she talked. 'In my second term, I think it was. Nobody seemed to be paying much attention to me, so I started trying to curry favour by making people's beds, and picking things up for them. I remember once picking up a book for a girl with pigtails – Alice Curran. She dropped it again right away on my toe and walked out of the room. It didn't teach me. I used to go round asking people: "Will you be my friend?" You can't wonder I was unpopular.'

Ben leaned against the slatted shelves in the warm little room which smelled of ironing, and lit a cigarette. 'I wish you wouldn't smoke in here,' Ella said. 'There's no ash-tray.'

'I don't need one.' He tapped the ash into the end of a matchbox, Navy style. 'If there's a fire, I can try out my new fire drill. Can you remember what it felt like to be unpopular?'

Ella stopped working to think again, and then shook her head. 'No. I can remember things like Alice Curran's name, but not how she made me feel. Why?'

'I just wondered. I remember when I was in a cruiser as a midshipman. We had the Germans boxed-up in the Norwegian fjords, and we'd been hanging about for months without seeing any action, and everything had slipped a bit, including the Old Man. Then he was relieved by a captain who talked through his teeth, like this,' he clenched them at her, 'and turned the ship upside down to get it back into shape. We had all become such a lot of slobs that we hated him for it. He didn't seem to care what anyone thought of him, but I'm beginning to understand how he probably felt. Are you listening, Ella?'

She was running her pencil down the laundry list. Her mind was apt to wander away sometimes in the middle of a conversation.

'Of course.' She sucked the pencil and looked at him.

'This is what it feels like to be unpopular, since you've forgotten. You feel cheated. Not hurt, or angry, or vindictive. Just cheated. When you haven't done anything wrong by your standards, it seems damned unfair that if people are going to dislike you anyway, you haven't had the fun of being really vicious. Don't you remember feeling that at school when you said Be my friend, and they dropped books on your toes?'

'I suppose so,' Ella said vaguely. 'I don't remember. You're not unpopular, anyway.' She was not interested in recollecting her own feelings when his appeared to need soothing. Ella was a great soother of feelings, but she usually managed to make you feel worse, like a clumsy nurse knocking into the end of the bed in her hurry to fetch something to relieve your pain. 'It's only that people think you don't know anything about the job; but I think you manage very well, considering you don't.'

'Thank you.' Ben changed the subject. 'How's the family?' He was always trying to get her to talk about her home.

'Oh, all right.' She sounded indifferent. How was that possible when she was privileged to be a part of Ben's provocative dream?

'It's a nice old place you have there.' He had been angling for an invitation ever since he had begun to work at the school with Ella.

'I suppose so. I like it, but I've lived there so long, I can't imagine what it looks like to a stranger.' She was going out of the door with a pile of towels for the boys' bathroom when she turned and said: 'That reminds me. My father told me to ask you over to lunch next Sunday. With Amy, of course. Or would she be bored?'

'She's never bored.' This was not true, but Amy was just as anxious to get into the house as he was. 'We'd love to come.'

Ella looked at him with her chin resting on the top towel and said: 'It won't be exciting. Just a family lunch, and I cook at the week-ends, which is bad luck for you.' Ella had acquired her housekeeper's post on the strength of a diploma from a domestic science school, but it was generally agreed that the diploma must have been forged.

As if she knew what he wanted to ask, she added: 'My sister will be there, anyway. You'll like her. She's the gay one. You know – at children's parties: "That's Laura Halliday, the gay one. The other one's Ella. She grew too fast." '

'Ella,' Ben said, as she turned away. 'You're gay, and I like you.' But she was gone, hurrying down the corridor and knocking into a very small boy who was below her line of vision under the towels.

It had never occurred to Ben that the younger sister Laura, with the short, pert curls and the slick figure would be married. It was some time since he had seen her from the train. He had not known that her figure would not be slick any more when he found her in the hall as he came in from the tour of inspection to which Mr Halliday subjected all new guests, if he could catch them between the car and the house.

'Pay no attention to me,' he said. 'You get like this when you're retired and don't have enough on your mind. It's just something I have to do once, and then it will be over.'

'But Amy and I want to see everything,' Ben said. Mr Halliday looked at him suspiciously, and when he saw that he meant it, he was so pleased that he enlarged the tour, and would have tramped Ben to the top of the second field to see the view if Ella had not caught him making for the gate, and called to him from the kitchen window.

As it was, he introduced Ben to almost every plant, of which not many were flourishing, and to the mushroom shed and the compost heap and the nursery bed dug out of the orchard grass, where the weeds were growing faster than the seedlings. Mr Halliday seemed to be quite pleased if he could find five or six struggling plants in a row where he had sown two packets of seed. This was the sort of gardening Ben understood, the only kind he had ever done, when he and Marion had the bungalow at Portland, and he could never stop her picking his few precious flowers as soon as they came frailly into bloom.

When they went into the house, Laura was in the hall in a yellow smock that stuck out in front like a half-open umbrella.

'This is my daughter Laura,' Mr Halliday said. 'Mrs Arnold.'

Amy kicked Ben lightly on the ankle, and when Laura turned away to get him a drink, she whispered: 'Bad luck, Daddy. Oh, what stinking luck.'

'Listen,' he told Amy quietly, for Laura was busy at the table under the window and Mr Halliday had left the room, having sublimated all his hospitable instincts in the garden, 'don't expect it all to be like we imagined. Nothing ever is.'

'That's what's so hateful about life.' Amy pulled at a loose thread on the back of a chair.

'It isn't. If everything happened the way you imagined it would, there'd be no point in ever letting anything happen. Because you'd know.'

She frowned uncertainly, then switched into a smile and said gently: 'Yes, Daddy dear', for Laura had come up behind Ben with a glass. Amy had evidently decided on the role of docile daughter for Laura's benefit.

Ella knew her at the school as anything but docile, for she was with the boys and copying them whenever she could escape Mrs Glynn's half-hearted supervision. Ben wondered how she would manage to combine the two roles when Ella and Laura were in the room together.

When Mrs Halliday came into the hall, which was the gathering-place of the house, Amy changed again. She had an uncanny way of knowing immediately what people would want her to be. She had sensed that Laura did not particularly like children and would prefer not to hear from them, and so while she was talking to Ben, Amy picked up a magazine and sat quietly with her ankles crossed. But when Mrs Halliday came in, waistless in a dun silk blouse not properly tucked into her skirt, she got up and began to talk to her about the horses, which she had broken away from the tour of inspection to visit.

Mrs Halliday, who was utterly and ineradicably horsey, although in a much gentler way than Ben had expected, welcomed Amy like Fuchs meeting Hillary at the South Pole; or rather Hillary meeting Fuchs, for Mrs Halliday had got there first. Everyone else in the house was tired of horses, but Amy was her disciple, sitting on a stool at her feet like the picture of The Boyhood of Raleigh, while Mrs Halliday, with a light in her mild amber eyes which may never have shone so tenderly for any of her babies, told her about the two horses which she trained as show hacks and took round to all the big shows in the summer. Since she was too fat to throw her legs across a horse any more, she rode side-saddle, which Ben was glad to hear out of the corner of his ear while he listened to Laura talking about herself.

'May I really?' he heard Amy say. 'Daddy. Mrs Halliday says I can go to some of the shows with her. She and George take the horse trailer and go hundreds of miles and sleep in the car.'

'George is the man who drives, and helps me with the horses,' Mrs Halliday said. 'My husband doesn't like it, but of course I sleep in the front of the car and George sleeps at the back.' She said this with a sort of anxious gravity. Her face, under the loosely-pinned swags of yellow-grey hair, was creased with the necessity that Ben should understand.

She was not tough and masterful at all, but disarmingly naïve. Ben had always thought of her as a leathery woman who would stand no nonsense from her horses or anyone else, but he saw now that what authority she had was confined to the stable, and that her horses had found themselves a lucky billet.

'You will let me go, won't you?' Amy got up from the low stool with a swift unfolding of her long legs and came to him, adding: 'Daddy, dear', for Laura's benefit. 'So now, you see, we must stay at the school.'

'Oh?' Laura's eyebrows, which were slightly out of drawing, went up. 'Weren't you going to?' She called across the hall to her sister, who came in from the kitchen flushed, with a lump of hair arched the wrong way over her parting: 'Ella – you didn't tell me Commander Francis was getting out. That's five bob you owe me.'

Ella wiped her hands on the dish-towel she was carrying and helped herself to a drink, stuffing the dish-towel between a cushion and the back of the sofa, where it might stay for days if this was the sort of house it seemed to be. 'Laura bet me five shillings you wouldn't stay more than a month,' she said, 'but I knew you would.'

'If only to win the bet for you,' Ben said. 'But how did you know?'

He thought she would say something flattering about his stamina, but she spilled a few drops of her drink on a table, swiped at it with the edge of her apron and said bluntly: 'Well, you told me what a hard time you'd had finding a job, and even Greenbriars must be better than living with Glenville Roberts.'

'Glenville Roberts?' Laura turned quickly to Ben. '*The* Glenville Roberts? You lived with him?'

'I *told* you,' Ella said wearily.

'You never tell me anything that matters. Do you know Glenville Roberts?' Laura looked at Ben as if she liked him better. 'He's one of my favourite authors. I read his last novel twice.'

'You would,' Ella said. 'It was revolting.'

'It wasn't. Nothing is revolting when it's good literature. It was realism, wasn't it?' She turned back to Ben.

Amy was looking from one face to another with interest, and he wished that they could stop talking about it before she popped up with some cosy detail of her life with Glenn. He said: 'I thought he went too far.'

Laura accepted this, since he had said it and not Ella. 'You know what he's like, of course. Is he really like that? I'd love to meet him.'

'You might. He's bought a house not far from here.'

'Will you take me over? Oh, please.' She put on a babyish, flirting face. 'I'd die if I met him. How exciting. We might ask him here, though I don't suppose he'd come. Elsie' – both daughters addressed their mother by her Christian name – 'get out the best silver. You might meet Glenville Roberts.'

'Who's Glenville Roberts?' Mrs Halliday had taken a steel curb-chain out of her pocket and was polishing it thoughtfully between the palms of her podgy hands. 'Why do you laugh? Should I know? Bernie.' She dropped the curb-chain in her wide lap and reached up to take her husband's hand as he came in from a room off the hall. 'The girls are laughing at me. Should I know who Glenville Roberts is?'

'No, darling, no.' He patted her hand. 'Why should you? You're much better off not knowing.'

'She will soon. He's coming here,' Laura said.

'God forbid. Make an appointment with the dentist for me that day, Ella.'

'You haven't been to the dentist since you lost your teeth,' she said, staring at him seriously.

'Don't be so literal. A surgeon will do. I'll have my gall bladder out.'

After lunch, when Ben and Amy went out to the kitchen to help with the dishes, Amy caught at his hand as they followed Ella down the passage. 'I see what you meant. They're not like we thought. We've had that. Now we have them. I like it here, do you?'

Yes, he liked it. And it was not so different. There was much that was familiar from his years of spying. As separate personalities they were different, of course, from what they had seemed when he had racketed by above them in the train; but together they had that casual, unquestioning family relationship which his imagination had treasured because he and Amy, in their different generations, had never known it.

The house itself was the house he had always known. He had never visualized its interior in detail. When he had thought of it, it had been scarcely more than a vague atmosphere suggested by the outside, but he knew now that if he had imagined it, he might have guessed at this kind of furniture; at the rugs, the older ones good, the newer ones less worn but uglier; at the large and inconvenient kitchen, which would be very cold in winter, with a table scrubbed white over the years and crusted bowls of half-eaten cats' and dogs' food in all the corners.

There should have been irony in his coming to the house after all these years. Having imagined them for so long a secure and stable family, he should have found them all at loggerheads, the arguments not harmless minor ones as unremarkable as breathing, but fierce and bitter quarrels, with people locking themselves in their rooms and torturing themselves for days over the futility of life.

Or, to make a morbid drama out of his dream, he should have come just too late ever to share the contented life he had

209

admired from the train. He should have arrived just as Laura ran away with a drunken poacher, or the father hanged himself with a dressing-gown cord behind the bathroom door, or Ella was killed trying to snatch a dog off the railway line, or Mrs Halliday was thrown from her side-saddle and turned into a crippled idiot for the rest of her life.

There was no irony. No drama. There was only truth. He had not been deceived. For some reason, the house had singled him out from all the passengers on the Southern Railway to show him something of the truth of the life that was lived within its walls.

After the first shock of finding that Laura was married, he did not mind that he could not be in love with her any more, because he would not have married her anyway, nor been in love with her, in any other than a dream world.

She was not as pretty as he had thought. Her curls were not bubbling, but dry and artificial. Her teeth were a little rabbity, and her eyes were not as blue as summer skies, or sapphires, or forget-me-nots. They were merely blue, with a shiny bulge above them where she had plucked out too much eyebrow. Her legs were a little bristly because she had shaved them and they needed shaving again. She was an average, unremarkable girl, neither captivating nor plain, and with no great amount of any quality in her temperament. She was fairly good-natured, moderately intelligent, only occasionally perceptive, and not very witty, although she went in for bold statements which were not as shocking as she thought.

She was, in short, a typical naval officer's girl friend, passable but not devastating; all right to take out, but not necessarily to marry, although heaven knew, lots of the poor creeps did marry her type, and it turned into a captain's wife or an admiral's wife with no perceivable effort. Ben might have done the same himself if he had got mixed up with someone like Laura before Marion . . . before Rose. . . .

Once in the train at night, Ben had seen the light from the french windows lying on the lawn like yellow moonlight. He had imagined himself in the garden and Laura stepping out through the window in a pale dress and coming into his arms with exactly the right words.

'I knew you'd come,' she would have said. Or: 'I've waited so long.'

He knew now that she was the type of girl you did not meet in a moonlit garden. You met her on the beach, or in the post office, or in some not very chic night-club, and what she said was not: 'I knew you'd come', but: 'I've been waiting hours.'

Laura's husband, who was a local doctor, came to fetch her after lunch, and she said to him: 'I thought you were never coming. I haven't felt too good', although she had eaten twice as much as anyone else and generally behaved like a healthy pregnant woman.

'Poor Roger, you're doing too much,' her mother said, in the gentle voice which came surprisingly from such a sturdy, open-air woman.

'You shouldn't kill yourself for these hypochondriacal females,' Mr Halliday said. 'Why have you been so long with Mrs Edgeworth? What's she got this time?'

Roger laughed. He had a bland fat face and a cheery air which was agreeable socially, but might be a little hard to take if you were dying. 'Oh – something feminine.'

'What?'

'You know I never discuss my patients, even with you, Dad.'

'Especially not with Daddy,' Laura said, 'unless you want the gynaecological details broadcast to the whole county.'

'How can I gossip? I never see anyone.'

'I wish you would, dear.' His wife picked up what was evidently her side of a long-standing issue. 'I wish you would get about more. You could come to some of the shows with George and me – and now Amy, of course.' She gave the child a private smile. 'All right, I know, I know. But at least it would give you the chance to get about.'

'How can I, Elsie, when I've all the work of this place on my shoulders? I'm not a smooth-tongued practitioner with a string of female patients inventing symptoms to pay my gardener's wages.'

He bared his long plastic teeth at Roger, who laughed, throwing back his affable head, and said: 'You have George, complete with nasal polypi.'

211

'That devil George never has time for anything but the horses.'

'If you'd rather do the horses,' his wife said sweetly, 'George can do the garden.'

'Don't tease him,' Ella said, and her mother looked surprised, as if her suggestion had been sincere. 'Oh, I'm sorry, Roger, I forgot.' Ella went out to the kitchen and came back with a plateful of lunch she had been keeping hot for him, looking pleased, because she had been thoughtful for a busy doctor, and Laura had not. But Roger had stopped somewhere for a sandwich, and did not want the lunch, so Ella put the plate down on the floor by her feet for the big yellow dog who looked like Nana.

Two days later, when Ben saw Ella in Mrs Morton's drawing-room, where the staff were obliged to forgather every other Tuesday to drink sherry, whether they liked it or not, he said: 'It was awfully nice of you to ask me to lunch. Amy and I had a grand time.'

Ella looked surprised. 'It was terribly dull. It was nicer for us than for you. We've got so used to seeing each other and the same old local crowd that it's good to have someone new. I don't count the strange people who come to talk horses with Elsie, because they mostly stand about in the yard with their heads down, talking at their boots.'

'That's odd.' Ben said. 'It looks like the sort of house where there are people in and out all the time, and always something going on.'

Ella shook her head. 'It was. When my father was still practising, there used to be more people – clients, and barristers on circuit – and of course when we were younger we were always bringing our friends home. But when people get older and get married and bogged down with babies, they don't want to come. Or if they do, it isn't the same.'

The sunless, uncomfortable room was full of masters and masters' wives. The younger masters wore tweed jackets and slacks and needed a haircut. The older ones wore bow-ties and grey flannel suits that did not go often enough to the cleaners, although laundry and cleaning were on the house. The wives wore anonymous summer garments that revealed upper arms

212

too bony or too massive and talked among themselves with the apathetic intimacy of women who live in a small and narrow community. The masters were mostly talking shop together, for they did not bother to make a social occasion of Mrs Morton's sherry hours. Mrs Morton herself, with her stick swinging dangerously on the crook of her arm, was talking to the games master, a muscle-bound man too old for his job whom she had pinned up against a bookcase to hear what she thought should be done about Sports Day.

Ben and Ella had found themselves in a corner with two glasses of sweet sherry and a dish of stale cheese straws, not deliberately ignored, but not quite part of the group. Ben's latest ideas on procurement planning, based on a study of requirements for the last five years, had not increased his popularity, and Ella was only invited as a sort of charitable gesture, since Mrs Morton considered her really one of the maids.

'When Laura married,' Ella went on, talking into her glass and not looking at Ben, 'I thought : Oh, good, here's some new blood. But Roger's not exactly a thrill. My brother's been married much longer, and he was engaged for ages, so we all got used to Betsy long ago, as if she'd been in the family for ever. She's just as dull as we are, but the children are all right, when she lets them alone.'

'I don't think any of you are dull,' Ben said. He was afraid that she would not invite him home again if she thought he had been bored. He wanted to explain to her how wrong she was, if that was what she thought. He wanted to tell her about seeing the house from the train, and what her family had meant to him, and what it meant to get on the inside at last.

He could not say it. He could not make any of the right words translate themselves into speech between his mind and his lips. He was afraid that he would not be able to make her understand, and she would frown at him and her brown eyes would grow troubled, as they had when he had tried to show her how to order soap and scouring powder on an annual basis without actually ordering a year's supply.

He said something about it being a shame that the railway was so close to the house, and with the memory of her in the garden looking up, he asked her: 'Do you ever look up at the trains and wonder about the people in them?'

'Occasionally. Sometimes I think it would be nice to be them. And perhaps,' she laughed, 'because they are them, they're looking into our garden and thinking it might be nice to be me.'

Now he could tell her. 'Listen, Ella,' he said eagerly, but she had caught the skirt of the maid passing with a tray and said out of the side of her mouth: 'Lucy, what are the chances of another sherry?'

'You've had two, Miss Halliday,' Lucy said, glancing towards Mrs Morton. 'That's all she –'

'We've only had one,' Ben said.

'Two, Commander.' Lucy looked at him as if he were lying drunk in the gutter. 'It's as much as my job is worth.'

'Don't worry,' Ben said. 'I'm the one who does the firing and hiring.'

Lucy blew down her nose, which had a lump of flesh between the nostrils, like a petrified drop. 'That's what you think.'

'You shouldn't have said that,' Ella said when she had moved away. 'She's one of Mrs Morton's spies. It all goes back to her.'

'Let it. I'm not afraid of her.'

'She can get you fired too.'

'Let her try.'

'Oh, she will.' Ella shrugged her wide shoulders and turned away from him as Mrs Glynn came up with her simpering, mumbling smile. 'How are you this evening, Ella, dear?' she asked, as winningly as if she really cared. 'I've never seen you looking so pretty. What have you done to your hair?'

'Oh – nothing.' Ella had brushed it neatly, but she put up a hand now and disarranged it.

'It looks charming.' Mrs Glynn, who was about a foot shorter than Ella, looked up at her, twinkling. 'What do you think, Commander Francis?' Although Ben and Amy were living in her house, she would never call him Ben. 'Don't you think we have a charming housekeeper?'

It must have given her a crick in the neck to stand looking up at them and turning her smile from one face to the other. When she smiled, which was nearly all the time, she pushed her lips in and out and twitched the corners of her mouth as if she were talking to herself.

'Very charming,' Ben said shortly. He knew that Ella hated to be discussed.

'I *thought* so!' If Mrs Glynn had been holding a fan, she would have tapped him with it. She had been trying, in what she thought was a subtle way, to marry Ben to Ella ever since he came to the school. Having had twenty-five blissful years with what she called 'My old Sweetheart', which was the collection of dried-up skin and withered muscles known as Mr Glynn, the physics master, she wanted to mate everybody. For a long time she had been trying vainly to marry Ella to the bachelor masters, Willis and Knight. No one would ever be able to explain to Mrs Glynn why she was wasting her time, and no one had ever tried to.

Chapter Fourteen

GREENBRIARS SCHOOL was less than three miles away from the Hallidays' house, and Ella went there and back every day on a tall old bicycle with a fraying basket on the handlebars. Sometimes when it was stormy, Ben would drive her home in the car which, now that he had a steady job, he had bought with some of the money with which the Navy had bribed him to retire.

Mr Halliday always gave him a drink, and Ben soon learned to ask for whisky, for Mr Halliday's dry martinis were made with vermouth distilled by himself from the puckered grapes in the greenhouse which rose among the nettles that were taking over the vegetable garden.

Sometimes he was invited to stay for supper. The Hallidays' food was not exciting, but it was preferable to the food in the school dining-hall, which the lack of cooperation between the cook and the dietitian and the dietitian and the bursar had done nothing to improve. Preaching economy all round the school, Ben had told Mrs Morton that she must cut down her food budget. He had also offered his opinion that the boys were not getting their parents' moneysworth in either quantity or quality.

'You can't have it both ways, Mr Francis.' Mrs Morton gave him that blank look as if she were not there behind her face. 'If you will explain to me how to spend less and feed them better, I shall be very much obliged.'

'That's not my province,' Ben said. 'You're the victualling officer. I'm sure it could be done though. As the Navy used to say during the war: The difficult we do immediately. The impossible takes a little longer.'

'It was the Americans who said that,' Mrs Morton said coldly. 'And I am neither in the Royal nor the United States Navy.'

Ben had hoped that time would mellow Mrs Morton, but it had not. They were still at war, although they were passably polite on the surface, and there had been one curious evening when he came to ask her something after dinner, and she had talked to him quite gaily and garrulously, almost as if she were drunk.

Old Hammerhead had been out at a meeting, and perhaps she had been hitting the bottle by herself for want of anything else to do. Ben would probably be doing the same thing himself by the time he had been in this place ten years. He had not told anyone what he thought. Mrs Morton was still, to all intents and purposes, the Admiral's wife, although he did not like her any better than he had liked that Admiral's wife in Malta who had spread the story about Marion and the Surgeon-Lieutenant.

With Mr Pearse and his little kick-backs out of the picture, the food budget was reduced, but the quality of the meals did not improve. Tilly Wicket tried her best, but her mother was failing up at the hospital and her ankles were letting her down this summer, and she declared that because of Lady Peg Leg, she was losing her heart for the job.

Ben exhorted her and sympathized with her over pots of tea, and even raised her pay. However, neither he nor Tilly could order Lady Peg Leg out of the kitchen, and she had acquired a habit of limping in at all hours to unnerve Tilly's kitchen help by standing at their elbows while they worked and giving them confusing orders in her dietitian's voice about washing their hands and boiling the tea-towels.

The boys, of course, fared worse than the staff, and the time-worn phrase: 'The food here is foul' had a new ring of truth in letters home that term. Ben ran a small tuckshop, and he served behind the counter himself, since the master's wife who was supposed to be in charge was visiting a married daughter in South Africa. He could tell that the boys were even hungrier than normal boys of that age. Most of them had generous allowances, and they would clean him out of baked beans and bananas and bars of chocolate so fast that he often had to close the tuckshop early because there was nothing more to sell.

He was sorry for the boys, and increasingly so as he came to know more of them as individuals instead of nameless parts of a scuffling, shock-haired crowd. Because he did not have to teach them anything, they talked to him more freely than they did to the masters, and in the tuckshop they complained to him about a lot of things, and principally about the food. Ever since he had scored a minor triumph by spotting a boy's missing camera in the back of Mr Willis's car and returning it quietly to the boy with the injunction that he would break his neck if he asked where it came from, the boys were always after Ben with their cry of: 'Can't you *do* something about it, sir?'

'I'll see what I can do, chaps,' he would say, but when he tackled Tilly Wicket about baked hearts for supper twice in one week, she would tell him: '*She* ordered them hearts. I only cooked 'em,' and when he tackled Mrs Morton, she would raise her smooth black eyebrows and say primly: 'You told me not to be extravagant. I'm only obeying orders.'

He longed to say: 'Oh, dammit, order steaks for them all tomorrow,' but he dared not give her that much rope.

When Amy went to meals at the Hallidays, she had two helpings of everything and went back to the school with cakes and rolls in her pockets. Mrs Halliday was only too glad to feed her and Ben any time they wanted to drive over, and it was during a Sunday lunch, when Roger and Laura were there, that a sudden lull in the conversation disclosed Amy saying to Ella: 'Of course, that was one of the older boys. I wouldn't let any-one less than a prefect do that to me.'

'Amy!' Ben jumped on her, and she looked so surprised that he wished that he had let it pass.

Laura made it worse by saying: 'That's right, Amy, never cheapen yourself,' and her mother said with unusual assertiveness: 'Be quiet, Laura. Amy, you needn't stay while we have coffee. Take some sugar out to the horse. Take a lot.'

She gave her the whole bowl of sugar, and Ella got up and went out for some more. Ella was always trying to do things that were thoughtful or quietly efficient. She was one of those people who never get enough recognition for what they do, because she was fated always to arrive with the wrong thing, or the right thing too late, as now when she came back with a packet of sugar and Laura had already reached backwards and taken another sugar basin from the sideboard.

'Who can't do what?' Ella asked, catching the fag-end of what her mother was saying.

'Amy. She can't stay at that school. It isn't proper.'

'Oh, Elsie.' Ella dropped the unwanted packet of sugar into a tarnished silver-plated bowl which her mother had won at a horse show. 'She was talking about swopping stamps.'

'Next time she won't be. You'd be appalled at some of the things I could tell you,' said Roger, who liked to hint at the unmentionable horrors of his professional experience. 'Elsie's right. It's a bad situation for the kid.'

'It can't be helped,' Ben said a little irritably, but Mrs Halliday sat up very straight and said rather loudly, for she was not accustomed to making bold statements: 'It can be helped. She can come and live with us.'

Flushed, and breathing rather quickly, she looked round the table at her family, challenging them to object.

They could not object, since Ben was there, so he said on their behalf: 'Oh, look, that's sweet of you, but she really couldn't.'

'Of course she could. No, don't interrupt me, Bernie. I know what you're going to say about not interfering in people's lives, but you're the last one to talk after what you did about poor Mrs Sykes and the council house.' She turned to Ben. 'I've been thinking about this for some time. I want to have her. Let me, Ben. She'd be so near, you could see almost as much of her as you do now. I wish we could have you here too, but –'

'Oh, he couldn't do that,' Mr Halliday broke in quickly, alarmed at the idea of his house being turned into a hotel. 'He

218

has to get his moneysworth of free board and lodging out of Morton. Couldn't let the old brigand get away with that.'

Ben looked at Ella. She was the one who would have most of the care of Amy if she came here. He wanted her to say something. She did not say anything, but when Amy's head appeared at the open window with the empty sugar bowl, Ella turned round in her chair and said: 'How would you like to come here and live with us?'

'You've spoiled it,' Mrs Halliday said with a little cry. 'I wanted to be the one to tell her.'

'I'm sorry.' Ella never spoiled anything for anyone on purpose. 'So did I.'

They looked at each other with understanding, and then they looked at Amy, who had shouted: 'Can I, Daddy?' and vaulted over the low window-sill with her hair flying like a blown flame to run to Ben and hug him. Ben sat with his arms round her thin body and thought that he had never been so happy for her since the morning when he had seen Marion with her beautiful hair damp and tangled on the pillow, smiling down at the new-born baby with the promise of the love he did not know she would not keep.

'I hope you didn't think,' said Mrs Glynn, her smile a little strained, as if she knew that he had thought it, 'that I did not look after Amy properly.'

'Of course not. You've been wonderful to her. But it isn't really the best thing for her to be here in the middle of a crowd of boys.'

'Little boys,' Mrs Glynn said distantly. 'How surprising that anyone should even think – Dear me, Commander Francis,' she pushed her smile in and out at him, 'what grubby minds some people have.'

'All right, then, it wasn't that. It was just that the Hallidays were so keen to have her. They love little girls, and Ella is very fond of Amy.'

'I love little girls too,' Mrs Glynn said wistfully, although she had never been particularly nice to Amy. 'But of course, I see which way the wind blows. With Amy there, you have *carte blanche* to go over whenever you like, and I know that the food is not the only attraction in *that* house.' She ogled Ben obscenely and went away to hang out Amy's blankets and scour her room as if the child had been a typhoid case.

Ben did go very often to the Hallidays, and although it was to see Amy and not especially Ella, he was always glad to see Ella, because she was so gentle and friendly. She seemed to be quite fond of him, and he was fond of her, sometimes with a sudden stab of tenderness when something went wrong for her, because she was so vulnerable.

With her careless, impulsive movements that might have been graceful in an adolescent, and the thick tawny hair that flopped over her eye when the pin slid out of it, she had something in common with the big shaggy dog that trailed her everywhere when she was at home. The dog was amiable and unassertive and would let puppies and cats take the food from his bowl right under his nose. Everybody loved him and called him Poor Old Geoffrey, although he was in the prime of life and perfectly happy.

Everybody loved Ella, and her brother Harry did frequently refer to her as Poor Old Ella. Ben loved her too, in a damnably brotherly sort of way which he was going to have to overcome if he was going to kiss her, as he planned to do, to see how they both would like it.

He picked a bad time to try it. Harry and his plump wife Betsy had come for the week-end with their three children. Betsy did not do anything in the house except be a mother, and Ella was rattled because she had too much to do.

Ben kissed her in the scullery, and she tasted clean and nice, because she did not smoke. She pushed him away with wet hands and said: 'Oh, don't start that, Ben. There isn't time.'

'What do you mean, not time?' He had never heard that raised as an objection before.

'I've got a lot to do.' She put her strong, rounded forearms back into the sink and her hair swung forward over her face.

She sounded neither annoyed nor surprised that he had kissed her, which was more deflating than if she had slapped his face. Piqued, he went away and left her to finish the saucepans by herself.

It was a rather unsatisfactory week-end, which did not work out in the way that Ben had hoped. It was the first time that he would meet all the family together, and he had planned that when Laura came on Sunday, he would tell them of his life-time's association with their house and them.

He imagined their surprise: how they would look, what they would say; which of them would perfectly understand, and which of them would think it more of a joke than anything else. Laura would undoubtedly be pleased at the idea of anyone watching her over the years. She enjoyed everything more if she had an audience. Even if she was only reading a book, she preferred there to be someone in the room, so that she could think to them: Look at me reading. If the family urged Ben to tell them all that he had imagined about them, he would have to think of some way of saying that he had always dreamed of being in love with Laura, without making it too obvious that a closer acquaintance had woken him up.

He would tell them on Sunday. Amy and he would tell it together. He could imagine all their faces looking within themselves and backward as they tried to remember some of the things they might have been doing when Ben sped by above them in the train.

Then Harry and Betsy arrived, and he knew that he would not tell them. Not this week-end at any rate. Perhaps never. With Harry came a breath of conscious sophistication. He was not just naturally urban because he lived and worked in London. He carried about with him deliberately, like a rolled umbrella, the aura of clubs and boardrooms and being welcomed by name by tail-coats in the best restaurants and white jackets in the more exclusive bars.

He was about Ben's own age, and he had grown from the stocky boy Ben remembered, who sometimes jeered rudely at the trains from a perch in a tree or on an outhouse roof, into a rather handsome man with hair slicked up above the ears, and a businessman's figure that would not look as good in swimming trunks as it did in a well-tailored suit.

He knew people. He dropped names. He had lunch with Chaps in the House, and dinner with the brother of a Character who played polo with Philip. He had a Jaguar, nominally owned by his firm, and his wife had a double row of real pearls round her soft, plump neck.

Ben knew that they were real, because they were a new acquisition and there was a fair amount of talk about them. Mr Halliday tested them with his teeth, and Ella tried them on and looked dubiously at herself in the mirror, and Mrs Halliday thought that Betsy should not wear them in the country.

'The old girl' – that was what Harry called his wife, 'the old girl' – 'is just as likely to lose them in London, and I rather hope she does, because they're insured for more than I gave for them.' That was the way that Harry had grown to be. It was not the beauty of the pearls on his wife's creamy skin that gave him pleasure, but the thought of what he could get for them. His life in London had put much more than fifty miles between him and the house by the railway.

You could clearly imagine him saying to his wife before this week-end: 'I suppose it's about time we gave the old folks a treat.' Once there, he was affectionate to his mother, teasingly familiar with his father, and good tempered to his sisters, but although he made himself very much at home, he had the air of a bird of passage, merely pausing there until it was time to go back to London.

He was quite affable to Ben, although plainly surprised at the frequency with which Ben arrived in the little car which he had to park well away from the Jaguar to stop it looking pathetic. He told Ben what was wrong with the Navy and how the cuts could have been avoided, which was a big help to Ben since he had already been axed. Then he told him what was wrong with Greenbriars School and how Ben should run his operations there.

After Harry had been in the house a few hours, Amy came into the garden where Ben was standing with his head back, watching a train go by and trying to capture the feeling of being in it and looking down at himself in the garden.

When the last carriage had whisked by and taken the noise with it, Amy said: 'Let's not tell them, Daddy.'

'Tell them what?' He had imagined himself so completely into the train that it seemed odd to find himself left behind here and not on his way to Waterloo.

'About seeing them from the train. I don't think Harry would understand. The others might, but he would think us silly. Or pathetic, that would be worse.'

'As if you and I were poor children outside a sweet-shop window. He might. When shall we tell them, then?'

'Let's not ever. When you've enjoyed something by yourself, it always spoils it if you try and share it. Like seeing a film you love, and then going again with someone else, and they won't cry too.'.

Harry and Betsy had three children, a girl of nine, a boy of six, and a two-year-old baby who was violent enough for a boy, but who was actually a girl with sparse hair. In theory, it was going to be nice for Amy to have someone of her own age to play with, but it was a mistake to imagine that because she and Penelope were both children they would have anything in common at all.

They had to share a bedroom, and after the first night, Amy told Ben that Penelope was an awful wet, stamped into her rubber boots and spent the rest of the day except meal-times out in the garden and the stable yard in the rain. Penelope stole Amy's new ball-point pen and complained to her mother that Amy had too much nerve and was trying to tell her what to do in her own grandmother's house.

She said it in front of Ben, and Betsy did not try to hush her. She seldom hushed her children, because she believed in the free development of character, and in this case the child was voicing her mother's own opinion. It was clear that Betsy resented Amy's position in the house, and it was not surprising, because Mrs Halliday, who could not dissemble, made it unintentionally obvious that she preferred Amy to her grandchildren. There was no Come to Grandma, or bouncing of the baby on her knee that week-end, because she had borrowed a pony for Amy, and spent most of the time standing in a muddy field in a sou'wester and gumboots with Amy and the pony describing cautious circles round her at the end of a long lungeing-rein. She could not wait until the rain had stopped or her visitors had gone to start teaching Amy to ride. The pony was there, so they had to start. Amy could not wait either. They were very much alike.

Penelope was terrified of horses, which was a blow to her grandmother, who had been wanting to get her a pony ever since she could walk. Betsy had forbidden it, but she now resented that there was a pony for Amy. She resented the intimacy between her mother-in-law and the usurping child, an intimacy that the querulous and neurotic Penelope had never shared with her grandmother.

Betsy resented a lot of things that week-end. Ella had always been supposed to be the perfect aunt, whose brother's children were 'like her own'. She was still attentive and affectionate towards them, but now Amy was her responsibility too, in a way that Penelope and Dorian and the monster Julia were not and did not need to be.

Amy's relationship with Ella went deeper than her bond with Mrs Halliday. That was centred round the horses. With Ella, it included everything. They had made a pattern of life together. Every morning, they bicycled to the corner where Amy caught her bus for school. Every afternoon, Ella was waiting at the corner when the bus brought Amy back. Mrs Morton did not know that Ella left Greenbriars half an hour early in order to do this. Ben hoped that she would never find out.

Ella fed Amy and washed and ironed her clothes and mended them with large, loose stitches that came apart again at the first sign of strain. She listened to Amy's involved prayers and tried to help her with her homework and administered discipline when it was necessary.

Betsy's children did not get discipline, because the book said that the only permissible discipline was self-discipline, which they would administer to themselves when they were ready for it. They got guidance instead, which meant educational toys and serious, repetitive talks which went on and on in Betsy's special voice for speaking to children. It was a slow, clear voice, hideous with patience and the conscientious determination to reach the child on his own level. When she first used it on Amy, Amy stared and said: 'You don't have to talk to me like that. I can understand if you talk the way you do to the grown-ups.'

Betsy flushed and forgot her child psychology so far as to call Amy a precocious little brat, which Amy repeated to Ben with glee. It galled Betsy that Amy, with no proper guidance in her life, was not a problem child who screamed at night and pulled the legs off frogs, but contentedly independent and well adjusted.

Adjusting was one of Betsy's favourite words. Penelope had to be guided to adjust to Amy, and in consequence never did. All three children had to adjust to living in a different house for the week-end, and Betsy's whole day, and part of her night, for the children went to sleep when they wanted to and not when they were told to, was given up to watching them and commenting on them and assisting them with their little problems. Since Julia had never been smacked for laying her rude hands on forbidden objects, Betsy's life was ruled by the necessity of watching this destructive baby to see that she did not brain herself or poison herself or set the house on fire.

Seeing how much trouble Betsy took over her children, and what a business she made of it, Ben wondered fleetingly whether Amy had been deprived by having had only the casual care that he and Geneva had given to her. Since she had more or less brought herself up, it was surprising how little trouble she was, but was she missing anything?

Sitting in the hall trying to read the paper while Betsy was reasoning in the patient voice with Penelope and Dorian, who were whining to go out in the rain, Ben looked out of the window and saw Amy tramping through the yard with a sack over her head and a load of hay as big as herself on the end of a pitchfork, and did not think that she was missing a thing.

The unremitting rain, which spoiled the plans for golf, picnics and the village fête, was not the only thing that went wrong with the week-end.

The oil heater in Mr Halliday's mushroom shed blew up, and the rickety little shack went up in flames, which might have spread to the stable if it had not been raining so hard. As it was, the fire turned to dense black smoke, which bellowed noxious fumes of overheated manure into the little crowd of amateur firemen who were sloshing about in the mud with hoses and fire extinguishers which they did not know how to work.

Mr Halliday was interested only in saving his mushrooms, which were his special thing this year and had cost him quite a lot for the spore. Mrs Halliday and Amy and George were interested only in the horses. When Penelope, who loved to bring bad news, had spread the alarm – 'I bet she lit it,' Amy commented, as she ran out – they had pulled the horses out into the yard, where they danced and circled at the end of halter ropes to the peril of the baby Julia, who had teetered out after her mother to see the sport.

To create more drama than there was already, Amy had tied a wet cloth over the pony's eyes, and having come out of the stable in spite of the cloth, it was now too wildly excited by the confusion to let Amy near its head to untie the knot. With the bandage slipped over one eye, it was plunging round in small circles with its head down, like a belligerent grey-haired pirate, with Amy gallantly swinging on the end of the rope.

'Let me have him!' George kept shouting to her, but Amy, breathless, spindle-legged, determined not to be beaten in her first challenge with horses, pulled the pony away from George, half-sobbing: 'I can handle him, I can handle him!' The pony plunged towards the baby, who was sitting in a mud puddle adjusting herself to the situation. Betsy screamed, Harry swung round and turned the hose on the pony, and Amy fell on her face in the mud as the pony tore loose from her wet hands and disappeared through the hedge and down the road towards its own home.

Ella appeared at Ben's side with a raincoat over her head and drops of water running down her nose, and said something to him which he could not hear because a train was racketing by. He looked up at the train and thought what a thrill it would have been if he had been in it and seen the fire, laid on for the benefit of his one brief glimpse. He would have seen the smoke and the horses and the figures of grown-ups and children slopping about in the pouring rain, and longed to be there with them, a part of what was going on.

He wondered if anyone in that train had rubbed a space in a steamy window and had noticed the excitement and wanted to be him, with an axe in one hand and an empty fire-extinguisher upside down in the other, and Harry in a sodden trilby jammed

226

on his head with the brim turned down all round shouting at him: 'Stand clear – she's coming down!' as if the little shed was a four-storey warehouse building.

'Amy's not the only one with an over-developed sense of drama.' He turned to say this to Ella, and saw that she was crying. There was so much rain on her face that he was not sure at first, but then he saw her distorted mouth, the bottom lip pulled stiffly down below her teeth. He dropped the fire-extinguisher and put his arms round her, holding the axe behind her back. 'It's not such a tragedy, Ella. I'll help your father build another shed. We'll buy him some spore for his birthday. There's plenty of manure, God knows.'

She stood stiffly in his arms, looking at nothing over his shoulder. 'It's one of the dogs. I'd shut him in the kennel because he was wet and I'd swept the kitchen floor. Penelope let him out. She told me she had. "All dumb animals should be free", she told me in that prissy voice. I couldn't find him, but knew where to look for him. He was on the railway.'

'Not Geoffrey?' Ben could hardly say it. The shaggy dog was a part of Ella, a clumsy, straw-coloured shadow who sat and rose and walked when she did, and lay watching her with his humble eyes in the middle of the kitchen floor where he could feel her when she stumbled over him.

'Oh, no, he'd never go on the line. It was the young one. The silly spaniel. Oh, Ben.' She put her face into his shoulder. She was taller than he, but it did not matter, because she was not always trying to make herself appear shorter, as Rose had done. If he were ever to kiss Ella properly, with her cooperation, she would not take her shoes off. She would just lower her face and it would all be quite natural and comfortable.

He shifted one arm from behind her to push her chin gently upwards with the butt-end of the axe handle. She looked at him with the vulnerable plainness of a woman in her thirties crying. He would try it now. No he wouldn't. Harry the fearless fire chief sloshed up with the trickling hose in his hand and said: 'God, what a place to neck. Why don't you go inside where it's dry?'

Ella pulled herself away from Ben and went to help her father, who was stamping about among the manure and charred

227

wood of the smouldering ruins, hoping to rescue some grilled mushrooms from the holocaust.

Nobody wanted tea after the fire. They all had a drink, and Betsy got mellow and forgot about putting her younger children to bed, and Julia crawled upstairs and into Amy's room and upset her ant farm.

The ant farm was one of Amy's dearest possessions. It was a narrow, transparent plastic case, half-filled with sand. In the top half, the silhouettes of farm buildings and silos and windmills stood on a ledge where the ants made their heap. They tunnelled devotedly in the sand of the lower half and brought it up grain by grain through a hole in the ledge, patting each grain carefully into place over the pieces of sugar Amy dropped in and the curled-up bodies of their less fortunate comrades who had not been able to adjust to life inside a plastic sandwich.

A reader in America had sent the ant farm to Glenville Roberts with a letter: 'You who have made an exhaustive study of the sex habits of the human race may find it even more rewarding to study the sex life of the ant.'

Glenn had given it to Amy. She had dug out some ants from a colony on Hampstead Heath, and six or seven of them had miraculously lived through being carried about the house and taken to school and moved to Greenbriars and finally to the Hallidays', where they had come to rest on a table by her bed where she could study them while she waited for sleep.

The Queen ant and the princes who mated with her had turned up their frail toes long ago. The half-dozen survivors were all barren female workers, who were labouring for nothing, since their world was doomed to extinction. They had made a marvellous network of sloping tunnels in which they could clearly be seen through the plastic, scuttling about on vital errands, playing ball with a grain of sand, washing their faces and tapping each other on the head with their feelers when they wanted to exchange a piece of gossip.

When the ants were first put in and started to work immediately, Ben and Glenn had the ant farm on the dining-room table and studied it at every meal, and bored all the guests with it. It was the sort of toy that was so fascinating for the first few days that they had wondered how they had ever lived without it, until they reached the point where they began to wonder why they lived with it. Having overdone their enthusiasm, they gave it back to Amy, but she had never lost interest in it.

She loved those ants. When the baby knocked them over and all the tunnels caved in, she was crying bitterly as she set the ant farm upright, because the ants had made their home and now they would have to start all over again, and she knew that they would start, shocked and aggrieved, but knowing no other way but to keep tunnelling. She forgot that she herself had knocked the ants over once, and so had Ella. She was furious with the baby. She smacked it, and was smacking it again when Betsy ran upstairs to see what the screams were.

'I would have thought you had enough sense not to smack it when its mother was in the room,' Ben told Amy afterwards, when the commotion had died down.

'I don't care. She should do it herself. She lets that little gorilla do what it likes just because it's two. As if being two made you God.'

Amy was not the sort of child who enjoyed younger children. Betsy, who had been a little mother to her small sisters and brothers, could not understand this. Ben was staying the night, and when he went to bed, he heard her discussing Amy with Harry, through a bedroom door ajar.

'Elsie shouldn't have her here. She's a peculiar child. There's something psychotic about her, if you ask me. All this play-acting. I can't think what they all see in her.'

'Oh, I don't know.' Harry was brushing his teeth. 'I rather like the kid. Did you see how she hung on to that pony? She's got some guts.'

'Oh,' said Betsy, 'so your own children have no guts.'

'Listen, Mummy, I never said –'

When Mr Halliday called his wife Mummy, it sounded nice, and she liked it. Harry was trying to mollify Betsy, but she snubbed him with: 'I am not your mother. I am the mother of your three children, to whom I devote every waking hour, the best years of my life. . . .' and so on, and so on. A regular married quarrel. Ben tiptoed past the door, feeling guilty because Amy had started it, which made it his fault too.

To crown an unsatisfactory week-end, Glenville Roberts arrived on Sunday morning to see Ben and Amy. He had been to the school, and Mrs Glynn, with many becks and winks, had sent him to the Hallidays' house.

The front door was open and he strode in, calling out: 'Anybody home?' Amy was outside and Ben was upstairs helping Ella make beds, since Betsy's domesticity stopped at motherhood, and she hardly did anything for Ella in the house except litter the kitchen with jars of half-eaten baby food with the sticky spoons still in them.

By the time Ben reached the hall, Mr Halliday had removed Glenn to view the remains of the mushroom-shed fire, and then on for a tour, since it was not raining at the moment.

Ben caught up with them in the greenhouse, where Mr Halliday was demonstrating his latest invention, the cardboard cylinders from inside toilet rolls stacked like a honeycomb in a seed-box as individual containers for seedlings.

'Ben, my friend!' Glenn turned with relief from a contemplation of withered geranium cuttings which Mr Halliday still hoped might take root. 'I can't tell you how glad I am to see you. Nothing has been the same since you walked out on me.' He put his arm round Ben and pushed him gently so that they could get out of the greenhouse.

'Honestly?' Ben was pleased.

'I swear it. You want to come back?'

'No fear,' Ben smiled at the security of not being tempted to accept.

'You should have stayed. I've had a marvellous time. Been half round the world since I last saw you, doing articles, and knocking around looking for ideas for stories.'

'And running away from Esther Lovelace?'

Glenn laughed. 'That too. But I ran myself into some more trouble, of course. If you'd been with me in Barcelona, you could have pulled me out of it. She was a princess. Fabulously rich, but a complete –'

'How is poor Esther?' Ben did not want to hear about the fabulous princess in Barcelona.

'I don't know. I haven't seen her, thank God. She's dead for all I know.'

'Who's dead?' Mr Halliday caught them up. 'Forgive me,' he said to Glenn. 'I'm insatiably curious. It's almost my only failing.'

'Quite your only one,' Ben said, and Glenn glanced at him sharply, surprised at the affection in his voice. 'It's an old girl friend of Glenn's. He was madly in love with her.'

'Well, it's sad when they die,' Mr Halliday said vaguely, not sure whether it was a joke or not. 'But if he had no further use for her –'

'There's only one girl friend I have any use for.' Glenn held out his arms as Amy came flying round the corner from the stable yard and jumped at him like a puppy. She was overjoyed to see Glenn. She dragged him off to see the pony, which had been brought back that morning, and would have kept him outside and to herself for the whole of his visit, but Harry, smelling a celebrity, came out with his personality smile and took him into the house for a drink.

Amy went too, and sat on Glenn's knee and rumpled his thick grey hair, and Ben saw that the family was surprised and a little disquieted to find her so friendly with him.

Apart from a mild gratification at having a celebrity in the house, they did not like Glenn very much. Ella did not like the way he stroked Amy's hair, and she invented an errand to get her off his knee.

'I will in a minute.' Amy said.

Glenn backed her up. 'Don't take her away from me. Can't she do it later?'

'She has to do it now,' Ella said in an unnatural voice that showed that she was making an effort, but was wishing she had not started it. When he saw that Ella was blushing, Ben ordered Amy to obey, and she kissed Glenn, got slowly down from his knee and stuck out her tongue at Ella as she went out of the room.

'The child is getting out of hand,' Glenn said with pleasure. 'She was never rude to me in my house.'

'You weren't supposed to be in charge of her,' Ben said. 'I was there, if you remember.'

'How can I ever forget? Priscilla – she's got acne now, by the way – never stops talking about you. She's still in love with you.'

'Oh, rot. She never was. Why don't you leave the poor girl alone? It was bad enough telling Esther Lovelace she was in love with you.'

'She probably is. When you're that desperate, anything in trousers will do.' Glenn laughed, the malicious, smutty laugh that Ben had heard before, and which sounded all wrong in this house.

Glenn's visit was not a great success. He showed off a little, as he always did with new people. Even though the Hallidays were clearly not in his world and could do nothing for him, he could not help trying to dazzle them with his well-oiled impersonation of a great man.

Ella did not know what to say to him. Mrs Halliday was still not quite sure why she ought to know who he was, and was worried because she did not know whether he expected to be asked to stay for lunch. Mr Halliday was disappointed because Harry would not let him make the drinks with his home-brewed vermouth. Betsy was huffed because Glenn paid so much attention to Amy and none to her children, and Harry quickly became bored with him, because in the duel between two men who both liked to hold the conversational floor, Glenn won.

Just when Harry got a chance to tell him what was wrong with the modern novel and why there was no future in cheap journalism, Laura arrived, enormous in a hot-coloured orange dress, and sat down to fascinate Glenn, with her back turned to obliterate the rest of the company.

'The Missus is well away,' Roger said contentedly. 'It's remarkable how she can talk all the stuff about books and things.'

But the Mrs failed to get anywhere with Glenn, who liked his women less obvious. After he had trapped her into admitting that she had not read a novel about which she was giving what she imagined to be clever opinions, he got up to leave, refusing the offer of lunch which Mrs Halliday hastened to make when she saw that he really meant to go.

'Come and see us when you're in these parts again,' Mr Halliday said. He had not liked Glenn, but he was going to enjoy discussing him after he had gone.

'I don't know that I shall be. I may sell the farm,' he told

Ben. 'It was all right when you were looking after it, but it isn't finished yet, and I can't face coping with these local idiots.'

'We could go over and supervise it for you,' Amy said, 'couldn't we, Daddy?'

Glenn said: 'Oh, Daddy doesn't want to get mixed up with me again,' and he and Ben laughed because it was what Ben had been thinking, and Glenn knew it. 'By the way,' he said on his way to the door, 'I saw your friend Rose Kelly the other day. She asked after you, rather tenderly I thought. She has a new boy friend. But she's probably had at least six since you.'

When he had gone, Laura pounced on Ben. 'I didn't know you knew Rose Kelly. How fascinating. What's she like? Is she as sexy as she looks.'

'No,' Ben said. 'That is – I mean, I don't know.'

Laura looked at him with a new kind of look, speculative, sucking in her lower lip, and Ben turned away to follow Ella out to the kitchen, because he felt that he must explain about Rose.

'Tell it to Laura,' Ella said when he started to explain. 'She's more interested than I am.' She did things noisily with saucepans and baking dishes, and then said reluctantly, not looking at him: 'Why didn't you ever tell me about Rose Kelly?'

'Why should I? It was all over and finished long before I met you.'

He told her a little about Rose, and when he had told her all that he intended to tell, Ella turned round and looked at him gravely. 'Fancy you being engaged to her,' she said, and Ben did not know whether she meant to be insulting or not.

Chapter Fifteen

THERE was a boy at Greenbriars called Neil Hardcastle, a small, pallid child with hair sprouting in every direction from a spot on the crown of his head and moist, wistful eyes on either side of a nose that would dominate his face when he was older.

He had been Amy's friend when she lived with the Glynns,

and when she left, he attached himself to Ben. He knew all Ben's movements in a routine day, and whenever he could escape he would be found lurking in corridors or waiting round corners or sitting outside the gardener's shed so as to be able to say: 'Good morning' or : 'Good afternoon. How are you today?'

'In the pink, thank you, Neil. How are you?'

'Likewise.' Neil would fall into step beside Ben and walk with him, making conversation, until a bell or buzzer sent him scuttling off to the next duty in his regimented life.

Sometimes on Sundays, Ben took him over to the Hallidays' house to see Amy, and the two of them would disappear into the tree-house with cakes and play seriously at being someone else until it was time for Neil to go back to the school.

Many of the parents came to take their sons out on Sundays, and Ben was expected to be on hand in the mornings to make himself known to those he had not met, and be greeted with confidential joviality by those he had; to escort anxious mothers to their sons' bedrooms, and if necessary to the kitchen, which was always scoured on Saturday night; to laugh at jokes about the bills, and rub his hands and be a bluff, breezy naval officer for the very rich, who seemed to like him that way.

Neil's parents never came. They were divorced. His father had married again, and lived in Ireland. His mother who was in the South of France, claiming to be an invalid, neither came to England nor sent for Neil to go to her. Both his grandmothers were dead. He spent his holidays with a married aunt in London, who made him feel a nuisance, or with a spinster aunt in Broadstairs, who did not provide anything for him to do. Once there had been nowhere for him to go for the Christmas holidays, and he had stayed at the school with Mr Horrocks, whose wife was the matron.

The Horrockses had been all right, he told Ben, and their grown-up children had come to stay and there had been a Christmas tree and presents, but they had left Neil alone to roam about the school and grounds by himself, and although he was not especially attached to any of the other boys, he had been overjoyed to see them all come back.

'I was the only one who was glad when term started,' he said, not with self-pity, but as an item of information.

His father had written to him that he thought of coming to England in July, and might come down for Sports Day, which was the big event of the summer term. Neil was holding on to this hope, and discussed the probabilities of will he, won't he, with Ben, *ad nauseam*.

'I hope he doesn't bring his wife,' Neil said. 'You wouldn't like her. She's very fat and she does her nails all the time and she doesn't speak properly to you until the evening, after she's had cocktails. You'd like my father though.' Partly why he hoped so much for his father to come was that he wanted to display him to Ben.

As the time went by, Ben began to know more and more of the boys, and was proud of having learned all their names. He made friends with many of them, but Neil was his special friend, his shadow, his dog.

The masters did not think much of Neil, who was brighter out of the classroom than in it, and who had an irritating way of dreaming off when he was being addressed directly from the blackboard. The games master had no use for him because he handled a cricket ball as if it were a rolled-up porcupine, and had once let go from fright half-way up a rope in the gymnasium and had fallen so clumsily that he had managed to sprain his ankle, even though there was a mat. Old Hammerhead viewed him with mistrust not only because he might have to superannuate him, but because Neil was what he called a slippery boy. When the others were in groups during leisure hours, Neil was mooning off by himself, watching a caterpillar eat a leaf, or squatting by the pond at the back of the old barn, stirring its murky depths with a stick to see what aquatic life came up.

Neil had been quite unhappy at Greenbriars. He did not care so much now. Now he had Ben.

One day, Neil caught a frog. He brought it to Ben in his hand and asked him how he could keep it. Ben got a tin basin from Tilly, and they put the frog in it with stones and weeds and water and covered the basin with a piece of wire netting.

There was an unused shed away by itself behind the garage, and Neil put the frog in there and caught insects for it, and miraculously it did not die. Then he caught a newt in the pond, and he and Ben put that in a basin too, begged from Ella this time because Tilly's ankles were playing her up. Presently some of the other boys began to get interested in what was in the shed, and two small fishes were caught, and another frog and brought to Ben in jars with the request: 'Could you do something about them, sir?'

'It's a proper aquarium,' Amy said, when she came over with Ben to revisit her old haunts and to console Neil, who had been confined to bounds for neither knowing nor caring about the Battle of Bosworth Field. All Sunday afternoon, when most of the boys were off with their parents eating big lunches in the local hotels, Amy and Neil fished in the pond with two of Tilly's kitchen strainers. They came out muddy to the knees with a few more hapless specimens of pool life, and that evening Amy got Mr Halliday to paint her a board which said Aquarium, and Neil tacked it up crookedly over the shed door.

The inmates of the makeshift aquarium were dying like the flies which were so assiduously caught for them, and since several of the boys were interested by now, Ben decided to do something about it.

The headmaster was surprisingly easy. Ben had him temporarily at a disadvantage, having recently discovered that the late bursar had been getting a higher salary than Ben was. When tackled about it, Mr Morton began to bluster about Ben's retired pay, and when Ben told him what he thought of that as an excuse, old Hammerhead had crumpled, and waved a flaccid hand at him and said: 'All right, all right. Don't shout at me. You're responsible for the salaries. Fix your own the way you want it, but don't bother me, with exams coming up.'

Having been detected trying to fiddle Ben out of a fair salary, which may have been his wife's idea, Mr Morton did not look him in the face for a while, and did not object when Ben asked him if he could buy a glass tank for the aquarium, in order to further this innocent and educational hobby. Ben and six boys went to the pet-shop in town on a wet Saturday afternoon when games were off, and spent a happy two hours setting up the tank and landscaping the bottom of it and filling it.

A boy named Grover, who knew a lot of things, but never told you where you were wrong until after you had made your mistake, pointed out the next day that nothing would live in

236

the tank without circulating water. Ben spoke to Mr Chivers, the handyman, who was graced on the school's brochure as Superintendent of Grounds and Buildings. Mr Chivers, who was as sympathetic to the overworked boys as Ben was, did a little plumbing job and hooked up the tank to the water pipes in the garage.

Mrs Morton had known about the aquarium all along. A group of boys out hunting for glow-worms had seen her limping up to the shed one evening in the dusk, and coming down the hill again with an inscrutable face. She bided her time. When more fishes were caught from the big pond across the main road, which was out of bounds, and Ben bought another tank and Mr Chivers hooked it up, she took action.

She sent a boy to fetch Ben to her. It happened to be one of the boys who was sharing in the project in the shed. He told Ben glumly: 'She's hopping mad, sir. If it's about our aquarium, see what you can do about it, won't you, sir?'

'I'll do my best.' Ben endeavoured to combine in his voice both encouragement and enough terseness to indicate that he could not discuss the headmaster's wife. Walking across the hall to her door, he felt almost sorry for Mrs Morton. She had not beaten him yet, and she was not going to beat him now. He had big plans for the shed. Stokes minor had caught a grass snake, and Neil had begged a ferret from the under-gardener, and the aquarium, if Ben had his way, was going to be enlarged into a full-scale zoo.

Mrs Morton was standing in her favourite position by the window with the light behind her, leaning on her stick; a stiff, narrow, and slightly ominous figure.

'Mr Francis,' she said, when Lucy had shown Ben in, lingered to hear what she could, and been dismissed with an impatient outward jerk of the cane, 'correct me if I am mistaken, but I have been given to understand that one of your functions here is to reduce the operational costs of the school.'

'Rather,' Ben said, falsely hearty. Was she going to ask him to sit down? She was not. He stood on the hearthrug, put his hands in his pockets, took them out again and settled their restlessness by folding his arms.

'In the pursuit of which undeniably worthy function' – Mrs

Morton talked like this sometimes; it came from living so long among schoolmasters – 'you have trodden on a great many toes, and caused a fair amount of understandable dissatisfaction, which you, no doubt, consider justified.'

'Oh, I don't know.' Ben felt uncomfortable before her empty stare. 'It had to be done. The chaps don't like not being able to order their own supplies any more, but they'll get used to it. All for the best in the long run, and all that sort of thing.' If only she would move, it would be better. But she stood there with her stick, like the statue of Roosevelt in Grosvenor Square, and made him talk as if he were one of the boys at Greenbriars, instead of one of the staff.

'Very well,' said Mrs Morton. 'It had to be done. Then how, may I ask, do you justify this – this what I can only call insane waste of money by having water running day and night for what I can only describe as a silly toy?'

'Oh, it's all right.' Ben unfolded his arms and put them back in his pockets. 'It's the same water going round and round. I bought a filter.'

'You bought a filter.' She limped towards him, and he thought for one wild moment that she was going to lay about him with her cane. 'With the school funds.'

'I'm responsible for the school funds,' he said, when she stopped walking and hung her stick on the mantelpiece. 'I've only spent very little so far, and I –'

'So far.' She considered him with her Egyptian gaze. 'You mean you plan to enlarge on this folly?'

'Sure. The boys are collecting animals now. They're going to buy guinea-pigs and rabbits with their allowances instead of baked beans. We're going to have a zoo. Oh, look here, Mrs Morton.' He grinned at her. Dammit, she was a woman after all, even though she was the headmaster's wife, and a queer customer at that. 'Don't you understand what a lot of fun the boys are getting out of this?'

'Fun.' She echoed the word mournfully. 'They can have fun in the holidays. Their parents pay us to educate them, not to play with them.'

'What's the matter?' Ben asked. 'Don't you want to understand, or do you really not understand?'

'I understand perfectly.' She sat down in a high-backed chair, which looked as unyielding as herself. 'I've told you what I think. Now, if you want to dig your own grave, please go ahead and do it. I for one shall not weep at your interment.' She smiled suddenly and relaxed, curving up her eyes. When she suddenly gave up the struggle for no apparent reason, it was more discouraging than if she had remained unapproachable.

'Well, if that's all,' Ben shifted his feet, 'I'll –'

'Not quite all.' She was still smiling. Her pale, pointed tongue moistened her lips. 'Why don't you have a drink with me now that you're here, just to show there's no ill feeling?'

He did not believe that there was no ill feeling, and he did not want to stay. It was only eleven o'clock in the morning. Ben was always ready to have a drink at any time, but not with her.

'There is some whisky in the dining-room.' She turned her sleek, narrow head towards the archway between the two rooms and held it in that position, her eyes following him as he went into the dining-room and opened the doors of the sideboard. 'And some soda, if you want it. You can pour me just a small whisky neat. I have felt a little faint ever since I got up, and my disappointment in you has not helped.'

'You never were anything but disappointed in me, as far as I can see,' Ben said, emboldened by being in the other room.

He came back with the two glasses, afraid that she would be rigid with offence, but she seemed not to have heard him. She watched the glass all the way into her hand, held it for a moment, looking at it, then took a swallow and shuddered.

'Like medicine, isn't it?' She looked up at him, took another drink, and set her glass down on a table beside her, keeping her fingers round it.

'Oh, yes, I hate the stuff.' Ben laughed at his own feeble joke, because she did not. He drank his whisky quickly, wanting to get away. He thought that when he had gone, she would get up and go quickly into the other room, perhaps without the cane, and reach for the whisky bottle with a hand that trembled. He did not want to think this. He did not want her to give herself away to him. He did not want to feel sorry for her.

He wanted to hate her, because she was trying to undermine all the things he wanted to do. He knew that she influenced the masters and their wives, who might have left him alone if they had not valued their jobs enough to want to climb on the bandwagon of her approval. They had started by laughing at his aquarium, but when the zoo got going, with the boys building cages and hutches and catching mice and buying rabbits and birds and hamsters, they stopped laughing and began to complain.

Ben had tried to be amiable with all of them. He got on all right with the desiccated Mr Glynn in his own house, and he had struck up some kind of pub-crawling friendship with Willis and Knight, who knew all the best bars for miles round; but he was not part of the scholastic group, and he felt that he never would be.

He was not sure whether they were deliberately excluding him from their club, or whether he was just naturally not equipped to qualify. Old man Glynn would chat with him now and then about the old days at Cambridge in his aseptic sitting-room where smoking was forbidden. Willis and Knight talked his own language when they were doing the pubs together in Knight's old racing Bentley with the outside pipes. But when Ben went into the common-room at tea-time, or at other times for company, it seemed as if they and the other masters conversed in a more esoterically academic way than necessary. Ben could not believe that they always spent their leisure hours discussing medieval church architecture, or the rise and fall of the European coalition under Pitt.

Encouraged by Mrs Morton, they now never missed an opportunity to snipe at Ben's zoo. If a boy's marks fell below the average, they knew where to lay the blame, if the boy was one of Ben's zoo-keepers. For boys who had pets in the shed, they delighted in finding some excuse to keep them in after hours, so that they would miss feeding-time.

The zoo was to be a show-piece for Sports Day. Ben and the boys had made up their minds about that. They now had about twenty-five pets of various kinds, besides the motley pond life in the tanks. There were two wire-netting runs outside the shed, and inside there were pens and cages and a glass-walled box labelled The Pit of Death for the harmless grass snakes wh. Stokes minor caught faster than they died. Ben was enormous proud of what he and the boys had done, and if it mean spending a little money on wood and glass and chicken wire and paint, it was well worth it.

The masters did not think so. Mr Horrocks, who was the assistant headmaster, said to Ben: 'Look here, Francis, I think you're taking a gross liberty, if you ask me. You've had the infernal cheek to tell us all we're wasting money, and here you go spending it like water on a ridiculous collection of tadpoles and white mice.'

'I'm spending it on the boys,' Ben said. 'That's the difference.' Mr Horrocks was one of those who had been making a good thing out of his deals with a wholesale stationery house, and he knew that Ben knew it.

'The boys got along very well before you came on the scene,' Mr Horrocks said. He was a moon-faced man in round pince-nez, with a voice like a creaking door.

'I don't think so.' Since his zoo had become such a success, Ben was not caring so much what he said to people at the school who were against him. The boys were with him. That was what counted. 'I think you all bother too much about what the boys do in the classroom and not enough about what they do outside.'

If Mr Horrocks had been the choleric type he would have turned crimson. As it was, his face remained the colour of Caerphilly cheese, but his pince-nez quivered a little, as if they had a life of their own. 'Since you know absolutely nothing whatever about the education of small boys,' he said, 'I consider that you have gone too far.' He was not a man capable of strong language, but he flung his head backwards and sideways and looked down his nose, as if he had said something very challenging.

'If you feel that way, why don't you complain to Mr Morton?'

'I have, of course, and I shall again.'

'It won't get you anywhere though,' Ben said. 'Since I told the old bird what a big hit this was going to make with the parents on Sports Day, he's all for it.'

le is?' Mr Horrocks lowered his head and pin-pointed Ben ough his lenses. Although he knew that Old Hammerhead greed with everyone to their face and then decried them to the next comer, he did not know whether to believe this. 'I'm sorry to disappoint you, and the Head, if you have trapped him into thinking that,' he said with a thin smile, 'but I don't believe the parents will be remotely interested. There will be so many other attractions. The sports, of course. The standard of athletics is very high this year, I understand. The concert after prize-giving. Quite a feature of our annual roustabout, as you will discover. And then, you know, we all have our displays in our own departments. The art gallery in the studio, the geology collection, the specimens in the lab. My own elaborate scale model of the first Pilgrim Settlement at Plymouth, Massachusetts, should attract more than a small amount of attention, I dare to think.'

'I see,' Ben said. 'You're jealous.'

'If you are a typical example of an officer in Her Imperial Majesty's forces, I'm glad my son was too delicate to do his national service.' Mr Horrocks' head, lowered with false modesty while he spoke of his Pilgrim Settlement, had gone up again to the duelling position. 'You are very uncivil, Commander Francis. You are also a – a –' he could not say a damn fool, so he said: 'a silly ass. With all this childish nonsense about a zoo, you are obviously playing for popularity with the boys. I've seen it before – masters who made fools of themselves because they wanted to be popular, and found that they were only despised. The boys are not your concern. Take my advice and leave them alone.'

'I can't,' Ben said lightly. 'They're the only decent thing about this place.'

Except Ella. Ella was all right. She took no part in the petty squabbles within the school. She had all she could do to handle the squabbles among her own domestic staff. When Ben came to her on the premises to rail against the anti-zoo faction, she said: 'Please don't drag me into it'; but in her own home, she listened to him, and let him voice his enthusiasm and his vexations, and was stoutly on his side, and had promised to lend Neil one of the puppies to display to his father in the zoo.

If Neil's father did not come, it would be a major trag Neil was not running or jumping or throwing anything in sports. He had neither instrument nor voice for the concer He had not won any prizes, and none of his paintings were displayed in the studio. But it was he who had started the zoo with his frog.

He was head keeper, and had an armband sewn by Ella to prove it. All the boys who were zoo-keepers had armbands, for Ben knew the value of even the hint of uniform, but Neil's was the widest and the brightest colour and had the words Head Keeper lettered indistinctly round it in marking ink.

Sports Day was to be a big social occasion, with a buffet lunch in the dining-hall and a slap-up tea in a marquee. Ben was overwhelmed with organizational details, but the last garnished touches to the zoo were the most important.

Mrs Halliday insisted on bringing Amy's pony over in her trailer, and Ben had to borrow sheep hurdles from a farmer to make a pen for it. Its name was Rusty, but Amy had re-christened it Phoenix on the day of the fire. Mr Halliday painted another board, and the pony's name was nailed to the hurdles as if it were a racehorse. The handyman's sister, who had been brought over from her nearby smallholding to see the zoo, had screamed gratifyingly at the snakes, clapped her hand over her mouth to smother her exuberant delight at the whole project, and had come back next day with a pair of bantam hens.

'A surprise for the boys,' she said, laughing again and stifling the laugh in an embarrassment of generosity.

Ben put the bantams into a hutch with a suspicious rabbit, and began to make a coop for them out of a wooden box, working quickly to have the hens installed by the time the zoo-keepers were let out of school and ran and hopped and shrieked and hurled each other joyfully to the ground, coming up the hill at feeding-time.

Squatting with his sleeves rolled up and a bunch of nails in his mouth, Ben realized how happy he was, and thought that perhaps Mr Horrocks was right. He was getting childish. It was said that Admirals began to go senile after they retired and suddenly had no authority. Perhaps the same thing happened to Commanders.

can't do it, Commander, I really can't.' Tilly Wicket sat ~vn at the end of the long kitchen table and put her bad foot ~ on a little stool. 'Even with extra help – and what kind of ~elp can you get round here that's any more use than a wet Saturday in March – I think it's too much to ask.'

'I thought nothing was too much for you.' Ben sat down and ran his finger along a knife scar in the table.

'It didn't use to be, but I'm not the same this term. Maids have come and gone here, and kitchen porters and the like, and they've said to me: "We admire that you can make do with it, Mrs Wickett, but that woman will get you down in the end." Well, now she has. My lady has overstepped the bounds this time, and if you won't tell her, I will.'

'Oh, I'll tell her,' Ben said. 'It will mean a row, but I'd rather she had it with me than with you.'

He did not mean that he thought he could win where Tilly could not, but he would rather Mrs Morton were rude to him than to Tilly. He could take it. She had already called him a penny-pinching, ignorant prig because he had said that her elaborate plans for the lunch and tea on Sports Day were too extravagant. Now when he told her that it was not fair to expect Tilly to rise to such heights of culinary display, she could only play a variation on the same theme.

He was not afraid of Mrs Morton any more. He thought he had got her number. She was trying to impress the parents. That was all right. Everyone was doing that, including Ben with his zoo, but Mrs Morton's plans for lobster salad and chicken in aspic and *foie gras en croûte* were not only to make a good impression, but to cover up the truth of how badly the boys fared on any day that was not Sports Day.

When their sons told them, hanging round the cars as they drove off, that the meals all term had been lousy, the parents would dismiss it as automatic schoolboy grumbling. 'Look at the spread Mrs Morton put on today,' they would say. 'The woman's a genius. If that's any indication of how you're fed every day, your standards of lousy are different from mine, my boy. When I was a lad –'

And the mothers would say: 'I think you must be exaggerating, darling. The lunch and tea were marvellous. If Mrs

Morton can cater like that for hundreds of extra people, it ~
be easy for her to feed a hundred boys well. You don't l~
exactly starved, either.'

'Well, I am,' the boy would say. 'There's such a thing a~
filling you up with bread and potatoes and porridge.'

And the fathers and mothers would laugh indulgently and
drive off in their shiny cars, confident in the fullness of lobster
and *foie gras* and excellent Chablis that they were lucky to have
their boys in the care of such an exceptional woman as Mrs
Morton.

She would be gracious and impressively ladylike on Sports
Day. Ben had seen her at that game with the parents who came
on Sundays. She would fool them all that she was the right kind
of cultured, well-bred, sensitive woman to have as headmaster's
wife, and she would take all the credit for the magnificent
hospitality although it would be Tilly's labour and Ben's
ability somehow to absorb the staggering cost into his budget
that would have made it possible.

If she were allowed to get away with it that was. Ben had not
given up the fight yet, and he advanced on Mrs Morton in
defence of Tilly.

'She's done it before,' Mrs Morton said. 'She can do it again.'

'She's never been asked to do so much before. She told me.'

'If you believe everything that fat megalomaniac tells you,
you are not as shrewd as you are always trying to make me
believe.'

'It's too much for her.'

'You're heading for trouble when you start coddling the staff.
If she doesn't like it, she can go. I can get another cook.'

'You'll never get another who works as hard as Tilly.' And
puts up with you as dietitian, Ben added in his head.

'Must we discuss the servants?' Mrs Morton smoothed her
hair with stiff, turned-back fingers. 'I find it very boring.'

'All right. We'll discuss the lunch again. I haven't changed
my mind. It's ludicrous, Mrs Morton. The school's in debt. We
can't afford it.'

'We were always able to afford it before you came.'

'Not on a scale like this. No, not only what Tilly told me.
I've seen the records. What are you trying to do – upset my

eting so that you can prove at the end of term that I
en't saved the school any money?'

'You're being childish, Mr Francis.' Why did everyone call
im that? Was it because they had been among small boys for
so long that the word nuisance was synonymous with child? 'A
little extra expense isn't going to matter once a year.'

'Once a year. That's the point. If we're going to spend extra
money on food, we should be spending it on the boys, not on
their bloated parents, who can get this kind of food any time
they want by paying for it.'

'You don't understand anything about running a school, do
you?' Mrs Morton looked at him, not with anger, but with a
kind of distant pity for his ignorance.

'I'm beginning to understand a lot,' Ben said, 'and much of
it I don't like. Now please give me the menus you've made out
for this feast, and we'll revise them together.'

'We'll do no such thing.'

'All right, then I'll plan the menu myself and get the orders in.'

She smiled at him in such a superior way that he added:
'And look here, Mrs Morton, if you try to cheat me by ordering
all this fancy stuff yourself, I shall tell the tradesmen that you
have no authority to give orders, and they'll have to take the
stuff back. That's going to make you look just ducky, isn't it?'

'Just ducky.' She fixed him with her eye. He tried to stare her
out, but she was looking at him as if he were a boy in the Lower
Fourth with egg on his tie and ink in his hair, so he turned and
walked off with what he hoped was a stern and resolute stride.
Now she could go away and get drunk.

When Mr and Mrs Horrocks had the week-end off, Ella had
to sleep in their room at the school, in their bed, which was
comfortable enough, but offensively connubial when you considered who normally shared it.

Since Mrs Horrocks was the matron, they did not live in a
separate house, but in a three-roomed flat at the top of one of
the wings of the Old Building, where Mrs Horrocks had her
sick-bay and her little dispensary stocked mostly with Milk of
Magnesia and ear-drops, and where she could supervise the
corridor where the smallest boys slept, three to a room.

The boys enjoyed Ella's occasional nights at the because she would gather them all together in one room read them a story, and she did not mind if they were ea chocolate in bed when she came to turn their lights out. Som. times she forgot to turn their lights out, and Mrs Morton seeing from her side window that there were squares of light on the garden where no squares of light ought to be, would call down one of the older boys and send him to Ella with an order disguised as a message.

On the night after his last battle with Mrs Morton about the lobster and Chablis, Ben was out in the garden late, walking back from the building where the maids slept.

Apart from a few steadies like Tilly and Lucy, who had been at the school for so long that they had forgotten any other way of life, the maids were always changing. The local girls got married, or got fed up, or got pregnant. Living-in staff were hard to find, and the numbers often had to be made up from migrant labour: strange, feckless girls who would steal anything if they got the chance, slow men, beaten down by misfortune or beer, sad-eyed women who were getting away from somewhere they did not want to be, negligent girls on the way to somewhere else.

They came and went, a constant worry to Ella, and also to Ben, who was responsible for hiring them and for finding replacements when they slipped cable in the night, with or without spoons or articles of someone else's clothing.

He had recently engaged a girl who did not seem right even by the low standards he had to make shift with. She looked like a prostitute, and a bargain-priced one at that, and she had not been in the place a week before Lucy informed Mrs Morton, who informed Ben, censoriously, as if it were his fault, that her appearance was not deceptive.

Since the girl was working well enough, and it seemed hardly worth looking for another so near the end of term, Ben made a trip to her room every night to make sure that she was not entertaining a man again. He hated to have to open the door and look in on the girl in bed, and the first night he had done so, she had welcomed him delightedly, until he explained the purpose of his visit. After that when he opened the door, she

avour him at the top of her voice with some colourful
ns of his virility, so he left his visits until as late as
.ble in the hope that she would be asleep.

his night, it was after eleven when he left the snoring lump
. girl in the bed which looked as if it was never made. He
wanted to go up to the zoo with his torch to visit the pets, but
they were so instantly aware and eager for food when you
woke them that it seemed unfair to disturb them. He walked
past the front of the Old Building on his way to the Glynn's
house. All the lights were out, except in Mrs Morton's drawing-
room.

The curtains were not drawn, which was unusual, for Mrs
Morton generally pulled them sharply across before the red
sun had given its last wink through the trees on the hill. Ben
stood for a minute or two and watched the window from a
distance. He imagined that he did not know the interior, nor
who was in it, so that the lighted room looked like a room in
a proper home, inviting, secure, because he was an outsider
looking in.

If he stepped closer and looked right into the room, the
attraction would vanish. The room would repel rather than
invite him, because of all the times he had stood on that hearth-
rug and tussled with Mrs Morton in that disturbing, unsatisfactory way which left him not knowing whether he had won
or not.

He felt impelled to sneak up and see what she was doing now.
It was unfair, and also dangerous, because she would have him
fired if she caught him, but the temptation to catch that inscrutable figure unawares was too great to resist.

He stepped softly forward over the lawn, holding his breath
as he crossed the gravel drive on tiptoe, then stood in a flower-
bed against the wall of the house and looked in sideways. There
was no one in that end of the room, which contained the high-
backed chair where Mrs Morton usually sat. Ducking down,
he passed beneath the window and slid a glance into the other
end of the room. No one there either. She had gone to bed and
left the light on. Wasting the school's electricity. He planned
words of reprimand for the morning, knowing he would not
say them.

He stepped out of the flower-bed and put out a foot to k over his footmarks, but drew it back. If the dents in the so earth started a scare about a Peeping Tom, it would make some excitement for the boys, who would start sleuthing, and give the old girl something new to worry about. Or better yet, she might think she had an admirer, who fed his love with secret glimpses. It was probably what she needed to make her human. Being married to Old Hammerhead had not helped her at all.

Passing the corner of the house, he saw that the side-door to the Morton's apartment was open. That, too, she had forgotten. She must have gone to bed tight tonight. Thank God she had the sense to do her drinking when no one knew about it. Or did everyone know? It had not taken Ben long to find out. You only had to see the way she handled a glass to know what the stuff in it meant to her. Perhaps the masters all knew, but were excluding him from the knowledge, as they tried to exclude him from their fraternity. It was not loyalty to Mrs Morton that kept their mouths shut. They were not that kind of team. Most of them were petty individualists who fed on gossip and spite. But they grudged Ben this juicy bit of gossip in the same way that they appeared to grudge him his position at the school.

He shut Mrs Morton's door quietly, in case she should awaken and cry Thief, and then he saw that there was a light on the top floor of the wing. A light from the Horrockses' bed-room. Ella's light. She was probably reading in bed. He had seen her in a dressing-gown at home when she got up to make early-morning tea, and had imagined what she looked like in the nightdress underneath it. He imagined it again now. She was strongly-built and big-boned, but she went in and out in the right places, and that time when he had held her crying against him in the rain, she had been satisfactorily soft, even through their two raincoats.

He pictured what she would look like sitting up in the big bed, which probably had a sag on Mrs Horrocks' side, for she was a good stone heavier than her husband. Ben knew, because he had seen her when she first got up, that Ella's lips without lipstick would still be pink, and her skin without powder would be rough and shiny. Her heavy, dark-blonde hair would be brushed back, but she would still be putting it away from her eyes with an automatic gesture of the hand. She might be eating an apple or a bar of chocolate in bed, or even drinking a mug of cocoa while she read. Unmarried women of thirty-five got into these habits. It was better than nothing.

The air was growing chilly. He would go. The bottom of Ella's window was open, and she probably would not shut it, even if it got colder. As Ben was turning away, Ella, fully dressed, appeared in the window with her arms raised to shut it. She saw him, so he called up Hullo.

'What are you doing down there?'

He wanted to say: 'I was looking at your window and imagining you in bed.' If it had been Laura, he would have said it. To Ella he said: 'I'm the new night watchman. Hadn't you heard?'

'I've just made some tea.' It was vaguely an invitation, but not so definite that he need accept if he did not want to.

'I'll be right up.'

They sat in Mrs Horrocks' parlour in which all the tables and shelves and chests had pieces of cloth laid over them. Even the mantelpiece had a white linen runner with lace hanging down at both ends, as if it was an altar. They sat on either side of the fan of paper in the fireplace in chairs that had extra pieces of material laid on the back and arms, and pretended that they were Mr and Mrs Horrocks, but had to give it up almost at once because they could not imagine what the Horrockses found to talk about.

'Do you always stay up so late when you have to get up early in the morning?' Ben asked. 'You look like a healthy girl who gets plenty of sleep.'

Ella made a face, and he saw that he had worded his compliment wrong.

'One of the boys has been having nightmares,' she said. 'He's been calling out and crying. He was afraid that I wouldn't hear him, so I promised him I wouldn't go to bed for a long time. I'd better go and look at him now.'

Ben went with her, and they stepped softly into the room where the three little boys were sleeping in strange attitudes in

250

their wooden beds. Ella had put a night-light by the bed o.
boy who had been dreaming. In the flickering light, he
sprawled outside the covers, his hands flung out, his spiky ha.
damp on his flushed forehead, his mouth as pure as a baby's.

'Much too young to be away at school,' Ella said as she bent
to pull the blanket over him and stroke the hair away from his
forehead.

'God, yes,' Ben said. 'Don't let's send our sons to prep
school.'

Ella stood up and looked at him doubtfully. 'Are we still
being Mr and Mrs Horrocks?'

Ben thought of all the times when he had meaninglessly
played at discussing marriage with Rose. You could not do that
with Ella. He sighed and said: 'I suppose so.'

Passing an open window on their way back to the parlour,
they heard a door below and to the right bang shut. Mrs
Morton's side-door.

'A night prowler?'

'It was open before,' Ben said. 'Perhaps I didn't shut it
properly, and it blew open.'

'There isn't any wind.'

Ella walked on down the corridor and Ben asked her back:
'Did you know that she was an alcoholic?'

'Oh, yes.' Ella shrugged her shoulders without looking round.
'Everyone knows it – except the parents. She's lucky she can
drink so much and that it doesn't show in her face.'

'It does show though,' Ben said. 'She has that look all the
time of not being there. You know how people look sometimes
at cocktail parties. She looks as though she were permanently
two martinis up on you.'

Ella sat down again in the parlour, but Ben remained stand
ing. 'I'd better go,' he said. 'If Mrs Morton sees your light and
comes up to tell you to turn it off, we'll probably both get fired.'

'Would you care?'

'Lord, yes.' He was surprised that she asked that, as if it
would be nothing to have fiddled about as a civilian for six
months and then lose the first decent job you found. 'I want to
stay here. I can make a success of this, I think.' He sat on the
corner of the table

251

body else thinks so. I'm sorry, Ben. I didn't mean that way it came out. I meant that they don't want to give you a ance.'

'Yes, I know. It's a closed shop. I'm an outsider, and a pompous naval officer, which makes me need to be taken down several pegs, and I've had the nerve to cut off some of their perks. They think I'll give in and go their way in the end, but I won't. I'm going to make a taut ship out of this place if it's the last thing I do.'

'Make a tight ship out of it,' repeated Ella, who was leaning drowsily back with her arms along the arms of the chair and not listening properly, 'and then get out?'

'Probably. There are better schools than this. If I do a good job here, I could go on to a public school with a bigger salary. I might even get into a college eventually.'

Ella smiled. 'You're very ambitious,' she said, as if ambition were a quaint idiosyncrasy.

'I'm not really. I'm making myself be. I wasn't ambitious enough in the Navy. If I had been, perhaps I wouldn't have been slung out. But the Navy's a feather-bed. You can be a nonentity and still draw your pay and be sure of your position. It's different on the beach. Nobody's going to give you the time of day unless you fight for it.'

She did not say anything. She sat with her eyes half-closed, her long, bare legs stretched out, the heel of one slippered foot rubbing gently on the instep of the other.

'What's wrong with ambition?' he said, irritated by her silence. 'What's wrong in wanting to push yourself a bit nearer the top?'

'Oh, nothing.' She opened her eyes and look at him mildly. 'But if you don't want so much, you don't get so many disappointments.'

'That's defeatist. You'll tell me next that a man who lives in a condemned slum with one cold tap in the yard is happier than a man who has a bathroom, because it doesn't occur to him to worry about keeping clean.'

Ella considered this, frowning at the cold, bare fireplace. 'He might be,' she said. 'It would depend on a lot of things besides the bath. The man with the bathroom might want a yacht, you

252

see, and not be able to appreciate the nice house becaus
couldn't have the yacht.'

'Therefore, the man in the slum is happier. *Q.E.D.* Y
should take over the geometry class, Ella.'

'Don't laugh at me, Ben. I wish everyone wouldn't always
laugh at me when I try to say what I think about life.'

'I'm not laughing. I agree with you in a way, not about the
bathroom, but about being happier if you don't want too much.
But I daren't let myself go on using that as an excuse for not
trying to get somewhere. A girl I knew once called me a
nobody. I hadn't minded being a nobody up till then, but when
she said it, it hurt.'

'Rose Kelly?'

He nodded.

'How unkind.' With her elbows on the chair, she linked her
fingers and looked down at them. 'All the s-same,' she said, with
the slight hesitation, not quite a stammer, which only checked
her speech when she was shy, 'you seem like the sort of person
who'll always be happier being nobody very special.'

'Thanks.' He slid off the table and put his hand on the top of
her hair. 'You said that in a much nicer way than Rose did.'

Ella jerked her head away from his hand and stood up.
'You'd better go. Mrs Morton is quite likely to come up.'

'She's probably blind to the world. But just in case –' He
went to the door and switched off the light. The moon was in
the room, and he sat Ella down on a terrible little settee by the
window, and the skin of her face and arms was young and
pearly in the cold light. Ben sat close beside her. She neither
held herself away nor snuggled up to him. He did not know
where they would go from there, but meanwhile it was very
peaceful.

'If she does come up,' Ella said, 'this will be worse.'

'Give the old girl a thrill.' He put his arm round Ella's waist
to see what she would do. She did not do anything. 'Why does
she hate me so much?' he asked.

'Didn't you know?' She turned to him so that her waist slid
away from his arm. 'Didn't you know about Mr Butterick?'

'My predecessor? Only that he left a bit of a smell behind
him.'

253

e had him fired.'

'What's that got to do with me? You mean she has to hate all bursars now because she didn't like poor Butterick?'

'Not exactly. She hates you because you're not him.'

'I don't get it.'

'They had a – well, an affair, I suppose you'd call it. About two years ago, it started. Everyone knew about it, including Mr Morton, but of course he wouldn't dare try to stop it. It was Mr Butterick who stopped it. He got mixed up with a girl who used to come here to give piano lessons – she doesn't come any more, of course – and so Mrs Morton saw to it that he lost his job.'

'You mean she won't have a bursar on the place unless he's prepared to take her on as well? Is that why she hates me – because I've never made a pass at her? My God, I'm not brave enough for that.'

'It isn't so simple. She got him fired, but now because he isn't here, no one else will do. I honestly think the poor woman was in love with him.'

'You sound as if you're sorry for her,' Ben said. 'You're sorry for everybody, aren't you? It must be very tiring.'

'I'm not. I wish I could be. But with the world so crammed with fear and misery, you'd die if you minded about everyone. It's like seeing those old pictures of concentration camps. If there was just one skeleton walking about, you'd care desperately. When there are thousands, you haven't enough pity to stretch far enough, however hard you try. But with her –' She bent her head so that her hair swung across the shining moonlit curve of her forehead. 'It's easy to be sorry for her because I can't help understanding how she felt. It isn't any fun to have a man you've allowed yourself to love calmly walk away from you with someone more attractive.'

'Who was the swine who did it to you?' Ben took her hand. 'I'll kill him.'

'You can't. He's in New Zealand. I don't care any more, anyway. I don't even remember much about him. It's funny. They say you remember the happy things and forget the painful ones, but the only thing I remember about being in love with him was the way I felt when I lost him.'

'Is that why you didn't want me to kiss you in the k
that day at your house – because you're disillusioned abou
men for ever? Through with sex, and all that?'

'Don't be silly.' Ella tried to pull her hand away and stand u
but he held her down and put both his arms round her.

'Why, then?'

She turned her head away.

'Tell me.'

'No.'

'Please, Ella.'

'No. Well then – it was because I thought you were only
trying to be nice because you were sorry for me because I'm
thirty-five and not married.' She turned in his arms to look at
him, and he saw that she was speaking the truth.

'That's neurotic,' he said. 'Why should I be sorry for you?
Are you sorry for me because I'm thirty-six and not
married?'

'It's different for a man. For a man, it's quite – quite glamorous to be unattached. It isn't for a girl.'

'Glamorous or not,' Ben said, 'at the moment, it's damn
convenient.' He shifted his arms to pull her close against him.
It was a wonderful kiss. The only thing wrong with it was that
they had wasted all these weeks by not kissing like this before.
'I've changed my mind,' Ben said. 'You're not neurotic.'

The settee was narrow and slippery and as unsympathetic to
their love-making as if Mrs Horrocks had instructed it to dis-
courage anything like this in her absence. Presently they slid to
the floor and stayed there quietly, not kissing for a while, but
just holding each other in the natural comfort of two married
people in bed. They began to talk about things they had never
told each other before. Without thinking how he would explain
it, Ben found himself telling Ella how he had been watching her
house nearly all his life, and what her family had meant to
him.

She listened as calmly as if she knew it already. He was glad
that he had waited to tell her alone. If he had told it in front of
all the family, there would have been questions and exclamations and jokes, and Ella's understanding might have been
swamped.

funny,' she said. 'I don't often look at the trains, except
ﾗﾉsionally to wish I was somebody going somewhere. But
ﾗｿe when I did, I saw a man looking out. Just for a second,
ﾗﾉt I saw what he looked like. It was the day you first came.
When I saw you standing in our front doorway, it was a shock,
because you looked like him.'

'I was him. I saw you washing the dog. You waved, and I got
off at the next station and came right back. I didn't know what
I'd say. Don't tell Old Hammerhead, but I'd no idea the school
even existed until your father suggested it.'

Ella knelt up and ran her hand over his cropped hair in the
gesture that Amy used when she was feeling tender. 'Like corn
in the moonlight,' she said. 'Your hair. It springs back after my
hand like corn does when the wind passes over it.' She stroked
it again and then dropped her hand and sat back on her heels,
away from him. 'You came to our house after all those years,
and then,' her voice flattened, 'you found we weren't a magic
family at all, but just ordinary, and you were disappointed in
us.'

'I wasn't. It was much better than magic. It was real. Darling,
I love you all. I love you, Ella.'

'You don't.' It should have brought her close to him again,
but she did not say or do any of the things he had thought she
might do when he told her this. 'You just enjoy kissing me,
and you say that because you think I'm the sort of nice
wholesome girl who needs to be told it before I can enjoy
it too.'

'Oh, yes,' Ben said bitterly, 'and the moonlight has gone to
my head, and I need a woman as much as you need a man. I've
changed my mind again. You are neurotic.'

'Go away.' She stood up and pushed back her hair. 'I – I –'
She stammered as she had stammered when she had greeted him
uncertainly in the doorway of her home. 'I wish you'd never got
off the train.'

She went towards the door, and stumbled over an upholstered
stool. Ben caught her and tried to twist her round to him, but
she was strong enough to break away, and she went into the
bedroom and shut the door.

For at least five minutes, Ben stood in a patch of moonlight

in the room and looked at the door. Then he went out sile
so that Ella would not know that he had been standing th
wondering whether to go in after her.

When he woke the next morning, he wanted very badly to
see Ella, so he dressed quickly and stepped out on to the cob-
webbed grass.

'Where are you going?' Mrs Glynn's head, shrunken by pin
curls and hair net, looked out of her kitchen door. 'I'm cooking breakfast.'

'Just up to the zoo.'

'You and that menagerie.' The head wagged. 'That's all you
think about these days.'

That's all you know, my good woman. Ben went across the
grass to the Old Building, but when he reached the door, he
thought: Why not? He would go up to the zoo first and then
see Ella. If she had watched his approach from the window, it
would do her no harm to be baffled by his sudden change of
direction. Keep 'em guessing, that was the way, he told himself,
although he knew that he would never be like that with
Ella.

But she would be chivvying the boys into their clothes now,
and tying ties for the smallest incompetents who had been
spoiled and nannied all their lives and suddenly pitched out of
the nest into prep school. He would catch her when the boys
had gone down to breakfast, and she was making tea and toast
because she hated to have meals in the dining-hall. He would
catch her alone and make her listen to him, make her believe
that he really loved her, force her to believe that she was
lonely.

As he went up the hill to the zoo, a small boy came running
down, stumbling, half-falling, crying so desperately that he
would have passed Ben without seeing him if Ben had not
caught him by the arm as he ran blindly by. It was Neil. He
was sobbing so violently that no coherent words came out. He
gasped something about: 'The zoo . . . our zoo!' and flung himself face down on the ground in a frenzy of grief.

The zoo was almost totally destroyed. The flimsy door with
its cheap padlock from some boy's bicycle had been wrenched
open. Inside, the pens and hutches were smashed or torn open.

doors gaped. The window of the Pit of Death lay in slivers
the bottom of the box on top of one dead grass snake whose
ck had been pierced by a spike of falling glass. All the
animals and birds were gone. The tanks were shattered and the
fish lay pale and dead-eyed in the damp stain where the water
had soaked into the earth floor. High up on a ledge under the
roof, a solitary budgerigar chirped and chattered to itself like
a madman chuckling over the end of the world.

There was no question about who had done it. Even if Ben
had not already known, there was the handle of Mrs Morton's
cane lying among a heap of splintered wood where it had
broken as she laid about her in her drunken passion.

When Ben went down the hill, Neil had gone. Ella looked
out of her window and called to him gently, but he could not
stop. Running, half-sobbing with rage, he burst through Mrs
Morton's side-door, calling for her at the top of his voice. He
did not care if Old Hammerhead heard him. He did not care
who heard.

Mrs Morton appeared on the stairs clutching a wrapper
round her, her hair hanging down her back like seaweed, her
face as white as the bellies of the dead fish in the zoo. When
she saw him, she did not go back or come down the stairs. She
stood motionless on the top step with her hand on the banister
while Ben stood in the hall and bellowed at her all the abuse he
could think of, and none of it was bad enough for what she had
done.

Chapter Sixteen

'YOU'LL have to go, of course.' The headmaster rubbed his
nose and squinted at his finger. He would not look at Ben.

'Of course, I realize that.' Ben stood and looked over his
head. He would not sit down and he would not call him sir.

Old Hammerhead cleared his throat. 'Do you want to stay
until the end of term?' he asked stiffly.

'I hardly could after what I said to your wife.'

'You could apologise to her?' Mr Morton looked up at him

tentatively. 'No. I see. Well, it's a pity. You were be₂
get a grip on things here, it seemed. Now I shall ha▾
well, no matter. But we shall miss you on Sports Day. ᴖ
of the parents have remarked that they thought you were
an asset to the school.'

'Thank you.' Ben bowed. 'Like the art gallery and the conce₂
and the mustard and cress in saucers and Mr Horrocks' Pilgrim
Settlement.' He wished that Old Hammerhead would stand up
and threaten to knock his block off for insulting his wife. If
the man had been a different shape, they could have fought, and
Ben could tell him what he could do with his school, and storm
away in a cloud of anger which would have been a more satisfactory end to this miserable thing than the unwelcome feeling
of pity with which he was forced to take his leave of the in-
effectual little man.

'I'm sorry,' Ben found himself saying, and his hand stretched
out across the desk.

Mr Morton tottered to his feet and shook hands limply. He
swallowed and said with difficulty, 'Thank you for apologizing
to *me*, at any rate.'

Ben did not disillusion him. The least he could do for the
Old Hammerhead was to let him believe that he was sorry for
what had happened and not that he was sorry for him because
he had to live with his wife.

Ben went up to London to stay with Geneva while he looked
for another job. The Hallidays would keep Amy until he had
found something and was able to make some kind of home for
her. He had no idea what he would find, nor how he and Amy
would live. They were back where they had started. Ben was
back on the books of the employment liaison officer at the
Admiralty, back with his hat in his hand in the waiting-rooms
of employers who were still sympathetic and still promising to
let him know if a suitable vacancy occurred.

It was like the sort of bad dream where you try to pack a
suitcase, or cross London to catch a train, or escape down a
corridor to save your life, and find that you can only stay in the
same place, making no progress at all.

Before he left the Hallidays' house, Amy had done a curious

_spondent, he had talked with her in her bedroom, _as the only place where they could get away from well-_ng people reviling the Mortons and telling him how sorry were. He could not raise any optimism for Amy, although knew that he should try, and after a while she had gone to _he table by her bed and with a calm movement of her hand, knocked over her ant farm.

She picked it up and set it straight. The tunnels were caved in. Most of the ants were submerged in sand. Two of them were running about in a panic on the top of their shifted hill.

'Now look, Daddy,' Amy said. 'They're going to start all over again, right away, and make a new city. They'll hate me for this.' She stroked the top of the plastic case lovingly with her finger. 'But I wanted to show you.'

Since Ben could not go back to the school, Ella brought Neil over in the car to say good-bye. Ben did not know what he would say to the boy, but when he saw him, Neil did all the talking. His father had telephoned from London. He would definitely be there for Sports Day. He was taking Neil back with him to Ireland for the holidays because his wife was going away.

'Perhaps she'll never come back!' Neil cried, making a song of it. He was bright-eyed with happiness. In the excitement of the imminent future, he had forgotten about the zoo, and forgotten to be upset because Ben would not be at Greenbriars next term. He could not see that far ahead.

When Amy reminded him, rather sharply, he said: 'I'll miss you terribly, sir. The boys are all sick as mud about what happened.' Then he began to talk extravagantly again about his father.

'Thanks for bringing Neil over,' Ben said to Ella when she came back from returning the boy to school.

'I thought you were a bit hurt,' Ella said, 'because he wasn't more upset about you going.'

'No. Oh, no,' Ben said quickly, because it was true. 'Thank God somebody's happy, at any rate. It was nice of you to think of bringing him.'

Ella blushed. They were walking back from the garage, where Ben had gone out to meet her when she came back with the car

'It was something I could do,' she said. 'I want to do s[...]
for you, but I don't know what.'

'You're keeping Amy for me.' They walked apar[...]
touching.

'Yes, but that's for myself. I want her. That's nothing.
books you always read about women who know exactly th[...]
right thing to do when there's a crisis. They boil water, or
appear suddenly with a tray of coffee and sandwiches, or if
somebody dies, they take all the children quietly away to the
cinema without being asked while the body is being got out of
the house. What do they boil water for? I don't even know. If
somebody suddenly started to have a baby with me, it would
be in a car, or in a railway carriage without a corridor, where
there wasn't any water anyway. If I made coffee, everybody
would want tea, or they'd all have gone somewhere else by the
time I'd cut the sandwiches. If I took the bereaved children off
to the cinema, I'd find people waiting impatiently when I got
back, saying: 'Where have you been? The children have missed
the train for Grandma's.'

'Silly,' Ben said. 'There's nothing wrong with you. I love
you.'

'I don't know.' They stopped outside the back door and Ella
stood on the worn stone step and looked down at him with her
gentle eyes. 'I think perhaps you say that because you need
someone to love, and you think that I do too. Ben, I'm sorry
I said I wished you'd never got off the train. I didn't mean it.
I'm glad you did.'

'So am I. Come with me to London, Ella. Marry me.'

She shook her head without looking at him. 'You've [...]
troubles enough now without me as well.'

He did not know what to say. He wanted to cry out his need
for her, but a deadening depression was closing in on him to
kill the words before he could say them. He had no right to ask
her now. He had no job. He had nothing but uncertainty and
worry and perhaps failure to give her. Why had he not asked
her when his job was secure at the school, when he was on the
upgrade, doing well, seeing a successful future before him? If
only he had not let that go. If only he had held his tongue. Why
was Mrs Morton ever born to wreck his zoo, his job – he looked

anding uncertainly, waiting for him to say something –

en Ella saw that he had nothing more to say, she turned
went into the house, and Ben did not follow her. He did
see her alone again. He said good-bye to her with all the
est of the family, and climbed into the little car to drive to
London and try to start building up his life all over again, like
Amy's ants.

On the day when he was to go for an interview with a large
manufacturing firm who were offering a job in their central
personnel department, Geneva woke him early and said: 'Your
Aunt Edna's on the telephone. She sounds very peculiar, even
for her.'

'Benjamin?' His mother's sister projected crisis shrilly over
the wire. 'Prepare yourself for a shock. Your father died in his
sleep last night. Yes, his heart. Thank God I was here.'

A big help you must have been, was Ben's first barely-
comprehending reaction. You'd be the last person I'd want if –
but, of course, it was much better that his mother had not been
alone.

'What . . . What?' Aunt Edna kept saying, as he was silent,
realizing the truth, feeling already the first scouting party of
remorse seeking him out, sniping at him because he had not
been kinder, had not gone down to see the old man for so
long. . . .

He asked to speak to his mother, but Edna, who was past-
master at her sister's brand of suggested reproof, said: 'Oh,
Benjamin, how can you ask that? How could you expect her
to talk on the telephone at a time like this? She wants you here.
You'll come at once?'

'Today? . . . Yes, yes, Aunt Edna, of course. I didn't mean . . .
I'll take the first train I can.' There went his interview, and the
job. Why should they hold it for him, with dozens of ex-officers
panting on their doorstep?

Ben did not want his mother to go to the funeral, and Edna
had said proudly: 'She's not able for it', but Mrs Francis
insisted that she must go, and even made Ben drive her into
Southampton to buy a black hat, since she had none that were

not gaudy. 'Your father would want me to look m. front of all his friends,' she said with shaky bravado.

She was being incredibly brave. She had wept to Ben he first arrived, but not again after that, and she had not spe at all of what her husband's loss meant to her.

All her life she had been heartsick and stricken to the core b, things that hardly affected her at all. Now that the substance of her life was dissolved, she had not words for it. She was not stunned into silence, as she had been when Matthew was drowned. Her quick sparrow energy was unslackened, and she never stopped talking all the three days that Ben was with her at Wavecrest, except when Edna forced phenobarbital down her and put her to sleep.

Edna did not approve of her being so normal. Her sister had wanted to break the news to Ben himself, but she had not let her use the telephone. In Edna's book, widows were desolate, to be treated like a cross between an invalid and a lunatic. If her sister went out of the room, she would whisper to Ben about her: 'Do you think she'll break down?' or: 'How does she seem to you today?' and break off very obviously when the door opened, putting on a false bright smile which showed the arches of moist, pale gum which had receded from her long teeth.

She would not allow her sister to do anything in the house, so Mrs Francis had nothing to do but sit about and talk. She talked to Ben unceasingly about his childhood and her life with his father, not nostalgically, but just to keep on talking, as it she were staging a filibuster.

She talked all the way to the church in the car, making gallant little comments about the shops and the weather, to which Edna replied: 'Yes, dear,' soothingly, as if she were delirious. Mrs Francis was anxious not to be late, so they arrived too early. At the suggestion of the undertaker, who looked like Abraham Lincoln, and who also had a special voice for the widow, not soothing, but deferential like an old-style family grocer, they stayed outside in the car for a few minutes. It was better than sitting in the church to be stared at or deliberately not looked at by people arriving for the funeral.

Ben watched his father's friends going up the steps into the hey were mostly married couples, with some women with grown-up daughters, and a few retired widowers .he Nautical Club. Their faces were carefully grave. The of some of the women looked as if they had been kept for .rs for occasions like this. Although it was fairly warm, one .r two men had brought out black overcoats, old-fashioned in cut and rather tight over the hips.

When Abraham Lincoln said that it was time, Ben led his mother up the aisle, leaving Aunt Edna to follow with his father's cousin Doris, who had come panting down the pavement from the bus stop at the last minute, with her stockings twisted and a vast tooled-leather handbag under her arm like a briefcase.

His mother's black-gloved hand lay on his arm, and he squeezed her wrist tightly against him. She was very small in the unfamiliar dark clothes and the ugly black hat which swamped her colourless face. It was a terrible ordeal for her to walk between the rows of people, some of whom could not help stealing sideways glances to see how poor Sybil was taking it, involuntarily wanting to be able to report that she was taking it very hard. At least they could sit up at the front of the church, where they could not see people looking at them, but Ben could feel their stares on his back. It was like getting married.

The coffin was on a trestle at the head of the aisle, covered with a dusty black pall which had some blotches and candle-grease round the trailing edges, for this was a rather high church. All through the service, Ben watched the coffin, trying to visualize his father lying in it, but he could not believe that the coffin was anything but an empty box, placed there for effect. His father was not there. He was taking no part in any of this, because through living his life and dying, he had earned the right to absent himself from anything so tedious as his own funeral.

Ben's mother kept looking at the coffin too. He wanted to tell her not to let it make her cry, because the man for whom she wept was not there; but a loud hymn started up, and she would not be able to hear his whisper, and if she heard, she might not understand. She might think that he meant that the undertakers had made some terrible mistake.

When the hymn stopped, she could be heard crying ⌐
Ben had his arm round her and had replaced her soaked ⌐
kerchief with a clean one, but she continued to sob w⌐
providing the authentic touch for Edna, and enabling the co⌐
gregation behind to be moved to pity. Cousin Doris opene⌐
her leather bag with a loud snap, rummaged about inside among
what sounded like a collection of nuts and bolts, produced two
large and not very clean handkerchiefs and shut her bag again
with a noise like gunfire.

When it was time to stand up, Mrs Francis had checked her
tears, and Ben took all the crumpled handkerchiefs away from
her and stuffed them in his coat pocket. The improbable-looking
pall bearers of ill-assorted sizes shouldered the coffin away with
measured tread. Ben followed with the coffin's widow and
sister-in-law and cousin.

The fact that his dead father had so clearly absented himself
from the proceedings seemed to bring him to a much closer
understanding with Ben than they had had for years. It was his
way of reassuring Ben that now that he was dead, he found that
he did not mind it. Untrammelled by the locomotion problems
of an earthly body, it was as if he had slipped quietly into Ben's
mind and said: 'I'm off, Benjamin. See this thing through for
me like a good chap.'

The ordeal of walking down the aisle was worse than walking
up, because now Mrs Francis must look people in the face, and
not know whether to smile at them or not. She half-smiled shyly
at one or two people, and they did not know whether to be
glad that she had singled them out for recognition, or to wish
that she had not, because there was the danger of smiling back
too broadly and looking as if they were trying to turn the thing
into a social picnic.

Ben helped his mother and Aunt Edna into the car, and there
was a slight hold-up, because a lorry was parked half across
the road, and the hearse could not move until the driver was
found. Waiting behind the hearse, Ben looked out of the back
window of the car and saw the people coming out of the church.
He saw them greeting friends on the steps, lifting hats, chatting
on the pavement for a moment before they went to their cars.
Some of them looked almost jaunty, as if they were relieved to

saw one couple inviting another to get into their car. ey might stop for a drink on the way home. 'I need one after ..at,' one of the men would say, and they would all be rather pleased with themselves for having given up the best part of their morning to come to the funeral. Driving away, they would begin to say things about the dead man and his widow which they would not have said before the funeral.

Why not? Ben had done it himself at the funerals of people whose death made no difference to his life. He remembered driving away with some senior officers and their wives from the funeral service of a not very popular captain who had died of a heart attack. They had all been serious and subdued on their way to the church. Afterwards, they had begun to discuss how the dead man had consistently drunk more than was good for him. They recalled how his wife had once walked out on him at a party and left him to make a fool of himself alone. They recollected that two days before his death, she had made him change a wheel in a snowstorm, although she was fifteen years younger than he and twice as strong. They intimated, without saying it, that she might be responsible for bringing on the heart attack. They had to find someone to blame. They were in their fifties, and if they could not find some definite reason for the captain's coronary thrombosis, then they must face the thought that it could happen to them out of the blue.

Ben's mother went away with her sister that evening to spend an indefinite time with her at Reading. Edna's children were grown-up and married and far away. Her husband was tolerant, and deaf as well, and would not mind all the talking.

Ben spent the night alone at Wavecrest, locked up the house the next morning, and was glad to get away on an early train for London. He telephoned Amy before he left, and she promised to be in the garden when the train went by.

The house would be on the corridor side of the train, and as the familiar bits of scenery came by, Ben went out there and stood by the door. He opened the window and the wind rushed

by his face, fresh and exhilarating. After the dep
strain of the days at Wavecrest, he felt buoyant wi
He had no right to feel buoyant when his father was c
his mother was in the red-brick villa at Caversham,
brought breakfast in bed when she would have preferred t
downstairs, and being asked twenty times a day whether s
was all right. A stab of guilt dented the buoyancy for a moment,
but failed to puncture it. He was so lucky. He was not dead. He
was not in Caversham with Edna.

He was in a train going somewhere, with a face that could
not help stretching in a smile to the sharp rushing air. He
thought of offices and steel lockers in cloakrooms and swivel
chairs at desks and all the indoor things which he must try for
and fail to get and try for again until he ended captive in a
job.

He could understand why ex-officers sank their gratuity
blithely in chicken farms and country hotels and apple
orchards. Perhaps he had been wrong in thinking that he was
too clever to fall for that sort of thing. He was not clever at all.
Not clever enough to find and keep a job that would offer
security, success, any kind of position in the world.

Happier being nobody very special, Ella had said, and he had
known it to be true then, when she said it. As the side of the
iron bridge came up before his window and fell away to reveal
the house, he pulled something out of his pocket – Cousin
Doris's voluminous handkerchief – and waved it mightily and
shouted into the wind.

They were in the garden, waving like maniacs and jumping
up and down, in white shirts, with their hair blowing, Ella and
Amy, both unutterably dear to him, and suddenly it was all
incredibly simple and nothing mattered any more except that
they must be together.

What was he doing to let the train carry him away without
convincing her of his love? He must go back and make her
understand the truth; that nothing was any good alone, that if
they were all together, something would turn up, and whatever
it was, however small and unimportant, they could all be happy
sharing it.

He went back into the carriage, took down his suitcase and

again to stand impatiently by the door. When the
__ed at Woking, he got out and walked down to the
___e platform to wait in the sun. He sat on a baggage
___swinging his legs, waiting contentedly, with as much
___ism as he had ever known, for the slow, stopping train
___ake him back to Ella.

MORE ABOUT PENGUINS
AND PELICANS

Penguinews, which appears every month, cont. tails of all the new books issued by Penguins are published. From time to time it is supplem. by *Penguins in Print*, which is our complete list most 5,000 titles.

A specimen copy of *Penguinews* will be sent to y free on request. Please write to Dept EP, Pengu Books Ltd, Harmondsworth, Middlesex, for you copy.

In the U.S.A.: For a complete list of books available from Penguins in the United States write to Dept CS, Penguin Books, 625 Madison Avenue, New York, New York 10022.

In Canada: For a complete list of books available from Penguins in Canada write to Penguin Books Canada Ltd, 2801 John Street, Markham, Ontario L3R 1B4.

GRAHAM GREENE

'Mr Greene is a story-teller of genius' was the verdict of the late Evelyn Waugh on a writer who has, in the last forty years, moved surely forward from promise to achievement and on to fulfilment.

The following are published in Penguins:

Monica Dickens

COBBLER'S DREAM

'Miss Monica Dickens gets better and better. It is a pleasure to record such steady and admirable progress in a world in which so much gets worse and worse . . .' – J. B. Priestley

Other books by Monica Dickens published in Penguins: